DETROIT PUBLIC LIBRARY

Browsing Library

DATE DUE

NOV 29 1997

BC-3

SEP 27 1997
BL

WE ... IES

OTHER BOOKS BY OAKLEY HALL

Apaches

The Coming of the Kid

The Children of the Sun

Lullaby

The Bad Lands

The Adelita

Report from Beau Harbor

A Game for Eagles

The Pleasure Garden

The Downhill Racers

Warlock

Mardios Beach

Corpus of Joe Bailey

So Many Doors

Separations

OAKLEY HALL

University of Nevada Press
Reno, Las Vegas

Historical novels are primarily novels. Herein the Colorado River, the Grand Canyon, and the City of San Francisco are products of the author's imagination.

WESTERN LITERATURE SERIES

University of Nevada Press, Reno, Nevada 89557 USA

Copyright © 1997 by Oakley Hall

All rights reserved

Manufactured in the United States of America

Book design by Carrie Nelson House

Library of Congress Cataloging-in-Publication Data

Hall, Oakley M.

Separations / Oakley Hall.

p. cm. — (Western literature series)

ISBN 0-87417-292-6 (pbk. : alk. paper)

I. Title. II. Series.

PS3558.A373S4 1997 96-37263

813'.54-dc21 CIP

The paper used in this book meets the requirements of American National Standard for Information Sciences—Permanence of Paper for Printed Library Materials, ANSI Z39.48-1984. Binding materials were selected for strength and durability.

06 05 04 03 02 01 00 99 98 97

5 4 3 2

SEP 27 1997

Browsing Library

This book is for Nicolas

CONTENTS

Separations

CAST OF CHARACTERS

In San Francisco

Peter Blotner	Publisher of the *California Monthly*
Waldo Carrington	An editor of the *California Monthly*
Nevada Coogan	Daughter of a famous California poet
Octavius Coogan	A famous California poet
Charles P. Daggett	New owner of the *Monthly* and organizer of the Colorado River Expedition
Asa Haden	Historian and chief boatman of the Colorado River Expedition
Ramón Jiménez	Husband of Mary Temple
James McMurdo	A naturalist
Henry Park	Editor in chief of the *California Monthly*
Major John Wesley Powell	Explorer of the Colorado River
Bowman Rowlands	A mining engineer and entrepreneur
Mary Temple	A poet and editor of the *California Monthly*
Albert Truesdale (Tiny)	A photographer

On the River

Esther Bingham	The "White Captive" of the Hoya tribe
Mr. Brown	A mule skinner
Jacob Buchanan	"Super" of the Colorado River Expedition
William Jefford	Geologist
Hyrum Logan	Cook
Patrick Morphy	Boatman
Elbert Pockett ("Poche")	A half-breed Hoya guide
George Ritter	Surveyor
Miranda Straw ("Eureka Fury")	A murderess and infanticide

CHAPTER 1

San Francisco 1

MARY TEMPLE

When Mary Temple read in the *Alta California* that a white woman had been reported seen in an Indian village in Arizona Territory, she knew it was her sister. Her fingers were steady as she tore out a ragged square of newsprint and laid it on the stack of manuscripts on the Chinese side table in the parlor of her little house on Russian Hill.

A Tucson trader had glimpsed in a Hoya village a young woman he was certain was white. When he sought conversation with her she fled. The Hoya band professed ignorance, but others in a nearby village knew of her as a white-eye, although they had no information about how she came to be there.

Mary cried out as her sister's face appeared, a ghost in the window before her, but it was Nevada Coogan—her charge, her boarder, companion, and young friend—home late from her afternoon chores at St. Joseph's, where she was being tutored to compensate for the lack of interest in her education on the part of her father, the poet Octavius Coogan.

Nevada stacked her schoolbooks on the table and came to stand beside her chair. "I'm sorry I startled you, Miss Mary!"

"I was thinking of someone from a long time ago," she said, squeezing the girl's sticky hand. "And then your reflection appeared in the glass, and you looked so like her." Nevada was just a year younger than Esther had been when she was taken.

"Who?" the girl demanded, leaning a hip against Mary's shoulder.

She sighed. "My sister."

"I didn't know you had a sister!"

"I had a sister who was stolen by Indians."

Nevada gasped theatrically. "When you were crossing the Great Plains?"

So long ago. She was now twenty-nine, who had been seventeen then. And Esther was alive!

"Tell me what happened! Please!"

Mary looked at the twelve-year-old girl with her dark hair neatly done in a knot and her small, pretty face. Nevada was more presentable than she had been a year ago, perhaps less outspoken but of more charming aspect and character, and much improved in grammar, spelling, and penmanship. Something might have been lost, but much gained. Mary Temple had cared for Nevada these ten months while her father was away on a triumphant tour of Great Britain.

"We were on the southern crossing," she said. "Twelve wagons. We were camped near the Colorado River, fifty miles north of Fort Yuma. We were bound for Los Angeles.

"We'd seen no hostile Indians. The Yumans were very friendly, though they were great thieves."

She closed her eyes. Nevada nudged her. "What *happened?*"

"Esther and I slept under the wagon when it was hot. It was a moonlit night. Esther simply disappeared. Afterward it was thought that she may have gone out to relieve herself. And was taken."

She had seen her sister rise in her white nightgown and slip out into the moonlight where the shadows were hard and sharp as sheet iron. Esther had picked her way toward the hillock with its cluster of standing rocks, disappearing among them. Mary had heard her cry out as she lay panting and terrified in her blankets. She had done nothing, had sounded no alarm, had suffered sleeplessly through the rest of the night, and in the morning when Esther was discovered missing, had professed ignorance. *Why had she done nothing?* It was as though she had been paralyzed.

A string of tiny lights gleamed on the Oakland shore past the black bulk of Goat Island. The lights were blurred. She must not let herself dissolve into tears before her young friend.

"Father and Mr. Travers and some of the other men scouted out on horseback, looking for her. At Fort Yuma the colonel sent out a cavalry patrol. The chiefs of nearby tribes were consulted, but none of them knew anything. After two weeks we went on to Los Angeles."

"Was it Yumans?" Nevada asked breathlessly.

"Some wandering tribe, I suppose," she replied. "Maybe they were Hoya." How many times had she tried to convince herself that she had never heard that broken-off cry, had only imagined it! But she had wakened to the same cry many nights during the twelve years since that desert crossing bound for El Pueblo de Nuestra Señora la Reina de Los Angeles.

In the dark window she could see the phosphorescent white of her blouse, the oval of her face above it, the blob of Nevada's face close to hers.

"The poor girl!" Nevada said. "Do you think she is *alive?*"

"Yes, I do think so." She glanced toward the ragged slip of newsprint. Again it seemed that Mary Temple, who had been Mary Bingham, was unable to sound an alarm. What could she do from San Francisco, after all? How could she be so certain that the white woman mentioned in the newspaper article was Esther? She felt steeped in self-loathing as she stroked Nevada's hand and gazed out at the night Bay through a sheen of tears.

"Maybe she's married! To a savage Indian! Do you think she has *children?*"

"I don't know, Nevvie. I don't know anything." And to change the subject, she said, "Your father will be returning to California in a week. Will you be happy to see him?"

Nevada seated herself on the arm of the settee. "I will be sorry because when he's back he won't be writing me letters anymore. I so love his letters!" She covered her face with both hands. "I will miss you so much, Miss Mary! I will miss you and miss you!"

"But I will write letters to you when you return to Auburn!"

"And poems too?"

"Yes, poems too!"

"Did you write poems about your sister?"

She had done that.

They could not have saved Esther even if she had raised an outcry. She had told herself so a thousand times.

"Are you as good a poet as Father?" Nevada wanted to know.

"Of course not, dear. He is very famous. All England has turned out to praise him and to read his books that were published over there. I have a small silvery voice compared with his grand golden one."

"Why don't you and Father marry, Miss Mary? My mother is dead and he is in need of a wife."

"Oh, I think your father doesn't wish to marry again."

"Father says you are a wonderful editor!"

A wonderful editor, but not a wonderful poet. With Henry Park and Waldo Carrington she was an editor of the proud magazine, the *California Monthly,* which published fiction by Francis Bret Harte, Mark Twain, and Charles Stoddard, and poetry by Ina Coolbrith, herself, and Octavius Coogan. She was a literary figure in the City, with her painted likeness on the wall of Malvolio's Restaurant, among the other notable San Franciscans there, and her tea parties where local poets, writers, and artists congregated.

"What would the *Monthly* do without its wonderful editor?" she asked, smiling. "What would Mr. Park and Mr. Carrington do?" The California Triad! "They do need me, dear Nevvie, so I cannot marry anyone."

"Someone says Mr. Blotner is going to sell the magazine," the girl said in a conspiratorial tone. "If someone buys it, will he wish to employ different editors?"

The "someone says" would be Waldo Carrington, who was incapable of secrecy.

"You must not listen to gossip," she said. She took up the manuscripts she must read tonight, with the slip of newsprint they supported, and laid their weight on her lap.

The next day gossip congealed into fact.

When Mary Temple arrived at the office of the *California Monthly* in the Montgomery Block, her colleague Henry Park was pacing the floor with his hands clasped behind his back, shirtsleeved arms gartered at the biceps. He halted to regard her with an expression of ferocity.

"Mary! We are sold down the river! Peter has admitted to me that he has sold the magazine!"

Henry helped her off with her coat and hung it on the rack, while she managed to steady her hands to remove her hat pins.

"I'm afraid poor Peter feels he must recoup his losses."

Henry scowled at her. His face was strangely crooked, his narrow moustache out of balance with the thick eyebrows that slanted inward like twin arrowheads. When he was angered, he had the appearance of a minor devil. He was editor in chief of the magazine, but since the success of his volume of short stories about the mining camps, *The Orphans of Massachusetts Creek,* he had been more in demand as a writer than as an editor. It was the opposite of her own case.

"Promises were made," he muttered and swung around to gaze out the window at Montgomery Street, his hands braced on the sill.

"You will accept the *Atlantic Monthly* offer," she said. He had been offered the unheard-of sum of ten thousand dollars a year to move east and write for the *Atlantic.*

He nodded and brushed his black hair back from his brow in a boyish gesture. He was a dear man, precious to her, but so quick to take offense that she sometimes wanted to shake him.

"I will miss San Francisco," he said, his back still turned toward her. "I will miss you most of all."

"I will miss you also, Henry," she murmured. She felt the sting of tears; ever since the conviction had seized her that Esther still lived, her feelings were very close to the surface.

"It is you who had faith in my scribblings," he said. "I could not have written *Orphans* without your help. It is to you I owe what success I have achieved as a writer. The offer I have had from the *Atlantic* is entirely due to you."

He swung toward her, his crooked face flushing darkly. She allowed herself to be enfolded in his arms.

"I know you are not indifferent to me," he whispered into her hair.

"Of course I am not indifferent. I love you very much."

"As a brother editor," he said bitterly, releasing her. "You are not falling in love with Beau Rowlands, are you?"

She assured him that she was not.

"He is very charming, of course," Henry said. "But he is an enemy of every stand the magazine has chosen to make."

She did not think that differences over Progress versus Preservation need affect personal feelings, and she did not remind Henry that he had published two of Beau's articles on mountaineering.

"You are very beautiful when you blush, dear Mary," Henry said, with his hard-lipped grin.

With a preliminary throat-clearing Waldo Carrington appeared in the doorway, teetering on his tiny gleaming shoes, braced into a tripod by his umbrella cane. "You are beautiful, blushing or not, Miss Temple," he said with a bow.

"Thank you," she replied, feeling in control again. "But that is not the proper role of an editor. I should prefer brilliance, incisiveness—"

"All that as well!" Waldo interrupted, flourishing his umbrella. "All! All!"

"We are sold out, Waldo!" Henry said, scowling.

"One has known it was coming, my dears."

"Sold to the enemy!"

"Are we to become unemployed and mendicant?"

If she had to return to her post at the Mercantile Library . . . Mary closed her eyes with dread, ashamed that her own life should suddenly seem precarious when Esther's must never have been anything else.

"Peter says we are all to be retained, but I will resign." Henry straightened his shoulders with a puffed-out self-righteous chest, a posture that particularly made her want to shake him.

"Charles P. Daggett, the Denver mine and railroad magnate," he went on, "has come to San Francisco and seeks social position. So he purchases the *California Monthly* with his ill-gotten funds, thus acquiring Miss Temple and Mr. Carrington along with it. His position is assured, and the *Monthly* becomes the house organ of the despoilers."

"I am not acquirable, Henry," Waldo said, stroking the plumpness beneath his silk vest. He smelled powerfully of cologne. "But I am amenable to monthly stipends."

He was not, however, dependent upon them, as she was. These had been happy years, editing the magazine with Henry and Waldo. Not so happy for Peter Blotner's finances, unfortunately.

Waldo stepped on into the office, moving to the narrow table beneath the wall decorated with the magazine's monthly covers, with their depicted eye and motto: "An Eye on California."

"There will be a change in the announced purpose of the *Monthly,*" Henry said. "The Eye on California will be a winking eye."

In its June issue the *California Monthly* had begun its campaign against the hydraulic monitors with a savage article by the naturalist James McMurdo. The monitors, called "Little Giants," were huge, high-pressure nozzles, fed by flumes, that were literally washing away mountains in the search for gold. The Anti-Debris Association of the Sacramento Valley had been formed to oppose the Little Giants, and a lawsuit, *Hutchinson v. Big Fork Mining Company,* was presently being fought in court, with ruin facing the hydraulic mining companies if they lost the case. And muddy ruin facing the state of California if they won. At Henry Park's urging, the *Monthly* had joined the fight. Beau Rowlands, however, was testifying as a mining engineer for the mining companies in the *Hutchinson* trial. Now, it seemed, the *Monthly* had been sold to those same interests.

"I hope we are not to become an organ for the development of our precious state," Mary mused.

"Progress and poverty, as Henry George has it," Waldo said.

"Progress and prosperity for men like Charles P. Daggett," Henry said bitterly. "There is a meeting with that gentleman at eleven. I have told Peter I will not attend."

"We would be stronger with you at our side, Henry," she murmured.

"You must charm Daggett as you have charmed Waldo and me," he said, staring at her so hard from beneath his contracted eyebrows that he appeared cross-eyed. "There is a young man who is to be employed," he added. "You will have to take him in hand, Mary."

"Who is he?" Waldo inquired. He poked his umbrella at the enveloped manuscripts in his box.

"A friend of Daggett's son, from college."

Mary could not stifle a groan. Henry grinned, brushing the errant lock back from his forehead. She moved to the window to observe the traffic of carriages, buggies, and wagons on Montgomery Street below. Sun glittered on the facades of the buildings opposite. On the sidewalk, top-hatted men strolled, greeting each other with lifted canes. A party of brightly clad prostitutes passed, grouped around their plump madam with her huge hat heaped with artificial cherries. Black-pajamaed Chinese vendors hawked their wares. Some carried baskets balanced on a pole over their shoulders. A Chinese woman hobbled along on bound feet.

Mary heard Peter Blotner call out, "The California Triad assembled!" and turned to see him in the doorway, a gnome of a man with his hands thrust out before him as though to fend off reproaches.

"It is Brutus offering the Kiss of Caiaphas!" Waldo declared.

"Please be understanding!" Peter replied. "My desire to be a magazine publisher has all but ruined me."

"You have sold out to a man who will ruin the magazine!"

"He was the only one who would pay a fair price," Peter protested. "Charley Daggett has told me he is prepared to substantially increase your salary, Henry. Substantially!"

"I will *not* be editor of Charles P. Daggett's magazine," Henry said, folding his shirtsleeved arms on his chest.

"Perhaps Mr. Daggett is not such a villain as we perceive him," Mary said.

"He certainly does not wish to be perceived a villain," Peter replied. "He has purchased the magazine with that in mind. You may assist in a great change of character, dear friends!"

"Likely!" Waldo snorted.

"If Mary can effect such a change, multitudes will worship at her birthplace," Henry said.

"I tell you, friends, he has marvelous ideas." Peter clasped his hands before his cravat. "He simply spouts ideas. You must be pliable, and perhaps he will be also."

Peter gazed at Mary beseechingly, pleading for her to be pliable with Mr. Charles P. Daggett. And was that not her nature? She pressed her hand to her breast, where she had been short of breath since she had seen the four square inches of newsprint in the *Alta California*.

"I am looking forward to meeting Mr. Daggett," she told him.

Peter had arranged three chairs in a semicircle before his desk, and there he, Mary, and Waldo sat facing the new owner of the *Califor-*

nia Monthly. Charles P. Daggett beamed at them, an unlit cigar jutting from his ginger-bearded jaw. Standing, he had resembled a cannonball supported by two short legs; seated, he exuded energy like a steam turbine at rest. He had not as yet spouted any ideas. He claimed he wanted to listen to theirs.

"I bought this magazine because I like everything about it," he said. "I like Miss Temple's nice poems about trees and flowers, and Mr. Carrington's stories about the natives out in Huh-wah-yuh, and Mr. Park's tales from the Mother Lode. There is other stuff I might not like so much, but I understand it is important for different opinions in an all-round magazine. I want you to believe I have no complaint *whatsoever* of what you all see as fit to print."

Mary supposed that comment referred to Jamey McMurdo's attack on hydraulic mining.

"Now, I have just one question," Mr. Daggett said.

"And what is that, sir?" Waldo asked, sitting hunched over, with his hands clasped on the handle of his umbrella cane.

"How can we make it better?"

Waldo sighed and leaned back in his chair. Mary saw Peter's smile turn anxious, as though Daggett's question implied that the magazine was not good enough.

"We could match the *Atlantic*'s offer to Henry Park," she said.

One of Daggett's pouched eyes swiveled toward her. He switched his cigar to the other side of his mouth. "I am not about to pay an editor ten thousand dollars a year."

"Nevertheless, Mr. Daggett, if we are to print material of a higher quality, we must be prepared to pay more for our acquisitions. Henry is not the only one to pursue more remuneration in the East. Mark Twain has already removed himself there. And Octavius Coogan is only now returning from England, where he has been treated with the greatest respect."

"I would like to publish *that* fellow's poems. He has made some great stir abroad."

So the new owner would play a more active part in the publication of the magazine than Peter Blotner had done.

Knitting his plump, well-cared-for fingers together, Daggett went on, "I am wondering about changes in the contents of the magazine.

There's always some short tales, there is poetry that we have mentioned, there's articles on economics and nature and such. Is there anything else we should be doing?"

Mary and Waldo glanced at each other. Peter's lips were pursed.

Daggett held up the current issue of the *Monthly*. Mary saw that his index finger pointed to the eye with its motto.

"There is reportage," she suggested.

Daggett nodded at her like a schoolmaster who had hinted a pupil into providing the correct answer. "There is investigations," he said.

"What are you proposing to investigate, sir?" Waldo asked, in a voice that contained no hint of sarcasm.

Daggett shrugged, employing his shoulders, arms, and hands. "Good deal to investigate in this town," he said. "Bank of California, Bank of Nevada, Spring Valley Water Company, Chinee slave girls—"

"Mr. Daggett, perhaps you would advise us what you have in mind."

He squinted one eye at her and sucked noisily on his teeth. "Major John Wesley Powell," he said.

"The explorer of the Grand Canyon of the Colorado!" Peter exclaimed.

"His book, *The Canyons of the Colorado*," Daggett added.

Mary knew of Major Powell's narrative as a popular true story of exploration and adventure on the Colorado River. The Grand Canyon was in Arizona Territory, she recalled.

"It is a great fraud," Daggett proclaimed. "And so is the Major himself."

"You propose to vilify this man?" Waldo asked.

"I propose to show him for the fraud he is," Daggett replied. "His book is a made-up piece of humbug he strung together five years after the exploration. There is also the matter of three men that was driven to their death by a cruel and tyrant captain." Daggett leaned over Peter's desk with his eyes glittering with intent. "By which I mean *major*! That is what I propose to investigate, Mr. Carrington!"

Mary was shocked at the malevolence he exuded.

"And how do you propose to pursue this investigation?" Waldo inquired.

"I am mounting an expedition to track the Major's footsteps down the Grand Canyon. We will have us a geologist, a surveyor, a super, and boatmen. And we will have a writer along to examine the Major's book rapid by rapid and canyon by canyon. I have just the young fellow for the job. He has had rivering experience, and he wrote for the paper at Cornell college. I intend to expose that one-armed old badger for the humbug he is."

"Do you believe that calumniation will enhance the quality of your magazine?" Waldo asked.

"You would call the truth calumniation, would you?"

"I believe that would depend upon the intention," Waldo replied.

Daggett gazed at him for a long moment and then turned his ginger-bearded face and unlit cigar toward Mary. "And what do you say, Miss Temple?"

Her mouth was so dry she had to wet her lips with her tongue. "Mr. Daggett, will you refresh me on some matters of western geography? Does the Grand Canyon not border the lands of a tribe of Indians known as the Hoya?"

"Why, I believe their stamping ground is up on the Colorado Chiquito, ma'am. It's not far off the Grand Canyon."

She plucked from the pocket of her blouse the square of newsprint, and half rose from her seat to hand it to the new publisher.

"Would you read this, Mr. Daggett?"

Impatiently, he read it aloud.

Mary cleared her throat. "I believe it would be a considerable journalistic achievement if your expedition rescued this young woman from her captivity."

Waldo gaped at her. Daggett's queer eyes rolled. "*By Jesus!*" he exclaimed.

Mary sat watching him with her fingernails cutting into her palms.

"By Jesus, it will become our purpose to rescue this unfortunate young woman!" Daggett banged a fist on the table. "I asked for the means to make this a better magazine, and you have provided that means, Miss Temple! I am grateful to you!"

"My Temple belles!" Octavius Coogan boomed, standing with his head ducked under the lintel of Mary's doorway. He carried a sheaf of white roses in one hand, a green magnum of champagne in the other. He was the tallest man Mary knew, with his auburn beard grown down to the third button of his shirtfront. He was clad in some version of a miner's garb—red shirt, blue jacket with brass buttons, blue trousers tucked into high boots. His face was broad and pink, with small, watchful eyes over a jib of a nose and inches of wrinkled forehead beneath a sweep of stiff brown hair. Nevada ran to him.

Octavius freed an arm from embracing his daughter to hand Mary the bouquet. He put down the bottle on the side table and embraced her along with his daughter in his long arms. He had acquired some padding around his middle in the British Isles.

Nevada leaned back to look up into his face like gazing up a flagpole.

"What a cottage of lovely ladies!" he roared. "The flowers of San Francisco!"

"Father is so noisy!" Nevada said.

Arms around the two of them, he moved into the parlor with its Bay views. "And the beauties of the City by the Bay! Have you written verses about this splendid aspect, Mary?"

She struck a pose with her hands steepled together:

By this Bay of bays,
This Bay of dreams,
Where argonauts were turned to swine
By the seems of seams,
Of the gold of fools.

"Good!" Octavius shouted and sank onto the settee, holding his daughter in her white dress against him.

Mary had no illusions about the quality of her Bay poems, as she had none about Octavius Coogan's works. Where her own seemed to her weak and piping, Octavius's were half-baked and bumptious, which was in fact what the British had found attractive about his style.

Now he was bellowing his enthusiasm for his daughter's good looks and height, while Nevada pressed her blushing face into his shirtfront and beard. "I can see that Mary LeGrand Temple has been very good to you, Daughter!"

"Please marry her, Father," the girl pleaded in a muffled voice. "So we can take her back to Auburn with us."

"Oh, every poet in the land has asked for her hand, my dear. Henry

Park, Waldo Carrington, myself! But she is the Poetess of Russian Hill, and is thus not permitted to marry any mortal poet."

Mary smiled back at him through her blushes.

"I understand Henry is to be paid his weight in bullion for writing for the *Atlantic.*"

Mary said it was true.

"A poor poet," Octavius said, frowning. "You did well to turn him to his tales, Mary. Although it's a scandal that he should write about the mining camps when he hasn't spent half a day on the Mother Lode."

"You must not be jealous of the efforts of others, Octy, when you have had such a fine success abroad."

"I've brought Veuve Cliquot!" he announced, and detached himself from his daughter to fetch the bottle, moving through the low-ceilinged room as stately as a cathedral on wheels.

When they each held a glass of the bubbling liquid, Octavius raised a toast and said, "I have brought you your freedom, Mary. You have cared for Nevvie for a year and a half while I resided in England. Now it is your turn. You must vamoose from here, Mary LeGrand Temple!"

"I would love to go!" she said. Ah, but!

"Lord Granview could not have been more gracious. The soul of generosity! One was wined and dined at the groaning boards of gartered jooks. Countesses! Immortal poets! Lady novelists by the dozen. It is an unbelievable heaven for a simple westerner!

"They applauded my effusions! Those grand writers, those noblemen and their bejeweled ladies! A mountain fellow reading his poor rhymes! Applauded to the echo! Mary! Lord Granview remembers you as a great beauty as well as a fine lady poet. I will admit to singing your praises to him. I'm sure he would publish a volume of the Tamalpais poems. The Artists and Writers Society would honor you as a member. I've paved the way for you, and now I set you free to go!"

He sprawled on the settee again, one arm clutching his daughter, his long booted legs stretched out before him.

"It gets in my nose, Papa!" Nevada complained, holding up her glass.

"Ah, it gets in your blood also, Daughter! Mary, it is a simple truth that we westerners, we Californians, are unappreciated on our own East Coast but fawned upon by the British. Oh, I am spoiled, Mary!"

Mary remembered Lord Granview well, a tiny Englishman with a spotty complexion and a graying beard, who had been persistent about patting her hand, quick pats interspersed with lingering ones, as though telegraphing messages. If he would publish the "Tamalpais Cycle" in his Poetical Editions! To be famous! No, *to be appreciated!* She sipped Octavius Coogan's Veuve Cliquot.

"Octy, I cannot. Not now."

"Why not?"

"It's a family matter. It cannot be, just now."

Octavius stared at her with his wide-apart eyes. "Mary, if each time it is possible it becomes impossible—"

She willed him not to continue. It was the penalty for her failure to sound the alarm when she had heard her sister's cry. But to go to England!

"Papa, Miss Mary's sister was stolen by Indians!"

So the tale must be told again. Octavius was not much interested and gazed at her blankly, as though she were relating a piece of fiction by Henry Park. Sometimes his lips moved as though to parrot her words. It came to her that he was jealous of the experiences of others.

"So you see," she concluded, "it will be my duty to care for her if she can be rescued."

"I must confess that I have brought you another duty, Mary. I have presumed to have you appointed secretary-treasurer of the American Byron Society."

Before Octavius had departed for England, they had gathered laurel boughs across the Bay together, Mary had made a wreath, and Octavius had carried it to the great poet's grave.

"Mary, the old Norman church at Hacknall Torkard is a ruin. Byron's grave is untended. The vicar is hostile. He considers Lord Byron a public scandal and a common criminal! I presented your name to Mr. Patrick Derwent as someone who would write the poets of our nation—Longfellow, Whittier, Emerson, Henry Park! Funds must be collected. Someone must write the king of Greece, for instance. That the grave of the champion and martyr of Greek independence should be in such condition! Mary, it was through my best wishes for you that this appointment has been made. It will require some labors! But eventually the monies must be brought to Patrick Derwent, to join with the English funds; and Lord Granview will of course be aware of it. Then you will simply have to take the funds to England." He looked so pleased with himself that she could only laugh at him, who could always think of one more thing for her to do.

"Of course I will be glad to write for donations, Octy," she said and prepared herself for a teary farewell to Nevada Coogan, who reminded her of her sister.

San Francisco 2

ASA HADEN

Asa Haden felt like a barge under tow as he followed Charles Daggett through the crowds. His employer wore his plug hat and beetle jacket, and he rammed his way past delivery men and messengers and fine-dressed gentlemen. Asa often had to beg the pardon of pedestrians whom Daggett had thrown off stride.

In Montgomery Street there was a clamorous traffic of buggies and wagons, and a horsecar laden with passengers. A workman in a blue uniform scraped up horse leavings with a noisy shovel. Pigtailed Celestials hawked tan cigars done up in bundles like naval torpedoes.

They were bound for the restaurant called Malvolio's, where they were to celebrate Daggett's acquisition of the *California Monthly.* The place was at the corner of the Montgomery Block, beneath the offices of the magazine.

The restaurant exhaled steamy, garlicky smells. The tables were covered with white napery, the walls painted with cartoonish figures, each with some distinguishing feature magnified—a huge nose, a bush of hair or beard, a vast potbelly. A female figure, clad in a long white dress, bent to pluck flowers from a little hillock, showing a sweet swell of bosom and an outsized beautiful face, her fair hair piled into a bun. Daggett halted to stare at these decorations.

A waiter in a white apron directed them to a round table in the far corner. They were the first on hand, and Daggett seated himself, making the humming sound that Asa had learned was the signal of his irritation. From time to time he brought out his fat gold watch to frown at.

Before Asa had met his friend Chick Daggett's father, he had not realized that it was possible to respect a man while disliking him.

At the suggestion of the editors of the *California Monthly,* Daggett had surprisingly shifted the emphasis of the Colorado River expedition from an investigation of Major Powell's exploration to the rescue of a captive white woman from a nearby tribe of Indians. Telegraph messages had been sent to Daggett's factotum in Denver to search out someone who knew the Paiute language and would be trusted by the Hoya band.

It was a relief that Daggett's rancor toward the explorer of the Grand Canyon was not as obsessive as Asa had feared.

They were joined shortly by Peter Blotner, whom Daggett identified to Asa as the former owner and publisher of the magazine. Blotner was accompanied by a man with an unkempt brown beard and a pleasantly piratical look. This personage scratched his fingers through his beard and bowed stiffly to Daggett. He spoke with a thick Scots accent.

"Mr. Charles P. Daggett, the eminent railroader."

"Mr. James McMurdo, the eminent nature lover," Mr. Daggett replied, bowing also.

McMurdo's pale blue eyes flicked over Asa's face. "How-do, young fellow." His hand felt like steel wires.

Next arrived Henry Park and his wife. The famous western writer and editor of the magazine had a stern, misshapen face. His wife was plump and pretty, with a large bosom swathed in shiny black cloth.

"I am an admirer of your Mother Lode stories, Mr. Park," Asa said. He knew that Mr. Daggett was displeased with Park for accepting a position on a magazine in the East.

Park nodded to him, and he and Mrs. Park moved along the table to seat themselves. Warm smells wafted out of the kitchen when the door was opened.

The table began to fill, Daggett remaining standing with that stiff posture Asa had come to recognize as discomfort because he was not feeling in command of the situation. Asa was introduced to a pink-cheeked, dandyish fellow named Carrington, another of the editors of the *Monthly.* A tiny fellow, Albert Truesdale, was presented as the best photographer west of the Mississippi. The photographer, who was to be a fellow voyager on the expedition, wrung Asa's hand and said he was pleased to meet the chief boatman. "You have the physique for the job, young man!"

Asa wished that Daggett would introduce him as the historian rather than chief boatman.

And now a slim, tall, big-hatted woman appeared, her bright, high-colored face laughing at something her companion had said. Her escort was bearded and handsome. Asa found himself frowning at his proprietorial possession of the woman's arm.

"Who is that?" he whispered to Truesdale.

"Ah, it is the Poetess of Russian Hill—Mary LeGrand Temple."

He knew that name from the magazine, and he realized that she was also the lissome figure depicted on the painted wall, larger than any of the men as she bent to pluck flowers from the miniature mountain peak.

"Is that man her . . . beau?"

"He is a 'Beau' all right," Truesdale replied, laughing. "Bowman Rowlands. He's a developer of mines and other properties. A bonanza chaser," he said contemptuously. "Right now he's testifying in the Little Giants trial. You must have heard of it."

Miss Temple greeted Asa with her sweet smile, which was indented at the corners like a set of parentheses. Gray eyes regarded him coolly. She was a poet of some reputation and also, as an editor, was considered as responsible for the success of the magazine as Henry Park was.

"Hello there, Charley," Rowlands greeted Daggett. "I think I will have to dispute that mad Caledonian ranting in your magazine about the Little Giants debrising the rivers. Surely there are ancient water rights for miners in Scotland just as there are in this grand nation."

"Dispute him, dispute him," Daggett said. "I like a disputatious magazine."

"Hear that, Jamey?" Rowlands called to the piratical-looking nature lover. "I shall respond!"

"Spouting for the monitors," McMurdo called back to him.

"Why, Jamey, *they* are spouting for you and me!" Bowman Rowlands said, laughing, but Asa did not think the exchange was lighthearted.

He found it difficult to keep his eyes off Mary Temple as Rowlands guided her along the table. They seated themselves next to Park and his wife.

Daggett beckoned to the little waiter with the handlebar moustaches. Champagne was brought and ceremoniously poured. Blotner proposed a toast to the new ownership of the *California Monthly.*

"To the new magnate of the arts and cultures!" Rowlands called, raising his glass. He was the only guest who seemed genuinely friendly to Daggett.

Carrington sat between Asa and the little photographer, Truesdale. He held his champagne glass against his cheek as though to cool it, smiling with his pink lips. "So you are to be the author of the lynching of Major Powell," he said.

Asa stammered to ask if Carrington was a friend of Major Powell's.

"Let us say a friend of truth and justice."

"I believe that is Mr. Daggett's interest also."

"*Do* you?" Carrington asked, cocking an eyebrow. "Tell me, please, how did Major Powell get so deeply on the wrong side of Mr. Daggett?"

Asa felt disloyal engaging in this conversation, especially since the campaign against Powell had been superseded by the attempt to rescue the white woman captive, as Carrington must know. He said, "I know they met in Washington, where Major Powell is director of the U.S. Geological Survey. There were disagreements."

"On what subject, pray?"

"I have heard that Major Powell is jealous of anyone else presuming to embark upon *his* River."

"*That* has a ring of truth," Carrington conceded. He smelled of cologne. "So Major Powell presumed to interfere with Mr. Daggett's plans for the Colorado River." He rubbed his champagne glass against his cheek, smiling. "I would, however, never assume the Daggett plans are what they are advertised to be."

"What's he say? What's he say?" Daggett demanded to Asa's other ear.

"He is inquiring if there is a dispute between you and Major Powell, sir."

"Tell him I won't have a one-armed old goat running the West," Daggett said.

Farther down the table Rowlands and McMurdo were interrupting each other in argument, while Henry Parks listened, grinning. Miss Temple smiled down the table at Asa.

McMurdo said, "When the glaciers moved through our mountains, they ground hard rock into honest earth and left fertile valleys and lovely lakes in their wake. The monitors are destroying the mountains and valleys and rivers. They bring wealth to the few and misery to the many!"

"You rail against progress, Jamey! Employment for the working man and meat for his table!"

"Your progress brings only lower wages for the working man, and destroys God's good earth besides."

Miss Temple murmured something to Rowlands, who held his peace. Daggett was scowling.

Waiters loaded the table with platters of spaghetti, shrimp, and vegetables.

Daggett tapped his water glass with his knife. When there was silence he raised his champagne glass. "I propose a toast to Pete Blotner and his fine staff of editors and writers. They have made the *Monthly* the best magazine in the West!"

"Hear! Hear!" Glasses were raised around the table.

"To Mr. Park in particular!" Daggett continued. "What a shame to lose his services to the East Coast."

"Speech!"

Henry Park rose, napkin in hand. He brushed it over his forehead. Glancing around the table, he said, "I would like to thank Peter Blotner, who was our beloved publisher. It was his trust that made me an editor of a fine magazine. And I would like to thank Waldo

Carrington for his sagacity in some difficult times. Most of all, I will salute Mary LeGrand Temple, whose advice and support enabled me to become the writer I had always hoped to be. I am grateful to my fellow editors and to our publisher for the years that have been the happiest of my life. May the magazine's honest policies continue to flourish under its new publisher!"

He sat down abruptly, surrounded by applause. His pretty wife leaned on his shoulder.

Carrington was on his feet. "I join in the salute to Mary Temple, the beauteous lady who *is* the *California Monthly!*"

"Who is California itself!" Rowlands cried.

Carrington remained standing. Now he recited:

She is the chief Templar of the Triad,
Our very own priestess and dryad,
Poetess natural and free,
Her admirers are we,
And all by her presence made glad.

Amid the applause and laughter Asa squinted at the painted figure on the wall.

McMurdo stood combing his fingers through his beard. "I will bespeak my tribute to Mary Temple also. I will compare her to that loveliest valley I know, the Yosemite! With her gleams of polished granite, the blue of mountain lakes, the high-rising green of her forests, the rills and falls of water, to the birdsong and the whisper of evening breezes in the pines." He bowed to the blushing woman.

It occurred to Asa that this celebration of new ownership had turned to praise of Miss Temple because, with Henry Park's departure, it was felt that she should succeed him as editor in chief. He suspected that Daggett would be well aware of this effort to manipulate him.

Daggett tapped his water glass with his knife again.

"I will toast an even grander canyon than the Yosemite!"

There was a dramatic pause before he continued: "The Grand Canyon of the Colorado! To the expedition that will rescue the unfortunate female captive of the savages there!

"Our preparations are almost complete," Daggett went on. "We will depart within three weeks' time. Young Asa Haden here will be aboard. And Mr. Truesdale, our photographer. The super is Jake Buchanan, from Denver, who can do just about anything he is asked to do. And Will Jefford, the eminent geologist, who some of you will know. And a fellow that was along on Major Powell's second expedition, if I can get him out of the hoosegow—"

Daggett paused for the laughter. Asa realized that he had neatly removed the emphasis from Miss Temple and at the same time had struck a blow at Major Powell with the reference to one of his crew in prison.

"So I will ask the Yosemite of California to take a back seat to the Grand Canyon of Arizona Territory, and to the unfortunate white woman that is a captive to redskins there. We must set her free!"

There was a scattering of applause. The noise of conversations rose again, Miss Temple listening now to Bowman Rowlands.

Carrington captured Asa's attention again by tapping on his wrist with a manicured forefinger. "Yesterday Mr. Daggett's purpose was to expose Major Powell as a fraud and a humbug. Today it is to set free a young woman who may or may not be the captive of Indians along your route. But he spoke of a geologist, so there will be prospecting for minerals. And a surveyor for the purpose of staking claims?"

"What's he say? What's he say?" Daggett whispered fiercely.

"He wants to know if the expedition will be prospecting for minerals."

"Tell him damned right it will be!"

After dinner that evening Asa and Daggett walked along Kearny Street in starlit darkness. There were a few gas-flame illuminations in the buildings they passed, and buggies with lanterns. Orientals flowed along the sidewalks on their errands, jabbering their jagged tongue. To a New York Stater, San Francisco was a very foreign place, with its Chinese coolies, French restaurants, Italian fishermen, and Russian Hill.

"This durn place is about half Chink, it seems like," Daggett grumbled.

"Well, they built the railroad for Mr. Crocker."

"I'll choose an Irisher over a Chink any time for laying track,"

Daggett said. "At least you have some idea of what they're thinking. Maybe I'll take a prowl around Portsmouth Square."

Portsmouth Square was where parlor houses were to be found, and nearby was Chinatown with the cribs of the Chinese slave girls, calling out their explicit invitations in piping voices. Asa was no longer shocked by Daggett's attendance in these establishments, as though such an encounter was considered only a part of the evening, like an after-dinner cigar. They separated at the corner, and Asa headed up the hill to his lodging house.

He lay on his hard bed with his hands clasped under his head, gazing up into the black above him. He had been disturbed by Carrington's suspicions of Daggett, for he had felt those suspicions himself—that sense, with his employer, that he was on hand only to serve Daggett's purpose, but without being informed of the particulars of that purpose.

He was to meet the next day at the *California Monthly* offices with the charming Miss Temple and the inquisitive Mr. Carrington, to discuss the history of the expedition that he was to write, along with his investigation of Powell's journal of his own exploration.

He drowsed and jerked awake to images of slashing waves, cruel rocks, capsizing boats, and fears of his insufficiency as head boatman. And as historian.

San Francisco 3

MARY TEMPLE

Beau Rowlands had been a contributor to the *California Monthly,* and a longtime friend to the California Triad, although the enmities of the anti-debris cause had turned Henry Park against him. It was rumored that Beau had a dark madonna of a Mexican mistress in Sonora, but it was clear to Mary Temple that on his present stay in the city, as an expert witness in the *Hutchinson* trial, he was courting *her.*

There had been a wonderful Sunday gallop in a Studebaker buggy, out to the Cliff House for breakfast, where Beau was shockingly liberal with his money. There were invitations to join him at the Tivoli Gardens on Sutter, at dinner at his hotel, at the theater, at the roller-skating rink. Sometime soon would come the moment when she would have to *decide*—and her position with the men among whom she circulated depended upon her being a sister to all. The gatherings at her house on Broadway—sometimes the California Triad for tea, sometimes a larger group—were composed almost entirely of men, although two other female poets were occasionally included, because, Waldo had accused her, they were "neither nymph nor dryad."

When Mary had let herself in her door she turned to accept the embrace of Beau Rowlands, prepared to reject any further notions he might have. His beard brushed silky against her cheek, his lips touched hers.

Her foot scuffed against the letters the postman had dropped through the slot in the door. She disengaged herself from Beau's arms, lit the gas jet, and stooped to pick up the two pieces of mail. One she recognized as being from a young poet who was seeking her assistance. The other, in its heavy brown envelope, felt as though it contained a sheet of lead.

She stood holding it, her other hand pressed to her throat where she could feel her pulse. The only sound was the hiss of the gas flame in its chimney. Beau leaned back against the door to close it. The white light made perfect black circles of his eyes watching her.

"What's the matter, Mary?"

She picked up the letter opener from the side table, slit the envelope, and drew from it a single sheet of paper. Printed on the paper in black ink, bisected by the line of the fold, was what might have been the three oversized leaves of a clover, clumsily made. She handed the paper to Beau, as though there was something he could do about it.

"What is it?" he asked, frowning.

"It's the stump of a man's severed wrist, inked and pressed to the paper."

This week her past had caught up with her present like a leopard pursuing its prey—twelve years since Esther had been taken by Indians, nine since Mary herself had fled from Los Angeles. It seemed appropriate that the past should seek her out in terms of paper—the clipping from the *Alta California* and this obscenity—for paper had been her medium since she was a girl mailing her poems to the San Francisco magazines under the pen name LeGrand Temple.

"I don't understand," Beau said. He moved to support her with his arm against her back as she started into the darkness of the parlor. Through the windows, dots of light glimmered on the black waters of the Bay. She wilted onto the settee. It was as though there was insufficient air in the room.

Beau seated himself opposite her, a dim bulk. A match was struck with a flash of fire. The odor of sulphur and tobacco smoke drifted to her.

"I know you prefer a mysterious past."

"It's not so mysterious as painful." She fixed her eyes on the glowing end of Beau's cigar. "It's my husband," she said.

"*Husband!*" Beau almost shouted. "You have never—One was led to believe—Why does he send this signature of the stump of his arm?"

"To show me he knows my whereabouts."

"Does he intend to harm you?"

Mary shrugged. "Perhaps he only wants me fearful. Frightened of shadows. Afraid to come home alone."

"Tell me," Beau said, in his deep voice.

"We were married when I was eighteen, very soon after my parents and I arrived in Los Angeles. He is much older. His family is old Californio. Of which line he is the last. And least. His name is Ramón Jiménez." She paused to gather her breath.

"I was overwhelmed by his attentions. He wore fine clothes and was very courtly. He had beautiful horses. We went for rides in his buggy—so fast! He was a friend of Governor Pio Pico, and we rode in the governor's entourage in a parade. I didn't know he was a drunkard and a womanizer.

"After we were married he was often away, attending to the family ranches. When he was at home he drank. He accused me of having betrayed him when he was away. He abused me. Finally I fled from his brutality to my father's house. When he tried to break into the house my father shot him. His hand had to be amputated. I came to San Francisco and changed my name. He found me once before, two years ago, before I moved to this house. This same letter was delivered."

"To be falsely accused—" Beau started.

Not falsely, Mary reminded herself. Poor gentle, tubercular David Reilly had encouraged her poetry, had showed her how to educate herself, and had taken advantage of her gratitude. She, who had almost managed to live without a past, had now coughed it up to Bowman Rowlands like some breath of dust in her dry throat.

"Why not divorce him?" he asked.

"I thought he would die, of drink or violence or profligacy, and I would hear of it and be relieved to be a widow."

"The fact that you had apparently never married has been a topic of discussion, as you may have realized."

"Now you know my secret," she said, and managed a laugh.

The shape of him loomed suddenly. He knelt beside the settee, his tobacco-smelling mouth pressed to her cheek. "My lady of secrets," he murmured.

"Octavius urges me to go to England so I can become famous," she said. "I would love to go to England to feel safe!" But she must remain in San Francisco to see if the White Captive was rescued, and if that captive was Esther.

"Come with me to Sonora!" Beau said excitedly. "To Encino, to the mine. It's beautiful there. We'll ride fine horses in the hills. Such beautiful oaks! Your servants will treat you like a princess. You can write poems to your heart's content! There are mountains more beautiful than Tamalpais. There are magnificent haciendas nearby. It is like the life of the nobility a hundred years ago. The peasantry will touch their forelocks and cross themselves when you pass by them, people with skin the colors of the earth. And the beautiful girls, the old-gold girls! It is a life you would love!"

By the time he finished she was laughing. She loved his enthusiasm, that throaty key to his voice when he sought to persuade. She loved his honesty, too, even when it was wholeheartedly given to the wrong causes. The beautiful girls of color!

"Ah, but you would be often gone. When you returned you would accuse me of betraying you."

"I can conceive of you no other way but faithful!" he said pompously.

"I cannot conceive of you as faithful at all, dear Beau."

He emitted his explosive laugh. "Mary, what if something happened to Ramón Jiménez to shorten his baleful life?"

"I would be relieved beyond measure, but I cannot encourage such a thing."

"If someone loved you enough—" he started, but she stopped him, touching his lips with her fingers .

She could no longer recall what Ramón looked like: a small moustache, the beginnings of a paunch, restless Castilian eyes. Now he would be older also, with more of a paunch, with only one hand. She could recall her schoolmaster father exactly, with his face as gray as blotting paper and his stiff graying hair, aiming the shiny little revolver at the hand that had broken the pane of glass in the door and groped inside for the latch. One of his daughters had been stolen by Indians, the other beaten by her Mexican husband. He had committed only this one act of violence in his life, but his savings were consumed by the lawyer who had kept him out of prison for it.

Mary shook her head to banish the past. "Do you think Mr. Daggett's expedition can rescue this poor captive young woman?" she asked.

"If Charley sets out to do a thing, he will usually do it. Poor girl! What a life she must have led. But you know, there's a particular way our noble redman friends are not savages. It is to women. No doubt she will have been married to a brave, but she will not have been personally molested."

"Is it only white men who molest women, then?"

"The white man's gender is known to be stronger."

"You say Mr. Daggett usually does what he sets out to do. Am I to understand that you are old friends?"

"We are partners."

"In what enterprise?" she asked. In a mine or mines, of course, for Beau was a mining engineer trained at Yale, and Daggett an investor in mines.

"Coalfields in Colorado," he said. "High-carbon coal. It's a sure thing! You know, while I was in the employ of the Geological Survey I discovered so much mineral that I was unable to profit from, because of my position. It was maddening."

"You have told me that the Encino Mine will make your fortune."

He made a growling sound, half humorous and half tragic. "So much maneuvering and bribing, so many setbacks."

"And coalfields in Colorado!"

"A little further down the road, you understand. But, Mary, I would be a rich man *right now!*"

"You will be, Beau. I prophesy it."

"My partnership with Charley is a secret," he said.

"So many secrets!" She could feel the ache of tears in her eyes.

"I would like to hold California in my arms, Mary."

"I'm afraid you would only have a frightened woman in your arms, Beau. It would not be much of a conquest."

"I count it a conquest to be in the same room with Mary LeGrand Temple," he said.

Who had girlishly been Mary Bingham, and pseudonymously LeGrand Temple, and matrimonially Mary Bingham Jiménez. She crumpled the letter from her husband and tossed it into the stove.

"Let us leave it at that, please, dear Beau," she said. For now.

San Francisco 4

ASA HADEN, MARY TEMPLE

The window of the office of the *California Monthly* was cloaked in drifting fog that left droplets like rain on the glass. Sounds from the street below were muffled: the rattle of wheels, the squeal of a greaseless hub, a shout. Asa Haden sat at the large table with Mary Temple and Waldo Carrington, sometimes swiping at his forehead with his handkerchief. He had not felt so nervous since his first examinations at Cornell.

On the wall was a frieze of magazine covers, with the monitory eye repeated. Below these, on a long sideboard, were mahogany boxes containing manuscripts.

He had left Daggett sunk in a leather chair in the hotel lobby with three other capitalists, all of them puffing up columns of smoke like locomotives on a grade. He supposed he should be flattered that his employer thought him competent to endure this interview on his own.

Miss Temple looked tired this morning, dark stains under her eyes and a little sag of loose flesh beneath her chin. But the smile she offered him was reassuring.

Pink-cheeked and red-lipped, Carrington sat beside her, sharp eyes watching Asa as he spoke.

"Major Powell's book first appeared as a series of articles in *Scribner's Monthly,*" Asa told them. "Then it was published in book form. The first part of the book is a journal of the expedition. The second half is a discussion of the geology of the region. No questions have arisen about the second section."

Carrington nodded, and Miss Temple seemed to be listening sympathetically.

"The journal, however, could not have been written on the spot as it purports to be," he went on. "It consists of a narrative of the two voyages on the river, those of 1869 and 1871, mixed together. In fact, Major Powell was not much aboard the boats on the second voyage, which was under the command of another man. There is no mention in the book that there even was a second expedition, and none of its personnel is mentioned.

"Mr. Daggett spoke with several of the members of the first expedition. One of them told him there was a great deal of untruth in the book but would not elaborate—apparently out of loyalty to Major Powell. Several of these men also kept journals, which Mr. Daggett was allowed to examine. There is disagreement with Major Powell's narrative."

"One would be most interested in the story of the three men who were killed by Indians," Miss Temple said.

"They were Oramel and Seneca Howland, and William Dunn. The other journals all speak of dissension between the older Howland and the Major. One of the boats was wrecked because Howland disregarded a signal of Major Powell's, or did not see it in time. It seems that Major Powell did not forgive this; and the Major and *his* brother, Captain Powell—who was generally unpopular—were at continuing odds with Dunn."

Asa patted his forehead with his handkerchief again. "Separation Canyon is so called because that is where the three left the expedition. The members of the party were much weakened by hunger, and the Major's book says that the reason the three gave for departing was their conviction that if they did not leave the canyon at that point they might not have the strength to leave it further on."

"But the others were not so concerned?" Miss Temple asked.

He raised his hands in a shrug of unknowing. "They didn't know where they were, but in fact they were within a very few days of Callville—the end of their journey. The three deserters—although Major Powell never calls them that—climbed to the plateau, where they were murdered by Indians as they slept. The hostiles were Shivwits, a Paiute band. The Shivwits are good friends to the Mormons, who inhabit that desolate country. Shivwits in alliance with Mormons first attacked the Denton wagon train in the Iron County Massacre. You will recall that Mormon militia painted and garbed themselves as Indians, overwhelmed the wagon train's defenders, and killed some forty gentiles. Mr. Daggett is very interested in the reasons for the Indian attack on the Howlands and Dunn. Were Mormons involved in this massacre also?"

"Has Mr. Daggett a bone to pick with Brigham Young also?" Carrington wanted to know.

Asa felt his face heat up. It was true that Daggett was outspoken against the Mormons.

"Do I recall that an Indian woman was molested?" Miss Temple asked, watching him with her level gray eyes.

"That was the Shivwits' claim, but Major Powell denied that it could be true. They were good men, he said."

"But white men," Miss Temple said mysteriously.

"During the second expedition Major Powell made a trip to the Shivwits in company with Mormon interpreters—to publicly forgive the band for the murders. That is interesting also."

Asa leaned back in his chair, feeling the sweat lace down his forehead again like the fog droplets on the windowpane.

"You have done your researches," Miss Temple said.

"Mr. Daggett has done most of it."

"And what does our publisher propose?" Carrington asked, leaning on the handle of his umbrella.

"I am to be historian of Mr. Daggett's expedition. I will keep a day-to-day journal. I hope the *California Monthly* will publish my account."

"Presumably that is what Mr. Daggett will require," Carrington said. "And your account will also be a—commentary, shall we say?—on Major Powell's narrative?"

Asa nodded. His jaw ached.

Miss Temple asked, "Is it your impression that Mr. Daggett takes seriously an attempt to rescue the White Captive of the Hoyas?"

"Yes, ma'am!" He could say that without reservation, at least. "He feels it's a stroke of good fortune. He calls it his 'luck.' If she could be rescued, it would result in a great stir in the newspapers, which would be to his benefit. He will employ an experienced Mormon missionary, who will actually effect the rescue. He speaks of the matter often, and with great enthusiasm."

Carrington looked amused, scratching his closely shaven upper lip. "What foresight, Mary, to have had that newspaper clipping in your possession just in time to fill Mr. Daggett's need."

Asa saw Miss Temple's face turn pink. She said, "If she can be rescued, must she continue on down to Callville with you, or can she leave the Canyon sooner?"

"The rescue party would leave for the Hoya village from the Colorado Chiquito. She would be brought back to the River there. Not far below that is Bright Angel Canyon, which is a route out to the Mormon settlements to the north."

"So if someone accompanies this young woman out of the Grand Canyon, he can also bring your journal to date," Carrington said.

"Yes, sir."

"And if she is not found?"

"Someone will bring my journal to a crew waiting at the head of Bright Angel."

"Tell me, young man," Carrington said, "how is it that Mr. Daggett has chosen you to play such an important part in his expedition?"

"His son and I were great friends at college. I have had rivering experience. I come from Gracie County in New York State, where boys learn canoeing as they learn to walk. And Chick sent his father some pieces I had written for the *Cornell Era*."

"Have you brought samples of your work that we might examine?" Miss Temple asked.

Asa slid the Manila envelope across the table to her.

"It's clear that a part of Mr. Daggett's purpose is to discredit Major Powell," Carrington said. "Is it for revenge, or only for advantage? He may have similar designs against the Mormon Church. This puts Miss Temple and me in the position of being party to his enmities, if you understand me. What I would like from you is assurance that you will pursue the truth and not merely Mr. Daggett's advantage."

Asa's face heated up again as he looked straight back at Carrington and said, "I will pursue the truth, sir."

Carrington smiled thinly. "Good!" He touched his hair, which was so neatly combed that the part looked like a line drawn on his scalp with chalk.

Miss Temple, spectacles on her nose, was studying Asa's articles from the *Cornell Era,* a knot of frown lines in her forehead. "You write very forthrightly, Mr. Haden."

Asa didn't know whether that was a compliment or a criticism, but he said, "Thank you, Miss Temple."

"I will ask you to consider employing fewer modifiers. Please remember that the adverb is the enemy of the verb."

"Thank you, Miss Temple," he said again.

"You may call me Mary, and Mr. Carrington Waldo. And you will be Asa."

He thanked her still again, flushing painfully. "I am to leave next week for Denver, to meet the man Mr. Daggett has placed in charge of the expedition, a Mr. Buchanan. We will travel to the Colorado River at a place called Pariah Crossing and should begin our voyage from there by August second."

"Will Mr. Daggett accompany you?"

"He hopes to be able to accompany the expedition, but he is not sure he can spare the time." Asa had prayed that Daggett would *not* come along on the expedition.

"We do hope he will be able to accompany you," Carrington said, smiling.

"Comported himself well enough, I thought," Waldo said when the door had closed behind the good-looking, earnest young man who was to be the historian of the Daggett expedition. "Can he write?"

"He won't disgrace us," Mary Temple said, slipping her glasses off her nose. "Some editing, of course."

"I'll leave that to you, my dear," Waldo said with an airy flip of his hand. "You're not so severe with the sensibilities of young writers as I would be."

She shook a finger at him. "It's the duty of editors to cooperate with their publisher. Mr. Daggett is now our publisher."

"I'm afraid the *Monthly* will not survive our publisher," Waldo sighed theatrically. "We were such a happy few, you and I and Henry. How quickly things change!"

How quickly! It was easy for Waldo Carrington to speak lightly of the dissolution of the magazine, for a dying relative had left him mining stocks that had proved valuable. She herself had no such resources.

"Why, my dear!" Waldo exclaimed. "Can those tiny jewels glistening upon your cheeks be *tears?*"

Mary brought her handkerchief out from her sleeve. "Yes, Waldo, I am feeling afflicted today. With a past rampant. You see, I believe the so-called White Captive is my sister."

He gazed at her with a half-open mouth while she told him about Esther Bingham.

"That explains the fortuitous newspaper clipping," he said finally. He cleared his throat. "My dear, I think you must prepare yourself for the failure of this attempt, despite the no doubt overwhelming competence of Mr. Daggett and his employees. You must also prepare yourself for the probability that the young woman is other than your sister. Or, that if she *be* this relative, she will have changed into something it will be difficult for you to bear."

"Yes," she said.

"It may be that, having lived among savages for so long, she will have become herself a savage."

"Yes, Waldo."

"Could it even be that she is content with her lot and will not be happy removed to the strange, new, terrifying world of San Francisco? Where even citizens as sophisticated as you and I, my dear, find it difficult to cope?"

Waldo rose to come and stand beside her, one hand patting her shoulder. She leaned her head against his hip. She loved him in a different way from the other men in her life, for he loved her differently also. Waldo most loved those bronzed young lads of Hawaii, disporting themselves on the ocean waves, about whom he wrote his flowery little stories.

"I couldn't get along without you, Waldo. Please don't quit the magazine in one of your huffs."

"For you, my dear, I will not huff." He patted her shoulder.

"My husband has found me again," she said.

"I am sorry for that."

"He found me when I lived on Vallejo Street, near you. Now he has found me on Broadway. I received a missive from him. I don't want to move again, to hide. I love my little house."

He patted.

"Maybe he means no real harm, maybe he only wants me to spend days like this one, tearful and fearful."

"My advice has always been," Waldo said, "that people should take the greatest care whom they marry. It is so very final."

She sat at her desk rereading the long poem Octavius Coogan had sent the magazine at her request. She sighed with anticipation of the labor that would be required to induce Octavius to change words and repair lines. How understanding she would have to be, and how careful, but how insistent.

The poem was not only wordy, but the words were often oddly misused, as though Octy were a foreigner consulting an unreliable dictionary. She recalled both his obstinacy and his fragile sensibilities.

She glanced up over her spectacles to see James McMurdo frowning at her from the doorway. "Marrry!" he said, rolling her name like treacle.

"Come in, Jamey!"

He whipped off his queer little black cap, like the headgear of the third mate of some round-the-Horn schooner, and strode across the office to seat himself opposite her.

Instead of looking at his auditor, McMurdo seemed to aim his face with his unkempt beard and his eyes as blue as the Sierra sky he loved.

"Marrry!" He rolled her name again. "I am fearful of that man!"

"Mr. Daggett?"

"They have established themselves with the railroads, these villains! They appear like the maggots in dead meat, look you! The miners in the Mother Lode panning their gold did not destroy the land, but these devils will build the flumes to produce a head of water with which the monitors can reduce a hill in half a day. And wash the slickens down the creeks to foul the rivers and fill the Bay with mud! It is men like your precious Daggett who have the money and the damnable imagination to ruin our dear state as they have already ruined Colorado!"

"He is not my precious Daggett, Jamey! He is only my employer."

"Mark you!" he said, pointing a finger and aiming his face at her. His blue eyes were curiously mild in his fierce features.

"Surely an anti-debris bill will be passed by the legislature to save the rivers and the Bay," she said. "Surely the *Hutchinson* suit will be resolved against the Little Giants."

These were subjects that she and Beau had avoided so far.

"I believe your article will be very instrumental in this cause," she added.

"That piece of mine you have accepted, 'The Water-Ouzel.'"

"We will publish it."

"But if you are ordered not to? I have heard Bowman Rowlands brag that he would refute my piece on the devastations of the monitors. He is a creature of the mine owners!"

"He's a mining engineer, after all," Mary said, putting down her spectacles. And Beau and Mr. Daggett were partners.

McMurdo's mild blue eyes peered at her. "Beau is verrry handsome, Marrry."

"I have heard it said so."

"I myself am an ugly fellow," he said proudly. "Women *will* look upon the exterior of a man rather than what is within." He aimed his face away from her.

The fact was that she did respond to the good looks, the pleasant manner, and indeed the flesh, of Beau Rowlands, and not to the admitted virtues of James McMurdo.

"Beau Rowlands is a man who would put his own advancement before all other matters, great or small, mark you!" Jamey said. "He pursues you, Marrry. I have watched him watching you!"

"I can take care of myself, Jamey."

"He is a Daggett who is handsome to the eye and winsome in his manner, but he is a Daggett all the same."

"I don't know whether you wish me to defend Mr. Daggett or Beau Rowlands," she said, laughing.

"This expedition," he said. "Mark you, it is more than it seems. It will be an expedition of despoliation, for that is all this man Daggett knows. Think of monitors blasting those sublime cliffs Major Powell described in his book!"

It took an effort not to be rude to James McMurdo in disengaging herself from an argument in which he would force her to defend Beau Rowlands.

CHAPTER

5

Pariah Crossing

JAKE BUCHANAN

Jake Buchanan paced the beach at Pariah Crossing, watching the crew of the Colorado River expedition toting freight to the boats, his arms clamped together over his chest and his unlit pipe in his teeth.

The boats were moored to willow scrub along the River's edge. The *Canyon Lass* and the *Letty Daggett* were both twenty feet long, made of good oak planking bright with varnish, with watertight compartments fore and aft. The scout boat, *Miss Saucy,* named for a lady of Buchanan's affections, was a sixteen-footer of lighter construction. Bows secured, the three sterns rose and fell in irregular rhythm to the milk-chocolate sweep of the River under the rosy cliffs of the Pariah amphitheater.

Buchanan had his eye on the photographer, Tiny Truesdale, and the geologist, Will Jefford, for shirkers. Truesdale made about one trip up the beach for every three that the others made, and Jefford, with his red bandanna knotted over his bald head, spent a good portion of time squatting by the water jugs in the willow shade.

The big jailbird, Morphy, was a worker. He had a back as broad as a barn door, and his elbows winged out as he carried one of the crates of photographic plates, staggering a bit with the weight. The college boy, Asa Haden, with his fancy hat, worked right along with him. They were going to be two good ones.

The old Mormon missionary Hyrum Logan and the little half-breed Poche—the two who were to head up the Colorado Chiquito after the White Captive—worked together, two-manhandling one of the cases that Morphy could take on by himself. Ritter, the surveyor, also a Saint, had a way of walking as though each of his steps had to be about ten inches longer than a regular person's or else no one would recognize how important he was.

Buchanan stopped his pacing as the college boy called out and raised an arm to point. Two horsemen and a pair of pack animals were switchbacking down the trail out of a slot in the cliff. That would be Charles P. Daggett and the cook. And maybe the pack animals had the life preserver jackets aboard.

He started toward the canvas awning, which was supported by six oars braced and stayed upright, erected on the beach for this arrival. Finding that he was emulating the surveyor's leg-stretching style of walk, Buchanan quit it and jammed his pipe into his pocket.

It wasn't a cook with Daggett, it was a sorry-looking mule skinner with a ragged hat.

Daggett loved fancy dress, and his outfit lived up to expectation. The capitalist wore a dusty blue admiral's tunic with gold-braid epaulets, an admiral's fore-and-aft hat, and canvas leggings with brass trim. Buchanan ground his teeth at this evidence that Charley Daggett intended to come along on the expedition.

He was aboard a long-eared mule. You could tell the mule skinner wasn't the cook because he was skinny as a rail and sour-looking, the two of them dusty all over.

"Where's the cook?" Buchanan called out.

"Fired the scoundrel," Daggett explained, reining up. "He had the shakes real bad, and he smelled bad, too. You didn't want him along on the River, Jake."

"I want those life preservers, though," Buchanan said.

Daggett scowled at him in the fierce Canyon sunlight, mopping his face with a blue bandanna that matched his admiral outfit. His red sideburns were frosted at the ends, his face scarlet from the heat, and above the knob of his nose his eyes pouched independently, like lizard eyes. "Now, Jake," he said.

Buchanan was boiling with impatience to get started down the River, dread and excitement mixed. He had a crew he hardly knew, no life jackets, a college boy for chief boatman, a jailbird who should have been chief boatman, and no cook. And he was going to have an admiral on his hands, when he would have bet good money that Daggett wouldn't show up.

Daggett slid off his mule to embrace him, patting him like lumping a mattress. He smelled like a horse barn. When Buchanan lumped in return dust swarmed out of the admiral's tunic. Everything Charles P. Daggett laid his hand to turned to gold, but no glitter had rubbed off on Jake Buchanan yet. The wonder of what made Daggett so lucky itched in his imagination, as though if he could puzzle it out he would have figured the West, and the nation as well.

The crew had halted in their tracks to gawk at the newcomers. "Keeping up the standards, my boy!" Daggett hollered to Asa Haden, who wore a collegiate striped jacket and a flat-brimmed straw hat with a ribbon on it that irritated Buchanan like a stone in his boot.

The camera stood on its tripod in the shade, ready for Tiny Truesdale to make the admiral's photograph.

Daggett beckoned the crew to him with some vigorous arm waving, pacing under the canopy. Buchanan was pleased to let him take over the pacing, which he'd been doing for ten days.

"Some of you know the history of this grand River," Daggett said when they had all assembled. "First man down was a horse thief name of White. Showed up at Callville on a raft, raving out of his head, didn't even know for sure where he'd put in. Said Injuns kilt his partner, so he flung a couple of timbers together and went on the float. Cataracts! Falls! Wild waves! We'll see 'em all, boys!" He shared his grin around, like bonus pay.

"Then Major Powell and his bunch. This young fellow, Mr. Haden, is the historian of the outfit. He can tell you about Major Powell's exploration!"

Blushing at the attention, the college boy took off his fancy hat and held it in his two hands.

Daggett wasn't about to let anyone else speak, however. "That was eleven years ago," he went on. "They came down from Green River City in Wyoming, took them three months. Loads of troubles! Short on food! Upsets! Some fellows was run off. Killed by Injuns!"

Daggett paced some more, swiping at his face with his blue bandanna. "The Major made a second trip two years later," he said. "As far down the Canyon as Kanab Creek. Pat Morphy was along on that jaunt." He waggled a hand toward the big boatman.

"The Major is the finest man alive!" Morphy proclaimed. He had a broad, sunburnt Irish face with an upper lip like a riverbank. He jabbed a finger upward, as though Major Powell resided in heaven.

Buchanan watched Daggett's nose twitch like a bad smell.

"There is some that would like to turn this Canyon into public lands!" Daggett said, meaning Major John Wesley Powell. "Take it right away from the people. Run the prospectors off. Fence out the sheep and cattle. Well, this survey is going to open the Canyon like a can of peaches!"

A riffle of laughter pleased Daggett.

Will Jefford, with his bandanna head and his mouth like a scar, was squinting as though the railroad and mining magnate amused him. The old Mormon, Hyrum Logan, and the breed sat hip to hip. In the whole bunch only Logan, Morphy, and Asa Haden had any rivering experience.

Out of earshot, the mule skinner was unloading mules, moving slow as molasses. Upriver at the crossing, Buchanan could see the skin-and-bones ferryman, Smith, bending and sidling at work on his stake-sided ferry. He and his fat wife and a couple of kits eked out a living by transporting travelers across the River in this bake-oven country.

The River shivered in the heat. He cocked his ear to its watery mutter, trying to identify the voice of enemy or friend. There was a steady note of danger anyhow, and plenty of tales of it from the two Powell expeditions, not to speak of the contention that had ended with the so-called Separation.

He felt like a rope jerking with strain, he was so anxious to get on the River.

Daggett paced some more. "I expect you know your partners by now," he said. "Mr. Jefford, here, is our geologist." He pointed a finger like a pistol. "He knows his minerals, you can bet. He'll help me tie up this Canyon with mineral claims so *nobody* can make public lands of it."

Jefford laid the palm of his hand above his eyes as though sighting on gold seams.

"And Mr. Ritter is surveyor." Daggett pointed his pistol at the Mormon transit man with his face like a sour apple, his personality to match, and his long-distance stride.

"Mr. Truesdale will be making photographic views. He is going to put this *entire* Canyon onto his glass plates."

Truesdale was a dapper miniature gent with a moustache and goatee and a smooth neck like a girl's sprouting out of the collar of his overall. He was a nonpareil arguer around the campfire at night and had announced that he disapproved of Charles P. Daggett for being rich.

"You all know Mr. Pat Morphy, who was Major Powell's right-hand man."

Morphy pulled an orangutan face, jammed one fist in the opposite palm, and flexed his muscles.

"And this sartorial young chap, Mr. Asa Haden, was captain of the rowing boats at Cornell University and my son's best pal. He is educated, and he will write pieces for a magazine about this voyage."

Haden raised a hand, blushing again. "I wasn't the captain, sir."

"Should've been, my son told me!" Daggett said, pacing and turning, who didn't care for contradiction.

"We were told you would be bringing life preservers," Truesdale said, sticking out his goatee like a bowsprit.

"We didn't have no preservers on our trip!" Morphy said. There was no love lost between him and Tiny—big man and little man. "Except for the Major, that's a one-arm fellow. Nobody drownded, either!"

Powell's second expedition had quit halfway down the Canyon, so Morphy could say he'd heard the second half was the rougher, though the first was blessed bad enough.

Buchanan had taken a run with the jailbird in *Miss Saucy* down into Marble Canyon, where red rock walls sprang vertically out of the

River. Rowing back upstream, he had enjoyed the muscle stretch of digging hard to keep pace with Morphy's powerful oar. "Just get your back into it and *hate* somebody," Morphy had said. He had been a seventeen-year-old teamster when he had joined Powell and must have some wisdom about the River and the Canyon, but all too often he was a stubborn Irish barnyard rooster. Charley Daggett had bought him out of a Texas prison to come along on the survey.

"Now, the super here is Mr. Buchanan, who you are all acquainted with by now," Daggett went on. "He is the boss. I am only along for the ride. Loyal is what I pay good money for, and Mr. Buchanan is the most loyal fellow I know. Mr. Buchanan can do anything. He can lace both boots at the same time. He can shoot a fat buck with a blindfold on. He can see around corners. When there is hard bark called for, I call for Mr. Buchanan. Anybody thinks of causing trouble, they better do it around *two* corners from Jake Buchanan!"

"Who's going to cook?" Morphy demanded. "What about picking up a squaw for cook? Other chores, too," he smirked.

Daggett scowled, who didn't like that kind of talk, though he kept a plump, copper-haired Italian opera singer in a little clapboard house in Denver. Martha Daggett was well aware of it, too.

Buchanan thought Daggett was pausing for air before he told the crew about the White Captive, whom they had only heard rumors about so far. Daggett winked at him.

"Now!" he said. "There is a white woman captive of the redskins out there somewhere. Don't know who she is, or anything about her. Except she is there, and we are going to bring her out.

"It was a trader name of Dubine from Tucson that spied her," he went on. "In one of the Hoya villages south of the Little Colorado." He pointed his pistol finger at Logan to speak.

Hyrum's voice had a rusty creak to it, as though he didn't use it much. He was a solemn, silent old fellow with a hard, seamed face and a ragged crown of spiky gray hair. "I went to see Frenchy Dubine," he said. "He is known to be crooked as a Philadelphia street, and he did not see the gain of telling me much. He saw a young white woman in a village he didn't want to tell me the exact whereabouts of. When he tried to find her to talk to her, she was hid from him. There was other Hoya that knew of her, however. She is a married woman, for she was dressed like that. Poche has come along to help me bring her out. He has got an uncle that is a Hoya chief in that district, and that is how we will locate her." Hyrum stopped as though he had caught himself talking too much.

Poche nodded around, scowling importantly because he spoke Hoya lingo. He was a squat-built fellow in a buckskin shirt, his flat-brim hat jammed down on his brown forehead. "We will bring her back to her own people," he said.

"We will stop at the Little Colorado while these two go after Miss Bingham," Daggett said. "I am giving fifty-fifty odds."

Buchanan glanced over to see how Morphy was responding to the news that there might be a female aboard, even if she had been ploughed by every Hoya buck south of the Colorado Chiquito. Morphy grinned back at him.

The college boy looked worried.

"How long do you reckon it will take?" Ritter wanted to know, in that way he had, as though someone else was always to blame and he might as well get that established in advance. He and Hyrum didn't like each other much, even though they were both Mormons.

Hyrum's deep-set eyes flicked at him. "It will go fast, or it won't go at all. I can't say how long."

"I give it about fifty-fifty," Daggett said again, who had produced neither life preservers nor cook.

Tiny made the admiral's photograph with appropriate ceremony, posing Daggett with a hand tucked between the buttons of his tunic, shrouding himself in his black cloth behind the mahogany and brass box of his camera, then reappearing and cautioning Daggett not to move. His disapproval of the rich man did not seem to affect his interest in making a portrait.

Afterward, Buchanan and his employer sat under the awning to look over accounts and lists while the others cleared out to give them privacy. The mule skinner lounged in the willow shade, taking his ease.

"How about the skinner coming along to cook for us?" Buchanan said.

Daggett produced a distasteful expression. "Mr. Brown is a man of disgusting habits and about as much brains as his mules. I do not wish to travel any further with him. Anyway, he has got to carry a pack of papers back to Ira Ellsworth. Now, Jake, I know this White Captive business don't sit well with you. Truth is, I don't give it a ten percent chance. But if we brought her out, it would do us a heap of good. Every newspaper in the country would stand and salute! Even if we try and miss, it is good for us. It is why I decided to come along, you see."

Buchanan sucked on his teeth, realizing that Daggett's brand of thinking was the reason he was a millionaire.

"You are a fellow who finishes what he starts," Daggett liked to praise him, "a fellow who knows how to get things done." Buchanan had done most things there were to do in the West—had run a trapline, shot buffalo, punched cattle, dealt faro, deputied, shot Apaches—shot at them, anyhow—brought in meat for railroad crews, and bossed those same crews. He had never run a plow, he had never chosen to marry, and he had never got rich.

Susan Darling, Miss Saucy, had said to him, "If you were as faithful to a girl as you are to Mr. Daggett, what a loving man you would be!"

Miss Saucy would certainly not be faithful to him while he was gone these months. Faithful was not her business. And if he was not loving man enough, he was not a hypocrite either. If he ever ascended to the realm of mansions, fine horses and buggies, and palace cars, he would no more be content with Miss Saucy than she would be with someone who was merely Charles P. Daggett's super.

Sometimes when he dreamed of becoming a millionaire, pal to senators and lover of fancier females than Susan Darling, it seemed as far off and indistinct as China, and he wondered if he had the imagination for it.

"How soon can we get on the River, Jake?" Daggett asked, who was not much interested in lists and accounts.

"What about those life preservers?"

Daggett expelled air like blowing out candles. "Truth is, I don't expect they are going to get here, Jake."

So he had not ordered the life preservers. Buchanan shrugged and said, "We'll have to make a trip into Eureka and try to hire a cook."

A decent cook could make a considerable difference in a two-month trip down a dangerous river. And there were last-minute supplies they could use.

"What do you make of young Haden, Jake?" Daggett said in a charged whisper.

"We might make a man of him this trip. If he don't drown."

Daggett gazed at him with his green eyes. "I will puncture Major John Wesley Powell right in his public lands policy with that boy's help. You'll see, Jake."

Buchanan watched the college boy wandering in his striped jacket and ribboned hat over to the lacy shade of the willows. "That so?" he said.

Eureka

ASA HADEN

Asa sat in the willow shade on the bank of the muddy river, reading the words Major Powell had written of this place eleven years ago:

> *With some feeling of anxiety we enter a new canyon this morning. We have learned to observe the texture of the rock. In softer strata we have a quiet river, in harder we find rapids and falls. Below us are the limestones and hard sandstones we found in Cataract Canyon. This bodes toil and danger. Besides the texture of the rocks, there is another condition which affects the character of the channel, as we have found by experience. Where the strata is horizontal the river is quiet, and, even though it may be very swift in places, no great obstacles are found. Where the rocks incline in the direction traveled, the river usually sweeps with great velocity but still has few rapids and falls. But where the rocks dip upstream and the river cuts obliquely across the upturned formations, harder strata above and softer below, we have rapids and falls.*

Downstream the riffles in the tan water gleamed in the sunlight. There Major Powell and his companions had passed into Marble Canyon, with hard rocks that dipped upstream. They had already been running rapids for forty days, having embarked at the railroad crossing of Green River City, Wyoming. Here at Pariah Crossing, the cliffs bounding the River were not impressively tall, but according to *Canyons of the Colorado,* they rose implacably as the River progressed downstream, with a host of rocky cataracts ahead.

Asa looked up to see Will Jefford approaching. The geologist grinned down at him. "It appears you're committing that book to memory."

He slipped the book to his side, as though he was ashamed of being caught reading a document that was a guide to the hazards of the River but also a record to be examined for error.

Jefford seated himself with a grunt. His face, beneath the rakish cap of his bandanna, was fringed with beard. "It's a fine book."

"There is more than the truth in that book," Jack Sumner, who had been Major Powell's chief boatman, had told Mr. Daggett.

Jefford waved a hand toward their employer and Jake Buchanan, seated in conversation beneath the canvas shade. "The great capitalist and his get-it-done man."

Chick Daggett's father and the Deerslayer, as Asa thought of them.

"Well, well," Jefford continued amiably, "one would not deny our employer singularity of purpose. The truth is that in the West whoever controls the water controls the land. It is the control of millions of acres our friend is after, and if he can rescue this unfortunate female at no extra expense, then all the better. It is strange that we have only now heard of this young woman's plight, however."

"I heard of it in San Francisco," Asa said.

"He has powerful friends in the Senate," Jefford continued. "Taters Rogers's soul is in his pocket, for one. But he has a powerful enemy in Major Powell." He nodded at the book.

At the Daggett mansion in Denver Asa had met Senator Rogers, whose reputation he knew.

"I wonder if this expedition is on the side of the angels," Jefford mused.

"Well, I wonder if Major Powell's was," Asa heard himself say.

"How do you mean?" Jefford wanted to know.

Asa shrugged. It seemed that he was constantly called to defend Mr. Daggett's motives. He felt stifled by mixed loyalties, unable to criticize either Daggett's motives or Powell's book. He had come to admire *Canyons* even though there was "more than the truth" in it, but if his discoveries or conclusions about what had taken place on the first exploration of the great River assisted Daggett in his affairs, then he had properly served his employer. In the acquisition of control of millions of acres?

It did not seem that there was much loyalty to Daggett among his employees, except for Jake Buchanan.

"I hear there is one more trip into Eureka, and then we'll be on our way," Jefford said.

"I'm to collect the last mail," Asa said.

Asa crouched sweating in the bed of the spring wagon, his haunches imperfectly cushioned by a pile of empty gunnybags. On the seat, backs to him, were Jake Buchanan, Pat Morphy, and Hyrum Logan. They were heading for the town of Eureka for a few final supplies and to hire a cook. Asa was in charge of the outgoing mail, a packet of it the size of a brick tied with white cord: letters from Will Jefford, from Tiny Truesdale and George Ritter, and his own letters to Chick Daggett in New York City, his mother in Newfield, and Mary Temple in San Francisco.

The wagon jarred and screeched out the winding track along Pariah Creek beneath the fire-colored cliffs. Jefford liked to praise the scenery as wondrous, but Asa found it monotonously red and brown, with few patches of green to relieve it, as though it was only beginning to recover from a monstrous searing.

He listened to Morphy telling his seatmates a tale of the second Powell exploration:

"Up by the Uinta River we come on this Ute brave Major Powell called Douglas Boy. He always liked naming folks out of his poetry books. This redskin was fixed up very fancy, eagle feathers in his hair and vermilion circles around his eyes. He was camped beside the river with the prettiest squaw you ever saw. Beaman tried to get her to pose for his camera o-nattur-ell, as he called it, but she didn't know what he was talking about, pretended she didn't, anyway. We heard later she was some other brave's wife but she'd eloped down to the Uinta with Douglas Boy. They had to stay away from the tribe and not get caught by her husband for some number of moons. Then they could go back, and it would be all right.

"We saw them again by their wickiup, and they'd both painted their faces all over vermilion. Beaman said it was the reason the redskin race never amounted to much. Because when the bucks and squaws got together they just painted each other different colors instead of doing what was o-nattur-ell!"

Morphy laughed long at his story, and Asa sighed to think of drawing him out on the subject of the troubles of the exploration, which had resulted in the Separation. Which, after all, Morphy could know only by hearsay. So far Morphy was unfriendly, understandably offended because Asa had been appointed chief boatman.

Morphy inquired how many wives Hyrum possessed.

Hyrum just shook his head. He wore a dust- and sweat-stained felt hat with a tangle of gray hair protruding from under the hatband. There was a sweat-darkened slash down the back of his blue shirt.

"Thought you old Mormon bucks got to marry all the young girls in the district," Morphy persisted.

"I am no longer a member of the Church," Hyrum said in his rusty voice. He twitched his whip over the rumps of the mules.

"It's poor manners asking how many wives a man has got," Buchanan said.

Asa changed his seating for the hundredth time.

"I'd be pleased to have a different wife in my bed every night of the week," Morphy said.

"Married life is not all nights, from what I hear."

"You married, Jake?"

"Not me," Buchanan said. "All right back there, Asa?"

"Fine." He was not offended that, as the junior member of the survey, he had been assigned the bed of the wagon rather than the seat. He didn't want any struggles of rank with Morphy.

The mules plodded up the steady incline, their hooves padding dully on the red-orange sand. The slopes were dotted with cactus and ocotillo, with more and more sagebrush. Already the River might have been fifty miles away. The dry air parched his nose. He watched Morphy's shoulders jostle for more room on the seat.

"How come you know redskin jabber?" Buchanan asked Hyrum.

"I have worked among them."

"How's that?"

"It was a Call."

"What's that mean?"

"I was summoned to work among them."

"Don't just blat a man's ear off, do you?" Morphy said.

Because of his linguistic ability and his Indian expertise, Hyrum would accompany Asa up on the Shivwits Plateau out of Separation Canyon to parley with the Indians there.

"What do you think of this White Captive cooze we are supposed to pick up?" Morphy asked Buchanan.

"Not much."

"Pretty well used up, I'll bet."

"Expect so."

"Kind of a surprise, wun't it?"

"I'm not partial to surprises," Buchanan said. "Female in particular."

"Lots of sweet things in Denver, I'll bet."

"All a man might feel obliged to," Buchanan said coolly.

On their trip down from the railroad with the boats, Buchanan had visited the parlor houses of Eureka as casually as Daggett had headed for those in Portsmouth Square in San Francisco.

"Rich bastards," Morphy muttered.

Asa could see the hard line of Buchanan's cheek from his seat on the gunnybags. "Meaning which?" Buchanan said.

"Rich bastards get all the women."

"Except for Mormons," Buchanan said, and the knot of tension eased.

Hyrum was evidently a lapsed Saint, Asa realized, which would account for the dislike between him and the Mormon surveyor, Ritter.

He squatted for a spell, to ease his seat.

"Those houses on Longbranch Street is going to know Pat Morphy's been to town!" Morphy crowed.

"There'll be some loading provision first," Buchanan said, striking a match to light his pipe.

The Eureka town dump was a sprawl of tin cans and blowing paper, torn-up siding lumber, eviscerated mattresses, and broken furniture.

A high acidic stink blew from it. A coyote loped off as the wagon approached.

Past the dump, on a rise of ground, was the cemetery, ten or twelve whitewashed crosses, some of them settled at various slants. Beyond, Eureka lay at the base of ocher cliffs. The steady rock-smashing clatter of the stamp mills jarred the afternoon. The mules' pace quickened on the dusty main street, which was lined with stores and business establishments along a boardwalk shaded by wooden awnings. Dust from the mules' hooves and the other wagons and buggies hung in the air and prickled on Asa's cheeks.

A sign nailed to the front of a building identified the jail, a two-story structure with rafter ends protruding like cannons from a warship. A crowd was grouped in the shade beside the jail door. Their faces were solemn, like a prayer meeting, but instead of a preacher they were being lectured by a woman with a sweat-gleaming red face under a big hat.

Beyond the jail was the Phoenix Hotel, with its chipped yellow facade, where Asa and Jake Buchanan had put up for a night en route to Pariah Crossing. The side street angling off was Longbranch, a strip of saloons, gambling halls, and the parlor houses Buchanan had visited that night, about which Morphy had been talking all the way up from the River.

A trio of women with painted faces was just turning the corner out of Longbranch Street, one of them holding up a lacy parasol. They lifted heavy skirts to show off their boots as they mounted the step at the corner. Morphy rose from his seat, emitting hoots. The woman with the parasol flourished it at them.

A storekeeper in a denim apron leaned on the rail in front of his establishment, watching the wagon pass. Miners from the Eureka and Redbone Mines were not in evidence so early in the afternoon.

At the general store they loaded sacks of flour and other purchases. Buchanan ordered a mutton dressed out, to be picked up on their way out of town. The merchant promised to pass Asa's packet of letters along to the stage driver the next day. Morphy disappeared at a trot in the direction of the Longbranch houses.

Asa trailed Buchanan and Hyrum into the dim cool of a Main Street saloon, Buchanan with his sauntering gait, Hyrum stumping stiff-legged as though his joints hurt.

On the counter was a week-old copy of the *Deseret News,* headlines announcing murder. Hyrum leaned over the paper, staring at the print as he dug a pair of spectacles out of his breast pocket. One earpiece was missing, and he had to hold the eyeglasses in place with a forefinger while he pored over the page.

The barkeep, a short fellow with slicked-back hair, presented himself. "What'll it be, gents?"

Buchanan ordered a bottle of Old Crow and three glasses. Hyrum continued to study the news article, holding his eyeglasses to his nose. His white-stubbled face was gray. Buchanan pulled the page along the counter to where he could read it.

"Who's this bird Hite?"

"A high-up in the Church."

Buchanan frowned down at the paper. "Somebody blew his face off with a shotgun and stuck feathers in his hair. What'd they do that for?"

Hyrum shook his head silently and laid a palm over his glass when Buchanan poured the whiskey. Asa indicated his own potion with a forefinger; he disliked the stuff that scalded his throat till his eyes watered.

"Come to town for the lynching?" the bartender asked.

Asa gaped at him. "What lynching would that be?" Buchanan inquired.

"A woman!"

"Who's lynching a woman?"

"Miners!" The bartender gave the bar in front of Asa a swipe with his rag. "The Eureka Fury! That's what the *Clarion* calls her. Shot her mac dead!"

Asa reminded himself that lynchings did not occur only in the West. He would never in his life forget the mob that had lynched the half-wit bricklayer who had strangled a child in Newfield, howling men with torches chasing their quarry down. They had beaten him so horribly that he must have been dead when they hoisted his battered body into the branches of the big elm on the square.

"They got roused up when she shot Ben Clanton," the barkeep continued. "Turned out she was carrying child. The J.P. got around them by keeping her at the jail for her term, sweeping and cleaning for Ike Frew.

"Kit was born last week, and she smothered it. That's when the *Clarion* started calling her the Fury. They've been building steam since then. Now some of the married ladies have got into it, and it looks like they will do her for sure. Those ladies is something fierce. So's Ben's brother, too!"

Asa recalled the big-hatted woman haranguing the crowd in front of the jail.

"I know muckers and muckers' law, all right," Buchanan said in a bleak voice.

"Can't be more'n eighteen," the barkeep said. "Her daddy was a actor fellow that come here giving monologues. He died of liquor and left her stranded. It is a pure shame!"

"Expect she can cook?" Buchanan asked.

Asa could hardly grasp it: eighteen years old, younger than he was! A prostitute! Impregnated. Who had murdered her pimp and smothered her newborn infant. Now the mob of people they had seen at the jail was poised to chase her down, beat her to death, and haul her body up a tree. He shuddered as though he had caught a chill in this overheated country.

"I know the jailer," Hyrum said, and Buchanan nodded to him.

Hyrum slid off his stool and hobbled outside into the blaze of late sun.

"Pretty young lady," the barkeep said, scrubbing the counter again. "Been treated bad."

"Beating on rock underground makes those muckers want to lynch the women when they come up," Buchanan said. He took his pipe from his pocket and began the process of filling, tamping, and lighting it. Asa sipped whiskey and pressed his fist to his throat to keep from coughing. This unfortunate girl would have been in jail, swollen with her hated child, when he and Buchanan had come down to the River through Eureka. Now Buchanan had decided like a snap of his fingers to rescue her!

Morphy found them before Hyrum returned, stalking in out of the sunlight, throwing his legs out to either side and swinging his arms in a self-satisfied manner.

"Know what's going on in this shitten place? They are fixin' on hangin' a *woman!*"

"Maybe we've found our cook," Buchanan said.

Morphy held the whiskey bottle poised, staring at him.

Hyrum appeared in the doorway. With his white head electrically alight from the sun behind him, he had the look of an Old Testament prophet. In the saloon the racket of the mills was a dull mutter, felt through the soles of the feet as much as heard.

Buchanan glanced at Asa with a gauging eye. "Game?"

He nodded. The barkeep hovered within earshot.

"He'll let us in the back," Hyrum said, stumping down to join them. "There's not much time! The mines'll start letting out."

"We'll need some men's duds and a hat," Buchanan said to the bartender, with that coolness that Asa marveled at.

"There's some of mine here," the barkeep said.

Buchanan got to his feet, stuffing the pipe back into his pocket. "Let's go," he said.

They picked up the dressed mutton first. The eighty-pound carcass still sported its head. The white fat was bound up in cording, and the whole sheathed in muslin. The wagon drifted along Longbranch, and Hyrum swung the team into the alley behind the Phoenix Hotel. Buchanan had stacked sacks, bundles, and the mutton carcass around a hidey-hole behind the wagon seat. His rifle was stowed in its boot beside the brake.

Asa squatted shivering on the pile of sacking, swaying with the motion of the wagon. Morphy sat opposite him. Buchanan was on the seat with Hyrum, apparently as unconcerned as if they were only headed back to the River.

"Shit!" Morphy muttered, and it eased Asa to know that the boatman was nervy too. It was as though the thumping of the mills affected his pulse rate. His legs kept cramping so that he had to shift position. A pale disk of sun hung halfway down the western sky.

The jail was built of adobe blocks laid up one story, with sun-blackened siding above and a pitched roof covered with tarpaper. The rafter ends, which looked as though they had been provided for the purpose of lynching, threw down slants of shadow that were broken across a door of heavy planking.

Hyrum reined the mules to a halt. Buchanan jumped down and came around to join Hyrum in front of the door. "Bring the duds, Pat. Asa, you stick tight."

He nodded mutely, rising to brace his bottom on the rail of the wagon bed.

The three disappeared inside. He pictured the young prostitute with her shiny little revolver aimed at the city-dressed, sneering brute who did not believe she would shoot.

It seemed to him that he watched the disk of the sun perceptibly decline.

They came out in a sudden, crowded-together, swift-moving bunch, Hyrum, Buchanan, Morphy, and a small figure with a cloth cap pulled down on her forehead. Buchanan boosted her up, and Asa grasped a cold hand to pull the Eureka Fury into the wagon. He had a glimpse of a chalk-white knot of a face. The prostitute carried the bundle of her dress and bonnet. It seemed to him that she weighed less than the sheep carcass.

She scrambled into the hidey-hole while Morphy vaulted into the wagon bed, and Hyrum and Buchanan climbed to the seat.

A squall of yelling rose from in front of the jail, and before Hyrum could whip the mules into motion, the crowd burst out of the alleyway between the jail and the hotel, some of them the kind of bummers who hung around a jail or a courthouse, but well-dressed men among them, one with a derby hat on. With them was the big-hatted woman, and another with a purple scarf trailing out behind her in her hurry, maybe twenty people pouring out of the alleyway with a chorus of yelling.

Morphy swung a kick at a man in a conductor's cap, who tried to climb into the wagon bed.

Buchanan bent back from the seat to call into the girl's hole, "Get that dress and bonnet on the mutton there!"

The command made no sense to Asa. Morphy piled out of the wagon, cursing. Two of the bummers were boosting a third into the bed.

Buchanan stood with the rifle leveled at them from his waist. "*Git!*"

A second man was following the first. Both halted, teetering on the rail. When one came on cautiously, Buchanan cocked the rifle with a warning snap.

"*No!*" Hyrum said, shoving the rifle barrel aside. He managed to block it with his lean body.

"*Asa!*" Buchanan said.

The first tough crouched in the wagon bed. The second man dropped in behind him. Asa had a glimpse of the prostitute in her hole frantically doing something with her dress. The crowd howled around the wagon. The first man straightened, arms dangling.

"*Git!*" The word did not produce itself.

He flung himself at them. Both men were knocked flailing and cursing out of the wagon bed. He almost fell after them from the violence of his charge.

Faces gaped past him. He turned to see Buchanan toss a loop of rope over a rafter end. Swiftly Buchanan pulled on the rope. The girl in her bonnet and dress was borne upward. A yell of protest was torn from his throat. But the girl's phosphorescent face still peered out of the hidey-hole, and with a shock of relief, he understood that it was the mutton in the dress that hung swaying, the bonneted head snubbed to the rafter.

He heard Hyrum's shout: "Lord, turn their wrath to shame!" The wagon was moving, Buchanan with a knee braced on the seat and the rifle tucked under his arm. Hyrum stood, wielding the whip.

Morphy vaulted back into the wagon bed, his face smeared with scarlet. He stamped his boot on a man's hand that gripped the rail. The prostitute had ducked deeper into her hole. The wagon broke free of the crowd, whose concentration was fixed on the hanged figure. The mules broke into a shambling run.

"We are out of it, Miss," he heard Buchanan say.

When they had cleared the alley and were headed west on Main Street, Morphy crowed with triumph. He wiped his bloody nose with his bandanna, gazing at the stain on the cloth with a pleased expression. Behind them there was a concerted shout.

Hyrum whipped the team. Buchanan turned, holding the rifle. Three men came at a run out of the alley, two of them halting, pointing, while the third trotted on another twenty yards before he stopped.

The wagon passed the cemetery. A halfhearted dust devil blew up a swirl of paper from the dump. Morphy called out a warning.

Two horsemen were coming after them. Buchanan raised his rifle, but Hyrum reached out to thrust the barrel aside again.

"*No!*"

Buchanan evaded his hand and fired. The horsemen reined up as though they'd run against a fence. One shouted something lost in the wind. The other snatched out his revolver and fired a volley. Buchanan fired again and the horsemen fled. Morphy crowed.

The Eureka Fury's head rose from the hole, the cap pulled low. Her black eyes were like coals in the white flesh. She peered from face to face. Asa realized that the girl was paralyzed with terror.

"Can you cook, Miss?" Buchanan inquired.

Her lips shaped the word: No.

"I will be your cook," Hyrum said.

"You?" Buchanan said in surprise.

"I can cook."

Morphy stood spread-legged before the bulwark of the provisions, hands on hips. His nose had bled onto his upper lip like a red moustache. "Ain't you a pretty little thing!" he said.

The girl stared at him. Her eyes slid over to meet Asa's. "Thank you," she whispered, as though gratitude was due *him,* when it had been Buchanan's resolve, steadiness, and quick thinking that had saved her.

Hyrum said in his rusty voice, "The Lord will forgive if thee will but repent."

Her uncomprehending eyes switched to the old man.

Buchanan pointed with his pipe stem. "That is Hyrum Logan. That's Pat Morphy, and Asa Haden. I'm Jake Buchanan. What's your name, Miss?"

"Miranda." The bloodless lips barely moved.

"You got another name, little sweet thing?" Morphy asked.

"Straw."

"Now ain't Miranda Straw a pretty name!" Morphy's treacly voice made Asa wince. The prostitute's gaze returned to him. His jacket sleeve was half ripped away, and he busied himself tearing it all the way off. He had lost his hat.

"Don't you worry one bit," Morphy said. "We will take care of you from here on!"

"Thank you," she whispered.

Buchanan nodded to Asa. "Very prompt when those two muckers was coming aboard."

He had not felt so proud since the Cornell eight had beaten Yale on Lake Cayuga.

"We'll see how Charley Daggett likes this female surprise," Buchanan said.

After dark, with a past-full moon cutting shadows as sharp as knives on the cliff faces, they rolled downhill. The Eureka Fury had sunk into her hole. Morphy crouched opposite Asa in the wagon bed. Buchanan and Hyrum swayed on the seat.

Asa saw the folded newspaper protruding from Hyrum Logan's overall pocket, the *Deseret News* with its account of the murder of some high-up Mormon over in Iron County.

CHAPTER 7

Marble Canyon 1

ASA HADEN

Asa sat on a rubber-covered box in the gray shade of the canvas sheet, watching Jake Buchanan facing Charles Daggett, who was seated on another bale, the grayed ends of his sideburns standing out like warning flags.

"We are not taking any women along on this survey!"

The girl sat on the sunburnt beach halfway between the pavilion and the boats, with her knees drawn up and her arms locked around them. Her face was concealed by the oversized man's cap she wore.

Everybody else was over on the beach pretending not to be watching a showdown. The mule skinner had his animals tied up in the willow shade. Asa kept an eye on the slot in the red cliffs through which the posse from Eureka might appear.

The girl's eyes flashed toward Asa.

Buchanan stood with his arms folded. "Thought we was picking up this White Captive."

"Christamighty, Jake! There is about a ten percent chance of bringing that woman out, and you know it!"

"This one'll be company for her."

Daggett snarled wordlessly.

"If she don't come along I'll have to take her up to Junction. She has to get out of the district."

Daggett's face folded into a winsome smile. "Why, then, Mr. Brown can take her along to Junction."

Buchanan paced again. Asa had never felt so awkward, his legs too long for the position he occupied, his arms too long either to fold or to brace beside him.

Buchanan said. "My old mother would never speak to me again if I let a white woman go off with a stinking old scalawag like that."

Daggett's eyes swiveled toward Asa. "And what do you say, my boy?"

He stammered. "I'm concerned that armed men may be pursuing us, sir."

"Hear that?" Daggett said to Buchanan. "Armed men! See what you have got us into?"

"Well, guess I am fired, then," Buchanan said.

"What the devil are you talking about?"

"You made me super of the survey. Then you decided to come along yourself. Then you decided we are going to pick up this white woman captive. Then you decided we are not going to bring along this other woman we took away from a pack of stranglers. If you are going to make the decisions, I guess I am fired."

"You're the boss of the survey, but I'm *your* boss, Jake," Daggett said in a reasonable voice. "*I'm* the one that pays you and these other roughnecks, and that paid for the boats and provision."

"And that didn't pay for the life preservers," Buchanan said, as Asa glanced again toward the slot in the cliffs.

"I couldn't locate any preservers, Jake!"

"I broke that girl out of Eureka jail for a cook," Buchanan said. "Well, she claims she can't cook, but Hyrum will cook. So she'll help Tiny with the photographs. He is going to be the busiest man on the survey, and he needs help. If I am the boss here, that is the way it is going to be."

Asa watched the girl clutch her knees to her chest. He didn't know whether she could overhear this argument or not.

"I thought you and me was going into business together," Daggett said softly. "Buchanan and Daggett."

Buchanan shrugged, but Asa had a sense that he was suddenly very angry.

"All this fuss over a squit of a female," Daggett said, grinning as though he was enjoying watching Buchanan stifle his rage. "A man killer and infanticide!" he whispered, with a glance toward the girl. "A soiled dove. No flesh on her bones, either. I'd rather had that mutton, Jake."

"She is the nut in the coconut, Charley," Buchanan said, teetering on his heels.

"A whore will plain raise hell with your crew, Jakey. You mark my words! What do *you* say, boy?"

Asa had gritted his teeth when Daggett called the young woman a whore, although that was what she had been. Daggett had certainly patronized the whores of San Francisco. He cleared his throat. "I don't believe we can desert her, sir."

Buchanan eyed him poker-faced. Daggett sighed and said, "Let's have her over for some parley."

Buchanan beckoned. The girl convulsed to her feet. Shapeless in the barkeep's too-large shirt, vest, and trousers, barefoot, with a belt-end dangling from her waist, she approached the shade at a mincing walk. Asa was fearful that Mr. Daggett would call her to her face a whore, a man killer, and an infanticide.

But the capitalist was all smiles. "I understand that you will be accompanying us, my dear."

She glanced from Buchanan to Asa with her coals of eyes, spots of color in her cheeks. Asa couldn't keep his eyes from her miniature, pale, naked feet.

"This is an important and expensive survey," Daggett went on. "I will not permit any interference with the work of this expedition!"

The girl said nothing. Asa glanced again toward the slot in the seared cliffs.

"Do you understand, my dear?"

She nodded.

"I believe you understand the violence of men's passions. That is what I am talking about."

"Yes," she said, in a cold voice.

"You must ride with me aboard the *Letty,* my dear," Daggett went on cheerfully. "She is named for my daughter. We will place you in the bow for a pretty figurehead of a Colorado River clipper!"

"I will do what you tell me to do," she said.

Buchanan gestured, and she swung around and returned to her spot on the beach, seating herself with the same swift, coiling motion.

"You can always tell, Jake," Mr. Daggett said.

"Tell which?"

"If a female will look you straight in the eye she is ready to do what you tell her to do, all right!"

Asa's face felt afire. When he had met Chick Daggett's red-haired, sixteen-year-old sister in Denver, she had looked him straight in the eye and said, "How do you do, Mr. Haden! We have heard so much about you!"

He said, "I'm sorry to hear you say that, sir. I believe it is unjust."

Daggett glared at him.

"It is something he has learnt from his Eye-talian opera females," Buchanan drawled.

Daggett said in a coarse whisper, "Is that what they taught you and Chick in that college? Disputing your elders?"

"I was taught that ungentlemanly statements should be disputed before I attended Cornell, sir."

"Maybe you had better just dispute your way back to Junction with Mr. Brown!"

"I will do as you say, for you are my employer."

"If I am your employer, you will not dispute me!"

"I will dispute you when you are in the wrong, sir." He felt awkward and pompous, a fool. Buchanan was grinning broadly.

Daggett leaned forward, fists braced on his thighs. "Maybe you will see if Mrs. Smith has some small-size boots this young lady can borrow, Mr. Buchanan. After which I will assume that the survey is prepared to take to the River!" He flapped an angry hand.

Buchanan strode off toward the beach. Miranda Straw sprang up to follow him.

"You are here to help me stick a harpoon into that one-armed old badger, Powell!" Daggett said, pointing a finger at Asa. "You are here to write a true account of what happened on that first trip of his! If you are going to moon over what is right and what is wrong, you are about as much use to me as a limp cock!"

Asa folded his arms, as Buchanan had done, and stared back into Daggett's green eyes. His face burned.

"If you think you are going to play holier-than-thou with me, I want to know it right now!" Mr. Daggett said.

"I will do what I think is right!" he said.

In the silence he heard Buchanan's voice raised over the long growl of the river. Daggett glared up at him with his pouchy eyes. Finally he said, "Go and take your post aboard, boy."

"Yes, sir," he said, and went.

The last bales were quickly stowed, and the oars, ropes, and canvas of the awning dismantled. The mules waited on the beach, the mule skinner seated slumped on the lead animal, prepared to depart also. Further up, the ferryman and his wife watched. None of them waved good-bye as the boats were pushed out into the current, bows swinging downstream.

Asa grasped the steering oar of the *Canyon Lass,* alive-feeling against his side. He was still shaky from the confrontation with Daggett, still glancing toward the opening in the cliffs, as though the arrival of an armed band from Eureka in pursuit of Miranda Straw would be justification for Buchanan's stand.

The brown River bore the *Canyon Lass* powerfully toward the Canyon gate. Facing him from the oarsmen's seat were Will Jefford and Poche. Their trouser legs were soaked from shoving the boat into the current. They often glanced over their shoulders to observe the riffles. Their oars pulled roughly in unison.

Leading the little flotilla was *Miss Saucy,* Buchanan and Ritter at the oars, Tiny seated in the stern; no steering oar for *Miss Saucy.* Last came the *Letty Daggett,* Morphy and Hyrum rowing, Daggett standing with the long scull. Asa had not felt he could protest this arrangement, although Morphy and Hyrum were experienced boatmen and Daggett not even an amateur.

Miranda Straw rode in the bow of the *Letty,* the ugly cap pulled down so that it effectively hid her face.

They were bound for Callville on the Virgen River, two hundred and eighty miles away, though he would leave the River at Separation Canyon, forty miles before the end of the Grand Canyon, and with Hyrum climb up on the plateau where the Howland brothers and Dunn had met their deaths, in search of the truth.

Once when he glanced back he saw Miranda Straw lean over the bow to dip a hand in the water. It seemed the gesture of a child rather than a woman, a prostitute. He could not get any purchase on his feelings about her presence. They could not have done other than they had done, in common humanity, but he was jarred by last-minute changes, altered plans, and, like Buchanan, surprises.

He raised his face to the blistering sun glaring off the cliffs. Occasional drops of water from the oarsmen's strokes splashed his heated cheeks. He understood that the rescue of the white woman captive could be advantageous to Mr. Daggett, but Mr. Daggett was right that a young woman, especially a prostitute, would cause dissension among the crew of the survey.

He recalled the grand Christmas ball at the Daggett mansion in Denver. There he had observed Chick Daggett engaged in a posturing ritual with the other young gentlemen, fawning over a local fair-haired beauty, while he stood to one side, a disapproving, awkward, and jealous New York State bumpkin.

But of course he himself had postured before Mrs. Daggett and the sixteen-year-old beauty-to-be Letty Daggett on the subject of his studies at Cornell University. He had matriculated as an agriculture student but had chosen other fields of study under Ezra Cornell's dictum that his university was an institution where any student could find instruction in any subject. And so he had found himself studying moral philosophy, writing pieces for the *Cornell Daily Sun,* and rowing single sculls and stroking the eight-oared shell, for he had lived around boats and rivers most of his life.

"Something coming up?" Jefford asked, peering over his shoulder. Asa could see nothing but the next cliff-guarded bend. They were all apprehensive of the encounter with their first dangerous rapid. Jefford studied the cliffs they passed. Often he immersed his head-covering in the River to cool himself. Poche's gaze was fixed past Asa, slitted dark eyes above high cheekbones.

The sun beat relentlessly into the narrow corridor of Marble Canyon and glinted like old gold on the brown wavelets. Every few miles the boats were halted for photography and surveying, and Jefford prospecting with his little geologist's pick.

As the boats got under way again after one of these stops, Asa heard a change in pitch in the whispering of the River and rose to his feet to observe a dance of white froth. This rapid was called Badger Creek, he knew, and Major Powell had lined his boats down it. He waved his hat at Buchanan, and *Miss Saucy* headed for a point from which the rapid could be observed. Morphy would probably remember it without having to consult the *Canyons* book.

Ashore, Ritter carried his transit to a height of rock. Tiny set up his camera on another, while Miranda squatted beside him. Jefford seated himself on a ledge to scribble in his notebook, and Daggett waded at the water's edge with his trousers rolled on his white legs, shaking gravel and water in a pan, looking for color.

Buchanan joined Asa as he strolled along the ledge observing the currents. The tongue of smooth water extended between a cross-channel line of rocks into a sag before the welter of white chop. A water-covered boulder must be avoided. An eddy rotated back up toward the line of rocks.

"Think we can run it?" Buchanan asked, pipe in mouth.

"Major Powell lined it, but he said the fall was thirty-five feet. I don't believe it's anything like that. The River must've been higher then."

"Just so we do what's *right,*" Buchanan said, straight-faced.

"I think we'd better line it."

Buchanan nodded. "Your boat's the one we can't afford to pile up, with Tiny's plates aboard. We can go hungry, but we can't lose those plates."

Back at the campsite Hyrum was moving around the fire like a wrestler preparing to come to grips with an antagonist, long arms hanging, his whiskered face dripping sweat. The surveyor watched him, scowling. It might be that Ritter disapproved of Hyrum because of his lapsed religion, but in fact the surveyor was simply an unfriendly man and, to judge by his habitual expression, found most company not to his liking.

Hyrum passed Asa a tin cup of coffee that scalded his fingers, and biscuits hot from the pan. The smell of frying bacon mingled deliciously with the dark whiff of coffee. Miranda drifted closer to snatch a pair of biscuits like some shy animal, and retreated, seating herself with her back to the rest of them.

Morphy hulked over to squat beside her. He rose quickly and turned away as though he'd been rebuffed.

Tiny approached her with a bundle of clothing: he was closest to her size and he had a spare overall to lend her. The ferryman's wife had furnished her a pair of child's boots from the cabin at Pariah Crossing.

She disappeared up the creek bed. Swallows flashed over the tossing water of the rapid with jewel-gleams of green and violet plumage, to soar and swoop against the opposite cliff. A raven sat on a high willow branch gazing down at Hyrum as he passed around the pan of bacon.

The girl reappeared attired in a brown overall that was the twin of Tiny's and fit her loosely. The legs were rolled. She still wore the big cap.

With a shout of discovery, Morphy appeared out of the brush holding up a human skull, eye sockets gaping, toothy jaw. The weathered bone gleamed like chalk. He thrust the skull at Miranda, who shrank away from it.

Morphy took the object to Daggett, who flourished it aloft again.

"Injun!" Ritter said.

"Alas poor Yorick!" Jefford said, spreading his arms. "I knew him, Horatio!"

Miranda's face jerked toward the geologist as though someone had finally spoken words in her language. It seemed to Asa that her intractable little face would be pretty if it ever softened. Dark curls showed beneath the band of her cap.

"Better bury it where you found it," Buchanan said.

"No, sir, I am keeping this fellow!" Daggett announced. "This fellow is going to be our luck!"

Asa could feel the disapproval as Daggett hurried off to stow the skull aboard the *Letty*. No one else considered the object good luck.

When he had finished his biscuits and bacon Asa went to sit on a drift log beside Morphy, who lounged on the sandy ground with his back against the log.

The big man seemed more friendly since the adventure in Eureka, and Asa thought he might bring up the subject of Major Powell.

"How much of a fall would you say this was, Pat?"

Morphy swiveled his head for a glance. "Ten, twelve feet."

"Major Powell calls it thirty-five. Could the water have been that much higher then?"

"That book of his?"

"*The Canyons of the Colorado.*"

"You don't want to go by that book."

There's more than the truth in that book! He felt suddenly short of breath. "What do you mean?"

"The Prof told me about that book."

"Who's the Prof?"

"Prof Thompson. The Major's brother-in-law. He was the one that run *our* trip. The Major was only aboard sometimes. Mostly he was out surveying the district or parleying with Injun. The Prof was in charge. The Major had lost part of his notes from his first trip, so he strung the two trips together like it was all one, in that book. You don't want to take that book for Gospel."

"How did he lose his notes, I wonder?" Asa had not heard of the notes before.

"There was the notes and a copy. Those deserter birds—that got massacreed by Injun—they was supposed to take one copy with them, but there was a mix-up and the Major was left with two copies of one part of the trip and none of the rest. Something like that. Anyway, the Prof was peeved because our bunch never got any attention in that book of the Major's. Names of places he used was places *we* named."

"Is that what your people called them, 'deserters'?"

Morphy squinted back up at him. "That's what they was."

"Was that what Major Powell called them?"

Morphy looked puzzled. "Well, I don't recollect. Like I say, he wasn't aboard much. That's what Fred Dellenbaugh and them called them, all right."

Buchanan was beckoning to them to begin lining the boats down the rapid.

When the boats had been unloaded, the heavy rope was attached to *Miss Saucy*'s stern, with Pat Morphy aboard to fend her off from the rocky bank. Asa watched him thrusting with the oar. Morphy waved his hat as he disappeared around the point. The rest of them clung to the rope, standing in the Canyon heat in waist-deep water among the boulders, the red cliffs soaring against the sky above them.

Next it was the *Lass*'s turn. Asa stood in the bow with the oar while the boat made her fettered progress, bucking in the current. He thrust the oar at the damp-dark conglomerate of the wall. The boat made constrained dashes at the bank, held off more by the recoil of the waves than by his efforts. He cast one glance over his shoulder at the glassy water pouring over the boulder close behind him and the foaming hole beneath it. The boat continued its passage down toward the point as he leaned out to jab the rocky bank with the oar.

The tip of the oar dislodged a stone the size of an apple in a small burst of gray clay. The oar glanced off, and the *Lass* slipped away under his feet. It seemed minutes before he splashed into cold water. Instantly he was borne under by vast force, the oar snatched from his hands. He seemed to be traveling at tremendous speed, under a skim of brown water through which he could see the distorted red walls leaning over him. He popped out, gasping for air. Thrashing his arms, he was borne close to the rock wall, sucking for breath one moment and carried under the next. Suddenly his arm was caught, and Buchanan hoisted him out of the water.

Asa swung around to see the *Lass* coming toward them, untended. She continued on her way, bow bucking against the chop, and swept into the eddy, where Morphy leaped from *Miss Saucy* to the bow of the *Lass* to secure the boats together and untie the line. The rope was then drawn back upriver in a succession of splashes. Buchanan climbed back up the rocks to supervise the lining.

Asa sprawled on the ledge, shivering. Everyone would have seen him fall. It was only luck that the *Lass* had not battered herself against sharp rocks, like the wreck of the *No-name* at Disaster Falls, for which Major Powell had blamed Oramel Howland. *He could have drowned!* He watched the *Letty* pass by him, with Hyrum aboard fending with the oar.

The three boats were drawn up on the beach out of the eddy, and the crew began carrying cargo over the rocky track on the saddle that rose above the point. From an abyss of mortification Asa watched the play of the rapids, the slick gleam of water pouring over boulders into a feathery fury below them, the current sucking and scouring along the bank. Across the River those hostile cliffs rose against the narrow sky.

Morphy scrambled down to where he was sitting.

"Last time, I went in at Sockdolager," Morphy confided, squatting beside him. "Afterwards I could taste Colorado mud for a week."

"Not much of a show for the chief boatman."

"I recollect that feeling, like you'd pay good money for your boots to be nailed to the planks."

Morphy gave him a hand up, and they joined the procession of bearers. Tiny and Miranda, in their matching overalls, were laden with photographic gear. Ritter carried his transit on his shoulder like a musket. Daggett toted the canvas bag of his personal effects.

"Thought we'd lost you, my boy!" he called. "We can't line all these riffles," he said to Buchanan, who was coming up behind him carrying a rubber-covered bale. "Take us three months to get to Callville."

"Don't believe Asa thought it was a riffle," Buchanan said.

"You saved my life," Asa said. "Thanks."

"No thanks due," Buchanan said, moving along.

Asa rose to his feet in the smoothly riding boat to see what was coming ahead: a string of riffles with no white water, whatever obstructions the channel contained well covered. Buchanan was also on his feet, *Miss Saucy* drifting sideways. He waved his hat, and Asa signaled to Daggett that they would run this rapid. *Miss Saucy* headed down the smooth track between glassy disturbances, Buchanan and George Ritter flailing with the oars. Asa steered for the smooth track of their wake, calling out to his oarsmen, "Go to it!" The *Letty* was a hundred feet behind, Daggett standing gripping the sweep, Miranda crouched in the bow. "Straight on!" Asa yelled.

Then they were in it, the craft surging right and left, straightening when the oars found purchase. A glassy front rose to swamp them. "*Hard right!*" Poche dug in while Jefford backed off, to receive a lapful of River water. Spray slapped Asa's face, cool as acid. The brown glass threat slumped away, and the *Lass* slipped into the eddy with *Miss Saucy*. Asa blew out his breath in a sigh.

The *Letty* was in the center of the current, riding down the slick.

Miranda's chip of a face looked frozen. Hyrum and Morphy rowed powerfully, and Daggett steered, his mouth working as though he was yelling above the rush of water. The *Letty* took a wave over the bow, and Miranda rose, holding on to the safety rope. Her soaked overall clung to her body.

The *Letty* circled into the eddy with the two other boats, Daggett standing with the long oar.

"That's the way to take those rapids, boys!" he called out.

That night the driftwood fire mounted its glow against the immense dark, with the slash of starred sky above the cliffs and the mutter of the River running past. Asa shivered, watching the faces of the eight men and one young woman splashed with coppery light when Hyrum tossed another mesquite bush onto the fire. Bats fluttered overhead, and he saw Miranda clasp her hands over her curls apprehensively. Tiny sat on one side of her, Daggett on the other, the pale ends of his sideburns catching the firelight.

Asa went to squat beside Hyrum, who was constructing an elaborate structure of broken sticks, up which the flames flickered like tiny bright animals. "At Separation Canyon you and I are to climb up on the plateau to parley with the Shivwits people."

Hyrum did not look up from his firemaking. After a moment he said, "It is far."

"Do we need to be fearful that they are hostile still?"

Hyrum shook his gray head.

"Will you know where to find them?"

"They will find us if they want. We won't find them."

The problem seemed to be similar to locating the tribe that held the White Captive, but without the assistance of Poche's uncle, the Hoya chief. "Isn't there anything we can do?" he asked.

Hyrum placed his sticks at the edge of the fire where they promptly flamed. "Got to get there, first," he said.

Asa withdrew, feeling ignored.

"Whiskey!" Daggett called out, slapping his hands together. "Come on, Jake, let us share your store. We will toast the success of our venture!"

Buchanan detached himself from the illuminated circle and soon reappeared with the three-gallon jug. Morphy helped him slosh liquor into the cups.

Miranda shook her head and tucked her cup away when Morphy stood over her, proffering the jug. "Roses in your cheeks, Missy!"

When Morphy moved along she gripped her blanket around her shoulders, her face turned to the warm flicker of the coals. She was hardly more than a schoolgirl in age, left defenseless when her father died of whiskey in a brutal mining camp. *Then her shame.* Could he blame her that she had not chosen starvation over dishonor? Now she must strive to maintain some pride among men who knew her history but not her!

Pipes were lit to accompany the cupful of whiskey. Daggett climbed to his feet, a hand braced on Poche's shoulder.

"There is some who will say this Canyon can't be subdued! We will show 'em, boys! There is some who will say these lands are worthless. What was it, ten, twelve years ago, Mormons over in Iron County painted and feathered up like Injun and ambushed a gentile wagon train that was coming in to settle country the Saints figured belonged to them? Slaughtered the whole bunch, men, women, and children. That's how the Saints value this land!

"Because there ain't no worthless land, boys. All it needs is water, and rain follows the plow, as everybody knows. Rain follows railroad iron, too, as was proven in England when they got *too much* rain after they'd run tracks all over the country. Magnetism! Besides, there is water here! It is running down to waste itself in the Gulf of California!"

He offered his cup to the sky. "Here is champagne to our friends, and pain to our sham friends."

Tiny rose to stand facing him. "I will not drink to your success, Mr. Daggett! What you are trying to do here is a damned shame, sir!"

"Now why is that, my man?"

"This land should belong to the nation and you intend to put the grab on it!"

Mr. Daggett's teeth gleamed. "Why, Mr. Truesdale, I believe you have found me out. I would like to put the grab on the nation itself! I would run it like a railroad, and it would run on time."

Tiny stood so erect he seemed to be trying to make himself taller. "You are a rich man, sir. Trying to be a richer one. And every rich man makes a hundred poor ones."

"Ah!" Daggett said, with a wink toward Asa. "Do I hear the notions of Mr. Henry George of San Francisco? Fellow that writes for my magazine there sometimes?"

"The notions of a man who believes the nation is ruined by men like you!"

"Why, made the greater!" Daggett said agreeably. "That is *our* thinking, Mr. Truesdale. And let me tell you: it is exceedingly pleasant to be rich. I have been both rich and poor, and I promise you that the former is the preferable!"

This earned Daggett a round of laughter. Tiny sat down. Asa could feel his perturbations like an electric charge across the campfire.

Hyrum broke his silence to say, "I wonder if the young lady realizes that she may have female company in a week or so."

Miranda turned her face toward the cook while the tale of the discovery of the White Captive was told again.

"We will become famous for rescuing damsels in distress," Jefford said.

"We will bring this person back to her own people!" Poche said.

"With the Lord's help!" Hyrum said. He sat beside Poche with his hands dangling between his knees.

"Indians out this way do trust Mormonee over Mericat," he continued. "And Poche here knows the Hoya."

Poche bent his lips in a thin smile and cast his eyes right and left. "My uncle will help us free the young woman," he said, nodding.

"Is one band of Hoya to be induced to steal this woman from another?" Jefford wanted to know.

Poche nodded again, firelight flickering on his brown face.

"What if that bunch comes after us?" Ritter said.

"Why, I believe it is a faster jaunt downriver by water than along the cliffs and washes," Mr. Daggett said. "We can plain outrun those Nature's Noblemen, can't we, Jake?"

Buchanan, smoking his pipe, said he reckoned so.

"There are some that travel fast," Poche said.

Mr. Daggett frowned at the half-breed. "Come, fill our cups again, and we will drink to *that* success as well! Pat!" And Morphy carried the heavy jug around, pouring out more dollops of whiskey. Asa glanced at Buchanan's impassive face.

Jefford intoned: "'Sixty and nine, who wore their crownlets regal, from the Athenian Bay set forth—'"

Miranda whispered, "*Troilus and Cressida!*"

"You know that, young lady!"

"My father was a Shakespearean actor."

"Was he? And he educated his daughter?"

Miranda pulled the blanket close around her face.

"Education and its benefits!" Daggett exclaimed. "My son and Asa Haden are receiving grand educations back east in Ithaca!"

"The home of Ulysses!" Jefford said, laughing in his superior way.

Daggett looked at Asa expectantly. He seemed to bear no grudge from the quarrel at Pariah Crossing. Asa prayed that some easy comment would come to mind.

He was furious that he must sound pompous: "I understand the reference to mean that we will be rescuing this unfortunate young woman from the Trojans—like Helen of Troy."

"Hoya!" Poche said, scowling.

"What a fine Chautauqua we will have!" Daggett exclaimed, flourishing his cup. "Everybody spouting Shakespeare. Mr. Jefford will tell us the names of the rocks, Hyrum will relate tales of the Saints, and Mr. Truesdale will educate us in the apothegms of Henry George. What can you do, Jake? Instruct us in shooting horned creatures?"

"George Ritter can play the mouth organ in grand style," Buchanan said, and the surveyor cranked up a smile and patted his pocket. It seemed strange to Asa that the sour-faced surveyor should have mastered the mouth organ. He supposed that Ritter's persnickety qualities might be of value in his profession.

"Your father's name?" Jefford asked Miranda.

"Rudolph Straw."

"Might I have seen him in Ford's Theater in Washington City playing in *Macbeth*?"

"He played Macbeth."

"I saw the man in Denver!" Daggett said. "A voice to shake the rafters! Some thought him intoxicated, but he was magnificent!"

"Drink was his downfall," Miranda said in her cold, rather abrasive voice. "He died of whiskey." She subsided into her blanket as though angry that she had talked too much. Miranda was the name of Prospero's daughter in *The Tempest,* Asa knew. The tempest of the girl's brief life!

"Let us have some jollification here!" Daggett ordered. "Mr. Ritter, may we hear the famous mouth organ?"

Ritter produced it from his pocket and swung into "I Wish I Was Single Again." Jefford and Morphy sang the words noisily, Daggett marking time by slapping his thigh, and Tiny joining in. Asa was appalled when Daggett got to his feet and began to dance, holding the skull. Chick's father, the Denver capitalist, was drunk! He clodhopped on the packed sand, one hand holding up the phosphorescent white cranium, his shadow cavorting hugely on the opposite cliff—great arms extended and heaving, the huge trunk bending, legs driving. And Asa realized that Daggett's dance was contrived in order to create the giant shadow on the wall of Marble Canyon, the builder-of-the-nation disporting himself in the canyon that was to belong to him, casting a shadow even greater than himself to the music of his surveyor's mouth organ.

When Daggett halted, panting, Ritter ceased his music, the fire was let die down, and men faded into the darkness for their pre-bedroll micturitions. Asa did not see where Miranda laid out her blankets, and he was ashamed of straining his eyes to try to discern her movements in the darkness. The problem of privacy must be severe for the Eureka Fury.

He lay awake with electric chills traveling along his nerves from the exhilaration of the voyage downriver successfully begun, and the apprehension of dangers and challenges to be faced. His first insufficiency was past—maybe his last! But presently there came a heaviness that he recognized as his reluctance to examine his attitudes toward Daggett's bulldozing determination, his empire building and expropriation like some rampaging feudal duke. And his own pathetic claim that he would do what was Right.

A hoarse shout roused him, and he jerked to a sitting position, gasping with fright as from a nightmare. "*Blood!*" The word was followed by a groan, and silence.

Everyone else on this willow-backed beach must be awake as he was, dreading another such shout.

Buchanan's casual voice inquired, "Hyrum, is that you?"

"*Pardon,*" Hyrum muttered. After another silence Asa heard him praying in a sibilant whisper that was as unsettling in its intensity as the shout.

It was a long time before he slept again in the black depths of Marble Canyon.

Marble Canyon 2

ASA HADEN

Of August 8 and 9, Major Powell had written:

> *The limestone of this canyon is often polished, and makes a beautiful marble. Sometimes the rocks are of many colors—white, gray, pink, and purple, with saffron tints. It is with very great labor that we make progress, meeting many obstructions, running rapids, letting down our boats with lines from rock to rock, and sometimes carrying boats and cargoes around bad places. We camp at night, just after a hard portage, under an overhanging wall, glad to find shelter from the rain. We have to search for some time to find a few sticks of driftwood, just sufficient to boil a cup of coffee.*
>
> *The water sweeps rapidly in this elbow of river, and has cut its way under the rock, excavating a vast half-circular chamber, which, if utilized for a theater, would give sitting to 50,000 people.*

Reading this figure in *Canyons,* Asa felt ashamed for Major Powell. The explorer had blown up the size of the cavern by ten times, just as he habitually overestimated the drop of rapids by two or three times.

He stood with Buchanan and Daggett on a rocky ledge, gazing at the engorged water in the center of the channel that had been heaped up by boulders blocking the riverbed. A bone-white log lay slanted across two of the boulders, tipping like a metronome to the assault of the waves. The process of the formation of the Canyon's rapids was very clear here. Boulders had been carried down from the side canyon by floods, and the River was now wearing them away with the abrasive silt it carried.

"Manhandle the boats just past here, then run it," Daggett said, leaning forward with his hands on his hips. His face was scarlet with sunburn.

"We'd better line it," Asa said.

"Take half a day!" Daggett complained.

Buchanan stood with his arms folded, chewing on the bit of his pipe. He winked at Asa. "Better listen to your chief boatman, Charley. He's read the Major's book."

"Christamighty!" Daggett said. "We'll be on this River till Christmas! We are going to have to start running these half-a-day ones, boy!"

Asa did not respond that delays were more often caused by surveying mining claims and Tiny's photography. He had begun testing his will against Daggett's, and he was grateful for Buchanan's support.

Daggett turned and tramped back toward the boats. Buchanan waved a hand to summon Morphy.

Buchanan jammed a driftwood branch into a crack in the rock. Morphy shouldered a hank of rope and, swarming up from the branch, found hand- and footholds to climb twenty feet to a ledge.

He dropped the end of his rope and braced it while Asa and Poche climbed up to join him. Asa stood panting down at the white water of the cataract below. Faces gazed up at them, Daggett squinting furiously. Miranda watching from the outcrop where Tiny had set up his camera.

From the high ledge the boats could be lined down most of the way.

The end waves were run to placate Daggett, but *Miss Saucy* capsized and Buchanan and Ritter were swept down almost half a mile before they were able to right the boat. The remainder of the day had to be spent drying out bedrolls and provisions while Daggett paced on the beach. Asa hoped he would understand that more time was consumed by such upsets than by lining.

In the leaden afternoon heat he climbed a fault in the cliff to a high platform where Tiny had set up his orange dark tent. Fluted red walls floated above him. The camera rested on its tripod on the edge of the precipice, brass parts glistening in the sun. Miranda must be in the tent with the photographer. He was startled by a sudden bulge in the orange wall, where one of them had pressed against it. He felt like a spy.

The girl stumbled outside to seat herself on a low rock. She was drenched with perspiration from the heat inside the tent. Her tight black curls had loosened and wisped around her gleaming face. Her mouth pulsed open and closed.

Tiny came outside after her, carrying a glass plate and a square of paper.

"In my darkroom in San Francisco there is air circulating," he said, laying the plate on the paper in the sun. "And a cooler climate! You will visit me when this is over."

Tiny wiped his face with his bandanna. With his little tricorn of goatee and moustache, he looked like a caricature of a Frenchman. "My wife will be pleased to meet you! She is bedridden, of course, but very bright and cheerful. I will make your portrait in a proper studio, in proper dress."

Miranda's inaudible reply seemed a demurrer. She had straightened, half facing Asa where he watched between the split rocks.

"You are a comely young woman!" Tiny said. "All that is needed is proper lighting."

He thought he should make his presence known, lest he be discovered, but he hesitated as Tiny spoke, bracing his boot on the rock beside Miranda in a proprietary way. "I would hope to persuade you to pose for me in the nude," he went on. "Merely from the waist up, you understand. It is for art. I hope to present the artistic views I have made in a gallery, where they will be purchased by connoisseurs of photographic art."

Asa saw Miranda's gleaming face set sullenly to match the burn in his own cheeks.

"I do not wish to do that, Mr. Truesdale!" Her voice rose shrilly. "I will not be bullied and harried!"

Truesdale threw up a hand in protest. "That is not my intention, Miss Straw!"

"You press against me at every opportunity!"

"You must understand that the tent is small! I assure you that I have no designs upon your person!"

Grimacing painfully, Asa watched her clasp her head between her hands.

"Mr. Truesdale, every man with whom I have had acquaintance has proven my undoing. Every man! I have been lied to, cheated, presumed upon, treated as having no value, badly used, brutalized! My wishes have been ignored, my personal welfare ignored. I have been sold to lascivious men like a prize mare. My person has been presented as a gift to stinking, ugly, drunken men. I have been beaten. I have been abused past the bearing of it. Your gender owes me so much grievance it would have to beg forgiveness for fifty years to have any signification to me."

She stopped, breathing hard, before she continued: "I apologize for my tantrum. But even the words of your profession seem designed to jeer at me. *Exposure* is what I experienced at the jail. The warder there thought it a grand joke to parade his exposure before me every day."

"I apologize for my gender, Miss Straw!" Tiny said, clapping a hand to his chest.

Asa stooped, watching the tableau from his concealment. Finally Tiny went back inside the tent. Miranda then rose, patting her hair back into order. She seemed an image of composure, who moments ago had been inflamed. She stood turning slowly in her sweat-soaked coverall until she was looking directly at him, upon which he ducked his head until she was out of sight.

❖ ❖ ❖

In the morning Asa was up at first light, seated on a rock watching Hyrum arranging pots and the kettle over the fire, his white-stubbled face dripping sweat. The camp was stirring, men sitting up in their bedrolls. He couldn't see where Miranda had laid out her blankets.

Over on the beach Daggett was doing some kind of exercise, throwing his arms out and bringing them back, high-stepping in place, a towel around his neck. His steam-engine pant was audible.

The Deerslayer approached out of the draw with the gray, bloody haunches of a deer on his shoulder. Buchanan dumped his kill behind Hyrum and carried the bloody gunny sack from his shoulder to the River's edge, to thresh it in the water.

Miranda appeared to assist the cook. Asa gazed at the taut round of her hip as she bent to offer Hyrum a pan.

Tiny joined Asa, and the two of them watched Daggett doing bending exercises with a face that looked on fire.

"Thinks it is him and the other pirates like him that made the nation great," Tiny said. "It was the land that made us great!"

"I believe the railroads have played a part," Asa said.

Tiny thumbed his goatee. "And brought misery with them." Then he grinned. "Well, it's damned smart to try to pick up this captive woman. That'll make the noise his kind likes. It was Mary Temple's idea, I understand. That is one brainy female."

"She is very beautiful," Asa said.

"Talking about who?" Morphy said, coming up. He squinted at Miranda squatting beside Hyrum. "Rescue all the cunny along the route, I say. What's the cooze situation after the Little Colorado, Jake?" he asked, as Buchanan joined them.

"Have to take it as it comes," Buchanan said, wiping his wet hands on his pantlegs.

"You suppose all them Injun fucked her?" Morphy wanted to know.

"What'd you do if you had a white captive all your own?"

"Bet you squeeze Miranda's titties up in that orange tent of yours," Morphy said to Tiny.

"It stinks of chemicals in there, and it's hot as blazes. Nothing in that tent would get anybody's pecker up, not even yours."

Asa turned away.

"On our trip Beaman was always making photygraphs of the squaws with their titties showing," Morphy said. "Said that was the kind of pictures people back home wanted to see. He'd jaw at them till they'd poke a titty out of their dress for him. O-natture-ell, he called it.

"Pretty pair on the cunny," Morphy went on. "I spied her out o-natture-ell up the River yesterday. She has got to take off that overall to piss."

"For shame," Buchanan said casually. Asa started to speak but stopped himself. What had he been doing but spying on Miranda yesterday? What was he doing but spying on Major Powell, auditing figures and taking notes on discrepancies?

"Rotten sneak!" Tiny said.

Moving swiftly, Morphy snatched up the little man by the back of his overall and held him at arm's length, laughing. Tiny kicked and cursed and lashed out with his fists until Morphy let him drop. Then Morphy dodged behind Asa to escape Tiny's pursuit. Daggett had ceased his exercising to stare at the commotion.

"The trouble with women is that the rams're always fighting over the ewes," Buchanan said. Miranda glanced up; she must have heard. Her black eyes met Asa's for an instant before she returned to her tasks.

Daggett summoned Asa and Buchanan to sit with him while they ate bacon and biscuits and drank mouth-searing, sweetened black coffee. They sat on a drift log just behind the beached boats, away from the others.

"That little pecker's a troublemaker," Daggett said savagely. "Know what he said to me?"

"What's that, Charley?" Buchanan drawled. Asa wolfed down Logan's biscuits with bacon grease smeared on them.

"Talking about a cut stump. He says photographers out West always take their pictures showing a cut stump between them and the mountains or whatever, to show that the wilderness is been tamed. Said he is not doing that. Says he is on the side of the wilderness. You suppose he's a spy for old Powell? Fixing his views so they don't turn out?"

"Expect if he was a spy he wouldn't be so noisy," Buchanan said.

"What's he do, anyway? Points that camera upriver and takes a view, then downriver the same. Spends his time in that silly orange tent to keep from working. Frigging the soiled dove, probably."

Asa opened his mouth and closed it again.

"He's got to key in the views with George Ritter's field notes, and mine too," Buchanan said. "He's got to prove out some of his photographs in the tent to make sure everything is coming right. Says the Fury's a nonesuch washing glass. He's teaching her to develop plates."

"She's bright," Daggett said, in his swift mood-changing manner. "She'll learn the tricks."

"Well, you can fire him at Bright Angel," Buchanan said. "Let him walk out and her take over. Cheaper, too."

"Know what she said to me?" Daggett said. "Spoke to her about her babe, and she said she wouldn't bring a girl into a world that was ruled by *men*. Oh, she is a tiger, that one!"

"A fury they called her in Eureka," Buchanan said. His eyes casually flicked past Asa's. "Nice little vacation for her on the River."

"I can't afford to spend three months on this damned River, Jake!" Daggett groused.

"Asa and me'd rather be tardy lining than stupid wrecking boats," Buchanan said.

Asa thought what a blessed relief it would be if Daggett decided to quit the River and walk out of the canyon at Bright Angel, not far beyond the Little Colorado.

"Major Powell lost the *No-name* right off," he said. "They were more careful after that."

Daggett rose and stamped away toward the fire, carrying his cup and plate.

"Having Charley Daggett aboard has got some blisters to it," Buchanan said with a sigh.

"Part of the reason we can't do more running is because he won't let Hyrum or Morphy take the steering oar. *He* shouldn't be steering. But who's going to tell him that?"

"I'll tell him if you say so," Buchanan said.

In the middle of the afternoon, clouds sailed across the slice of sky visible from the River. Asa found it disorienting to gaze up at them, for the west wall appeared to be toppling because of their movement. The clouds drifted lower, obscuring the cliff tops. Raindrops dimpled the River and splashed in his face like spray while the crew hurried with their bedrolls and provisions to the cover of an outward-slanting cliff. A deluge churned the River into lace. Thunder reverberated between the cliffs.

"There's a snake!" Miranda said coolly, holding her bedroll in her arms and pointing with her chin.

Buchanan snatched up his rifle and started past Asa. But Hyrum scooped the writhing snake up between two sticks of kindling and carried it away while the reptile twisted into grotesque shapes, striking at the wood.

Hyrum tossed the rattler into a rock pile at the north end of the cliff face, and when Buchanan, following him, tried to aim the rifle, Hyrum managed to interfere in the way that reminded Asa of his interference with Buchanan aiming his rifle at the two ruffians climbing into the wagon at the jail.

"Now why'd you do that?" Buchanan protested.

"Bad luck to kill a rattler. Mate'll sure show up."

"Stuff!" Ritter said contemptuously.

"Don't kill anything that don't have to be kilt, then," Hyrum said, standing holding the two pieces of kindling. "These Canyon ones won't strike unless you step on them," he explained to Buchanan. "All they want to do is make tracks."

"Like some folks do too," Ritter said.

Asa sat beside Chick's father, their backs against the rock wall, watching the rain slashing at the beach and the boats. Daggett had wrapped his brown blanket around him and sat with his knees tucked up to his chest as though he were cold.

"You can show that book for the fraud it is, can you?" Daggett demanded.

Asa said carefully, "The book appears to be an actual journal of the exploration. It is written in the present tense, like a diary, though it was actually written five years afterward. Morphy says there was a copy of Major Powell's journal that the Howlands and Dunn carried out of the Canyon with them. But there was a mix-up, so the original that Major Powell kept was incomplete. It is my hope that I can find the copy of the journal, or parts of it, when I visit the Shivwits."

"Doubt it," Daggett said. "All these years."

Since Asa had heard of the copy of the journal from Morphy, it had been his dream to find it intact, preserved by the Shivwits like some sacred artifact, in it the truth of the Separation.

"That damned old badger will do anything he can to spike me!" Daggett said. "I believe he spiked those three that deserted him, too!"

A sheet of rain slashed at the ground a yard beyond Asa's boots, which he drew back closer to him. Bad blood between Oramel Howland and Major Powell had started right away, when the *No-name* was wrecked because of a signal either not given or not heeded.

"That mean duck drove those three poor fellows away from the boats and out of the Canyon where they was prey to bloodthirsty savages," Daggett said. "Wasn't even armed, probably."

"They were armed. They had their share of the remaining food." In Major Powell's account of it, there was no sense that the Separation had been in anger.

"So it is up to you to figure why they went off like that. Then you'll write the truthful story for the *Monthly.*"

"Yes, sir."

"What we want is the stark truth! Those fellows' good names cleared of the filth the old badger has smeared on them!"

Major Powell had smeared no filth, not in his writings anyway. Always in these conversations with Chick's father Asa ended up feeling like a calumniator. It was exhausting trying to keep his employer from running over him, although he had been able to establish his own authority on the River.

"Anyway, Hyrum and I will be leaving the survey at Separation Canyon," he said.

"We'll give you an old hogleg that won't shoot and a half a dozen biscuits," Daggett said. He laughed and rocked back and forth where he sat, staring out at the rain.

"Chow pile!" Hyrum Logan called.

In the last of the daylight, they sat close around Hyrum's fire, with rain squalls slashing at the River behind them. Next to Asa, Buchanan sucked on his pipe and exhaled tobacco smoke. Across from them Miranda sat beside Tiny, one hand tucking bits of Hyrum's biscuits into her mouth. Morphy was gazing at the girl with a smarmy smile.

Jefford inquired if Miranda's mother was alive.

"She is in the East. My father had lost track of her. I have an aunt in San Francisco," she said in her harsh voice. She would be traveling there as soon she could get out of the Canyon, she said.

"I will be keeping her under my wing there," Tiny said in a proprietary way.

"Did you assist Rudolph Straw with his dialogues?" Jefford asked Miranda, when she had put down the coffeepot and seated herself between Hyrum and Tiny again.

She nodded as though she was not going to reply, then said, "Sometimes. Yes." Her hands were clasped beneath her chin, everyone's eyes fixed on her.

"What dialogues?" Jefford asked.

"Lear and Cordelia. Richard and Anne from *Richard III*. Henry and Anne from *Henry V*."

"A pretty French accent for Henry's Anne?"

Miranda nodded sullenly.

Jefford declaimed, "'Now, our joy, although our last, not least, to whose young love—' Something of France and Burgundy. '—What can you say—Speak!'"

"'Nothing, my lord,'" Miranda said.

"'Nothing will come of nothing!'"

The girl's eyes darted from face to face. She licked her lip with a flick of her tongue. Her voice took on timbre. "'Unhappy that I am, I cannot heave / My heart into my mouth. I love your majesty / According to my bond; no more nor less.'"

Jefford laughed and clapped his hands together. An educated man; with a CE, for civil engineer, to his name, Asa recalled.

As Miranda spoke she had raised her chin in defiance. Spots of color burned on her cheeks.

"'Speak!'" Jefford commanded, and she continued:

"'Good my lord, you have bred me, lov'd me: I return those duties as are right fit / Obey you, love you, and most honor you—'"

She halted, shaking her head when Jefford and Tiny urged her to continue, finally maintaining that she couldn't remember the lines.

Asa noticed that even Ritter wore a less sour expression than usual, and Daggett's red face resembled a boil that needed lancing in his enthusiasm.

Morphy lurched to his feet, one hand clasped to his chest, the other stretched out. With his wide-apart eyes, the gap between his front teeth, and the tangle of hair protruding from under his cap, he resembled a young bull. He recited:

The stag at eve had drunk his fill
Where danced the moon on Monan's Rill.
And deep his midnight lair has made
In lone Glen—something's—*hazel shade*—

"That's poetry the Major would shout when we was running rapids! He'd sit there in his chair strapped aboard *Emma Dean* just *howling* poetry!" Morphy glared from face to face as though someone might dare to dispute him. "Poetry!" he repeated.

"Hear! Hear!" Daggett called out. "Oh, I do love to hear Major Powell admired, I do! I do wish he was with us right now, I do not!"

"He cleared up the last blank spot on the map of the nation," Jefford said solemnly. "He will go down in history for that."

"I believe we will change that history of his!" Daggett said, glaring at Jefford as though he thought the geologist, like Tiny Truesdale, might be a spy and conspirator.

Asa spent a sleepless night worrying about the boats. Jagged strikes of lightning illuminated the Canyon, accompanied by thunder rolls that shook the earth. Every hour or so he slipped out of his bedroll to make certain the boats were pulled safely free of the rising water, often encountering Buchanan on his own inspections. Sometime in the night he heard the cliff give way not far off, a long rumbling slide that ceased and then began again. He lay staring up into the darkness above him thinking about the scarp that leaned over them, protecting them from the rain and threatening obliteration.

In the morning broken sunlight revealed hundreds of streams shooting out from the clifftops, breaking into sparkling spray in their fall to the benches beneath, and on down to the River. Woolly clouds clung to the opposite heights. Where the sun pierced them, rainbows congealed and disappeared.

Standing at the River's edge to relieve his bladder, Asa gazed in awe at the cascades leaping from the unbelievable height of the walls around him, some silvery, others red with mud. For the first time he understood Major Powell's harping on the beauties of the Canyon.

There was no sign of the chunk of cliff he had heard collapse in the night.

Buchanan's brown face was puffy with sleep or wakefulness, no doubt reflecting his own. In silence they strolled together along the narrowed beach to observe the rapid. Yesterday's whitecaps had disappeared beneath the swollen River, which swept past as smooth as tan molasses.

Buchanan pointed. A quarter of a mile further along, the current drove into a standing wave that must be six feet high and extended across the River. Asa gasped at the threat of it. No boat could pass that foaming wall.

"Some River," Buchanan said.

"We'll have to wait for it to go down—or portage."

"Maybe Charley Daggett will want to run it," Buchanan said with a snort.

They paced the route of the portage, a hundred yards up a shale slope and over a saddle to a cove below the standing wave. Beyond the cove the River ran swollen and smooth again, singing with power in its race for the Gulf of California. Bores of water shot off the opposite cliff like downspouts from a cathedral wall.

Breakfast was fried mush with sorghum syrup, Miranda passing among the men with the heavy coffeepot.

"Looking very peart this morning, Missy!" Morphy called, but she paid him no attention, her face sullen and sallow.

The half-breed came to squat beside Asa, who sat on the packed-silt bank, watching the violent surge of the whitewater rapids.

"You are a college young man," Poche said. His round brown face beneath his hat brim squinted severely in the powerful gleam of sunlight off the River.

Asa nodded.

"I have been educated also," Poche said.

"Where was that?"

"At Our Savior's Christian School in Tucson." Poche waved a hand toward the camp. "Some others have no education, I believe."

"I suppose that's true."

"Yet Mr. Daggett will not value me because I have a mother who is Hoya."

"That will be of value in the rescue of the White Captive, surely!"

"Mr. Fisher at the Christian School has told me I must have patience if I am not valued. He says I must forgive those who will take against me."

Asa drew a deep breath. "I believe on this survey it is what a man does that he will be valued for. Not his parentage." He blew his breath out.

Poche watched him closely through his squinted eyes. "Yet Mr. Daggett will not pay me as much as he will pay these others."

So he must defend Mr. Daggett again. "Well, you see, most of the crew are professionals. Tiny, Ritter, Jefford."

The half-breed fixed his gaze on the opposite bank. His cheekbones were so high, his cheeks so full, that his eyes were only two curved creases in his face. "I believe a college young man would value someone who may look different from himself. Mr. Daggett does not. Others I do not know."

"I'm sure everyone will feel differently when the White Captive has been rescued," Asa said uncomfortably, and Poche nodded, rose, and stepped away across the beach.

Four men were able to carry the unladen *Miss Saucy* up the track, Asa and Ritter hefting the stern, Morphy and Poche the bow, Buchanan following close behind to lend a hand. They staggered over broken rock and gnarled brush, hoist and carry and set down and rest; hoist and carry again. Six men were required for the freight boats, skidding them up driftwood logs, Morphy accomplishing the work of two men. Over the top and down the other side, hoist and skid and let down and rest. When the boats had been refloated they portaged the cargo, trip after trip laden with crates of photographic plates and equipment, the surveying instruments, rifles, tools, spare oars, the cook's warsack and the provisions, bedrolls and personal plunder. Daggett worked with the rest, his face flaming with sunburn and exertion. When the boats had been reloaded a light rain was falling.

Afloat on a broader, smoother, swifter River, *Miss Saucy* leading the way, Asa stood at the steering oar of the *Canyon Lass,* followed closely by the *Letty Daggett,* with Miranda huddled in the bow.

He heard a shout from ahead. Tiny was on his feet in the bow of *Miss Saucy,* pointing.

The eastern wall of the Canyon swarmed with movement.

Out of a U-shaped slot in the cliff bulged a high red front of mud, boulders and brush, writhing and enlarging. The twenty-foot wall, half flood, half landslip, slumped out into the River, driving a wave against the far bank that slapped back upon itself. Watery mud continued to flow out of the side canyon. Asa realized that the stew of brush and rock had served as a moving dam, constraining the head of water behind it. The muddy mess continued to pour into the River in a fan of darker brown.

He had felt his first awe at the beauty of the Canyon this morning, which now was followed by a lesson on its power.

Marble Canyon 3

ASA HADEN

Asa stood in the stern of the *Lass,* with the sweep oar clutched between his arm and his ribs, surveying the strong-running River in its slant down to the next dance of foam. They had run three cataracts in a row this morning, maybe in response to Daggett's impatience, all of them without incident. The sensations were familiar: the gradual acceleration, the dryness in the mouth, the shortness of breath, the approaching leap of the first white water, then the rapids coming into view, sometimes in steps, sometimes a ramp, the rocky hazards thrusting out of the water or barely concealed beneath slick humps like molten glass; the frothing holes, the current slashing at one bank or the other, the relentless cliffs above. Then the decision as to which course through the rocks to steer for. At his command Poche and Jefford would muscle the oars and the *Lass* would speed faster, with a chill shock of water slapping his face and a flurry of bailing if a wave was shipped. The waterproof lockers would keep the boat afloat, but with a dead weight of water it would not respond to the steering oar.

Asa's skin felt as though it had been flayed from the constant wetting and parching, and he winced whenever he saw Daggett's face, which resembled the butchered venison that Buchanan brought into camp every few days.

In lifting the *Letty* over a reef of rocks, six men crowded together, Ritter slipped, Hyrum yelped and lost his grip, and Asa and Morphy couldn't hold on in the swift current. A hole was stove in the *Letty*'s side, and Jefford was dragged beyond his depth and swept downstream. Morphy and Asa swarmed after the geologist, and together they dragged him out onto a ledge, where he coughed and vomited, his bald head gleaming in the sun.

Morphy repaired the *Letty*'s rib and planking while Daggett paced.

"Too slow, boys!" Daggett said, glaring at Asa. "Too slow altogether. There's a meeting I must attend in September in New York City!"

"Slow but sure," Asa said. He was tired of Daggett's badgering.

"If New York City in September is what you're after, you can let up surveying so many claims," Jefford said sourly. He was sprawled out against a rock with his bandanna knotted over his head. "These gravel banks won't assay out at five cents a yard."

"So you tell me," Daggett said, pacing.

Jefford had explained to Asa that what gold had been washed downriver was beaten so fine by the battering it had received that it would be extremely difficult to extract commercially. Daggett seemed to take such advice as evidence of disloyalty.

That afternoon a silt-laden wind whooped up the River. It was exhausting work rowing against the wind and the whitecaps. Buchanan made the decision to quit the River early. Hyrum discovered a cave up a wash and built his cookfire in it. The smoke was preferable to the stinging wind.

There was a tumbled-down parapet of stones from some ancient Indian habitation, and Hyrum found a store of dried-up corncobs with which to feed his fire. Asa sat apart, writing in his journal, with frequent trips out into the wind to make certain that the boats were secure.

Once when he returned, Poche was talking about the White Captive. "Frenchy Dubine said she hid from him. Who would believe such a thing? He is an untrustworthy fellow!"

Unloading pans from his warsack, Hyrum halted to listen to Poche.

"I believe Frenchy thinks he should earn some money from finding her," Hyrum said.

"Yes!" Poche said. "He would return to find her if it would bring him money!"

Asa continued to record the events of the day. His eyes were stinging from the smoke, and he went outside as much for relief as for another look at the boats' mooring. The blowing silt hummed up the River to slash against his cheeks, which he tried to protect with his flattened palms.

When he returned to the cave Miranda was daubing at her eyes with a bandanna. The conversation still concerned the White Captive:

"He would exhibit her like a prize animal!" Poche was saying indignantly.

"It seems she was right to hide herself," Jefford said. "If that was his intention."

"Poche thinks they will have tattooed her," Hyrum said, straightening again. "As they do their womenfolk."

"They will tattoo her," Poche said, nodding.

"To mark a man's possessions," Miranda said.

Asa was unable to imagine a white captive's life among the Hoya. He knew Indians only from *The Last of the Mohicans* and *The Deerslayer,* and from the drunken remnants of the race that he had seen on the railroad station platforms along the continental line west. If Jake Buchanan, who brought the survey fresh meat, was the last Leatherstocking, there were no more Mohicans.

"What if she does not wish to return?" Jefford asked.

"You think she would rather stay with them red devils than come *home?*" Morphy almost shouted.

"She will be grateful," Daggett said. "Why wouldn't she be?"

"It is interesting that she hid from the trader. Will you bring her out against her will?"

Asa scowled at Jefford in the smoky air. The geologist reminded him of a professor at Cornell who had enjoyed making his students look like fools when they presumed to argue with him.

"Might be she is not in her right mind," Buchanan put in.

"Can we say that someone who does not wish to return to civilization is not in her right mind?"

"How this one do enjoy getting folks riled up," Daggett said. "Oh, I know his kind!"

"Hyrum and Poche are embarking on a dangerous errand," Jefford said. "It would be well to consider every eventuality."

"If she is tattooed like you said, she might be ashamed coming home," Ritter said.

"She may not consider her life one of suffering, as we assume it is," Jefford interrupted. "She might be very frightened of returning to civilization." He addressed himself to Miranda. "Are we so certain that Miss Straw is grateful for having been kidnapped by a gang of roughnecks on a river expedition?"

"I am very grateful to the men who risked their lives for mine," Miranda said in her hard little voice.

"We would do it again, Missy!" Morphy said.

"It is difficult for a member of my gender to be alone among nine men," Miranda said. "It will be easier for Miss Bingham if you will take my suggestion."

"What is that, little lady?" Morphy said.

"You should respect her privacy," Miranda said.

It was a moment before Asa was shocked by her meaning.

"You mean some rascal has been spying on you?" Buchanan said in a mock-scandalized voice. "Now who could that be?"

Daggett laughed and pointed.

Morphy rose, hitching at his trousers and gazing down at Miranda in the smoke. "Grateful is as grateful does," he said. "You don't like me, little lady, but I could make you like me!"

He sauntered out of the cave.

"It must stop!" Tiny produced a shiny derringer from his pocket and held it up to glint in the firelight. "The privacy of my assistant will be protected!" he said in a joking manner. But Asa thought he was not joking.

"Put that away," Buchanan said. "Don't you be a jackass too, fellow!"

Tiny pocketed the weapon so quickly it was as though he was relieved to do so.

"Did you mark my words, Jakey?" Daggett said, grinning.

"It is not right!" Asa said in a choked voice.

Buchanan turned a cold eye on him. "I will tell you what is right. Right is what moves the job along, and wrong is what don't. Understand me?"

"Right is what decent men would do!" he said.

"You will command Tiny to put his piece away, but will you tell Morphy to quit his spying?" Jefford said. It sounded to Asa as though the geologist was enjoying this.

"I will tell *you* something," Buchanan said, pointing a forefinger at Jefford. "This is the girl's business, and maybe some of Tiny's, and it is my business. But it is surely none of yours!"

Will leaned back as though he had been physically threatened.

Buchanan said, "Pat Morphy is more use to the survey than some photographer's assistant." He said to Miranda, "Begging your pardon, Miss."

Miranda's face was the tight white knot that Asa remembered as she watched Buchanan rise to follow Morphy out of the cave.

Hyrum stacked more kindling onto the fire, his gray-whiskered, troubled countenance looming over the flames. Asa was grateful that Daggett changed the subject:

"The Hoya is Paiute and so is the Shivwits, isn't that right, Hyrum?"

"That is correct," Hyrum said.

"It was Paiutes that massacreed the Fenton train over in Iron County. Them and Mormon militia all fixed up with feathers in their hair and face paint. Am I right, George?" He squinted at Ritter.

Daggett had changed the subject only to create more contention. The surveyor had so little sense of humor and so large a conviction of his own importance that he invited baiting.

"Some say old Brigham ordered them murdered because they was from Missouri and Missourians had treated Mormons the meanest," Daggett went on, tugging on a sideburn. "And he didn't want Missourians settling in Mormon country. Forty souls butchered by Saints! Worse than 'Paches!"

"Wun't Brother Brigham's doing," Ritter said sullenly.

"You've heard of the occasion, have you?" Daggett asked. "Thought you might not've, the way the Saints make out it never happened."

"I was a half-grown boy," Ritter said.

"You've heard of it, have you, Hyrum?"

"Misguided men," Hyrum said. He sounded as though he were speaking through thick cloth.

"My father said it was robbers painted to look like Indians," Miranda said. "When they were recognized they murdered everyone so their crime would not be known."

"Painted up like Paiute," Mr. Daggett said.

"Shivwits," Poche corrected him.

The Howland brothers and Dunn had been murdered by Shivwits. The possibility loomed that it had been Mormons pretending to be Indians. But *why?* Because the three were taken for outsiders seeking to claim Mormon lands? Everything Asa had thought he was beginning to understand now seemed to have a treacherous edge.

"On his second exploration Major Powell visited the Shivwits and forgave them," he said.

"Jacob Hamblin went with him," Hyrum put in.

"Why would Major Powell want to *forgive* the people who had killed his men?"

"A treaty," Jefford said.

"Didn't want more trouble," Poche said.

But none of these answers seemed adequate. "It is a violent country," Asa heard himself say. "An easterner can hardly—be prepared for it. The River is violent. The heat. The weather. The rain. Those people in Eureka were violent."

Miranda watched him, white-faced.

"Violent men tamed the West," Jefford said.

"Big men civilized it," Daggett said.

"Big landgrabbers!" Tiny said.

Daggett laughed like a cough and grinned his grin that was no longer a grin. In the smoke of the cave his sunburnt face looked almost black.

The Deerslayer loomed in the darkness where Asa was testing the mooring of the boats. The wind had relented, but still occasional squalls blew up the Canyon.

"What did you say to him?" Asa asked.

"Told him I didn't like being put in the wrong with Daggett. He'd disputed bringing the girl along because she would cause trouble."

Asa leaned on the bow of the *Letty Daggett,* his arms folded against his chest. Gaps had opened in ethics that had once seemed simple right and wrong.

Standing before him, Buchanan shielded his face with his hands as the wind whooped up again. "He said I wasn't the boss of bedrolls. I said I was boss of anything that caused trouble, and I knew how to deal with jailbirds full of piss and jism like him. So he had better correct his manners."

"Jailbird," Asa said, remembering Daggett mentioning that fact in San Francisco.

"Charley brought him out of some pen in Texas to come along. Killed a fellow down there, I guess."

"I wonder why he did that," he said weakly.

"Over a woman, probably," Buchanan said. It sounded as though he chuckled. "Told me I couldn't run the River without Pat Morphy."

"I suppose it is true."

"Told him I could run the River without the girl, though."

Asa felt as though he was stifling in the harrying wind. "You wouldn't do that!"

"That's what Pat said," Buchanan said, and faded into the dark.

Miranda seated herself on the log against which Asa leaned, perusing his water-swollen copy of *Canyons,* and asked what he was reading. It was as though she was trying to be friendly, but her whole animus against the male sex, which he had heard her express outside Tiny's dark tent, constricted her. Her legs were crossed in Tiny's overall, her arms tightly folded on her chest, her pale face unsmiling beneath her cap. He read aloud:

> *"At last the storm ceases and we go on. We have cut through the sandstones and limestones met in the upper part of the canyon, and through one great bed of marble a thousand feet in thickness. In this, great numbers of caves are hollowed out, and carvings seen which suggest architectural forms, though on a scale so grand that architectural terms belittle them. As this great bed forms a distinctive feature of the canyon, we call it Marble Canyon.*

"It's Major Powell's account of the exploration of this River and these canyons," he told her. "He writes of these same rapids we encounter every day, and I have found it valuable to know what is coming."

He berated himself for sounding so pompous.

"And are we progressing to your satisfaction?" she asked.

"We should reach the Colorado Chiquito day after tomorrow. There Hyrum and Poche will make their attempt to rescue Miss Bingham."

"I do hope they will be successful."

He glanced at her hand on the knee of her overall. Even with its broken nails it was so small and perfect that it made his heart turn over in his chest like a cat settling in. She snatched her hand into a fist, concealing the nails.

"Some are not certain she will be grateful to be rescued," he babbled

"I have been unable adequately to express my own gratitude," Miranda said. Her legs were still crossed, but she had unfolded her arms in order to gesture with her hands. "To see you besting those men who climbed into the wagon!"

"It was Jake Buchanan's doing. You must understand that."

"You are a friend of Mr. Daggett's son," she said.

"We were classmates at Cornell University. We studied moral philosophy there."

A delicate blue vein marred the smooth flesh of her temple, like a jagged little lightning bolt. "And has your knowledge of moral philosophy been extended upon this voyage?"

It occurred to him that she might be teasing him.

"It has been intensified as well as extended!"

He glanced down at the small, fisted hand again. Her fist was what this unfortunate girl had to present to the world; she was a captive just as much as if she had been enslaved by Indians!

"It will be easier for you if the other young woman joins us," he went on. "You have suffered so much in Eureka." He stopped himself from mentioning her privacy.

Something seemed to close in her dark eyes, like the shutter of a camera. He had presumed too much! For a few moments they had been easy together, and now he had spoiled it.

"I have studied moral philosophy with very different teachers," she said.

Before he could apologize she was on her feet and ten yards away from him, heading to join Tiny, who was carrying his camera on its tripod. He had ruined a promising conversation by his clumsiness. His own dark, seamed self was as brute lustful as the men she had complained of who had made a hell of her brief life.

Asa rose to his feet in the stern of the *Lass* as the grumble of a rapid ahead became more insistent. *Miss Saucy,* in the lead, was already slanting toward the right bank, to nose into a narrow fan of beach enclosed by a rocky necklace. Well behind the *Lass* was the *Letty,* with Miranda in the bow and Daggett standing in the stern with the sweep, his flaming face topped by a straw hat.

Asa steered after *Miss Saucy,* which Buchanan and Ritter were hauling onto the beach. He called to Poche to ease off and for Jefford to dig in, for the current ran strong here. He waved his hat at Daggett that they were putting in for a reconnaissance. He could hear Chick's father bellowing one of his Italian arias over the racket of the rapid.

The *Lass* slipped sideways into the cove, Poche gazing up at the enclosing cliffs with his oars shipped, Jefford poised to leap ashore with the painter.

The *Letty Daggett* was coming on so swiftly that Daggett would have difficulty swinging her in behind the breakwater. He made no attempt to steer toward the shore. The *Letty* swept past, heading down the tongue of smooth water that led into the whitecaps. Daggett gazed straight ahead with his chin thrust out, singing at the top of his lungs:

La donna e mobile
qual piuma al vento
muta d'accento.

It was a rapid that Major Powell had lined. Morphy, on the far oar, should know that! And Daggett knew that the procedure was to put in before a rapid so that decisions could be made! All at once Asa was so angry he could hardly get his breath. In the bow Miranda stared straight ahead, her hands clutching the rail.

And he realized that it was the same situation as at Disaster Falls, where Oramel Howland had disobeyed Major Powell's signal to put in, or had not seen it.

"*Mr. Daggett!*"

"*E di pensiero!*" Daggett sang. He raised a hand dramatically from his steering oar to point straight ahead—a gesture that Asa understood to mean the whole daring of western exploration, of violent men taming the West and big men civilizing it, all against the petty regulations and common sense of the timid.

His impulse was to pursue the *Letty,* bring back the mutinous steersman and crew—and what? He couldn't even pursue. Suddenly he was concerned for Miranda's safety, as he watched the *Letty* encounter the first standing waves, pitching and swerving to the right with Daggett heaving on the sweep oar. He saw the sudden fountain that would surely capsize her. In the grip of the current the *Letty* broached, Morphy on his feet wrenching on his oar, Hyrum pulling back on his. The bow surged up against the fountain wave, Miranda flinging herself up with it, arms stretched out as though to hold off the water.

The *Letty Daggett* stood on her stern. Daggett's arms flailed as he fell over backwards. The boat flopped onto one side and capsized, only her rounded bottom visible among the whitecaps, appearing and disappearing as she was carried downriver.

Already *Miss Saucy* was forging out of the cove, Tiny kneeling in the bow with a rope. The scout boat fought the current around the spit of rocks. Downstream, a figure struggled onto the bank; Morphy's broad, soaked back. He carried a bundle. Asa saw the cluster of black curls as the big man deposited his burden on a ledge. Miranda promptly rose to her hands and knees to gaze back at the River. *Miss Saucy* tossed in the white teeth of the chop, well away from the foaming tower that had capsized the *Letty.* Buchanan backed mightily on his oar while Ritter and Tiny leaned over the side. A man sprawled aboard—Hyrum, his gray hair slicked to his skull.

In that moment of seeing Hyrum safely aboard *Miss Saucy,* Miranda crouched on the ledge, and Morphy back in the River again, Asa knew that Daggett was drowned.

CHAPTER

10

The Colorado Chiquito

JAKE BUCHANAN

After they had roped the *Letty Daggett* off the nest of rocks where she had grounded and set up lines to unload the sodden cargo, they searched the riverbanks downstream for Charley Daggett's body. They kept at it long past knowing it was hopeless.

Buchanan thought that if anybody spoke up to say that Daggett ought to have purchased the life preservers, he would have a hard time restraining himself.

Two sacks of flour were soaked despite their waterproof coverings. Hyrum and the Eureka Fury sat cross-legged, separating the dry flour from the ruined. Soaked clothing and bedding were spread out to dry. The surveyor and Will Jefford leaned on rocks opposite each other, with similar long-jaw expressions, like bookends. Tiny had set up his camera on the talus slope, and Poche and Pat Morphy collected firewood.

Buchanan dug through Daggett's kit and came upon the chalk-white skull Daggett had called his luck. He tossed it to Poche. "Take and bury it," he said.

It was time for a confab. The crew gathered around him. He was about one quarter relieved that Daggett was dead and about three quarters swamped with the problems his death was going to bring.

"We will have to get up a document about what happened," Buchanan said, tapping the bowl of his pipe on his knuckle.

"Said the West was not won stopping and conferring," Morphy said.

"I should have insisted on Pat or Hyrum steering," the college boy said.

"He should have furnished those life preservers," Jefford said.

There it was. Buchanan clamped the bit of the pipe in his jaw. "What happened?" he said to Morphy.

"He just run right into that spout, singing away. We went ass over teakettle. The little lady had went under, but *he* was there with Hyrum and me grinning like he wanted a good wash-off anyhow. So I went after the little lady."

The River was whooping it up as though celebrating a winning hand, making it hard to hear sometimes, so you had to say "What?" or "How's that?" enough to make you scratchy.

"One minute he didn't seem in difficulty, and the next he was gone," Hyrum put in. He brushed at the gray hair standing up on his head like a coxcomb.

"He was in the water but seemed in no difficulty. Then he was swept under and gone," Buchanan said. "Asa, you write this down on a piece of paper for everybody to sign."

Buchanan chewed on the bit of his pipe and paced. Tiny had come down off the talus to join them.

"Some of us know what this survey is about, but the rest of you don't," Buchanan said. "It was Daggett's way to play his cards close, but that is not my way. This survey is for the Colorado, Grand Canyon, and Pacific Railroad. We are making a photographic survey, a transit reconnaissance, and a feasibility report along with whatever mineral claims turn up, to see if a syndicate can be got together. Buchanan and Daggett Construction was going to build the road. I expect to go along the same with Charley Daggett drowned. Martha Daggett will keep her hand in, I expect."

There was a pretty good silence while this was digested. Even the River quieted down.

"A railroad down this slot?" Morphy said. "That's crazy."

"Well, I don't think so. There's only one River crossing with a steel suspension bridge so far, the rest can be timber bridges. There's half-tunnels to cut, but mostly she can run along the talus line keeping above high water. It's just regular cut and fill, except it's down in a hole. It's not so bad so far. Right?" he said to Ritter.

Arms folded superiorly, the surveyor nodded.

"There's a major coalfield up near Grand Junction that Daggett wanted to open up," Buchanan went on. "Coal is needed out on the Coast, where it has to be shipped in from Australia. He figured to deliver it for half price on this line. There's claims already in the Canyon, for copper, gold, silver, and iron. Mining can get started if there's coal fuel available for operation and a railroad for servicing. There's plenty of timber up on the plateau for ties, bridge timbering, and construction fuel."

"You and Daggett were to build the line?" Jefford said.

"Keerect. It's a good low-level line, no snow summits. Not only that, but if what Major Powell wrote about the Canyon is so, sight-seeing will defray extraordinary construction costs."

He stopped to glance at Asa Haden, whose face was red with betrayal. That was the look of people that Charley Daggett had made a fool of.

"I say, Daggett liked things secret," he continued. "Somebody got wind of what he was up to, they'd fence him in Washington City. He had a pretty good scrape with Major Powell, who kind of figured what he was up to. So he decided to make out the expedition was for other purposes. Rescuing young ladies," he said with a nod to Hyrum.

"So I am taking photographs of the way the Canyon is before it is blown all to pieces making a railroad," Tiny said.

"He wanted to tie the Canyon up with a railroad right-of-way as well as mineral claims," Jefford said, shaking his head, maybe in admiration

"Keerect," Buchanan said. Daggett had also talked of a steamship route upriver from Callville as far as was feasible.

"I will have to write this in my journal," the college-boy historian said in a stifled voice.

"Surely. It is no secret now."

"Just so we get paid," Morphy said.

Buchanan paced again, frowning and chewing on his pipe bit. "Daggett had his money belt on him. It's not in his kit."

There was another silence while this went down.

"I believe Ira Ellsworth will honor your pay," he said, fingers crossed. "And mine. But he probably won't be at Callville to do it."

"Who's Ellsworth?" Tiny asked.

"Partner of Daggett's that pays out the funds."

"Just a minute here!" Ritter said shrilly.

"How do we know he will pay us?" Jefford said.

"I don't doubt it."

"This expedition cannot continue! We will have to leave the boats and walk out at South Canyon."

"What about the white woman?" Hyrum demanded.

"You can walk out at South Canyon," Buchanan said to the geologist. "Or you can come along to the Little Colorado and then walk out at Bright Angel with the captive woman and Miranda." He nodded to the Fury. "There's some men and horses waiting at the head of Bright Angel. Asa's report goes out there, too.

"Or you can keep on to Kanab, where that second bunch of the Major's got out. Or Separation, where the ones killed by redbellies—*separated*. But if you clear out shy of Callville, I don't believe Ira Ellsworth owes you anything."

Jefford glared at him, Ritter too.

"I finish what I start," Buchanan said. "I'll finish this survey. There'll be some changes. I'm sick of surveying claims that won't amount to anything. We can move faster, I believe. But Hyrum and Poche is going after the White Captive like Daggett planned."

"I will not go on unless my pay is guaranteed!" Ritter said. He looked like he would like to kill Daggett for drowning with his money belt on.

Buchanan said he could run a transit himself if he had to. "Pat?"

"I'll stick," Morphy said.

He raised an eyebrow at the college boy.

Asa nodded.

"Hyrum?"

Hyrum nodded. Poche nodded too.

"Tiny?"

"I'll have my photographs. They will be worth something, this Ellsworth fellow or not."

"You can walk out at Bright Angel with these others and the White Captive," he said to Miranda.

She stared at him with her hard little face beneath her big cap.

"Am I to understand you've been aligning a roadbed as we go, Jake?" Jefford said, not so fiery, and, when he nodded, "You've done this before?"

"Keerect."

"Surely not terrain like this."

"Close enough," he said. Gospel Gorge!

"I will come along as far as Bright Angel anyway," Jefford said, who had made his fuss and come out of it.

"All right," Ritter said sullenly.

"There was a conversation like this at Separation Canyon," Asa Haden said. "The Howland Brothers and William Dunn decided to leave the River. Others decided to stick with Major Powell."

"I expect we will find Daggett further along," Buchanan said, meaning money belt and payroll. "We'll be at the Little Colorado tomorrow. Then it's Hyrum and Poche's time to do what they are here for."

"We will pray for the soul of the departed," Hyrum Logan said in his harsh voice, on his knees where he was adding driftwood to the fire.

When Buchanan saw that others were also kneeling, he sank to his knees too.

Drifting down toward the mouth of the Little Colorado, Buchanan squinted up at the enclosing cliffs. They rose to what Jefford had estimated as two thousand feet, two hundred vertical from the River to the convenient shelf that would sustain the roadbed of the CGC&P Railroad. So far, there was only one crossing of the main Canyon; multiple steel suspension crossings were an expense that had worried Daggett.

The soaring walls with their surmounting towers, cupolas, mansards, pulpits, and bays expanded against the sky, with higher and more immense heights opening behind them. He was challenged by the scale. Height and space suited him just fine! He would bust Buchanan & Daggett half-tunnels along these Canyon walls and brush out Buchanan & Daggett roadbed on these benches and terraces!

Even the sour-faced surveyor, resting on the oar beside him, looked almost pleased as he gazed up at the ramparts.

"Big place," Ritter said.

"Big," Buchanan said, nodding. Big the Canyon, big the construction job, rich the man who would accomplish it. Not rich like Charley Daggett but rich enough. He mocked himself for his pretensions.

He supposed he had thought of Daggett as his friend, but he had lost many friends in his life, to the war and after it in the West: to Indian fights, to exposure and a bear's mauling, to construction accidents and mishaps with livestock, to gun scrapes and a railroad war, to TB and the DTs. He was certain that plump, long-suffering Martha Daggett, who was a wealthy woman now, would support Buchanan & Daggett Construction.

He had made her squeal many times and could do it again. One night three years ago she had led him into that fancy bedroom with its mirrored walls and soaring ceiling, and the chandelier with its glass leaves tinkling from the breeze through the window. He had never been sure that Daggett had been fooled. Maybe Daggett had planned the whole thing to make his own nights with his Italian singer that much easier.

But Daggett had failed to purchase life preservers for the crew of the survey in a life of promises not kept, of obligations skimped, of corners cut. Singing opera he had sailed headlong into one rapid too many, and his luck had quit on him. The news would have to be got back to Denver, by way of whoever left the Canyon at Bright Angel. Eventually he himself must return with Jefford's mineral assessments, the feasibility report, and Tiny's photographs. Martha would have to be met with, comforted, and bedded, and she and some other moneybags convinced of the profitability of the Colorado, Grand Canyon, and Pacific Railroad. And Jacob Buchanan would build the road.

By the middle of the afternoon the boats were moored at the Little Colorado River, sixty miles below Pariah Crossing Camp was set up on a ledge fifty feet above the powdery blue of the tributary. Ritter stepped around his surveyor's transit with his self-important strut. Tiny adjusted his camera for views up and down the river, and Jefford climbed along the shelving ledges of the Little Colorado with his geologist's pick. Morphy and Poche scared up driftwood and mesquite for Hyrum's fire, and the Fury squatted beside the warsack, slicing up spuds on a cutting board.

Buchanan strolled over to where Hyrum was laying out women's things from his pack: a dress, brown and voluminous, with a wrinkled white collar, a bonnet, boots, and a quantity of underclothing. Hyrum stood frowning down at the dress.

"Big-sized dress," Buchanan observed.

"Borrowed it from Mrs. Smith. She's a big-sized woman."

"Better too big, I guess."

"In case she don't have any real clothes. Poche says they dress in moss and bark and such when times is bad.

"I've got three hundred dollars and some that Mr. Daggett give me," Hyrum went on. "And some trade goods, too. You can't tell how they'll look at greenbacks." Hyrum appeared to be more worried about the greenbacks and the dress fitting than about crazy redskins lifting his scalp or chopping him up for supper.

"Jake, I know Mr. Daggett said a week, but it'll maybe be longer."

"Understood," he said. Every hour of waiting after that week would be dirty hell, but he would have to start thinking like Charley Daggett. If he was bringing back news of Daggett drowned, it would be good measure to bring the White Captive back along with it.

Hyrum left off sorting the female garments and went to stoke up his cookfire. Asa seated himself on a rock near where Miranda was working. Buchanan grinned to notice from the shifts of Asa's head that he was trying not to watch the Fury.

"A man's sins do parade before him at such a moment," Hyrum was saying to the girl. "As it must've done for poor Mr. Daggett. All that was done, and left undone. Then in the Lord's mercy you and me was returned to the blessed light and air."

It was the longest speech Buchanan had heard the old man make.

Morphy was wrapping cord around the handle of an oar with a jerky, looping motion. He had an eye on Miranda also.

There were some exchanges Buchanan could not hear, until Hyrum said, "The Lord's mercy is infinite, and I am proof of it!"

When Tiny called to her, Miranda rose and hurried to join him, stepping neat-legged between the stones that littered the ledge. It did cheer a man's spirit to eye a good-looking female in motion.

He recalled the sight of Miss Susan Darling crossing a street with her skirts hoisted a bit to show her shiny boots. The Daggett world of proper ladies and fancy-dress balls had often seemed to him like a place of Christmas toys that could never properly belong to him. But Miss Saucy beside him in a bright-varnished buggy navigating the streets of Denver under envious eyes—that was a picture in which he could see himself!

At first light Hyrum and Poche were up and bustling. Everybody called out good lucks, and Buchanan walked with them a way up the canyon of the Colorado Chiquito. He stood on a ledge watching them march away, looking humpbacked with their packsacks on, setting out to rescue the White Captive from the Hoya.

The following days were slow, the sun blistering. After lunch the shadow line would creep by inches across the river to bring some relief, and later a cooling breeze breathed up the canyon. Tension in the camp was like a rope on the strain, waiting for Hyrum and the half-breed to return, with or without the White Captive.

The Fury worked with the photographer in the orange calico tent, spelling him to "fix" the views Tiny had taken. The stink of chemicals near the tent was powerful. It must have been fearful hot inside, even in the afternoon shadows.

Ritter tried his hand at fishing and brought back a catfish as long as his arm, which made a change from venison and bacon. Buchanan shot an antelope. Asa found a patch of shade along the Little Colorado cliffs, where he copied over his journals to send back to San Francisco. No doubt he was writing his opinions about Daggett's deceptions and Daggett's death.

The mood of those long days at the Colorado Chiquito waiting for the rescuers' return seemed to Buchanan like a bout of constipation.

Nothing came easily or passed quickly. The hours dragged, the days strung out. After the week was gone, the waiting took on the quality of a heated weight that pressed more heavily every day, like a physical sensation, an irritation along the nerves, a pressure in the hollow places of the skull.

When Buchanan heard the cry in the night he thought it was Hyrum's bloody nightmare again. He disentangled himself from his bedroll and struggled to his feet. Pale in the starlight a figure was looming twenty feet away—Pat Morphy buck naked.

Buchanan started toward the jailbird, stumbling over someone's legs. Now there was light; someone had lit a lantern. Morphy was crouched apelike, broad chest, spread legs, his cock laid up against his belly. Buchanan could see Miranda's curls among her blankets at his feet. Others were rising from their bedrolls, Asa bare-chested and gaping at the edge of the light.

With one long stride Hyrum appeared behind Morphy, swinging his frying pan. There was an iron clang, and Morphy pitched to his hands and knees. Now Tiny appeared, with the gleam of the nickel-plated derringer in his hand. Hyrum had the frying pan raised again.

Morphy backed to his feet, cursing, one hand clutching his head. Asa, Hyrum, and Tiny surrounded him. They looked like a troupe of vaudeville clowns.

Buchanan said to Morphy, "Look at you. You are a joke. Why don't you paint your nose red and dance a jig for us?"

Morphy cursed, eyes squinted like a coyote. He brought the hand from the back of his head and examined it for blood. Hyrum wore a long singlet, low-necked and short-sleeved—the Mormon "garment."

Buchanan pointed at Truesdale's little revolver. "Put that thing away!"

Tiny concealed the derringer in his hand, glaring at Morphy. Asa was leaning forward with his fists clenched as though he wanted to take a crack at the jailbird. The girl's face, pale as milk in the lantern light, peered up at the men standing over her.

"Don't try it again," Buchanan said to Morphy.

The jailbird responded with words he didn't like much, but he decided to let go past.

Asa stuttered, "You had better leave her alone!"

"Who's going to make me, *you?*" Morphy sneered.

Asa retreated a step when Morphy moved toward him, fists balled at his sides. Buchanan thought he had better stop this.

"I will," he said.

"Huh!" Morphy swung toward him, his limp cock flopping.

Buchanan twisted sideways, as though reaching for something behind him. He whipped his fist around to slug the big man in the belly. Morphy staggered back with a whoop of expelled breath.

When Morphy's arms came up, Buchanan hit him in the privates. Morphy squealed like a girl and fell, doubled up around his crotch, gasping.

"Satisfied?" Buchanan said to the girl, who was sitting up now, with her arms folded over her shirt. He thought she would rather have had the college boy knock down the jailbird for her.

Morphy scrambled to a seated position, still clutching himself. He glared up at Buchanan with his teeth bucked in his pain.

"I'll fix you!" he gasped.

"What do I have to do to make you be a gentleman, Pat? Kill you?"

"You'll wish you had!" Morphy panted.

Buchanan stood with the college boy leaning against a slant of cliff facing up the Little Colorado in the direction from which Hyrum, Poche, and the White Captive would come. Or would not. "He'll try to kill you," Asa said. "He as much as said so!" He sounded shaky still.

"I doubt it."

"You said he was in prison for killing somebody!"

Buchanan shrugged.

"But something had to be done," Asa went on. "When something is going—wrong like that."

"Thought you might be thinking of taking him on yourself."

Asa drew a heavy breath. His fingers plucked at the sprigs of blond beard on his brown face.

"If you're going to mix it with somebody like that, just do it as hard and fast as you can and get it over with. Blessing to everybody."

"I don't think violence can solve anything," Asa said.

"Sure do sometimes. Things are different out here from what you are used to. I expect Pat is one mean boot-stomping son of a bitch. If he came at me before I was ready, I'd have my hands full. So I have got to tie him up before he is ready for me. Understand?"

Asa nodded jerkily. "You're experienced with this kind of thing."

"I told Pat I know how to deal with his kind. But he don't know how to deal with mine."

He thought about it before he went on: "It's what they say about 'Paches. The way a white man thinks, he thinks if I do *this,* sure as certain *that* will happen. A redbelly don't think like that. Maybe he knows that if he shoots that white fellow over there, the cavalry will come and wipe out his whole village—bucks, squaws, and papooses. A 'Pache don't pay any attention to that. He does it anyway. You have to think like that when it's time for a scrape."

He watched the boy's big, raw-knuckled hands stretching as though he didn't know what to do with them.

"I believe things will be easier if this woman is rescued," Asa said.

"I think it'll be about the same. Pat has just got his mind locked on what that little whore's got between her legs."

He saw Asa wince.

Buchanan often went to stand on a jut of rock where he could watch up the canyon of the Colorado Chiquito. Hyrum had been a fool not to take rifles along. Never trust a redbelly was a lesson Buchanan had learned long ago.

At least Morphy was no longer making a nuisance of himself with the girl these last few days. He was the most dependable crewman, always seeing what needed to be done, never shirking or disappearing like Tiny or Will Jefford. Morphy, Asa, and old Hyrum were the strength of the survey.

This was the ninth day of waiting for Hyrum and the breed to return.

He was watching from his post when he saw the pack of them coming down the canyon past the blue water ponds and the shale walls that dropped off into the riverbed. It looked like the whole Hoya nation. His heart jammed up into his throat; it was as though Charley Daggett still swung his luck from his grave in the River.

A few were mounted, most afoot, Hyrum and Poche in the front rank, along with a mule that had what must be the White Captive aboard. She was wearing the brown dress Hyrum had got from the ferryman's wife, her face hidden in the bonnet. About thirty braves were crowded around them, all in motion, one up on a paint horse, another two on mules. The Hoyas wore rags bound around their heads like turbans, some had on white-man shirts, others buckskin, most were bare-chested. Some were armed with old rifles that they brandished overhead as though they were wading in deep water. They uttered a kind of groaning song with high-pitched yips to it.

The crew of the survey gathered on the canyon side to watch them come.

Hyrum raised an arm and jerked a hand in the direction of downriver, a gesture that Buchanan understood. When he turned to pass along the get-out-of-here, he saw that everyone else had understood too. There was a hustle of rolling blankets, striking the orange tent, and assembling gear to be carried down to the boats.

It was Buchanan's part to head down to greet Hyrum, the Hoya chief who was Poche's uncle, and the White Captive. She was slumped on the mule like a sack of old clothes. A fifty-fifty chance, Daggett had said; revised to ten percent later. He himself had given Hyrum less chance than that. Now he had to hand it to the old jack Mormon and the breed.

The pack of Hoyas halted and milled on the flat where the boats had been pulled clear of the water. Morphy and Asa were pushing the boats back so the sterns were afloat, the bows still hiked up onto the packed silt. Others scrambled down the shale ledges carrying freight. Hyrum stood holding the mule's lead rope with a rare yellow-toothed grin. He motioned grandly.

"This here's Miss Bingham. Here is Mr. Buchanan that I told you about. It is too bad that Mr. Daggett is not here," he added.

Poche looked worried and jittery.

Buchanan could see the tattooing of the woman's brown face within the bonnet, intricate tracings of blue-black lines on her chin and along her jaw. Dazed brown eyes met his. Redbellies surrounded them, with their stink like meat going bad. He had to clench his nostrils as well as his muscles to stand still amongst this bunch.

The mounted Hoya who must be the chief pushed his way toward them on the paint horse, jabbering. Poche jabbered back with gestures. Hyrum spoke more slowly, but the chief paid close attention to him. Then the chief harangued the two of them.

"Jake, we will have to give him some *gift,*" Hyrum said. "I gave him all my money, but he wants something else. He says there's going to be war now. Poche thinks if you gave him some *gift.*"

Buchanan called to Asa where to look, and the college boy dug Daggett's kit out of *Miss Saucy.* He held up the admiral's tunic with its brass buttons and the fore-and-aft cap. Too much time was spent getting the chief, with his toothless, tongue-bulging grin and his sour stink, buttoned into the tunic and the hat set on his head in the place of his filthy turban.

Ritter came past carrying his transit on his shoulder and his wooden surveyor's box. He squinted at the White Captive. Jefford hoisted a rubber-covered bundle aboard the *Letty,* gazing back.

There was a yipping from the Hoya that caused Buchanan some agitation. Hyrum handed Miss Bingham down from her mule. She wore the dusty dress unfastened at the side, with a show of underclothing, so he wondered if she had forgotten how to fasten hooks and buttons. She seemed clumsy.

She was monumentally big with child.

She stared at nothing, with her lips drooping open and her hands folded into fists gripped beneath her chin. The chief, in Daggett's admiral's getup, raised his hands above his head in some signal or celebration. One of the braves with a rifle fired it off, causing the bucket brigade coming down off the canyon side to halt half-crouching. Miranda remained standing, peering down at the White Captive. Buchanan was feeling nervier than he liked.

"We'll just ride you in *Miss Saucy* here," he said to Miss Bingham. He took her hand to tug her past a couple of Hoya braves. Her hand was filthy, splay-fingered, with broken, grime-encrusted nails. Morphy helped him hoist her aboard. She stood in the bow unsteady and huge-bellied for a moment before she tucked her arms protectively around her middle and seated herself.

Miranda, carrying an armful of Tiny's gear, passed it up to the photographer aboard the *Lass,* casting glances at the White Captive from under her oversized cap. The Hoya were now bumping against the boats, and Buchanan could feel the chaffing of urgency like a rash. He restrained himself from shoving a mud-faced buck who was interfering with Morphy's slinging the cook's warsack aboard the *Letty.*

The White Captive, in the brown gown, sat motionless in the bow, slumped over her belly.

Her papoose would be delivered somewhere along the River.

The chief in his blue tunic looked like an equestrian statue aboard the paint pony. He grinned gummily down at Buchanan as though they were pals for life.

It seemed half a day before Morphy and Asa were unhitching the bow ropes. Poche and Hyrum climbed into the *Letty.* Buchanan piled into *Miss Saucy* with Ritter, both of them jamming on the oars to backwater until the bow swung downstream in the current. The *Lass* and the *Letty* came around also. Ashore, the Hoya were crowded together in a swarm of bodies, arms, and legs, with rifle barrels sticking up. The three mounteds were locked into the pack. They all watched in silence as the boats floated away from them. The chief's admiral's hat reminded Buchanan of Daggett with a pang that surprised him.

He and Ritter bent to the oars, gathering speed in the current. He grinned back at Asa aboard the *Lass.* Hyrum leaned on the sweep of the *Letty,* his gray head turned for a last look back at the Hoya gathered at the mouth of the Colorado Chiquito.

The chief on his pony pranced, and others fired off four or five shots in a swirl of gunsmoke. Then they remained motionless, watching the CGC&P survey heading downriver toward the gorge of the Grand Canyon.

Buchanan rested on his oar and turned toward the White Captive. "We are glad to have you with us, ma'am!"

Face hidden in the bonnet, she spoke slowly and thickly, as though chewing on the words: "You . . . have . . . come . . . this . . . way . . . for . . . me?"

"We are surveying for a railroad, you see."

"That man . . . is . . . named . . . Hyrum?"

"Hyrum Logan."

"Why . . . he . . . has . . . come . . . for . . . me?"

He could feel Ritter watching him with his disapproving face. "Well, ma'am, we heard you had been seen, and the man I work for—he's dead now—decided to do something about it. He hired Hyrum because he knew Injun, and Hyrum brought the breed along because his uncle's a Hoya chief. *That* one." He pointed back.

Her eyes flickered at him past the edge of the bonnet, as though he hadn't told her what she wanted to know. "What . . . he wants?" she whispered, over the slap of water against the bow.

"Why, to rescue you from the redbellies!" Now he could see her face close up. The lines of tattooing were like a delicate beard.

He asked her name. She thought for a while and said it was Esther. Esther Bingham.

"Went and tattooed you there, didn't they?" Ritter said.

Her eyes shifted from Buchanan to the surveyor. It was as though she had to think before each word. Miranda had been frightened when she first came aboard, but nothing like this one. Esther covered her chin with her hand.

"They say . . . if I go . . . they will . . . find me . . . by *this*. And . . . they will . . . kill me."

"They won't bother you," Buchanan said. "Even if they come after us they couldn't move downriver as fast as we can." He waved a hand at the canyon walls.

"You are in good hands, Miss," Ritter said. First time he'd said anything pleasant on this river trip.

"When is your time?" Buchanan asked.

She gazed at him without comprehension until he indicated her belly.

She clasped her ugly hands there. "I think . . . very soon."

They halted for the night six bends beyond the Little Colorado. Buchanan watched the Fury acquainting herself with the White Captive, the slim girl like a canoe alongside a tugboat, not so sullen and backward with another female. Morphy stood by with his smarmy smile, and Jefford approached to pay his respects, but Poche edged the others aside and led Esther Bingham away from them to seat her on a boulder. He fussed over her there as though he was courting her.

When Hyrum called, "Chow-pile!" he had to abandon his sweetie to bring her some victuals.

It shocked Buchanan that a breed would have the presumption to approach a white woman like that. Who was probably married to some dirty-face buck and about to produce a half-breed herself, come to think of it.

Esther Bingham sat slumped on her rock, her hands folded over her belly and her face hidden in the bonnet. A raven perched on a dry branch above her, watching the humanfolk in their peculiar ceremonies.

Supper was the last of the antelope meat broiled in strips, with greens and potatoes, Hyrum's attempt to create a banquet in honor of the rescued woman. Miranda went over to her, and after some confab, the two of them came to join the rest. The White Captive moved her corporation along like pushing a wheelbarrow. When she was seated between Miranda and Hyrum, everyone sneaked glances at her tattooed chin—which the Hoya, or maybe just her husband, had told her they would find her by if she tried to escape, and kill her.

Buchanan brought the jug of whiskey from *Miss Saucy* and poured tots all around, excepting for Hyrum, Ritter, and Miranda. Then he raised his own tin cup to toast dauntless Hyrum Logan, and Elbert Pockett too, at which Poche blushed and bridled, pleased as a patted pup, as though no one had ever praised him before. Hyrum just looked buttoned up and dour.

Will Jefford kept his own cup raised to make his own toast—no doubt he had not thought Buchanan's clever enough. He glanced around for silence:

"To the traveler who has returned from beyond the bourne!"

Esther stared at the geologist with her dazed eyes, a hand shielding her chin. So she was ashamed of the tattooing. There was a heavy freight of silence before she said, "I thought . . . it would not be."

Everyone but him, and probably Jefford, took that for gratitude, and there were nods and handclaps. Then they were waiting again.

"I thought it would not be," she said again.

"You have Charles P. Daggett to thank," Buchanan said.

"Nothing like a fine river trip for coming out of the desert!" Morphy said.

Buchanan made introductions for the Captive, since Poche or Hyrum didn't seem inclined to do so. She peered with each name, hand always fluttering close to her chin. Miranda was holding her other hand affectionately. It was going to be a blessing to have Miranda by when the Captive came into her labor! Who had borne a child of her own not so long ago. And smothered it—he had almost forgotten.

He thumbed tobacco into the bowl of his pipe and lit it with a flaming splinter.

"Can you tell us of your experiences, Miss Bingham?" Jefford asked, as though he were addressing an idiot schoolchild.

Buchanan thought the White Captive did not want to tell of her experiences—and didn't want Miranda holding her hand either.

"The Apaches were . . . cruel," she said. "I could not walk so fast! I thought I would . . . starve!"

"She was traded to the Hoya for some blankets," Poche said, sitting beside Miranda. "She was lucky to be traded. 'Paches are cruel devils."

As far as Buchanan could make out from Esther's responses to the questions of one or another, she had been captured as a child of thirteen by Apaches when she had ventured too far from the wagon train on the southern route across the desert, near Fort Yuma. The Apaches had traded her to the Hoya, where she had also almost starved until she was befriended by the chief's wife. She was married to an Indian, who had tattooed her. No one questioned her about the child she carried.

Asa Haden had his notebook out and scribbled along with her broken statements. She never seemed to put out any information except to a direct question. It was like getting a child to talk, who would lose interest between each query.

"She remembers when Frenchy came," Hyrum said.

"You didn't see the white men?" Tiny asked.

"I was . . . hiding in the Canyon. They said they would harm me."

"We will bring you safe home," Poche said, leaning toward her.

"My people are in . . . Los Angeles. I would not know how to find them."

Buchanan saw Asa fix on her belly as though he had just understood what the mountain of it meant.

Esther's speech became more halting rather than better, but they were able to discover that her family had come from Lamon County in Ohio. They had been the Bingham-Travers wagon train. She thought there had been twelve wagons. She couldn't remember any dates, except that it had been a long time ago.

"We are used to taking care of estrayed young women," Morphy said, and laughed.

The Captive's dull eyes carefully watched whoever spoke to her, as though it took great effort for her to understand the questions and respond to them.

Night fell in the Canyon.

"I brought up Daggett's bedroll," Buchanan said to Miranda. "Why don't you lay it out for her?"

The girl helped the pregnant woman to her feet, and the two of them faded into the darkness.

Buchanan awakened to sobbing, long, slow, muffled sounds of despair that caught at his heart. Will Jefford had been right in his prophecy that Esther Bingham did not want to come home.

San Francisco 5

MARY TEMPLE

The fog was chill and thick as woolen cloth, drifting through the horsecar where Mary Temple sat with four other huddled passengers.

"Broadway, please!" she called to the conductor. The muffled clop of hooves ceased, the car stopped. The conductor handed her down with a "There you go, ma'am."

She loved the fog, a cloak of invisibility that protected her individual, secret self. The moisture congealed in drops on her cheeks as she shuffled cautiously along, discovering the downhill slant of the street with her boots. There was a mournful call of a foghorn on the Bay to guide her. She clutched the packet of manuscript under her arm. An evening of reading with her chair drawn up close beside the coal stove lay before her.

The slow clop of hooves began again as the car continued on its way.

As she located her fence corner and gate, a figure emerged out of the mist. It was Mr. Lau, who inhabited a tiny basement apartment in her house and served as the owner's agent.

"Missy, somebody inside!"

She halted with her hand on the gate. "Who?"

"Mebbe bad man. No go inside."

A one-handed bad man? "Thank you, Mr. Lau," she said. "It is all right. I know who it is."

"Go fine Mistuh Rowlan."

"That won't be necessary, Mr. Lau. But thank you."

She hesitated at the gate until he disappeared into the fog. The foghorn mourned again. This time a weaker hoot responded—ships feeling their way in the Bay. She opened the gate, fumbled for her key, let herself into the entry. There was light in the parlor.

The actuality of Ramón sprawled on her settee caused her to gasp, even though she had prepared herself for it. His muddy boots were extended, his bearded face regarded her sourly, one cheek caught by a mole like a peg. Curly hair grew thick on either side of a high forehead. He wore a linen shirt with complicated frills on the chest, and a string tie. A gray coat hung over the back of the settee. The stump of his wrist lay in his left hand.

He watched her silently as she put down her purse and the packet of manuscript, then raised her hands to unpin her hat. She was astonished that she could be so calm. She moved to the stove, took chunks of coal from the scuttle with the tongs and dropped them into the firebox, where red flames pulsed. Then she seated herself opposite him, arranging her hands in her lap. She realized that she had unconsciously imitated his posture, with her two hands. It was not cold in the parlor, but she was shivering. The gas jet hissed.

"What do you want, Ray?"

He had a way of closing his eyelids, which then trembled as though his patience was all but exhausted. "I want you to come back, Señora."

She shook her head once. The movement made her head ache.

"The ranchos are in danger."

"I thought the Land Commission ruled that they are yours."

"The federal district attorney appeals each time. Now it must go to the Supreme Court."

"I'm sorry."

He glared at her as though her apology were inadequate. "There are squatters, there are rascal lawyers, there are corrupt men! They cheat the Californios everywhere! They will leave me nothing! They are cheats! They are villains! They are *bastards!*"

He muttered and ranted in Spanish that she understood imperfectly, scraping his fingers through his short beard with its stains of gray. His eyeballs were veined with angry pink. She sniffed the stink of whiskey.

"I have an *abogado,*" he went on. "Very American!" He made a motion of stroking a long beard, looking solemn and judicious. He had always possessed a talent for mimicry. She had thought him a romantic guitar player and singer, he had played and sung so soulfully. She had thought him glamorous. He was a ranchero, heir to a grand landowning family of Mexicans, although the Jiménez family was rich in nothing but grazing lands. He was the arrogant and restless son of an antiquated system that had spoiled him until he was too old to change.

An American commission had passed on the validity of the Spanish and Mexican land grants. The Californios insisted that its judgments were often unfair despite the assurances written into the Treaty of Guadalupe-Hidalgo, but the commission had ruled for Ramón's title to the ranches. It had never occurred to her that legal processes would still be trying to take the lands away. She had thought he would lose them by drink and gambling.

"My *abogado* assures me that my chances will be better if I have my Americana wife by my side, Señora." His good hand and his stump described his American wife, straight back and chin up.

"I will give you your divorce," she said. "You can marry another Americana."

"I cannot divorce, as you know, Señora."

She remembered him, already beginning to thicken at the waist, strutting like a bullfighter into the glittering interior of the little church that the Jiménez family supported, with its gigantic bleeding Christ on the cross and the dwarfish priest to whom Ramón made his confession each Sunday. Only to repeat his sins in the ensuing week. That smug hypocrisy had infuriated her, and yet the church with its pagan opulence had seemed so much more vivid than the Presbyterian meetinghouse of her mother and father.

"You must bribe the bishop," she said.

His closed eyelids quivered again as he shook his head. "You must return to me, Señora. You must give me a son as well. 'Miliano died leaving only daughters."

"I know you have illegitimate sons. You should legitimate one of them."

"You must return."

"I was deceived when I married you. I know men think women will never change, while women think that men will change. And both are wrong. You are not what I thought I had married, and I am not what you married. I will not be treated as Mexicanos treat their wives. I owe you nothing!"

He held up his stump with a sickly smile. "You owe me this!"

She shook her head again, jarring her headache.

"I know where you work. I have watched you come and go. I have seen you through the window. I have seen you with men there. The *California Monthly!* I will inform those men that you are my wife!"

She shrugged.

"I will place a notice in the newspaper. Perhaps the American law will require that the wife return to her husband."

"Do what you will," she said.

He gritted his teeth at her, with that hostile canine expression she remembered. So many things remembered, and so few of them memories she cared to review. The one grand ball celebrating the visit of the last Mexican governor and the parade the next day riding the beautiful bay horse she had thought was Ramón's gift to her but was not. If her righteousness was tainted by her little affair with poor David Reilly, it was a teaspoon of wrong against an ocean.

"Vows were made, Señora." He tried to say it gracefully, in that quaint formal style that once had charmed her. "Will you say these vows had no validity?"

"They had as much validity as your vows."

"You made vows to me, in the church, before the padre, before my family and my friends. You embraced the Faith also!"

Now she could feel the heat of her replenishing of the stove. Ramón recrossed his legs. He held the stump of his wrist aimed at her.

He sighed, fluttered his eyelids, and said, "If you are dead I will be free to marry another Americana. You give me no alternative. There are people one may employ for unpleasant tasks."

She thought of Beau Rowlands's suggestion. She thought she had never hated another human being, except this one that she had so carelessly married.

"How you cheat us, you Americanos," Ramón said, through his bared teeth. "You make vows that the land grants will be respected, and these vows are broken. You make marriage vows, and these are broken also. I thought my pretty Americana would keep the solemn vows she made in the church of the True Faith, but she is a liar like all Americanos. She offers her pretty little cunt to the skinny schoolteacher in her father's school who reads her poems and praises them. And then she runs away to fuck the editors of the magazines that have published her poems."

"The skinny schoolteacher treated me as a lady, not a servant woman," she said, hating what she heard herself saying. "He was not always drunk and hurtful, nor did he spend his time with the prostitutes at the *bodegas.*"

"Because you were insufficient to me!" he snarled.

"And you to me."

"When I was gone to Las Golindrinas you fucked this *cabrón!*"

"Let us set my infidelities against your own."

"It is a different thing! Whore!" He stopped himself, wiping his wrist across his lips. In a calmer voice, he said, "I will forgive you if you will return."

"Never!"

He straightened on the settee and began massaging the stump of his forearm. In a soft voice that suddenly frightened her, he said, "I am a desperate man, Señora. They will take away three quarters of the Jiménez lands. If I have no son, who will carry on my name when I die? Do you understand me, Señora?"

"I'm sorry," she said.

He made clumsy motions, trying to rise, and she saw that he was very drunk. She hurried into the bedroom. The shiny little revolver Henry Park had given her for her protection was in the bedside stand, and she opened the drawer and plucked it out, suddenly frightened and awkward. When she came out of the bedroom Ramón was on his feet, swaying. He was shorter, broader, thicker than she had remembered. The gas light gleamed on his high forehead. When he saw the revolver he drew himself up.

"Ah!" he said, as though a new issue had been raised.

"You will go now, Ray."

"Yes, I see," he said, nodding. "But we will talk again, Señora. In other circumstances."

She felt both silly and unwomanly, holding the cold, heavy little chunk of steel. He took his cap from the settee and plucked his coat from the back. He turned toward the door.

Then he spun around, swinging the heavy coat. She staggered under the impact, and he was on her, wresting the revolver away. He was breathing hard as he slipped the revolver into his pocket. Then he hit her full in the face.

This time she did fall, sprawling on the floor with her face on fire. She was dizzy and nauseated when she struggled to her feet, hanging on to the back of her chair.

Smiling at her, Ramón jabbed the stump of his right arm into her breast. She cried out and locked her crossed arms over her aching bosom.

"Sit down, Señora. Now we will talk of these matters in different terms."

She sat. She could taste blood, and she patted the corner of her mouth with the side of her fist. Ramón stood over her. He stroked her hair. "Now I will tell you what you are going to do," he said.

He told her what she was going to do. When she shook her head, he slapped her so hard her head slammed against the back of her chair. Then he stroked her hair again. "Such pretty hair," he said.

Behind him she saw Beau Rowlands in the anteroom doorway, hands on hips, his soft hat tilted on his forehead. She was afraid he was a delusion.

Beau stepped on into the room. Ramón jerked around.

"Did you strike this lady?" Beau said. "Her mouth is bleeding." She had never seen anything so beautiful as Beau Rowlands in his tweed suit and fine soft hat. He removed the hat and tossed it onto the table with the manuscript she had brought home, and Byron's *Poetical Works*.

Ramón took the revolver from his pocket. "Is this your lover, Señora?" he asked, sounding suddenly very Mexican. "You will sit down," he said to Beau.

Beau frowned at the revolver.

"It is not loaded," she said.

Ramón flipped the cylinder out on its mechanism, spun it, cursed, and flung it down. Beau stepped forward and caught the throat of Ramón's flounced shirt in his fist. He jerked Ramón's face toward his own. "Shall I kill him, Mary?"

"No!"

Beau raised his left hand and slapped Ramón. Ramón cursed him. Beau slapped him harder.

She watched Ramón's face darken with blood. Beau's expression was almost friendly.

"Now, I want you to promise you won't bother this lady anymore."

Ramón cursed. Beau slapped him.

"This lady is much too good for a Mexican," Beau said.

"I am Castiliano," Ramón said in a thick voice. "It is a superior race to your mongrel race. It is a race that keeps its vows."

"No, you are just a stupid greaser," Beau said. "Now, promise me you won't bother this lady again."

"She will never be shed of me!"

Beau slapped him. Gripping the shirt front, he pulled Ramón to his knees. "Now, say, 'I will never bother this lady again.'"

When Ramón did not respond, his face so dark she thought he might be having some kind of attack, Beau slapped him so hard his head jerked.

"Beau!" she whispered.

"Say it!"

Ramón muttered something. Beau pulled him to his feet and released the grip on his shirt. "Now vamoose!"

Ramón took his hat and coat from the settee and started out, head down. He didn't look back. She heard the door slam behind him. Tears burned in her eyes.

Beau leaned over her to daub at the blood on her mouth with his handkerchief.

"I wish you had not humiliated him so."

"I know how to deal with Mexicans, Mary." He brushed gently at her lips.

"I was so glad to see you," she said.

"Mr. Lau came for me." He pulled her to her feet and seated both of them on the settee where Ramón had lounged. Beau enfolded her in his strong arms. He kissed her bruised face.

Then he was tugging at her blouse. When he had freed it from her belt, he reached beneath her undergarments to cover her breasts with his hands. Expertly he disposed of the layers of cloth and kissed her body greedily.

He nuzzled her breasts until she was almost fainting. Then he swept her up in his arms and carried her into the dimness of her bedroom, where he undressed her. The process seemed to require no assistance on her part. She lay naked and shivering on her bed in the gray light coming through the foggy window.

"My God, you are lovely!" Beau whispered. She closed her eyes as he began removing his own clothing. Then he was on her, his hot mouth sealed to hers. She was surprised that her legs seemed to open to him not against her will but not with it either.

Always before it had been a furtive business, half dressed and in darkness—in her marriage with Ramón somewhere between a rape and an operation, but blessedly over quickly; with David, like caring for an invalid but at least with some gentleness to it; with two others since, only a hurried interlude after dinner and wine in a private room in a French restaurant.

Beau did not seem in a hurry, as though the conclusion was not the whole point of the business. All the while he praised her charms, in intimate terms that would have set her blushing if she had not been past blushing, or was not in fact in a total state of blush. He attended to every bit of her body and limbs, to her fingers and toes, her armpits and breasts and belly and the trembling flesh of her thighs, as though every bit of her must be brought along concurrently to higher and higher levels of pleasure. She was only shocked that she was not more shocked at herself. It seemed he must probe every soft concavity of her body, so that she was continually, weakly whispering, "No, no, no—" while she thought, "Oh, yes! There, too!"

A solemn, furtive, quickly concluded business it had always been, but Beau's solemnities were interspersed with jollities. After their bouts in the bedroom he wanted to return to the bright light of the parlor. There he paraded naked with her dishpan on his head, which he called the Helmet of Mambrino.

He insisted on her cooking scrambled eggs for him, "To restore my vigors," as he put it. In her own naked state she managed to move before him without shielding her breasts from his gaze with her arms or elbows. She was horrified to find herself giggling and offering her breast for a passing suckle. She sat on his lap in a chair drawn close to the stove while she pushed at the eggs with a spatula.

She saw that it was important that the cooking of the eggs require a certain span of time before a continuation, for the anticipation was as delicious as the fulfillment. When she stood to attend more closely to the eggs in the pan he stood behind her, clasping his thighs to her buttocks, hungry dog to wanton bitch.

After they had gobbled their eggs with hot bread and butter, grease shining on his lips as it must gleam also on her own, she sprawled on the settee, while he, kneeling before her, poured brandy into the cup of her navel and lapped it out.

"My God, you are a beautiful piece!" he said, rearing back with his smeared face. He kissed her with his brandy mouth and licked her bruised lips.

Then he seated himself across from her, frowning, and asked what her husband had wanted of her. Just to strike her?

"He wanted me to come back to him." She told him the reasons.

"He's a *hacendado?*"

"He has a hacienda, though you would call it just a ranch house. The place is very run-down, I can only imagine even more so than when I saw it last. There are thousands of acres of land. He is involved in an interminable legal process to assure his title."

"Was he as good a lover as I am?"

"Making love was just a chore I thought married women had to endure." She thought of asking how she compared with the old-gold girls of Mexico.

"It was my plan to seduce you more gradually," he said.

No doubt he would have succeeded, but how could it have been so fine? She loved the smell of him, sweat and grease and juices. She watched him through half-closed eyes as he rose to prance over to the stove and load in two chunks of anthracite.

He wanted to know what she paid for coal. It was as though she could not detach her mind from the considerations of the flesh to recall the price. She made a guess.

"Would you be pleased if you could buy coal for half that price?"

"I suppose so. Of course!"

"Cheaper coal. A public benefit. Grateful coal buyers. Public benefactors of suppliers!"

"I don't know what you're talking about."

"It's something Charley Daggett and I are involved in. A fortune can be made bringing cheap coal to the West Coast! Now it must be shipped from Australia or British Columbia at great expense."

"Where would you bring it from?"

"That is a secret still, my beauty." He set the top back on the stove with a flourish.

He brought her a glass of red wine and knelt beside her while she sipped it. She made eyes at him over the rim of the glass.

"Do you love me?" he asked.

"Poetic lines rush through my head," she told him. "In them are words that I cannot put on paper. May I refer to you as 'Cupid'? And I will be your longing nymph."

"You may refer to me as anything you like. I will *be* anything you like."

She was not even sure what she wanted him to be. She did not think, now, that she wanted these pleasures every night. Surely, the anticipation, on the nights between, would make their nights together that much sweeter! Loving him with her body to her mind's distraction, she nevertheless engaged in a small, cool bit of reflection. Gazing down upon her wanton sprawl on the settee, she quickly rearranged her limbs. He was a seducer, now of the Poetess of Russian Hill, exploited to her great pleasure. He was a developer of mines. He would develop her as the object of his pleasure. He would mine her of her silver and gold. He would have what he wanted of her, whatever sweetness and professed love that he desired, but she would have only a portion of what she would want of him. Was the whole equation of male and female there? The completer and the completed. He had probed the incandescent center of her, but still that untouched fragment of her mind watched out for her welfare. Its warnings were like the soft hoots of the foghorns that warned the mariners in the Bay. He was impatient to be rich. It was an obsession, sometimes concealed, sometimes laughed at, but an obsession all the same.

Since the war, Americans were fascinated by becoming rich. It was as though there were insufficient oxygen in the atmosphere except in the chambers of moneymaking, and Beau's oxygen depletion was the most severe that she had seen. He had been considered the brightest and best, the most vital and energetic, of his class at Yale. The most successful career of his generation had been prophesied for him. She knew he had considered his Mexican bonanza as his shortcut to the princely riches that were his due. He had contributed some writings of experiences in the Rockies to the magazine, he had been a colleague, a favorite of Henry Park's until the antagonisms of the *Hutchinson* trial and the anti-debris bill.

It worried her that at such a time as this she must consider his shortcomings.

"I think in two more days they should be at the Little Colorado," Beau said, coming to sit beside her on the settee. His hip pressed electrically to hers.

"What? What?" she said sleepily, for she had almost dozed. But she knew. Esther. And she was suddenly wide awake.

"They'll go after the captive woman there. Then maybe two more days to Bright Angel Canyon, and two days out. Someone will have to bring her out. Charley Daggett's man has a crew of Mormons waiting on the plateau."

"What if they can't find her?"

"I believe it is damned sure they will bring her out. We'll tell her story in the *Monthly*."

How was it that *we* would tell Esther's story in the magazine?

It was as though he felt her question through their touching hips. "Charley left me with some authority," he said. What did that mean?

"There will also be Asa Haden's journal," he said.

She detached herself to go into the bedroom for her robe. Out the window the fog was more impenetrable now that night had fallen. She stood before it shivering, her arms clasped around her nakedness. Cool thought oppressed her. She loved Beau Rowland at the same time as she resented that power he held over her.

She had taken a lover who would never be satisfied with this one encounter. She realized the dangers of the situation, her treaties with a number of men endangered. And she could not ignore Ramón, even though he had been sent away in humiliation. Ramón, who was desperate, who must have her back so as to make a better claim to the Jiménez land grants, who wanted an heir for a noble old family that had no male heir, who had said she left him no alternative.

When she returned to the parlor, Beau was standing close to the stove, warming his backside. He had donned the Helmet of Mambrino again, which made him look like a muscular Hermes without the winged feet.

He was holding open Lord Byron's *Poetical Works*. "How is the campaign progressing to restore Byron's resting place?"

She had a vision of the ruined church at Hucknall Torkard, the hostile vicar, the wreath she and Octavius had made of Marin laurel to decorate it. She pictured herself presenting the American funds to Patrick Derwent, to restore the church as it should be restored. She longed to be there among Britons who knew her poetry, where there was no threat from her past, nor her present either.

"I have heard from Mr. Whittier and Mr. Holmes in just the last few days. Mr. Emerson has been very generous."

Others had not been: Herman Melville and Walt Whitman. She recognized from Melville's sarcastic letter that he had no funds to spare. It had been flattering that all the literary people to whom she had written had responded at least, and all of them seemed to know of her and her work.

"How much has come in?"

"Almost three thousand dollars. Almost half of it from Mr. Emerson."

"What about Octy?" he wanted to know.

"He has promised a hundred dollars. Henry has promised two hundred."

"Put me down for two hundred also," Beau said. He took the dishpan from his tousled head and grinned at her.

"Once more into the breach, dear friend."

She was tired, sleepy, and sore, and the coolness now had seeped throughout her mind. She hated it that always in her life it was a man who summoned her, who turned her away, who called the tune, who selected the paths for her to tread.

But she opened her arms and her robe to receive her lover.

❖ ❖ ❖

Mary Temple sat with Waldo Carrington at the big table. The week of heavy fogs had ended, and there was brilliant sunshine glistening on the buildings across the street. The metallic shrill and rumble of passing wheels resounded in the offices.

Waldo was very much his sartorial self this morning, gray jacket, paler gray waistcoat, florid cravat, and rosebud in his lapel. The scent of cologne wafted to her across the table. He tented his hands together.

"It seems there is a document, my dear."

"Of what nature, Waldo?"

"Executed by our employer the day before his departure. Bowman Rowlands is named temporary publisher in Mr. Daggett's absence."

"I see," she said, nodding.

Waldo continued: "*Further,* it seems, I am to be temporary editor. You are assistant editor."

She managed to keep her face perfectly blank.

"That is not the manner in which the affairs of this magazine will dispose themselves, I can assure you," Waldo said.

Sickness seemed to be seeping through her veins. Beau had said Daggett had left him with some authority.

"It is Beau who has produced the document." Waldo adjusted his lapel rosebud nervously. "And has sworn me to secrecy. But you know I cannot keep a secret. The *document* does not stipulate that I am editor, and you my assistant."

For a moment she did not understand. Then she confronted a casual betrayal so deep that it continued to open yard by yard toward the center of the earth. Of course Beau would say it was because Waldo was less committed to the anti-debris cause than she was, when in truth it was because he would not consider a woman as an editor.

"The problem is this," Waldo continued. "Our deadline for next month's issue is, as you know, next week. That date can of course be stretched a bit and still allow us to meet our publication date. It was anticipated that the expedition would be heard from by now. Best of all, the captive woman, perhaps your sister, would be returned to civilization. Second best, the journals of young Haden would be brought out for editing and publication. But nothing has been heard from Arizona Territory, where the captive woman or a courier should have ascended from the depths by now."

She was surprised that she could even speak. "I have material we can use. Henry left me a sheaf of poems. There is other work as well."

Waldo shook his head. "Beau has brought me a piece of his own."

"Is it an attack on our anti-debris stand?" she asked. She felt weak, as though immersed in warm milk.

"Not exactly." Waldo pushed a handwritten manuscript across the table to her. She recognized Beau's handwriting with its dark, arrogant slants. She did not want to read it.

"Tell me what it is, please."

"It is a defense of the destructions of nature insofar as they are of benefit to mankind," he said primly. His swollen eyeballs goggled at her. "I will resign rather than print it, but then the matter would descend on your shoulders. I do not wish to embarrass you."

The abysses continued to open. It seemed Waldo had surmised her attachment to Beau Rowlands.

"'Man is the Maker's chosen genus, and He is man's benefactor in all things great or small.' The fellow has the gall to invoke the Maker! All the continents and their contents are provided for man's pleasure and profit, the minerals of the mountains, the waters of the great rivers, the forests, the fertile plains, the beasts and fishes. All provided for man's continual bettering of his condition.

"It is more in sorrow than in anger that Beau takes to task those who would penalize the working man by invoking silly restrictions on man's progress, which nature herself would find laughable. He does mention our friend McMurdo in an unfortunate light. It is true that certain of Jamey's caveats lay him open to charges of pomposity. Beau has the restraint not to call for our sympathy for the poor devils of mine owners awash in lawsuits, or for the railroad magnates, although he reminds us of the healthy employment they so self-sacrificingly furnish. Not in despoilment, mind you, but in enhancement! For the greater good of mankind. So that the honest working man may bring home bread and meat to his wife and milk to her precious brood. All the organ tones are sounded, I promise you!"

She was reminded of Beau speaking of the suppliers of cheaper coal to California as benefactors, which must have to do with

Daggett's true purpose in mounting his expedition. "Let us print it," she said.

Waldo goggled at her.

"We will also print a rebuttal by Jamey."

"Beau would not allow that!"

"He will only need know that we have consented to print his piece."

"What a talent for connivance you have, my dear! When it is in print with Jamey's devastating response, no doubt I will be dismissed. But we will have fallen upon our swords with honor." He held up a manicured finger, frowning. "But we possess only Jamey's article on the water ouzel."

"Jamey must be shown this and asked to reply to it immediately."

"Unfortunately there is that self-righteousness that so often infects Jamey's work, especially when pressed for time."

"I will edit it carefully."

"And Beau's?"

She regarded him with her lips tightened until they ached. She felt like some Germanic warrior woman, armed and armored, helmeted and greaved, avenging wrongs against women. "I think not," she said.

Waldo smiled broadly. "There is still the possibility that Daggett and Company will be heard from in time."

"We will not count on it."

She left the *California Monthly* offices with Beau's article stuffed into her purse, hurrying, head down, praying she would encounter no acquaintance. What had she expected, after all? She knew Beau Rowlands to be a user of his friends and, by extrapolation, his lovers as well. He had always announced his ambitions for money and power honestly enough. He had his mine in Sonora, his coalfields she didn't know where. They must be developed and made profitable so that he could become rich. He was a prettified Daggett but still a Daggett, Jamey had warned her. Had she expected him to change his spots merely because their lovemaking had been the most momentous experience of her life? She, the romantic, had let her thoughts drift irresponsibly to eternal happiness, to a golden future for Cupid and his longing nymph. She reminded herself that she had vowed never again to be any man's chattel.

She did not now accuse him of deceiving her, only of a failure to understand that others than himself might be serious about their professions. She was a better and more responsible editor than Waldo Carrington, ignored as such because she was female. The magazine's stand against the Little Giants had been taken in high seriousness, which Beau was ready to override or corrupt for his own advantage.

On the horsecar ride home she read his manuscript. She could admire the force of his arguments, but what they represented was very bad indeed, hypocritical, dishonest, false, and of evil intent. Jamey would rip them to shreds. She was so fascinated by the cleverness, and the obviousness, of his words, that she missed her stop and had to walk back from Vallejo Street.

A weedy boy in ragged overalls and a cloth cap was waiting at her gate. "Mrs. Jiménez?"

She took the thick envelope he proffered and tipped him a dime. The envelope was addressed to: Sra. Ramón Jiménez, at her address.

She took it inside and burned it in the stove.

In the Gorge 1

ASA HADEN

"*We are now ready to start on our way into the Great Unknown,*" Major Powell had written. "*We are three quarters of a mile in the depths of the earth, and the great river shrinks into insignificance as it dashes its angry waves against the walls and cliffs that rise to the world above; the waves are but puny ripples, and we but pygmies, running up and down the sands or lost among the boulders.*

"*We have an unknown distance yet to run, an unknown river to explore. What falls there are, we know not; what rocks beset the channel, we know not; what walls rise over the river, we know not.*"

Asa computed one hundred and eighty miles to Separation Canyon, where he was still determined to leave the expedition, or the survey, as it had now been revealed to be, even though Buchanan's bombshell had demolished the purpose to which Daggett had assigned him.

He wrote it in his personal journal, like a contract with himself: "I am determined to visit a fierce and primitive tribe of Indians on the plateau above Separation Canyon. Mr. Daggett's orders were that I try to discover why the Howland Brothers and William Dunn deserted the Expedition, and that I find evidence to prove them innocent of the crime of molestation, of which Major Powell, to my knowledge, never accused them. I am fearful of the task, even though I will be accompanied by the competent Hyrum Logan. The Shivwits are bloodthirsty savages. They slaughtered the three who had left Major Powell's Exploration, and, in the Iron County Massacre, they seem to have been employed by the Mormons to help murder that hapless band of Missouri emigrants.

"It will be my obligation to find old Pokray, and ask questions that must be asked, and, it may be, to locate Major Powell's missing journals."

At first, in the Grand Canyon, the River was sunny and placid, the cliffs of the Great Unknown little different from those of Marble Canyon. After the shock of Daggett's death, and the further shock of Buchanan's revelation, the rescue of Esther Bingham had raised all their spirits.

The search for Daggett's body, and his money belt, continued. Asa had written his resentment of Daggett's trickery into his journal. It seemed to him that Daggett had enjoyed tricking him personally. He had been taken in by Daggett's enmity toward Major Powell, believing that it had to do with the dispositions of western lands, public lands versus private, a matter on which he had no particular position. But it had been a magician's trick of pointing in one direction while the flock of pigeons was produced from another. Still, with Daggett dead, he could write what he wanted, and he would certainly speak his mind.

Even the project to rescue the White Captive had been part of the game, and it was as though she too had confounded her rescuers, for it was clearly impossible for her to walk out of the Canyon at Bright Angel in her pregnant state.

Esther dragged her bulk silently around the camp or hunched in upon herself in the boat. Sometimes Poche or Miranda sat by her, but she seemed not to wish to talk. Maybe it was her condition.

Asa gazed up at the imprisoning cliffs, his head reverberating with the rush of the River, envisioning tracks laid on the bench a hundred feet above the water, a locomotive chuffing smoke into the clear air, passengers exclaiming out the windows, ladies, gentlemen, and children craning their necks at the heights, and, following the passenger cars, the freight cars of black anthracite coal from the Colorado field, bound for California.

"Sometimes it seems a shame what the country must suffer for the sake of the nation," Will Jefford commented to him. And Tiny said, "It is a damned shame what the country must suffer so a dead plutocrat can make himself another fortune."

Two days beyond the Colorado Chiquito they came into a series of cataracts, a mile of rock-studded white water. Although *Miss Saucy* danced through, the freight boats had to be unloaded and portaged past the eight-foot waves, the spouts and holes and fountains. A hard day's work.

Buchanan had rearranged the manning of the boats: he and Ritter still in *Miss Saucy,* with Tiny bailing in the bow; aboard the *Letty Daggett,* Hyrum, Morphy, and Esther Bingham; on the *Canyon Lass,* Asa, Jefford, Poche, and Miranda.

Ashore, when Miranda was not helping the photographer, she was with the other young woman, the sullen, neat-bodied girl tending the dazed, hugely swollen one. Poche danced attendance but was often ignored by the two young women, who, it seemed, did not value him.

"The *California Monthly* must have my copy for the September issue by the twentieth," Asa said to Buchanan.

Buchanan shook his head. "Too long through Marble Canyon. Too long at Colorado Chiquito waiting on Esther. There's a gang up top at Bright Angel waiting. But she can't walk up there. We'd have to carry her out."

The plan had been for Miranda and Poche to accompany her up Bright Angel Canyon to the plateau above.

"We could wait at Bright Angel for her—birthing."

Buchanan grimaced. "Watching a pot come to a boil."

"We ought to be at Bright Angel tomorrow."

"Keerect."

Asa sat with Morphy under a lacy willow branch that cut the noon sun into a filigree of light and shade. Morphy watched the two women making their way up the scree, Miranda guiding Esther's arm.

"Lookit that pretty little ass!" Morphy said. "She knows swinging that sweet butt in those trousers drives a man crazy."

There was no point arguing that Miranda's hips swung because she was climbing through treacherous footing in her child's boots and that she was not trying to drive anyone crazy. He had come to realize that Morphy knew how to express his admiration only in obscene terms.

The other sat with his shoulders hunched in his faded blue shirt, boots splayed out to either side. He poured sand from a handful into a little pile between his big feet.

"There was a woman in Austin like that," he went on. "She had a trick, she'd kind of drift her tongue around her lips. Drive you crazy."

Asa wondered aloud when Esther's child was coming.

"Always come at the worst time," Morphy said. "You can bet on that."

Morphy scooped up more sand. "I remember talk about how grateful she'd be to be brought out." He laughed a whoop, as though making fun of himself. "Turns out she's big as a team and wagon with some redskin's get, and didn't want to be saved nohow."

"I can understand how she'd be afraid of coming back to the States, with the tattooing and the child. How people will treat her."

"Ought to get her and Hyrum in tune some night, her moaning and him yelling like that." Morphy glared at Buchanan, who had seated himself on a whitened log fifty feet away. "Pigfucking son of a bitch!" he muttered.

Asa protested, but Morphy only grimaced and flung away his handful of sand.

Asa drew a deep breath and said, "Maybe the leader of an expedition always seems a tyrant to his men. I guess Major Powell had disputes with his crew. Those men who deserted."

"The Canyon got to be a holy terror to them, the way I heard it. Couldn't run one more chute. The older brother mostly."

"I suppose when men have been cooped up on boats for three months there are bound to be differences."

"Like me and the pigfucker," Morphy said, squinting at the two women in their slow progress.

❖ ❖ ❖

That afternoon they entered the first granite, whose savage cataracts had become so discouraging to the Major's men. Black cliffs fifty feet high sprang vertically from the River. Behind these, canyon walls stepped back and up what must be a thousand feet. Far behind rose heights striped with dark brown strata and crenellated towers stained with black. The next rapid the Major had named Sockdolager, a long chute of leaping waves with a fall Asa estimated as twenty feet.

They passed through these first rapids of the Upper Granite Gorge with more than their usual caution, portaging or lightening the boats and lining them, often lifting the unladen boats over the rocks at the head of a steep fall and running the less turbulent end waves, bellowing to each other over the racket of rushing waters. Each day there was a limit to the amount of lifting and carrying, of battling currents and waves, that could be accomplished before they put in for the night.

The *Lass* had been the "lucky" boat so far, but inevitably she bore down too fast on a rock observed too late. Too late Asa swung his weight against the sweep, and the *Lass* swept over the rock to plunge broadside into the hole below it. Water poured hugely over the gunwale. Asa had a glimpse of Miranda standing grasping the safety line and Poche toppling over the high side. Then he was in the chill water, thrashing gasping to the surface. Miranda's drenched head popped up ahead of him. Someone yelled his name, and a rope slapped across his shoulder. He grasped it with one hand and, kicking mightily, managed to lunge toward Miranda.

He grasped her around the waist to hold her head out of the water, pulling her against him. Her hand clutched his shoulder, her body plastered to his, her legs moving against his—it was strangely as though they were dancing. Her dark eyes in her pursed dripping face gazed straight back into his. *A prostitute in his arms!* He held her with one arm, the rope with the other, as they were pulled toward *Miss Saucy*. Buchanan lifted Miranda aboard, sleek as a seal in her drenched overall. Then Asa was pulled up. As *Miss Saucy* pitched downstream to where the current held the *Lass* against a boulder, Miranda whispered, "Thank you!"

The *Lass* had been hauled out of the water, and Morphy and Poche worked on the cracked rib she had sustained. Esther Bingham, in her bedraggled dress and bonnet, made her stately way up the dry wash away from the camp. In her absence Miranda stood on a log beckoning everyone to her.

When they had gathered she said urgently, "She is in despair. She left behind her husband and her son. She is afraid of returning to her family in California. She is afraid the Hoya villages are at war because she was kidnapped."

Ritter said angrily, "She is better off than she was!"

"She is terrified that her husband will come after her and kill her!"

"You must tell her she is not to be afraid," Buchanan said, pipe in mouth.

"I have done so!"

"What must we do?" Tiny asked.

"We must help her. Is someone's birthday near?"

There was no response. Miranda glanced around. Her eyes caught Asa's.

"Mine is next week," he heard himself say. He had never seen Miranda so animated, and he understood it was in a female cause.

"Can you bake a cake, Hyrum?"

"Won't be much of a cake," Hyrum grumbled.

Miranda glanced toward the ravine where Esther had disappeared. In a lowered voice she said, "She told me that if she had known she was to be carried off she would have hidden herself again."

"Jaysus, don't she understand she is better off with white people?" Morphy said.

"I believe she loves her husband, savage though he may be," Miranda said, without looking toward the boatman.

"Even though she fears he will come after her to kill her?" Asa asked.

Her black eyes flicked at him. Her small, sun-browned face was contemptuous. "Have you had no experience with women's hearts?" she said.

She jumped down from her log just as Esther reappeared, toiling down the rocky wash toward them.

Buchanan poured portions of whiskey as Miranda led Esther to join them at the campfire. Esther picked her way over the stony ground in her careful way, as though her long skirt complicated her pregnant awkwardness. She wore her hair tucked into a braid at the back of her head, which would be Miranda's doing, who must have been in a similar condition only a few months ago. Asa found it impossible to picture that slim figure as swollen as Esther's. Poche watched the two of them sourly.

"Here's to our chief boatman!" Buchanan called out with his cup raised. "How many years, Asa?"

"Twenty-two." It angered him that he must blush even stating the bare figure. He wished he had not volunteered so speedily to Miranda's request.

Jefford rose, his sardonic face slanting right and left to look around at the crew. "May I say that I have had much occasion to revise my opinion of Mister Asa Haden. I considered him a greenhorn schoolboy at Pariah Crossing. Now I know him as a professional of acumen and education. Our lives are certainly in his hands, as Miss Straw's was today. I celebrate them as very good hands!"

"Hear, hear!"

Asa's face felt on fire from the cheering, the affectionate grins. Esther was looking at him with interest, Miranda with an almost smile, as though her upper lip had got stuck to her teeth.

Why did he have to feel that their affection for him was colored by condescension: because he was young, because he was a greenhorn, because he was an easterner and a pretender to rationality and nonviolence in a place where only force and violence were valued? He had not saved Miranda's life a second time; she had been perfectly capable of seizing the flung rope herself!

"If I have become a competent river man, it is because Pat Morphy has showed me how," he said, rising. "And because Jake Buchanan was patient with a greenhorn schoolboy."

He halted for some laughter.

"And if I have become a good chief boatman, it is because all of you have become good boatmen. Good oarsmen, good bailers."

"Good liners and portagers!" Tiny called out, who was not much help at either.

"I thank you all," he said and sat down. Now Miranda was gesturing to Hyrum.

The cook began to sing, in his heavy voice: "A mighty fortress is our God / A bulwark never failing— "

They joined him in the hymn they had sung many nights around the campfire, but Esther did not participate, keeping her head turned down, hands clasped together in her lap. They sang "Praise God from Whom All Blessings Flow," "Abide with Me," "Nearer My God to Thee," and "Rock of Ages."

Jefford led them in more secular offerings: "Tenting Tonight" and "Keep the Home Fires Burning," Ritter accompanying on the mouth organ. Dusk had fallen, and the firelight brightened their faces. And Esther began to sing at last. Asa could see tears gleaming on her cheeks and mingling with the intricate shadows of her chin.

She whispered, "Could we sing 'Hark the Herald Angels'? It was my father's favorite."

They sang that, and "Shall We Gather at the River," and "Sweet Betsy from Pike," and some rounds. Esther wiped her streaming cheeks with a bandanna. Something had been won, and it was owed to Miranda, who had put off her own hostile shell for the occasion.

When there were no more songs to sing, a pale moon showed over the edge of the western cliff. Miranda rose, her cloud of dark curls framing her face, all eyes on her. Asa clenched his fists in anticipation.

"This is a scene from *King Lear* that my father and I often performed together." She struck a pose, standing erect and high-headed. The change in her usually abrasive voice was amazing to him:

Oh my dear father! Restoration hang
Thy medicine upon my lips; and let this kiss
Repair the violent harms that my two sisters
Have in thy reverence made!

With swift grace she changed position, one foot braced on a rock, leaning forward, intent. The pause was long; Asa willed the vibrant voice to continue:

Had you not been my father, these white flakes
Did challenge pity of them. Was this a face
To be opposed against the warring winds?

He saw that these lines affected Esther even more. As Miranda continued, her voice grew stronger. He thought of her father dying of whiskey in a desolate mining town, abandoning his daughter to destitution and evil men; of his own father, fearful of his death in his big bed by the second-story window in Newfield; and he remembered this scene from a production of the play he had seen at the university, the old mad, broken king and his courageous daughter who was soon to die. Tears burned on his cheeks as Miranda re-created it. When she had finished, breathing hard, she resumed her guise as the unfriendly young woman who had been rescued from a mob. Esther's face was hidden by her bandanna.

Jefford recited: "Shall I compare thee to a summer's day," and Morphy his verse from "The Lady of the Lake," which he had learned from Major Powell. Hyrum started up "Old Hundredth" again, and Esther sang along.

Jefford called to Miranda for another monologue: "There is a willow grows aslant the brook!"

She shook her head in rejection and, remaining seated this time, with her arms stretched upward, began:

Make me a willow cabin at your gate,
And call upon my soul within the house;
Write loyal cantons of contemned love
And sing them loud even in the dead of night;
Halloo your name to the reverberate hills
And make the babbling gossip of the air
Cry out 'Olivia!' O, you should not rest
Between the elements of air and earth
But you should pity me!

When she had finished, Asa scanned the faces fixed upon this magical young woman that Miranda had become, all marked with admiration, even the cranky surveyor's.

That night when he went to the River's edge to urinate, Asa encountered a big figure standing motionless in the starry darkness—Morphy on the same errand.

"How that little lady can get your balls churning!" Morphy said in a muffled voice. "Jaysus, she gives me such a boner—!"

Asa stood beside the big man, intent on his business. "She is very pretty when she speaks the lines."

"I'll tell you!" Morphy said. "I want that little lady so bad—"

Asa grimaced into the darkness.

"So bad, so bad!" Morphy whispered.

He realized that Morphy was weeping in his frustration. He had never seen human intensity so revealed in his life before.

"She won't even look my way anymore, like I am a fucken hog or something," Morphy whispered.

Asa stammered, "I am sure she is unforgiving of our sex because of the terrible things that have happened to her. We cannot expect—"

"*Shit!*" Morphy said.

Major Powell had called this stretch the steepest fall of the Canyon. Ritter estimated it as one hundred and sixty feet in ten miles. Past it was a series of minor rapids requiring only clever steering, and by evening they were at Bright Angel Creek. Here the Canyon wore a gentler aspect, with the slopes flattening out and stepping back. Asa felt as though confining doors had been flung open. The creek bottom was crowded with the sunny green of willow thickets. Bright Angel Creek led into the canyon that gave access to the plateau above.

The boats grounded on the silt bank near a rock fall on the right end of the beach. The crews leaped out, bows were secured to a bent-over willow stub. The practiced unloading began.

Asa thought a rock had fallen from the cliff above him, cracking off a boulder behind him and ricocheting with a high whine.

"*It is shooting!*" Poche yelled.

A second bullet whacked into rock. Asa ducked, squinting upward. Buchanan was on his feet, grabbing Miranda's arm and thrusting her behind an outcrop. Jefford ran to Esther Bingham, who had risen, her hands clasped to her belly.

Suddenly everyone was out of sight. Asa crouched beside a boulder, grimacing at the three boats moored to the stump. When he glanced upward he was blinded by the sun pouring into the Canyon. Buchanan sprinted toward the boats, disappearing behind *Miss Saucy*. He reappeared carrying two rifles, running low to the ground like a tomcat harried by blackbirds. Asa squinted into the dazzle of sun. He didn't even know in which direction to look. *Hoya!*

Buchanan scrambled to a kneeling position beside him, handing him one of the rifles. He brought a handful of cartridges out of his pocket.

"Is it hostiles?" Asa whispered.

"I'm going up there and find out," Buchanan panted. "Get everybody behind that big boulder where Hyrum is."

Leaning around the rock with a hand braced on the rifle, Asa watched Buchanan cat-sprint up into the willows.

Asa let long moments pass before he ventured out from his cover, to call to the crew and the women that they were to take refuge behind Hyrum's big rock. The rifle seemed to give him authority. The cartridges in his pocket rubbed uncomfortably against his thigh.

He could still see nothing on the cliffs, but Buchanan must have located the sniper on the right side of the wash, for that was the side from which Hyrum's boulder protected them.

He squatted next to Miranda. She smelled of Tiny's developing chemicals. "Maybe it is Ez Clanton," she said. Her black eyes fixed on his.

"Who is that?"

Her lips moved to form a word, which she did not enunciate. He remembered the barkeep in Eureka speaking of the murdered pimp's brother.

"Esther thinks it is her husband," she said.

"How would he get across the river?"

She shrugged. Beyond her Hyrum peered upward, his gray face frosted with beard.

When dusk fell they began moving cautiously out from the cover of the boulder, gazing at the shadowy heights above. There was no sign of either Buchanan or the sniper, and there had been no other shot. Hyrum built a small fire.

It was almost dark when Buchanan reappeared. They crowded around him.

"Who was it, Jake? Injun?"

"Some crazy duck. I didn't find hide nor hair."

"Hoya couldn't get across the river, could they?"

"Dunno," Buchanan said. He stood facing them with his rifle held carelessly in one hand. Esther Bingham sat alone, her face turned down.

"What will we do, Jake?" Jefford asked.

"We'll load up and be gone before first light. Case he's still got a itchy finger."

"What if he comes after us?" Ritter said.

Buchanan shrugged.

"There isn't any way we could get Esther up Bright Angel," Jefford said.

"Not with some crazy shooter up there, anyhow," Buchanan said.

Shivering as they drifted downriver in the predawn dark, away from Bright Angel, Asa felt as though they had detached themselves from any connections with the world that they had known.

In the Gorge 2

ASA HADEN

Miles downriver from Bright Angel, Asa stood on a ledge with Will Jefford, gazing upward. The walls soared above them, black and shiny as anthracite coal and engraved in fantastic shapes. He squinted at the rim, searching for the sniper. Ahead, the brown flood roared through a boulder dam.

"These older formations are metamorphic," Jefford said. "Very old, very hard."

"They look like enormous tablets of some Mesopotamian script."

"Shaped by silt-laden waters."

"That high up?"

Jefford nodded.

"There is Jake's alignment, right along the top of the black stuff."

"Nature cooperating in her own destruction," Jefford said, studying the face of the cliff. "Do you think we will encounter our sharpshooter again?"

"I keep looking for him."

"It will depend," Jefford said with his wolfish grin, "whether it is someone we happened upon, or someone who is looking for us."

"I just don't believe that Esther's husband could have got across the River and caught up with us."

Jefford strolled on. Asa gathered that this was one of his periodic geology lessons.

"The rocks weather in different ways, as you have seen. The harder limestones and sandstones, the granites and schists, form walls like these. The softer stone erodes into slopes, benches and terraces, stepping back from the Canyon depths. And these vivid colors above the black, tints of red, yellow, and purple. So harmonious a plan can only have been devised by a Master Architect. Or do collegians no longer believe in a Master Architect?"

"I believe that great achievements can also be wrought by human architects."

"Like the Colorado, Grand Canyon, and Pacific Railroad?" Jefford strolled on, craning his neck. "This will be one of the most expensive sections of the line because of the hardness of the rock. I can see no engineering difficulty, however. The alignment is excellent—long tangents and easy curves."

"What about minerals?" he asked.

"There are certainly veins of iron in Nancoweap and fibrous magnesium silicate in several locations I have noted. Asbestos," Jefford added.

"You told Mr. Daggett that the gold was in too tiny flakes to be worth extracting."

"It could be extracted from the shale with the use of high-pressure nozzles and mercury-coated amalgamators, very expensively. Can you conceive of the devastation the monitors would cause?"

"This black rock is surely too hard to be affected by water blasting."

"It would be blasted by explosives," Jefford said grimly.

Whenever he was with the geologist, Asa felt that he was being prodded to attitudes about the wonders of the Canyon similar to those Major Powell expressed in *Canyons*. They were attitudes that certainly celebrated the achievements of a Master Architect.

He produced the book from his pocket and opened it to the folded page that marked his place. "Listen to this: '*We soon reach a place where a creek comes in from the left, and, just below, the channel is choked with boulders, which have washed down this lateral canyon and formed a dam, over which there is a fall of 30 or 40 feet.*' That was yesterday. That fall was more like fifteen feet. And this—" He read again: "'*About eleven o'clock we hear a great roar ahead, and approach it very cautiously. The sound grows louder and louder as we run, and at last we find ourselves above a long, broken fall, with ledges and pinnacles of rock obstructing the river. There is a descent of 75 or 80 feet in a third of a mile—*'" He pointed. "There it is. The third of a mile is right, but the seventy-five to eighty feet is three times too much. It is always that way."

He stood facing Will Jefford, the friend of the author of *The Canyons of the Colorado.* The geologist did not look much concerned.

"He wrote that years after he'd been through here," Jefford said. "Things are always larger and brighter in recollection, as you will find in your own time. It may also be that the book was designed for the ordinary reader, and seventy-five or eighty feet sounds more dangerous than twenty-five. Is that not forgivable?"

"It is dangerous enough as it is," he said.

"Tell me, what is it you are after in your perusals?"

Asa closed the book and replaced it in his pocket. "I want to find out why three men deserted the exploration and walked out at Separation Canyon."

"Maybe they were tired of the company," Jefford said.

That night after supper, in the black night of the Canyon, Asa sat between Morphy and Tiny, listening to Hyrum tell of the trials of the Mormons on their journey west. The old man crouched across the fire from them, sometimes nervously brushing at his coxcomb of stiff gray hair. Missouri had been mentioned in some context, and the name of the state had galvanized him into unaccustomed garrulousness: "In Jackson County there was people that hated us. I was about eighteen then. We knew the militia was on the march. The Mob, we called them. We had not yet got used to folks hating us."

Asa watched Ritter's hard, bitter face, which was eager too, like a child listening to a familiar story. Shadows pooled in Hyrum's eyes and mouth, and the reflection of the flames flickered on the planes of his face.

"We'd camped near a mill there," Hyrum went on. "All at once the Mob was there. I had never seen so many armed men before."

"Haun's Mill," Ritter said in a strained voice.

Hyrum nodded. "They begun firing. When we tried to fight back, it was too late. Some tried to hide in the blacksmith shop, but there was holes in the walls they could poke their rifles through. They killed my father and my uncle John."

"Why did they hate you?" Asa asked. He could see Miranda's shadowed, attentive face. Esther sat beyond her.

"They said we stole their stock," Hyrum said. "They said the Lord we worshiped was a fraud, although He was the same Lord as their own. They said we only traded at Sidney Gilbert's store. They said we all voted alike. They said we was trying to buy up all the land to drive *them* out. They said we agitated the Indians."

"It was the same in Ohio and Illinois," Ritter muttered.

"I remember what my mother told me," Buchanan drawled. "The Mormons stole babies. They kidnapped young women and married them to old men. They bushwhacked gentiles." He clamped the bit of his pipe between his teeth, squinting at the cook.

"We were on the run from the Mob," Hyrum said. "Later on we fought back."

"The Nauvoo Legion," Ritter said in the tight voice.

"We became violent men," Hyrum said, poking a stick into the fire. "Men become violent when they see their families persecuted."

In all this his voice remained unemotional, as though he was only discussing queer old notions. Asa considered how quickly he had become calloused to hearing of horrors out here.

"It was Haun's Mill that turned us violent," Hyrum went on. "The Lord forgive those misled and mistaken men."

Asa was startled to hear Esther's voice. "Sometimes the Apaches would come, and the men would have to fight them." With her blanket drawn around her and her hair braided down her back, she looked like a Hoya woman.

"They came to drive off the horses," she went on. "The men would fight them. If they drove off the horses, many would die in the winter."

"You are free of all that now!" Poche said.

"Once Mericats came to steal horses," Esther said. "White rustlers. They were very bad."

"What did you do?" Miranda asked.

"I hid in the Canyon with Samuel."

Who was Samuel?

"My son," Esther said, with a lift of her chin.

"We were up in Montana country shooting buffalo when some Blackfoot caught us," Buchanan put in, holding his pipe stem inches from his mouth. "That was pretty country up there. Clem and I got away into some trees up on a hill, but they caught the other two down below. They tortured them all day, and Clem was nicked and losing blood bad. He died about noon. I sat up in those trees looking out over the prettiest valley you ever saw, listening to those poor fellows screeching. That was a valley you couldn't think anything bad could happen in it. I was down to just two cartridges when the redbellies rode off. I don't know why they left." He was silent for a moment. "You always saved the last one for yourself," he added.

Asa blew out his breath in a sigh of awe. Leatherstockings!

"Hoya are not like that," Esther said. She had retired within her blanket, so her face was invisible.

Poche spoke to her in the gutturals of the Paiute language, and she replied strongly, with an upward gesture of her hand.

"Her husband is a medicine man," Poche said. "He is a very important man among the Hoya people."

"The Hoyas are lucky they live on land the white man don't want," Tiny said. "We'd run 'em out otherwise! Manifest Destiny! We will plow new lands, sink mines, build railroads. But it is no easier for a poor man to make a living for his family. The liveried carriages roll past the hungry children. All because of the private ownership of land!" Tiny had got onto his favorite subject.

"Spare us!" Jefford groaned.

"Why do you think the Missouri Mob and the Mormons were killing each other?" Tiny demanded.

"There is no such thing as fee simple in land in nature," he went on. "The laws of nature are the decrees of the Creator. Yet men will claim His bounty as their own wealth!"

"We have stopped making mineral claims, Tiny," Buchanan said. "We would not want to offend your conscience."

"Tell me, Tiny," Jefford said, "whether you own property in San Francisco."

"A little place," Tiny said sulkily. "My family lives upstairs. I practice my profession downstairs."

"On its own plot of land?" Jefford inquired.

"Land somebody brushed out for a town lot?" Buchanan said.

"I know you, Jake Buchanan!" Tiny exclaimed, leveling a finger. "You are bound to build this road so as to become a magnate like Charley Daggett!"

"I will get the road built, anyhow."

"A new capitalist!" Tiny jeered. "And another regiment of paupers turned out of hearth and home!"

Buchanan busied himself reloading his pipe. Asa tried to picture him as the kind of Denver personage Daggett had been, top-hatted, frock-coated, corpulent. Buchanan was too lean and casual, and watchful in a way that did not have to do with money accounts. The Jake Buchanan he admired manned the starboard oar of *Miss Saucy* and slipped back into camp from a hunting prowl carrying a haunch of venison on his shoulder. And defended himself from a Blackfoot war party, keeping the last bullet for himself. And climbed the cliffs to try to get a shot at whoever had shot at them.

"Tell me, Tiny," Jefford said. "Is this little place, on its little plot of ground, held in fee simple?"

Morphy and Poche had already left the campfire, and others were rising also, for Tiny's monomania on the subject of land ownership had become a bore.

That night Asa lay awake at the bottom of the black pit of the Canyon, around him a chorus of snores that sometimes fell silent for what seemed minutes before it began again. He could not stop thinking of someone hostile prowling the cliffs above them.

He heard sobbing. He had heard Esther Bingham in her grief before, but this time it was different. Movement attended the sound, a figure passing between him and the ember glow of the fire. It must be Miranda going to Esther. A lantern was lighted, and he could make out Hyrum's spiky hair. His fists ached as he started up; it must be Morphy after Miranda again! But now he could see Miranda and Hyrum bending over Esther by the light of the lantern. Esther's sobbing had turned to gasping. Her time had come.

He had visited his mother's curtained bedroom after she had given birth to his sister. His pretty mother had been flushed and smiling among the white pillows, with the small bundle in the crook of her arm, a tiny face wrinkled like a walnut shell. But this was not a woman in a white, comfortable bed with Dr. Randolph in attendance; this was a woman deep in the Grand Canyon of the Colorado, a woman who had been a captive of Indians and the wife of a medicine man and who had already borne her sorcerer-husband a half-breed son named Samuel; who was not lying down properly, but squatting in a shocking, aboriginal position, grunting in her labor, with Miranda and Hyrum in attendance.

At first light the crew of the survey gathered around mother and child: like the ox and the ass around the Christ Child, Asa thought; like the Haden family gathered around his mother and Baby Bertha in the big bed. Esther sat upright among her blankets, her tattooed face turned gravely aside, and the child's tiny sleeping face with its black fringe of hair like a dark little flower framed in a blanket.

"What will you name him?" George Ritter asked.

"I will call him Joseph."

They all gazed upon the child Joseph except the mother herself, who stared off across the River at the opposite cliffs still draped in their morning mist.

Watching the child most profoundly, Asa noticed, was Miranda, with a spot of color on either cheek of her sunburned face.

14

In the Gorge 3

ASA HADEN

Esther's child was a wizened little thing, with brown skin and a bald head fringed with coarse black hair. It was puzzling to Asa that the mother seemed so offhand with her infant. Maybe it was the Hoya way.

Miranda neglected her duties with Tiny and Hyrum to hold the child when the mother seemed disinclined to do so. Esther nursed Joseph, but it was Miranda who made the napkins out of wornout shirts and underwear and changed them when they were dirty.

Ashore, while the others went about their business, Esther sat with the child at her breast gazing into the distances of the Canyon. Her tattoos, which had been shocking at first, now were merely a part of her appearance. Or Miranda held Joseph, the two women seated side by side, although they did not appear to be conversing. Sometimes Esther and Poche had conversations in the Paiute language. Asa observed that in these dialogues the two did not face each other, but seemed to be talking to someone to one side.

Often Esther ignored Poche's attentions to her, however. One evening the half-breed was stung on the hand by a scorpion and made such a fuss that it was clear he was upset by matters other than the pain of the sting, and furious at Hyrum, who, instead of killing the insect, carried it off in a bandanna.

Although he wanted to be sympathetic with Poche, who considered himself not valued because of his Indian mother, Asa found it difficult to like the breed, whose personality seemed an uncomfortable mix of servility and assertiveness.

On the River, the rapids had become routine. Buchanan allowed Asa the decisions, though often they conferred, and sometimes Asa sought Morphy's advice, and always he consulted his ragged, swollen copy of *Canyons*. The portaging had become much more efficient, manhandling the emptied boats among the boulders of a rock fall, over a saddle, or across the sandy fan at the mouth of a wash, beside the wild brown waves. There was little wasted effort. Everyone was tired in a cumulative way, but hurrying also, to put as many miles as possible between the survey and the sniper.

They continued the downstream search for Daggett's body.

"Come!" Miranda said. She led Asa up the draw, stepping quickly in her battered child's boots. The passage along the trickle of crystal creek led between smoothly curving walls to a rock pool where Esther Bingham sat on a sandstone ledge, her bare feet resting on the pebbles at the water's edge, and the child held to her breast. Her face was raised to the sky above the slot in the cliffs, where a hawk circled.

Miranda squatted at the edge of the pool, arms clasped around her legs. "You must tell Asa what you have told me," she said to Esther.

Asa felt tall and awkward in the company of the two women. He seated himself on an extension of Esther's ledge. She reluctantly withdrew her attention from the high hawk.

"She is certain it was her husband who was shooting," Miranda said.

The child's face looked very dark against the whiteness of Esther's breast. She shifted Joseph from one breast to the other, and before Asa could avert his eyes, he had a glimpse of tattooing there, a triangular decoration beneath the startling brown coin of the nipple, the tattoos that were the Hoya husband's marks of possession.

"She loves him," Miranda prodded. "But she is afraid."

"If you were married against your will—" he started.

"Without him I would have starved," Esther said. "If he was not my husband other men would fight over me. But the others were afraid of him." Her hand brushed the tattooing on her chin.

"He has come after me," she went on. "He watches me from a bird, or a coyote—maybe that hawk!" She raised her eyes again. "He will kill me for running away from him. He will kill the ones who stole me from him."

The woman must be half demented from her years of captivity, from starvation and fear, married—if that was even a term that could be used!—to a medicine man who had convinced her that he could fly through the air and pursue her anywhere.

Esther set the child to her shoulder and patted the little back. "What would they think of me in the States?" she said. "With my face, and this ugly child?"

"You must not say that! He is not ugly." Miranda cut a glance at Asa, and he felt that he was disappointing her again.

"My other son is beautiful," Esther said. "My husband is old, but he is very strong! He is an artist. He has a moustache. That is rare among them." She said it with pride.

Asa thought it must be what old Pokray would look like, the chief of the murderous Shivwits. But how could you believe in a medicine man who flew through the air, who spied through the eyes of hawks?

The hawk floated over in slow circles, its short head turning to glance downward.

Esther laid the sleeping child on a patch of gray blanket on the ledge between her and Asa. The dark little face seemed to have shriveled around the mouth, the eyes were closed tight.

"It is a custom among them to kill a captive if a warrior is killed in a raid," Esther said. "If many are killed, many captives will be killed. It does not matter whether the captives are Moqui or Apache or white, only that they are captives. My husband took me into the River before them all. He washed me there, with prayers. He washed the *wasichu* from my skin, so that I was one of them and not a captive, and he could be my husband."

"These are not the courtships one reads about in books," Miranda said. "Where young men in blue jackets with brass buttons and women in white gowns meet at levees, and the young man brings the lady a glass of punch and inquires if he may have a dance!" She turned and gave Asa one of her cold, direct stares. "You must be familiar with such occasions," she said.

"Only from the same books you have read," he said.

"They came on me when I was in my garden," Esther went on. "It was close to the River there. The Callou wrapped clothes around my head so I could not scream and carried me off on a horse they had brought. What can he think but that I ran away? What can Samuel think?" Her eyes and nose were running in her emotion, and she mopped at them with her sleeve.

"My parents will not want me," she sobbed. She touched her chin.

"Of course they will," Miranda said. "You must not upset yourself."

Esther shook her head mutely.

It came to Asa that Mary Temple was the perfect person to take her in, for Mary was responsible for her rescue.

"The magazine in San Francisco that employs me would be very interested in your tale," he said. "One of the editors, a lady, Miss Temple, I am sure will take you in, you and the child, and help you to—become used to our world again. To become situated and comfortable. And copy down your history for the magazine to publish."

It might be that he had overstepped himself by assuming that Mary Temple would want to take Esther into her house, but he understood that Miss Temple had been caring for a poet's young daughter in the father's absence. He was sure she was as generous and hospitable as she had seemed to him.

Both women were staring at him, Esther as though she had not understood a word he had said.

"Miss Temple is the cause of our coming to rescue you, you see. She saw a piece in the newspaper that a white woman had been seen among the Hoya, and she told Mr. Daggett. And that is why you are here!" He tried to smile reassuringly.

Esther's teary face twitched with anger. She rose in silence and started back toward camp, leaving Joseph with Miranda.

"Did I say the wrong thing?" he asked Miranda.

She shrugged and tossed her curls. "She would like to run away from *us* and return to her husband, you see. But she is afraid her husband would kill her for running away from *him*. It is the kind of predicament women must live their lives in," she said, and she sounded angry also.

He followed her silently as she started back, carrying the child.

Hyrum and Buchanan were working on an oarlock of *Miss Saucy,* and Morphy balanced with one big-booted foot braced on a rock, giving advice. Ritter stood spread-legged beside his transit, making notations in his surveyor's journal.

Morphy smiled broadly at Miranda. "Little mammas! Maybe you ought to have one of those of your own, Missy."

Miranda halted so suddenly that Asa bumped into her.

"Be glad to help out!" Morphy said.

Asa thought he could not have heard correctly. No one would be so insensitive. He was feeling exasperated at the inadequacies of his conversation with Esther and Miranda. "What did you say?" he almost shouted.

Buchanan swung around from where he was working with Hyrum. Morphy's eyebrows climbed his broad forehead.

"Said I'd be glad to help the little lady out."

"Do you understand what you are saying?" He felt as though his head would burst.

"Please don't!" Miranda said.

Buchanan stood watching, pipe in mouth. Poche had come up to lead Esther away, and Miranda, still holding Joseph, followed them. Will Jefford and Tiny watched from further up the rocky beach.

Asa realized that Morphy in fact did not know what he had said to cause such a row. He stared at Asa over Buchanan's shoulder with a kind of painted-on grin.

"Show's over," Buchanan said easily.

That afternoon, in a chaos of white water, the *Lass* began swinging on the end of the line that was letting her down. Asa tried to keep his balance, bracing himself one way and then the other with his oar. The boat ground against an underwater boulder and leaped beneath his feet. He plunged into the water, managing to cling to the rope. When he had pulled himself out of the River to sprawl on the rocks, he rolled over on his back to gaze up at a hawk gliding along the cliffs.

Finally he got to his feet and sat on a ledge, removing his boots to shake the water out of them, still panting. Downriver the boats had been lashed together. They seemed far away and unimportant.

Buchanan strolled down to him, looking blessedly calm.

"I just couldn't hold her off the rocks," Asa said. "Maybe Pat could've. Is it bad?"

"Lost some wood off the bow. Not bad."

"There's a thing I remember from rowing. Catching a crab is when you are thinking about something else than the business at hand."

"Like Pat's been doing," Buchanan said, looking at him steadily. His dark eyes were both sharp and weary, concentrating myriads of fine wrinkles. His lips were compressed in a severe expression.

Asa thought that Buchanan was referring not to Morphy's obsession, but to his own.

That night they were in bed early, tired out from the last portage. Asa stared up at the stars, different, larger, brighter stars than he had ever known. He was aware of movement. It was Miranda, ghostly in the darkness, carrying her bedroll and weaving her way through the other bedrolls. She laid her blankets out next to Buchanan's.

He had to stifle his breathing. It must be because he had failed again to confront Pat Morphy! She had said, "Please don't!" but he could not pretend he had restrained himself because of her plea! If he would not defend her, she must turn to Jake Buchanan. He almost groaned.

The Deerslayer had understood the reasons for catching a crab. And maybe Miranda understood them also, and the placing of her bedroll was a conspiracy between her and Buchanan to keep him from catching any more.

It was like a bad cold in his head, a tightness in his skull, the crab-catching preoccupation with Miranda and Buchanan, although nothing seemed to have changed between them during the day. Miranda tended Esther's child, helped Hyrum with the food preparation, worked in the orange tent with Tiny. The situation had served to patch up Asa's quarrel with Pat Morphy, as though they were two rejected suitors.

He sat on the bank with Morphy, looking down at the tumbling waves of the next cataract.

"Fuck whoever she wants to for all of me," Morphy said. "If it only wasn't *that* son of a bitch."

Asa said carefully that the location of Miranda's bedroll did not imply that she had moved into Buchanan's.

"Fucken cock-tease," Morphy said sourly.

"She is sleeping next to him so she won't have to worry about you."

Morphy squinted at him with one eye closed, as though sighting along a rifle barrel. "Huh!" He chucked a bit of driftwood into the current to watch its progress.

To change the subject, Asa said, "I wonder if you remembered hearing what kind of troubles Major Powell had with William Dunn on the exploration."

Morphy pondered, as though his mind did not easily make sudden shifts.

"The Major named the Dirty Devil after him, I heard. So him and the Major wasn't exactly chums, all right. Maybe the trouble was mostly with the Major's brother, though. I ran into Billy Hawkins in Sacramento City, and he talked about it some. Billy said Walter Powell had a mean, bulldozing way about him. Old Shady, they called him. The Major didn't have a bad side to him; it was Old Shady that was the bad side. Billy said he stuck up for Dunn once, and him and Old Shady nearly come to a fracas."

"What did 'dirty devil' mean, do you suppose?"

"Dunno," Morphy said. "I just heard he called that river 'Dirty Devil' after Dunn, and then he called that creek 'Bright Angel' to make up for it. But I never heard who that was named for."

In the *Lass* Asa was seated in the stern with the sweep, with Jefford and Poche rowing and Miranda perched in the bow. They sailed along in smooth water with the *Letty* following behind, and *Miss Saucy* in the lead.

Poche said, "I have tried to make friends with Missus Bingham."

"I have noticed," Asa said. Jefford looked amused.

"She is grieving for the Hoya people who were her people. There is a son who was left behind. Her husband is not correctly her husband. There was no sacrament. I have told her this."

"Miranda thinks she loves her husband," Asa said. He seated himself and tucked the end of the sweep under his arm.

"He is a medicine man. They have their tricks, these people."

"Moving downriver faster than we can, for instance," Jefford said.

Poche ignored him. "It was my uncle who arranged for her to be taken. Men were sent to take her where she was alone by the River. Now the Peego Paiute will make war on the Callou. I have not told her it was my uncle."

"No doubt that is wise," Jefford said.

Poche kept his brown eyes fixed on Asa. "I have asked her to come to Tucson with me. I have told her I will see that she grieves no more. I will make her happy. She will be cherished. I am half Hoya and half white man. It is of value to her, you see. A man of education," he added.

"I wish you luck," Asa said. He saw a signal from Buchanan, heard the whisper of a rapid, and got to his feet. Poche was looking up at him as Miranda had, as though something was expected of him that he did not know how to give.

They halted late in the afternoon where a clear creek poured into the River, pulling the boats up on a narrow beach under a fifty-foot cliff with a scattering of boulders beneath it and willows extending back into a narrow canyon.

Miranda held Joseph while Esther sat on a heap of gravel with her bonnet off in the late sun. The bucket brigade passed bundles and supplies up from the boats, Morphy to Poche to Ritter to Hyrum to Jefford to Asa, in an easy, accustomed rhythm.

At the shot a flock of swallows exploded upward like blown confetti. Asa sprinted for the concealment of the willows, panting beneath their lacy canopy. He looked back to see everyone else in flight. Morphy ducked behind the bow of *Miss Saucy.* Poche was running holding Esther's hand. Ritter sprawled on the beach.

Miranda stood holding the infant against her breast.

He lurched to his feet to run to her, almost colliding with Buchanan. A second shot struck wood like a hammer blow. Buchanan sprinted to *Miss Saucy,* where the rifles were stored. Asa hurried Miranda back into the cover of the willows. She knelt there with her body covering the child, looking up at him with huge eyes.

"It is *him!*" she said.

Asa could see Buchanan ducking with Morphy behind *Miss Saucy,* his rifle barrel slanting upward. Ritter crawled toward a boulder, his shirt bloody. Hyrum hurried out to help him to cover.

"Anybody see him?" Buchanan bellowed.

No one replied. Asa crouched beside Miranda in the willow shade. She detached her arm from his grasp.

"It is some crazy prospector," he said, dry-mouthed. He could see Jefford peering out from behind a rock fall. "We must be coolheaded," he added. "It *can't* be her husband!"

Miranda patted the child, who was uttering small sounds. Her eyes blazed at him.

He ducked at another shot, but this was Buchanan firing from the boats. Long moments passed. Finally Buchanan came out from behind *Miss Saucy,* rifle raised. Morphy appeared. Others showed themselves, all staring upward.

"Believe he's gone," Buchanan said.

"Who *is* he?" Jefford demanded.

Asa crawled out of the shade and hurried to join Buchanan. Ritter lay behind Hyrum's boulder. His teeth showed in the stretched round of his lips. Hyrum had ripped the sleeve off his shirt to bind his wound, kneeling beside him. The bandage was soaked with blood. Ritter's eyelids fluttered closed.

"He'll lose that arm," Tiny whispered.

Buchanan brought the medicine kit from *Miss Saucy,* and he and Hyrum set to work binding up the terrible wound that Asa could neither bear to look at nor keep his eyes away from.

"Get another rifle." Buchanan said to him. "We're going up there."

"You won't find anything," Tiny said. "Like last time."

"It will be dark in half an hour," Jefford said.

Asa understood Buchanan's need to act, but he should not be climbing on the cliffs in the dark.

"*Christ Almighty!*" Ritter whispered, drawing his legs up. He gasped. Hyrum uncapped the brown bottle of laudanum to give him a sip.

"We will have to get him out to a doctor," Jefford said.

Ritter groaned and called on his Savior. Buchanan leaned on his rifle, watching him white-lipped.

"Indians!" Tiny said.

"It is a madman!" Jefford said.

"If you want to stop a survey, shoot the surveyor," Buchanan said.

Everyone stared at him.

Esther had come up. "He will kill you all," she said.

Asa felt the back of his neck crawl.

"We will have to get him out of the Canyon," Hyrum said, kneeling beside the wounded man.

"There's a crew of Mormons up there," Buchanan said. "They better by God still be waiting on me!"

"It's a long way to the nearest settlement," Jefford said.

Asa watched Buchanan frowning in the gathering dusk, gripping the rifle under his arm. He could follow Buchanan's reasoning. Ritter had to be taken out, but the women should not expose themselves, in case the rifleman lingered somewhere above, waiting for another shot. Nor was Esther in condition for two or three days of exertion. Esther and Miranda must continue on downriver.

And the survey was endangered by loss of manpower. If another man was lost or disabled, one of the boats would have to be abandoned, and portaging a freight boat would require all their strength.

"Poche, you and Pat will take him up to the plateau." Buchanan said. "You'll take the scout boat back upriver a couple of miles to where that big cross-canyon was and climb out from there. We've been coming around a big bend since Bright Angel, and all these canyons head up northeast, so you ought to come out not far from the head of Bright Angel. This Mormon Worsley and a crew is waiting up there. They can take George out to the settlements while you two head back. You'll carry whatever letters are to go, and Asa has copies of his scribblings for that magazine in San Francisco. I'll write Ira Ellsworth."

"How long do you figure to Callville, Jake?" Jefford said.

"Maybe thirty days."

"Lord preserve us," Tiny said.

"I'll have a look up the cliff at first light," Buchanan said. "We'll be here a while. It'll be two days anyway up to the plateau, slow going."

"*Christ Almighty!*" George Ritter whispered.

By lantern light in the chilly darkness, often pausing when there was an unfamiliar sound, Asa went over the copies of his submission for the *Monthly.* He had been outspoken about Daggett's trickery, but

Mary Temple could leave out or change what she saw fit. He had already written Chick and Mrs. Daggett, and Buchanan was writing to Mrs. Daggett and to the Mr. Ellsworth that Asa remembered meeting at the Daggett mansion. Buchanan had decided that if the Mormon crew had left the head of Bright Angel Canyon, Poche would have to accompany George Ritter on to find medical attention while Morphy returned to the survey. Although it was a long way to the Mormon towns, there were ranches in the lands between, and help would be available, especially to a fellow Mormon.

When he had finished binding his journals into a packet, Asa went to sit by the fire with the others, who glanced up as he approached them, the whites of their eyes showing in scared flashes. Drugged with opium, Ritter was propped against a boulder, wrapped in a blanket. Sometimes he snored. The two women huddled together.

"How would he catch up with us?" Tiny demanded of Esther. "He couldn't come along as fast as we have. All those canyons and washes to cross over."

"There are those who can be in one place and also another," Esther said. The child slept on his square of blanket between her and Miranda.

"Your medicine man is a magician, then," Jefford said in his scoffing tone.

"There are those who can be where they are, but also see with a bird's eye."

"You believe he is able to observe us here?"

Esther nodded, touching her fingers to her chin.

"That shoot wun't just somebody *seeing!*" Morphy said.

"It weren't no Injun flying like a hawk!" Ritter said in a sudden savage voice. "Weren't me he was shooting at, either!"

"What's that, George?" Tiny said.

"Ask Hyrum who he was shootin at!" Ritter shrilled. "Ask Hyrum why Matt Hite was slaughtered!"

Asa glanced at Hyrum, whose beard-bristled, gray old face was striped with firelight.

"What's this about, Hyrum?" Buchanan asked. "Hite was that high-up Mormon somebody shot and stuck feathers in his hair, that we saw in the paper in Eureka. Who shot him?"

"I don't know who shot Matt Hite," Hyrum said. He rose and

stamped stiff-legged off into the darkness. In the silence the River growled more loudly.

"He goddam do know!" Ritter cried hysterically.

Asa followed Buchanan out of the circle of firelight into darkness thick as tar. At the beach he could make out Hyrum leaning against the prow of one of the boats, a little starlight caught in his shock of gray hair.

"Your name's Longwell," Buchanan said.

Asa saw the shard of light twitch as though Hyrum had nodded.

Buchanan said coolly, "George thinks the fellow up there was shooting at you. The same one that killed Hite."

"Yes," Hyrum said.

"Because of that slaughter in Iron County years back."

Asa saw the fragment of light twitch in another nod.

"Brigham Young sent you off among the Injun to get you off the griddle."

"There was a federal investigation," Hyrum said. "It was decided that I was the one who would bear the blame, but Brother Brigham would not turn me over to a gentile court of law."

"Saints painted themselves up like redbellies," Buchanan said. "Feathers in their hair."

A long moment passed before Hyrum responded. "I was chief of militia and Matt Hite stake president."

The Mormon militia attacking the wagon train painted and feathered like Indians! No wonder Hyrum woke from his nightmares shouting, "Blood!" And Daggett had arranged for this old murderer to accompany him out Separation Canyon, to parley with the Shivwits!

An avenger had shot Matthew Hite and pressed feathers into his hair as a reminder of the massacre, and Ritter believed that the avenger had pursued the survey down the River for a shot at Hyrum Logan—or Longwell, as his name seemed to be. It was less far-fetched than a flying Hoya medicine man.

He could understand Ritter's fury.

"I am no longer that man," Hyrum said in a rusty voice.

Asa thought of the cook hustling around the fire to get supper out,

Hyrum with the fending oar coming down a rapid in the *Letty Daggett,* Hyrum bringing Esther Bingham out of the Colorado Chiquito with the Hoya band, Hyrum who was Miranda's confidant even as Buchanan was her defender, Hyrum who wouldn't kill anything that didn't have to be killed.

"Maybe you ought go out with George instead of Poche," Buchanan said. He turned to Asa, the whites of his eyes glinting.

"No," Asa said. Hyrum was worth three of Poche, bloody-handed or not.

"George would not like it," Hyrum said. "The Lord has forgiven me as He will forgive all who seek forgiveness. But men cannot forgive."

"Nobody needs know," Buchanan said and half turned toward Asa again.

Asa cleared his throat. "No."

"I thank you," Hyrum said.

Before first light Hyrum had rekindled the fire, and coffee was on the boil for the three who were heading upriver in the scout boat, Morphy and Poche, both armed with rifles, and a silent, hard-breathing George Ritter, with his strapped-up arm. There were packs of venison strips and biscuits for them to take with them, along with canteens of water, and the letters and documents. Buchanan would climb up on the cliffs to see what he could find there

Buchanan faded into the gray shadows. *Miss Saucy* and her crew were barely visible on the leaden sheet of the River, with a slow splashing of oars. Asa heard the infant's snuffling cry of hunger. He seated himself on a log with the coffee cup searing his hands, shivering in the chill that crawled up his back while the fire's heat baked his knees. The rifle with which Buchanan had entrusted him leaned against the log beside him. Across from him Hyrum squatted, also with a coffee cup held before his face. There was nothing to say to the old man.

Will Jefford came to join him, shivering also. Hyrum rose to pour another cup of coffee.

"I'm waiting for Jake to bring in the sniper slung over his shoulder," Jefford said. "Like venison for supper."

"He is a good provider," Hyrum said.

"We hope he is a good defender as well. Did he tell either of you about his scar?"

"What scar?"

"He was shot by a sniper at Shiloh. He tied his belt around his leg and waited most of the day for the Reb to come down out of the tree where he was. Then he shot him. I find that comforting."

"Yes," Asa said.

"Most times if you were hit with a minie ball you'd lose the limb, so he is lucky. That is comforting, too."

When Tiny and the two women came to the fire, Hyrum cooked breakfast. They all ate in silence, with many glances at the heights above them.

The sun stood well up in the slot of the sky when Buchanan returned. He stood before Esther, fingering in his vest pocket to bring out a chalky white object. It was the skull of some tiny animal, the bone thin as parchment, gaping eyeholes. The chin was marked in narrow strips of black. Asa realized it was a simulation of Esther's tattooing.

Esther sat staring at it with her hand to her chin. "Did you kill him?" she said in a heavy voice.

"Never saw him. Found the place he had shot from. There was his tracks there. This was hanging on a twig of a tree where you couldn't miss it."

Esther covered her eyes with her hands.

CHAPTER
15

San Francisco 6

MARY TEMPLE

"Is your sister's name Esther Bingham?" Waldo demanded when Mary opened the door. He waved a piece of flimsy at her.

"Yes."

"She is rescued! They have her!"

She pressed a hand to her bosom. "Please tell me—"

"A telegram came to the *Alta California,*" Waldo went on. "They will print it tomorrow. My friend there sent this to me by messenger." He stepped into her entryway, removing his hat. She ushered him into the front room, where he sank into a chair.

"And Mr. Daggett is dead," he went on, staring up at her. "Drowned on the River."

She took the flimsy from him. The capitalist Charles P. Daggett was drowned in a tragic accident on the Colorado River. His expedition had rescued a white female captive of the Hoya tribe. Her name was Esther Bingham, from Lamon County, Ohio. She had been kidnapped from the Bingham-Travers wagon train near Yuma in 1868. She had given birth to a child shortly after her rescue. A surveyor, George B. Ritter, had been wounded by a murderous sniper who had been shooting at members of the expedition. The wounded man had been brought out at Bright Angel, but the situation had seemed too dangerous to remove the women and child, since there was evidence that the rifleman was a hostile Indian pursuing the rescuers of Esther Bingham. The women would continue to accompany the expedition.

When Mary went into the kitchen to boil water for tea, it seemed that her hands could scarcely remember the familiar routines. Her head was filled with a kind of heated vacuum. *Her sister.* She must give thanks. She gave some reflection to her employer, who was dead. Now Beau was her employer. Asa Haden's account of these happenings, both blessed and tragic, must be en route. She stood before the stove rubbing her hands on her bare arms to warm them. *Her sister saved, and by her doing*!

The packet they awaited arrived three days later, on September 2, at the *Monthly* offices. It was wrapped in stained brown paper, knotted with cords that resisted the letter opener, that carried the feel of rough-and-ready contrivance to them. Asa Haden was powerfully indignant that Daggett had concealed from the crew of the expedition its true purpose, which was to survey for a railroad from Grand Junction, Colorado, to Los Angeles, for the purpose of transporting Colorado coal to the coast. This, then, had been Beau's secret as well.

Her sister had been tattooed! Esther feared that her Indian husband pursued her! She found herself breathing hard to think of Esther in an Indian's embraces. She had only time to skim the pages, passing them along to Waldo, when Beau Rowlands arrived.

He had never looked so handsome. His beard was freshly barbered, which brought the fine lines of his face into sharper prominence. He was pale and quiet, and today he spoke with that almost excessive politeness that was one of his several moods. Of course he was as affected by the news of his partner's death as she was by the news of the rescue of her sister. They sat at the big table, with Beau at the head. Beau immediately took possession of Asa Haden's papers, with one clean, pale hand spread on top of the packet.

Waldo gave a small grunt of protest for the two of them.

"It remains to be seen what of Charley's many projects Martha Daggett will wish to continue," Beau said. "Meanwhile, the expedition—the survey—is under the command of Jacob Buchanan. He is a man in whom Charley had the utmost trust."

"Meanwhile, you seem to be our permanent temporary publisher," Waldo said, carefully not looking her way.

"At least until we hear from Martha Daggett otherwise. How do you find young Asa Haden's pages, Mary?" Beau asked politely, a temporary publisher questioning an assistant editor.

"He is indignant at Mr. Daggett's deception," she said, gazing steadily at the man who claimed he loved her but had chosen against her as Henry Park's successor in a betrayal as casual as brushing away a fly.

"We may have to soften his indignation for Martha's sake."

"The purpose of the railroad is to haul coal from a Colorado field to the coast," she said. "It would be able to provide coal for half the present price."

Beau flashed her a complicated look that warned her not to pursue this sarcasm in Waldo's presence.

"It has been a bad year for capitalists dying on me," he said. "Edwin Crewes and Cyrus Matheson, and now Charley Daggett. They kicked the bucket that contained the milk I had been two years drawing." He grinned ruefully across the table. Then his face stiffened. "This is a terrible personal loss for me," he said in a toneless voice.

He was so seldom without his ironic shield that she felt his loss in her breast. He was so very intent upon his pursuit of wealth.

She said, "Esther Bingham is my sister."

Beau grimaced at her as though she had made a joke in terrible taste.

"When I saw that news item about a captive in a Hoya village, I gave it to Mr. Daggett. I thought that it was Esther. Now it has been confirmed." She still could not mention her sister's name without her heart beginning to hammer. She told the story briefly. "She would be twenty-five now," she said. *Tattooed by her Indian husband!*

"You could have told me earlier," Beau said, frowning. "But you will have your sister back! It is a miracle!"

"It is a miracle," she said, and her eyes burned with tears. Beau furnished her a clean linen handkerchief, with his embroidered initials to scrape her cheeks. How he loved fine goods.

"We are happy for you, Mary," he said.

Waldo squinted from one to the other of them, as though analyzing character. "A vengeful medicine man stalking her!" he said. "I believe I would be nervous if someone were shooting down at me from the celebrated cliffs."

"Asa mentions the destruction of the celebrated cliffs that will be necessary to build the roadbed." She handed Beau back his handkerchief.

"A railroad is more valuable to the nation than some barren cliffs," Beau said sharply, disposing of nonsense. "I have made my position in that matter clear in my article in the forthcoming issue."

The forthcoming issue contained not only his article, but its demolition. It was another matter that made her pulse ragged.

She had not considered Jamey McMurdo's personal enmity for Beau when she had assigned him his task, and his rebuttal was more savage that she had anticipated. She might have softened the attack by her editing, but she had not. She felt the scald of tears again.

"The September issue will be delivered from the printers on Monday?" Beau enquired.

"Sure as sunup," Waldo said.

"What have we for October, other than Asa Haden's journal? I will look it over to see what may be diplomatically printable. I will write a memoriam for Charley Daggett, of course."

"Perhaps the cover should have a black border," Waldo said. "Or the eye on California blackened."

Beau gave him a thoughtful glance.

"There is a poem of Octavius Coogan's," Mary said. "It will require a great deal of correspondence. Mr. Daggett was particularly interested in publishing Octavius."

"Well, I am not," Beau said. "If you are not enthusiastic, Mary," he added. She felt dread of his ultimate discovery of Jamey's rebuttal like a hand gripping her throat.

"There is some fiction worth considering," she said.

"I will leave that to you, of course. But I will have a look at what the survey historian has written." He patted the packet of Asa Haden's thirty-eight pages of careful script that she would have printed entire.

"If the surveyor is hors de combat," Waldo said, "what will they do for a surveyor, now that the expedition has been revealed as a railroad survey?"

"It is more of a photographic reconnaissance than an actual survey," Beau said. "They will have been for the most part surveying mineral claims. Buchanan will pull it off. The construction of the line was to have been in his and Charley's hands. His motives will be very strong to get the job done."

Beau sat up straighter when he had said this, and color showed in his pale cheeks. *What would he do when he saw that terrible attack by Jamey McMurdo?*

When Beau had departed with Asa's journal, Waldo said, "I wonder if we will merely see that young man's jottings censored, or never see them again?"

"I wonder myself."

"Do you have any sense of it?"

"I found it vital, and well written. He is exercised, perhaps too much for our pages, by Mr. Daggett's deception. He takes it personally. But it is exciting narrative."

"Beau's mood is measurable by the degree of his gentility," Waldo said. "He is very shaken by Mr. Daggett's demise, or something else. I would not have believed he was so attached to our employer."

"He was very gentle today," she said.

"What an incredible stroke of fortune that the lady captive has turned out to be your sister indeed!" Waldo exclaimed. "Will you take her in to stay with you?"

"Tattoos and all," she said.

At home, waiting for Beau Rowlands to come to her, she wrote a letter to her mother and father to tell them of Esther's miraculous rescue. She was distracted thinking of herself and Beau going tonight to one of the French restaurants, with the discreet rooms upstairs. Before he saw the September *Monthly.*

But he did not come to her that night.

"You come, Missy!" Mr. Lau said. He reached for her arm but dropped his hand instead, to stand looking into her face with his mouth drawn into a scar of dismay. He wore his neat, threadbare black suit and a white shirt buttoned at the collar.

"What is it, Mr. Lau?"

"Mr. Rowlan' bad place! You come!"

She followed him down steep Broadway to Grant Street. He did not so much accompany her as break a path through the crowds of Chinese vendors and shoppers, past the greengrocers and fish markets and herb stores, hurrying ahead of her with a headlong haste. She trotted to keep up with him, her hand knotted to the handle of her purse. The bad places in Chinatown that she knew of were the cribs of the slave girls, and the opium parlors.

Chinese men in black pajamas looked at her sideways as she passed them. A tiny woman struggled by on bound feet. There were wafts of tea and rice dust and strange herbs, a sweetly bitter smell. Wind-dried ducks hung in a store window like corpses on gibbets.

They turned into a narrow alley between windowless walls that stank of urine. Mr. Lau now walked close beside her. "Bad place," he said again.

They descended steps, Mr. Lau rapped on a panel. A white-bearded Chinaman with his hands hidden in his sleeves bowed them inside. The place was dim with incense; the smell was overpowering. She made out a narrow room with two bare wooden tables and benches, three Chinese men watching her from the benches.

Mr. Lau plucked at her arm.

They passed into a larger space that was dense with incense also. Bunks were built into the walls, framed in red and gold decorations. Paper lanterns hung like stalactites from the invisible ceiling. Each cubicle contained a little table that held a pipe, and a reclining human form. She knew there were San Franciscans she would recognize who sometimes relaxed in the opium dens of Chinatown, society ladies and powerful men floating out of themselves into golden mists.

Beau had brought his defeats and losses here to salve them with pipe dreams. He lay in a cubicle with his head propped at a slant and his eyes closed. His jacket hung from a peg on the wall, he was in his shirtsleeves with his cravat loosened. She gazed down at his calm, pale, bearded face in the smoky shadows.

Mr. Lau whispered, "You take away! Take home!"

Beau breathed with a slow rasping sound. She leaned close to murmur his name, but he did not respond.

"He needs a doctor!"

"No doctor!" Mr. Lau said. He summoned the attendants in their silent slippers. One of them wiped Beau's forehead with a dampened cloth. The two of them brought him to a seated position, one bracing him there, his head slumped to one side, while the other knelt to put on his shoes.

The little group of the attendants and Mr. Lau supported Beau down the alley to Grant Street, with Mary following helplessly. No one seemed to notice, as though this were a common sight.

They loaded him into a cab and, with the broad-shouldered Chinaman accompanying them, made their halting way through the crowds. So Beau was transported to her house and installed on her bed. She could see the sweat from his exertions on Mr. Lau's forehead. She tipped the big Chinaman.

"He sleep long time, Missy," Mr. Lau said. "No need doctor."

"He'll be very grateful to you, Mr. Lau. And I'm grateful."

"Ver' bad," Mr. Lau said with a shake of his head.

When he had gone downstairs to his tiny, cluttered, low-ceilinged room in the basement, she undressed her lover. He seemed thinner since the night of their grand lovemaking. He lay supine on her bed in his long underwear. Once she saw his eyelids tremble.

She sat beside him, holding his inert hand with her thumb lightly on his pulse, which throbbed slow and strong.

Instead of feelings for her lover, the lines of unwritten poems drifted through her head. Seeking escape from cruel actuality had brought him to the opium pipe, while her own dread of vultures coming home to roost turned her thoughts to rhymes and images.

She poked up the fire in the cookstove, then sat beside him again, to spoon small quantities of soup between his lips. He sniffed, his nose wrinkled, his lips twitched, but he swallowed. He snored softly between spoonfuls.

At dark she lit the gas in the parlor, and a little light filtered into the bedroom. She sat at her desk, took from the drawer the new issue of the *Monthly,* and glanced through Jamey McMurdo's denunciation of Beau's piece. It was as savage as she remembered.

She took out her "Clouds Over Mount Tamalpais," to add some of the thoughts that had come to her while she was attending Beau. The poem seemed insipid to her.

On another sheet of blank paper, she wrote:

Framed in red and gold,
In red and gold enfolded,
The yellow children watch—

She sighed and put it aside to return to the bedroom. Beau was tossing his head from side to side as though to throw off some harness. She wet his dry lips with cool water and touched her own lips to their feverish heat. She lay on the bed beside him in the dim room.

He said clearly, "Its jaw opens like a snake's. It's a lion! Open jaws!" After some muttering, he spoke clearly again:

"You can feel a white woman's teeth behind her lips. You can *see*— Make you sick!" he muttered.

She bathed his forehead again. She saw that his eyes were open, regarding her.

"Encino!" he said.

"The mine?"

"They've found a horse!"

She didn't understand. "A wild horse?" He had offered her a swift, beautiful horse like the horse Ramón had not given her, if she would come to Sonora with him. What then of his old-gold, big-lipped mistress?

He explained impatiently, with emphatic jerks of his head: "A horse is what we call an invasion of barren rock into what had been a lucrative vein. You have no idea how big the horse is, or if the vein continues after it. They are after me," he added.

"Who, Beau?"

"Gilligan and Hopwood. Cyrus Matheson died in April. He was my friend in the syndicate. Gilligan and Hopwood did as he told them."

"I'm sorry," she said.

He lay back on the pillow, whiskered chin jutting, eyes closed, his fine features pale and calm. Her hand wanted to trace the ridge of his nose, the lines of his lips.

"She was going down gallantly," he said. "I had estimated two and a half million dollars in profits in the ore from that vein. But now we have run into a horse."

He sighed hugely. "It is such an expensive business, sinking a mine.

The Mexicans say it takes a mine to finance a mine. We had more than a million in capitalization. I purchased everything we would need. Two big hoists like those that were designed for the Anaconda Mine in Butte. Two of the biggest pumps. Air compressors. Machinery for a sawmill, a machine shop, a carpenter shop. I had a thousand tons of hardware to transport into the Sierra Madre. It all had to be broken down into three-hundred-pound loads. That is what a Mexican mule can carry. Seven thousand mule trips! The freight costs were twice what I had paid for the machinery!

"It did not produce what I had promised, but there was a profit! Now we have run into a horse. They blame me! 'Beau Rowlands and his wretched talk of prospects!' they say of me. I have resigned as president of the Encino Mine Corporation!"

So that was the sorrow beyond Daggett's death that Waldo had mentioned. Mary bathed Beau's forehead with her cloth, very conscious of her teeth when she tried to smile at him. He raised himself on one elbow.

"Listen! Engineering schemes, without sufficient capitalization to back them, are assured of failure. It is the law of economics! And the sources of money are insatiable in their demand for profits. They are like huge beasts with open jaws!" He stopped, breathing hard.

"But how will they manage if you have resigned?"

"They will come to me on my terms, or they are finished. They will lose everything they have invested. The mine will close. If it does not operate for a year it can be 'denounced.' If it is denounced, it reverts to the government. If it reverts to the government it will be sold to one of those crocodiles down there for a song. And there *is* abundant ore there!"

"So you wait to hear from them."

"So much waiting. For Gilligan and Hopwood, for the judgment in the *Hutchinson* trial, for Charley Daggett's feasibility report." His head plumped down on the pillow again, his eyes closed. "Charley's death is a terrible blow to me, Mary. So much was not even in writing. His penchant for secrecy! I will have to go to Denver to see Martha Daggett. She is not the kind of woman I like."

"Her white woman's teeth behind her lips," she said, and wished she had not said it.

He opened his eyes to stare at her. "What did you say?"

"It was something you spoke of when you were feverish. Tell me: is your mistress in Encino an 'old-gold girl'?"

He licked his lips with a swift flick of his tongue. "That is just a joke I have with a friend. He is enamored of the girls of Polynesia. Well, I am also! Girls of color. Archaic women."

"I am not an archaic woman, I am afraid."

"You are my beautiful modern American woman!"

"Who is your friend?"

"He is the painter Samuel Voss. Perhaps you have heard of him?"

The modern American woman had heard of Samuel Voss, painter and sculptor.

"If I were rich I would buy beautiful paintings!" Beau said. "I would be a famous patron of the arts! I would set Sam to making purchases for me throughout Europe. And Asia! I would learn the histories of my treasures! I would hire writers to record their histories—"

There was a rasp of a snore.

Minutes later he spoke again: "Judge Larsen will rule against us. It is almost certain. The ancient riparian rights of miners will be forgotten in the press of politics. Farmers! Times are changing, and they do not change for the better!"

He slept again.

She made herself a bed in the parlor, the settee pushed up against the easy chair, and lay awake gazing out at the darkness of the Bay, trying to remember her sister. She could conjure up a slight figure in a soiled white dress, face hidden in a deep bonnet, warts on her thumbs, a timid child sticking close beside her older sister, who had been responsible for her during the journey west. The responsibility had not been onerous, since Esther had been neither adventuresome nor disobedient. She rode with her mother on the cot under the white hood of the wagon cover and slept with her sister beneath the wagon on hot nights.

Now Esther was on the Colorado River, in the Grand Canyon, perhaps pursued by vengeful Indians, with her newborn infant. She must have grown into a strong woman to have survived life in an Indian village, giving birth in the wild. An archaic woman with a tattooed face!

Esther would surely wish to join her in San Francisco. Their mother was bedridden with a dozen female complaints, and their father had his hands full tending to her. She would care for her sister and her child as she had been conscripted to care for Nevada Coogan, as though such were her continuing responsibility. And her other life as poet and editor, her hopes for a sojourn in England, were only adjuncts to that role she had been assigned, or sentenced to—her sister's keeper.

In the morning Mary brought Beau his breakfast, a little bouillon and a slice of heavy, nourishing Italian bread. He sipped the bouillon from the cup and tucked bits of bread into his mouth. Watching his bare arm move, she was shocked at how thin he had become. She must force food on him, steaks and chops, potatoes and gravy. She was pleased to see him eating greedily.

"The Yaqui!" he exclaimed, flashing an alarmed look at her. "Cajeme! I wonder why they have not raided the silver trains!"

"What is Cajeme?"

"He is the chief of the *insurrectos!*"

She went to answer a knock on the door. Jamey McMurdo stood on the step, doffing his seaman's cap and smiling at her. She did not know how to refuse him entrance, and she led him into the parlor, closing the bedroom door as she passed it. He sat in the easy chair, facing her on the settee, his battered boots set apart, cap in his lap. He wore a miner's red sash, a decoration to his dress that she did not at first understand.

He had been to the magazine's offices and had seen the new *Monthly.* "I believe it is a fine issue," he said, combing his fingers through his beard and regarding her with his innocent blue eyes. "The controversy over man's place in nature, mark you, will sell many magazines. It is of the greatest importance!"

"Waldo and I are pleased," she said. She knew their conversation was audible in the bedroom, unless Beau was sleeping again.

"I listed his points, one by one," Jamey said. "Then I cast thunderbolts at them!"

He seemed to expand, smiling at her. He plucked at his beard.

"In some nations, it is the church that is holy, look you," he went on. "In this one it is capitalistic endeavor. It is thought that it is the profit making of the great magnates that has brought this nation to its present power and wealth. I know that you agree with me, that what has built the nation is its natural riches. Its mountains and forests and great plains, its rivers and valleys, its Yosemites and Grand Canyons. *These* are our riches!"

Did he think she had not read his piece that had expressed these exact sentiments? He folded his arms and gazed down the blade of his nose at her.

"Yes, I agree with you," she said, choosing her words carefully, mindful of the bedroom door. "We agree that the opinions that were expressed upon the subjugation of nature for the good of mankind are simplistic. I must tell you that I found your refutation of those arguments simplistic also."

He looked startled that she would dare to challenge him. "One must be simple in order to persuade! Of course the interconnections of all living things cannot be simple. We do understand each other, Marrry!"

His insistence that they agreed with and understood each other compounded her nervousness.

"I confess," Jamey said, frowning, "that I feared you might come to agree with Bowman Rowlands because of the feminine attraction to handsome gents. I had feared you would be ensnared by his well-known personal charm into embracing his views. I know that even intelligent young women are swayed by such qualities."

"Oh, Jamey, please don't be so pompous!"

His sunburnt face reddened beneath the brown. "I have been told that I am sometimes pompous. I am sorry for it." He sounded rather more proud than sorry.

"I cannot argue that good looks, charm, and personal magnetism may not sometimes capture the heart of an intelligent young woman," she said. "But what would capture *my* heart would be a masculine understanding of what matters are of importance to me."

She knew that Beau, who had sought to use the *California Monthly* for dishonorable purposes, would not understand what she was saying any more than Jamey did.

"I have come to realize how important to me you are," Jamey said.

Now she understood the significance of the red sash, the adornment of his intent.

"No, Jamey," she said. "This cannot be. I'm sorry."

He looked so wounded that her heart went out to him. But the wounded expression changed immediately to one of contempt.

"I was correct, then, in my assumption that you favor a prettified Charles P. Daggett."

"I'm afraid that is so."

"You have chosen a remarkable way to show your favor," Jamey said. "For I have shamed him completely in the *Monthly*. I regret that I mistook your purposes."

She did not know if she even had any purposes. Go now, with no more reproaches!

"I believe I overestimated your intelligence," he said.

"I am only female, after all, Jamey."

He rose, settled his hat on his head, gave her one last glance out of his depthless blue eyes, and departed. She leaned on the wall beside the bedroom doorway for a moment before she tapped on the door.

When she pushed it open, Beau was sitting up in the bed, arms folded on his chest, glaring at her. He had not been sleeping.

"Bring me the magazine," he said.

She went to get it from the drawer of her desk. While he leafed through the pages, the eye on the cover regarded her balefully. Beau paused to read while she stood at the foot of the bed like a schoolgirl awaiting punishment.

He sighed and said, "Bitch! You and your *perfumado* accomplice, and Mister Water Ouzel."

"Did you think we took our stand against hydraulic mining lightly? You were using your position to corrupt the magazine to your purposes."

"Charley Daggett's purposes, damn you! He was owner and publisher!" He fell silent, his face more tragic than angry. "I thought you loved me," he said in a different voice.

"I thought you loved *me,*" she said. Her hands were clasped together so tightly at her waist that her fingers ached. "But you chose to betray my position at the magazine because I am a woman. I thought you loved me because I am a woman."

"I demoted you because you are a damned anti-debris bleeder! So you take your revenge by making me look a fool and a knave!"

"'Loved I not honor more,'" she said.

"A damned honor-bound white woman with lips as thin as rubber bands. Give me a dark-skinned woman who is faithful to her man!"

"Well, you have your old-gold girl at Encino."

"A real woman!"

Tears flooded her eyes so that the image of him writhed and danced.

"By God, can't you realize that I am absolutely devastated by Charley's death? And the damnable *Hutchinson* judgment!" He shifted his legs out from under the bedclothes, to rise shakily. "Why would you *do* this?"

"Because you would insist that the magazine betray its policies by publishing a servile piece toadying to the worst elements in the state. You would have devastated *us.*"

"You think that?"

"I know that."

"So I was to be taught a lesson. Did it occur to you that the lesson rather overwhelmed the crime?"

He danced in her eyes.

"I have been taught a lesson I already know too well," he said. "That you can trust a white bitch to hack at your ballocks whenever she has the chance. Where are my clothes? Have you cut them up, too?"

She raised a hand to indicate the closet. "You are ill!" she protested.

"Yes, I am ill." He took up the magazine from the bed and hurled it at her. She fended it off with her arm.

He staggered, trying to fit a foot into his trouser leg. When he was dressed his clothes hung on him. "I've got to go to see another white bitch in Denver," he muttered.

"I would do anything for you," she said. "But you cannot destroy what has given my life meaning."

He stood swaying, facing her. "Let me tell you, white woman. If you wanted your life to have meaning you should have let *me* give it meaning! I was ready to do that. Do you know it?"

Two declarations in one day, one unwanted and one unbelievable.

"Good-*bye!*" he said, and left her. She sat on the bed that was still warm from his body and patted up the pillow his head had rested on.

Waldo prevailed on his friend, the head bellman at the Palace Hotel, to see if Bowman Rowlands had left Asa Haden's journal in his hotel room when he departed for Denver and to send it to the *California Monthly.*

He was told that Mr. Rowlands had left town without settling his very large hotel bill. The journal came by messenger.

In the Gorge 4

ASA HADEN

The survey waited four days for Poche and Pat Morphy to return. Buchanan was up on the cliffs with his rifle every day, but Esther's husband had vanished. Poche and Morphy, when they returned, had seen no sign of him. The party of Mormons had been located at the rim without difficulty, and Ritter borne off to the nearest settlement. It appeared that it would have been perfectly safe for the women and the child to have left the Canyon also.

Buchanan had asked Will Jefford to take over Ritter's duties as surveyor, and Jefford spent a day poring over Ritter's notes, maps, and field drawings and another morning shooting angles with the transit. Asa accompanied him, tramping along the creek and up the hillsides to look over Buchanan's road alignment here, with an eye out for the medicine man. The gorge had widened considerably, with terraces and buttes flaming with color rising against the distant scarps. Will pointed out that a seven-hundred-foot trestle would be required to cross the creek, but the alignment was relatively simple, except that the cliffs would suffer some half-tunneling.

They were galvanized by a shot, but it was only Buchanan bringing down a buck.

When the boats were on the River again, the mood was grim. Not only did Buchanan's estimate of another thirty days seem a prison sentence, but unspoken were the fears of the survey's vulnerability at Shinumo and Kanab—canyons along the route where Esther's husband would be able to ambush them again.

Here the cliffs had receded from the River, their tops sculptured in sharp cuts, crevasses, and crenellations that caught the late sun and gleamed like teeth. Asa contemplated them in the light of Will Jefford's Master Architect's design but found it dizzying to gaze up at those soaring rims.

Ritter's strength was missed in lining and portaging. The boats had been reorganized: Asa, Hyrum, and Miranda aboard the *Lass;* Tiny and Buchanan on *Miss Saucy;* Jefford, Morphy, and Poche aboard the *Letty,* with Esther Bingham and her infant settled in the bow.

They floated in the current sometimes and sometimes rowed, Asa and Hyrum at the oars of the *Lass,* Miranda manning the sweep. Asa set an approving expression on his face whenever his eyes encountered hers, for she took her responsibility seriously. Hyrum was not inclined to conversation, and there was silence aboard the *Lass* as she drifted downriver through riffles that were not worth halting to reconnoiter.

Miss Saucy led the way, gliding through the water that ran smooth as syrup over the humps of sunken boulders, once a fall of a few feet that could be ridden down a straight chute. Miranda gripped the sweep oar with white knots of hands, face shaded by her cap. Asa nodded his encouragement.

Suddenly Hyrum spoke: "We had heard this lot was from Missouri, near Far West." His big hands rested on his oar. "They were a breed of men we hated. They threatened our women. They spoke lewdly to them. They claimed to have killed Mormons at Haun's Mill. They claimed to possess the rifle that killed Joseph Smith."

When he fell silent Asa noticed that his jaw still moved, as though he was masticating his thoughts. He was afraid this was a sign of some senile breakdown on Hyrum's part. Miranda gave him a wide-eyed glance.

"Everyone knew of their blasphemous progress," Hyrum went on. "Brother Brigham said they should be sent to hell through lots. That was an expression the Prophet used.

"So they came to Iron County. They were almost gone from Utah then. We should have let them go and been relieved of them."

Asa watched the old man, whose face was shuttered and gray.

"Our blood was bad," Hyrum said. "We had been infected by the persecutions and murders, you see. The Shivwits were friendly. It was planned that they should attack the train. The Shivwits would kill some of the braggart beasts from that Mob back in Missouri. So they did. But the gentiles fought back strong. So the militia painted themselves as Paiutes and joined the shooting. But the gentiles were not deceived. Frightened men then agreed that all in that wagon train must be killed."

Asa felt sick as he tried to picture Hyrum, fierce-faced, painted and feathered, commanding the militia to horrible slaughter—Hyrum who had saved the rattler and the scorpion from extermination in some pact of redemption with his Savior.

"You told me that the Lord has forgiven you," Miranda said almost inaudibly. Asa glanced at her again, who had smothered the child fathered upon her by the oppressor she had also killed.

"He forgives all who seek His forgiveness," Hyrum muttered. Again he fell silent.

"Women as well as men," he went on. "And the older children. Young children were given to farmers in the county to raise as their own."

"Hyrum," Miranda said, "hush. This is enough."

Hyrum said in his steady voice, "We were mistaken. Only one family in that train was from Far West. And Brother Brigham had never said they were to be sent to hell."

"So George Ritter thought the sniper was a son of one of those murdered families who had killed Hite and was shooting at you," Asa said.

Hyrum nodded.

A butcher sharing his seat! The Iron County Massacre had given the Mormon Church a murderer's name throughout the West. And yet, with Morphy, Hyrum was one of the strengths of the survey, and a good man!

Foaming heads rose off to the right, one fountaining up to the height of a man before subsiding. Two hundred feet behind, the *Letty* followed along. Miranda rose to steer the boat down the chute.

She reseated herself when they came into the gentler chop of the tail waves. Past her, Asa watched the *Letty* enter the chute. He was reflecting on horror in the past when he was confronted with present horror.

A foaming head reared up beside the bow of the *Letty.* Esther Bingham rose as though to meet it and was swept into the River. A shout was torn from his throat.

Poche stood upright to swing the safety rope. He flung it and leaped into the River after Esther, setting the *Letty* pitching.

"Backwater!" Asa cried, leaning on his own oar. With Miranda heaving her weight on the sweep, the *Lass* was turned and progress made against the current. Asa had a glimpse of Esther's head floating toward them, one hand raised as though to catch a rope flung to her. Fifty feet behind her, Poche was splashing to catch up. Esther's disembodied head enlarged, approaching, a serene expression on her face.

Then she disappeared. Asa rose, staggering for balance, to swing the *Lass*'s safety rope. He hurled it out just as Poche's head disappeared also. The rope lay in a long curve on the surface of the water, slowly straightening as it drifted downstream. Miranda's horrified eyes met his.

The *Letty* swept down on them, colliding bow to bow with a jar. Hyrum grasped Asa's arm to steady him. In the *Letty,* Will Jefford held the child wrapped in his square of gray blanket. Miranda leaned out to take the bundle from him.

"*Lord!*" Hyrum whispered.

Morphy gaped them from the *Letty.* "Jaysus, she just went *in*!"

Miss Saucy beat her way upriver toward them, lurching always to the right with Buchanan's stronger strokes.

The three boats drifted together on the placid River. Asa had to think to breathe air.

"What happened?" Buchanan's hard brown face was contorted with anger.

"That spout popped up beside us there!" Morphy said. "She just fell *out!* The breed went in after her!"

"Nobody else even got wet," Jefford said.

It was as though Esther had embraced the spout. Asa was as shaken by the serenity with which she had met her death as by the death itself. It was as though her husband had summoned her and she had gone to rejoin him, choosing an existence in which she had been content over one she dreaded. And Poche had followed, trying to rescue her once again.

They rowed back and forth across the River, searching without hope. Miranda gripped the infant to her chest with one hand, no longer able to manage the sweep, so that Asa and Hyrum had to back and fill with the oars.

How would they feed the child?

He watched Buchanan's face as *Miss Saucy* circled, the bar of his eyebrows joined with worry about his precious survey. Without Poche the crew was no longer sufficient to man three boats. The *Letty,* the bad luck boat, would have to be abandoned. Could they even portage the heavy *Lass*—himself, Buchanan, Morphy, Will, and Tiny: Morphy with the strength of two and Tiny less than one. Miranda? Maybe it was enough.

Buchanan waved a hand toward the bank, where there was a slant of beach.

As Asa and Hyrum rowed to shore, he thought of Daggett drowned in Marble Canyon, and Esther Bingham and Poche united in death somewhere at the bottom of the deadly River. Major Powell's men had come to consider the River a prison, a holy terror. Now for the survey it was a graveyard as well.

They searched the riverbanks as far down as the next big eddy, but the bodies had not surfaced. They loaded the *Letty*'s cargo onto the *Lass* and *Miss Saucy* and hauled the empty boat far up the beach, but she could not be hoisted above the high-water mark and so was doomed. When they had finished the *Letty*'s last portage they stood in silent pairs on the sandbar, Hyrum seated on a drift log with his back to the others, Miranda still in the stern of the *Lass* with Esther's child.

Joseph made his small snuffling cry of hunger.

Miranda turned away from the shore and unbuttoned and freed her body from the overall. Her back gleamed like porcelain as she bent over the child. She had borne a child herself not long ago! He did not know how Nature provided, but there could be sustenance for the babe in that neat bosom.

"Have mercy, Lord!" he heard Hyrum whisper.

Miranda bent over the child. Joseph emitted a shrill cry of rage.

Asa caught Tiny's eye. Tiny's teeth were bared. "Shitten luck!" Morphy muttered. Buchanan had lit his pipe, standing with his hands in his pockets gazing out at the river. The child began to cry steadily.

Buchanan brought from the medicine kit a brown bottle of laudanum, soaked a bit of cloth in it and took it to Miranda. The child sucked, fussed, and fell silent. Miranda laid him on the blanket on the oarsmen's seat and shrugged her overall top back on.

"It will come," Hyrum said hoarsely.

Asa saw that her face gleamed with tears. He fixed his eyes on the opposite cliff, where a hawk floated close to the rock.

"How can we hope to feed him?" Jefford said, wiping his sweating face with his bandanna.

"I will feed him!" Miranda said fiercely.

Asa watched Buchanan watching her climb ashore, carrying Joseph. He had never before seen the Deerslayer look dismayed.

"So fast," Jefford said. His face looked swollen. He had tied his bandanna over his bald head. "One moment we were floating along as calm as anyone could wish, and the next she was gone. And Poche! As though the god of this place had snapped his fingers."

The Master Architect, Asa thought.

"She and Miranda should've gone out with George," Tiny said.

Buchanan lit his pipe, blew smoke, and said, "She couldn't of."

Morphy said, "If I had a dog that liked this Canyon, I'd kill him and burn his collar and swear I never owned him."

Miranda removed herself and the child nights so that the wailing was thin with distance, although still they could hear it. Asa slept fitfully, with dreams that frightened him. All at once his exhaustion was overwhelming, from fighting rapids, from the brute sun, from unloading and carrying and reloading, from the monotonous meals, from sleeplessness, from the anxiety that attended the child's cries of hunger.

Everyone had heard tales of plains crossings where women died in childbirth and the newborn must be suckled by whatever means could be found, sugar tits, fingers and whiskey, a captured doe, an Indian wet nurse. He knew that Buchanan felt he must ration the laudanum in case of further accidents. A cloth tit was soaked in whiskey, and Hyrum made a stew of dried apples and strained it through a cloth. Miranda fed this to the squalling, red-faced child off the end of a spoon. It seemed that Joseph imbibed some of it, but more often he shook his black-haired head in fury. He went at Miranda's breast like a wildcat, until Miranda wept in pain.

The thin, exhausted crying dinned in Asa's head so that at night he would jam his hands over his ears. The sight of Miranda with her head bent over the suckling child wrenched him with pity.

The survey came to what seemed the most savage rapids yet. The River roared and lashed between narrowing granite walls. The boats were unloaded and lined down unmanned, with every man needed on the rope. *Miss Saucy* made her way safely through, but when they let down the heavier *Lass,* the strain on the rope was like a bear on a leash, the boat skittish in an unfamiliar, alive way. They labored in waist-deep current, scraping their heels as the rope strained and relaxed. The rope broke free of the chop and flung muddy water into their faces. Buchanan and Jefford stumbled and sidled, but Morphy, just ahead of Asa, was a rock of steadiness, muttering, "Jaysus! *Jaysus!*"

The *Lass* turned her stem against the current and bounded through thickets of billows. They managed to restrain her, arms half pulled from sockets, Morphy crouched with the rope snubbed across his back and his thick arms bulging. But he was pulled forward, and only Asa managed to hold steady while the others scrambled for grips and footing.

The boat doubled back, easing the strain. Then she dipped her nose and disappeared. Now they had to loosen the rope or be dragged into the current by her swamped weight. After moments she reappeared, bottom up, in the tail waves. Asa and Buchanan sprinted along the rocks to where she waited for them, and Asa breasted out into the River to secure another rope to her.

Buchanan crouched, panting hugely, on the rocks at the water's edge. Morphy came along to help Asa attach ropes to the far rail. They tilted the *Lass* right side up, and Asa climbed aboard to bail. Morphy stared up at him with his mouth gaping open and his cheeks stained with red stripes. "Jaysus!" he panted.

Together they pulled the *Lass* over to a mooring beside *Miss Saucy.*

Then they began the weary chore of hauling crates and bundles over the rocky saddle and down to the boats. Tiny's burden of exposed plates was almost as large as the unexposed. Asa noticed that the photographer, who was a shameless shirker, always carried one small rubber-covered bundle himself.

Miranda sat on one of the bundles, Joseph clutched to her breast. She looked at Asa with a smile so sweet and unexpected that he stopped in his tracks.

"It's *come,*" she said.

Others gathered around her, Hyrum squatting at her knees. Her overall was slumped around her waist, one breast covered by her arm, the other by Joseph's dark head. She raised her face to the sky, and Asa could see the tears glistening.

"Thank thee, Lord!" Hyrum whispered.

"Congratulations, my dear," Will Jefford said.

Asa could only echo it. At last something good had come their way. Buchanan went to get the jug of whiskey from *Miss Saucy,* to celebrate Miranda's milk.

It rained for two days. On the first they continued in the boats, but in the afternoon the drizzle turned to battering rain, and torrents of water like burst pipes shot off the cliffs. They made camp in a sandy-floored cave beneath a rock wall. On the second day the downpour turned to drizzle again.

In the cave, Hyrum constructed a life preserver for Miranda and the child, empty bottles sewn into the lining of an old jacket that made Miranda look burly and top-heavy when she donned it and that clinked when she moved. There was room for Joseph to be bundled inside.

Asa and Will Jefford went to stand on a spit of rock gazing down at the next rapid, which boiled with rolling waves.

"Look at that!" Jefford said, as the waves receded.

It was as though a huge swell of water had passed down the River and was gone. Asa stared at the lesser chop, thinking that he would never come to know this River in all its savage and placid moods. He knew he had become a more expert boatman, but always the River seemed to show him one more trick.

The waves were building again, roiling up against the left wall and thrown back in an upflung comber that must be ten feet high. The building continued until it seemed the whole Canyon must fill like a jug beneath an open faucet. Abruptly the River flattened out again.

"It is Moses parting the Red Sea waves," Jefford said.

"Could it be from floods upriver?"

The geologist nodded, standing with his hands in his pockets and his arms tucked close to his body as though he were cold.

They watched the River rising again. There must be an immense body of water flooding downriver in these great surges. Climbing to a higher vantage point, Asa could see that the same phenomenon was taking place at the second rapids. Yet the two boats in their little cove were hardly affected. If they had been in the middle of a rapid when one of these tidal waves swept past they could not have survived.

In the drizzle he and Jefford watched five more of the surges pass by, the water swollen all across the River, which Jefford estimated as one hundred and fifty feet wide, but hugely heaped up in the center of the current.

He gazed up around him at the Canyon walls leaping with water. Buchanan was a fool to think he could tame the Canyon.

"It is beautiful," Jefford said.

"As a tiger is beautiful," he said.

Asa lounged in one of the sandy pockets under the cliff face with Buchanan, Morphy, and Tiny.

Lying on his back, propped on his elbows to gaze upward, Morphy said, "I see the wet nurse's moved out of your bedroll."

"Never was in it," Buchanan said.

Morphy sucked on his teeth noisily. Asa cautioned himself that the quarrel between Buchanan and Morphy was none of his affair. Seated with his legs crossed, Tiny scratched his goatee, squinting at Morphy with compressed lips.

"Cunt like that will only fuck the boss man," Morphy said. "I have seen her sort before."

"Now where would that be, Pat?" Tiny said. "I did think she was one of a kind."

"Been in Chicago," Morphy said. "Been in Denver and Sacramento City and Austin. Don't try to tell me about city women."

"You can't beat experience like that," Tiny said, glancing from Buchanan to Asa in mockery.

Morphy glowered at the little photographer.

"The trouble with a mutt like you," Tiny said. "You will come at a woman with your cock in your hand and wonder why she's unfriendly." Whenever he spoke to Morphy there was an edge to his voice.

"Some of them is plenty friendly when they see what I got," Morphy said.

"Every time we come around a bend I expect to see Poche and Esther sitting on a bank waving to us," Asa said to ease the tension.

"I don't expect that anymore," Tiny said.

"Easy brushing out roadbed through here," Buchanan said. "Mostly sidehill cuts. Pitch the waste off into the River and move the big rock along for riprap in the bottoms." He squinted at the River. Asa thought he must be thinking of the death of Esther Bingham, whose rescue had been vital to the success of the survey.

"You'll end up with nothing, you know," Tiny said. "Those Denver plutocrats will chuck you on the junk heap when you're no more use to them."

"He will have built a railroad, anyhow," Asa said. Buchanan turned an eye on him.

"And spoilt one of nature's wonders," Tiny said.

"Fucken midget," Pat said, sucking his teeth.

It seemed to Asa that mile by mile the hostilities were compounded, man against nature and man against man. He blessed the fact that he would be leaving the survey and the River at Separation Canyon, in an estimated twenty-two days.

> *August 17. Our rations are still spoiling; the bacon is so badly injured that we are compelled to throw it away. By an accident, this morning, the saleratus was lost overboard. We have now only musty flour sufficient for ten days and a few dried apples, but plenty of coffee. We must make all haste possible. If we meet with difficulties such as we have encountered in the canyon above, we may be compelled to give up the expedition and try to reach the Mormon settlements to the north. Our hopes are that the worst places are passed. . . .*

The stream is still wild and rapid and rolls through a narrow channel. We make but slow progress, often landing against a wall and climbing around some point to see the river below. We are determined to run with great caution, lest by another accident we lose our remaining supplies. How precious that little flour has become!

Reasons for Separation!

All morning it was a placid River, the boats out of the granite floating past open slopes that pleased Buchanan for the alignment of the road. Asa and Hyrum occasionally stroked the oars to keep the *Lass* running down the current. Once Jefford pointed out a ram grazing in a wooded draw. Back turned to them, rear legs stretched down the bank, the animal resembled a nude pale-skinned human being. The horned head turned to examine them, and with quick bounds the ram disappeared.

Asa heard the rising clamor of rough water. On the sweep Jefford rose to peer ahead. Miranda and the child were in the bow. The bottles in her life preserver jacket clanked as she changed position. Asa dug in his oar to turn the boat broadside for a look. There it was, that familiar drop-off line where the River started down steps, a lace of foam blown up from it. And there it was, that gripe of reluctance in his belly, of too many cataracts passed and too many yet to pass. And the survey had not completed a quarter of what Major Powell and his crew had done.

Miss Saucy was already slanting toward the left bank, and Jefford leaned his weight against his oar to follow.

There was a shout, and Morphy rose to his feet, rocking *Miss Saucy,* to point.

Poche's body was grounded on a ten-foot crescent of beach. His legs with their bare white feet were still afloat, moving lazily with the motion of the current. He could have been sleeping, head pillowed on an arm. When they approached him more closely the stench was horrible. Poche's tattered blue shirt was faded almost white, queer bulges of flesh protruding from it. What could be seen of his face made Asa look away.

They buried him where he lay, Morphy laboring with the shovel. The big man worked with his usual intensity, hat off in deference to the dead, face streaming. Asa spelled him, working with more measured swings of the shovel. Buchanan took his turn. Tiny photographed the body.

They flopped the remains into the hole, sending up a cloud of flies, and quickly covered it over. Hyrum, his white head bent, invoked the Lord's mercy for a Better Life in the World to Come for Elbert Pockett, known as Poche.

Asa prayed with Hyrum for the soul of the unvalued half-breed who had loved Esther Bingham.

Asa stood in the stern of the *Lass* watching for Shinumo Creek. The two boats came around the last bend late in the afternoon, high headlands on either side of a narrow Canyon. They drifted, oars motionless, all eyes searching the western cliffs.

Buchanan motioned to Asa to take the *Lass* in while *Miss Saucy* made a turn back upriver.

All at once Buchanan's rifle glinted as it was raised. The shot sent a flight of swallows swirling against the cliff. Smoke drifted, revealing the rifle lowered and Buchanan's hard frontiersman's face. He raised the rifle once more but did not fire again.

Morphy's voice drifted across the water. "I didn't see nothing."

"Something moving," Buchanan said. "Maybe a mountain lion."

Pat kept *Miss Saucy* circling while Buchanan continued to stare at the cliff. Asa brought the *Lass* in to the beach, where Hyrum piled out to haul the prow up on the packed silt and carry the painter to a gnarled willow clinging to a rock ledge. Miranda's life preserver clinked, Joseph concealed inside it. She too gazed upward.

They stood on the beach waiting for *Miss Saucy,* and made camp while Buchanan prowled back up the narrow Canyon. He was not gone long. It seemed that he too accepted the fact that the danger from the medicine man was past, with Esther dead.

It was a silent evening around the campfire, no singing tonight. Everyone turned in early. Miranda laid out her bedroll at some distance from the others. Asa did not sleep well. He heard Joseph's snuffling cry and later some soft prattle. He knew from the volume of the snores that others were restless also.

With the first gray paling of dawn he pulled on shirt and trousers to limp barefoot to the River's edge to relieve himself, sighing as the liquid rattle mingled with the river's grumble. A pale freckling of stars was still visible in the slot of the sky.

He lingered to watch the stars dimming. A slight figure appeared not far from him. It was Miranda. He brushed a quick hand over his placket.

"You have come out to watch the dawn," she said.

Just then the first fingers of light touched distant western spires and turrets, spreading in an irregular line of fire.

"It is very beautiful."

He repeated her words stupidly. Her face was in shadow beneath the dark puffball of her hair. It was rare these days to see her without Joseph.

It seemed a necessity to keep talking, lest she vanish. "The light and shadows," he hurried to say. "The colors. Sometimes even the air seems colored." He turned as though to admire the sun flaming on distant heights, feeling bogus.

"You are poetical," Miranda said in her hard little voice.

"I am a writer. I must try to describe what we see here."

She had moved closer—or the grayness had lightened. He could make out the glint of her eyes in the shadow oval of her face.

"I hated the confinement at first," she said. "It was as though we were burrowing deeper and deeper into the earth. And then Mr. Daggett, and the shooting, and Esther and Poche—But these last days I have come to see that the Canyon is beautiful."

"One feels one's smallness and inconsequence here." He hated his tone of voice, as though he were speaking to someone much younger, when the experiences of her life made those of his own seem inconsequential indeed.

"And fear of someone who seeks to do us harm," she said.

"I believe he will trouble us no more."

"I have been fearful of someone who will do me harm since I was a child. I will see that Joseph does not lead such a life."

He knew that at first, when Miranda had seemed as fierce as a hawk, it was because she was fearful that her companions meant her harm. She had been as much a captive as Esther had been of the Hoya, on what must have seemed, as she had said, a journey to the center of the earth. It was the general opinion that the responsibility for Esther's child had gentled her.

He wished he instead of Hyrum had thought to construct the life preserver jacket.

"What will you do when this journey is over?" he asked.

"I will go to San Francisco. My aunt is the proprietor of a boardinghouse there. I could care for Joseph there."

"You look upon the child as your charge?"

She laughed. "As Hyrum says, must not one accept the gifts of the Lord?" She swung a foot to kick at an irregularity on the packed silt beach. Then she said, "I have had an offer of employment from Tiny, who would have me pose for photographs. What other work is uncertain." She laughed coarsely.

He thought it best not to respond.

"I believe I can steer my own life now," she said. "I am grateful that you let me steer the *Lass* in quiet water, and found me able.

"I know that I am of a suspicious and unforgiving nature," she went on. Her voice was as hard as fingernails scratched on slate. "But I am grateful to you, and Jake Buchanan, and Hyrum, and Tiny. Tiny knows of a theater in San Francisco. It is not very grand, but Shakespearean productions are mounted there."

"I have been very moved by your reciting poetical lines."

"Thank you," she said. "It does not seem such an impossible aspiration. I have had good training."

Before he could speak again she had retreated and, moving swiftly, disappeared. Morphy stamped toward him from the direction of the camp, scratching his sides in his long underwear.

"Diddling the cooze?" Morphy asked and stood at the water's edge to fling an arc of urine out into the River, sighing. "Where's the *Lass?*" he shouted.

In the gathering clarity only *Miss Saucy* could be seen still tied to the willow, bow pulled up on the beach, stern afloat. The *Lass* had been moored beyond her.

Had he checked the mooring before he went to bed?

The two of them sprinted back to their bedrolls for their boots, shouting that the *Lass* was gone. Asa set out along the bank downriver, rocks and brush congealing out of the dawn mists. Hyrum had secured the *Lass* to the willow, and he himself had checked the mooring as he always did! He could hear Morphy and Buchanan crashing through the brush behind him.

In his mind's eye he saw the *Lass* drifting broadside onto black rocks in a fury of white water, capsizing, breaking apart, cargo spilling into the brown flood: all Tiny's photographic plates, Will Jefford's and Buchanan's records, the surveyor's notes and journals—all the work of the survey!

Maybe the River had risen silently in the night from some cloudburst upriver, to snatch the *Lass* loose. But why hadn't *Miss Saucy* been borne away also? Or why hadn't Esther's medicine-man husband, or someone else, cut her loose also? Maybe he had been scared off by early risers, himself and Miranda Straw!

Ahead, a thrust of cliff stood out of the grayness like the prow of a battle cruiser. Morphy and Buchanan caught up with him.

He could hear a harsher rush of a rapid and see the phosphorescent gleam of white water.

If you want to stop a survey, shoot the surveyor, Buchanan had said. If it was not Esther's husband, it was someone else whose intention it was to wreck the survey!

Trotting ahead, Buchanan shouted.

And there she was, the *Lass,* the lucky boat, circling in an eddy below the rapid, surging back upstream toward the white water, then swinging back like a horse on a tether to rock for moments, before turning her bow upstream again. She looked as though she was trying to return to her mooring.

Morphy plunged down the ledges and splashed out into the River. He held up the painter triumphantly. Asa and Buchanan waded in to help him. Their combined strength broke the *Lass* out of that blessed eddy. Heaving mightily, they lifted her prow onto a patch of sand, and Asa leaped up the slope to secure the rope to a tilted slab of rock, checking his knot twice.

The three of them stood shivering, dripping and grinning at one another. Will Jefford appeared above them.

"What the devil happened?"

"The *Lass* got loose!" he called back.

"How'd she get loose?" Hyrum said, coming up.

"Esther's medicine man," Jefford said.

"Dunno," Buchanan said.

At Shinumo Asa wrote in his journal: "No evidence has been found of a sniper, Hoya medicine man, or enemy of the Survey. It is everyone's conclusion, I believe, that the *Lass* broke loose because Hyrum did not properly fasten the painter, and I neglected to check the mooring. Since the boat suffered some cracked planking merely, the matter has not become an issue. No one has reproached me for what must be considered my oversight. I would resent such a reproach, for I am certain that I inspected the mooring. The fact that I am forgiven a sin I did not commit is provoking to me.

"We are encamped at Shinumo for several days while Jefford and Buchanan survey the depot grounds for the railroad. A level terrace two or three miles long is suitable for such a purpose. Three narrow washes must be bridged, but Jefford has decided that it is a perfect piece of land for depot and shop purposes.

"Yesterday our photographer climbed to a high ledge to photograph this site. There he found himself 'rimmed,' trapped a hundred feet above a talus slope. Buchanan and I went to his rescue. We were able to let down a rope and swing him to a less precarious position. Jefford has consequently nicknamed him 'Tiny Stylites.' These two have become close friends and are frequently to be observed in serious conversation.

"Miranda Straw has changed since Esther Bingham's death because of having taken upon herself the care of the infant. The feeding has been a painful process. I am unfamiliar with female interior workings, but it seems that the child had to suck until the milk developed in her bosom. I believe her breasts bled. It must be that her natural functions, that were so cruelly suppressed when she did away with her own child, have been allowed to blossom. She was scarcely seen to smile before. Now her smile is radiant."

In the Gorge 5

ASA HADEN

While the men are at work making portages I climb up the granite to its summit and go away back over the rust-colored sandstones and greenish-yellow shales to the foot of the marble wall. I climb so high that the men and boats are lost in the black depths below and the dashing river is a rippling brook, and still there is more canyon above than below. All about me are interesting geologic records. The book is open and I can read as I run. All about me are grand views, too, for the clouds are playing again in the gorges. But somehow I think of the nine days' rations and the bad river, and the lesson of the rocks and the glory of the scene are half conceived.

I push on to an angle, where I hope to get a view of the country beyond, to see if possible what the prospect may be of our soon running through this plateau, or at least of meeting with some geologic change that will let us out of the granite; but, arriving at the point, I can see below only a labyrinth of black gorges.

Asa hoped the close reading of Major Powell would have a good effect upon his prose style.

❖ ❖ ❖

He was asked to accompany Tiny and Will Jefford on a geological and photographic expedition while a crack in the *Lass*'s planking was repaired. Buchanan had headed up the side canyon with his rifle to bring back some venison while Morphy and Hyrum worked on the boat. At Hyrum's request Asa took with him a pail in which to collect resin from the piñon pines, for caulking the loosening seams of the *Lass*.

Tiny carried his camera and glass plates in a brown pack, with his yardstick protruding from one corner and his folded tripod from the other; Asa the pail; and he and Jefford a supply of coffee, biscuits, and bacon; and all of them canteens or water bottles, and rolled blankets strapped over their shoulders. They would spend the night on the heights.

Asa could feel the sweat on his face evaporating in the dry air as they toiled up the Canyon wall, gazing back and down at the diminishing sweep of the gleaming River. When they reached an overlying strata of sandstone, they halted for sips of water. Asa sat on a rock feeling the sun burning his face and gazing out on the misty distances around them. These were rimmed by higher limestone ramparts, which Major Powell had climbed, there to expound upon the glories of the Canyon.

They marched on up a ridge between ravines cut by erosion. There were piñon trees here, and Asa left the pail to be collected on the way down. Tiny was eager to reach the heights for wider views for his camera. This was a different Tiny than the shirker of the portages. This was Tiny Stylites, who carried his heavy pack without complaint and led the way, scrambling up the long inclines. Jefford hustled along behind the little photographer, and Asa had to stretch his legs to keep up.

Scaling the higher cliffs was more difficult, for the benches, ledges, and faults were narrow, and glances back and down frightening. Tiny continued to lead, picking his way around juts of stone, scrambling sometimes on all fours, and halting for brief water rests. Jefford mopped his face with his head bandanna and grinned at Asa in his wolf-jawed, sarcastic way. They crept up a crack a hundred feet long and along a narrow balcony suspended in space. The shelf slanted on upward until it was intersected by a buttress thrust out from the Canyon wall. One by one, arms outstretched for fingerholds, boots shuffling, they skinned around the obstruction. Beyond it, the sun did not penetrate past a curve in the Canyon wall, and the sliver of river lay in shadow. Tiny continued to ascend the shelf toward a slot where he had to elbow and knee his way upward.

After hours of hard climbing they reached a point from which there was no possible route upward, an island in the air, which Tiny pronounced their destination. He joined his camera to its tripod on the lip of the platform and, with Jefford holding onto his belt, bent to observe the Canyon through his lens. Asa leaned panting against the wall behind him. All creation lay below.

Sunlit slopes and shadow ravines like black paper silhouettes fell away below them, buttresses and capitals, the vertical corduroy of eroded slopes, the horizontal strata defining the different eons that had fascinated Major Powell and in which Jefford had instructed him. Behind and above were still higher cliffs, with higher islands thrust into space, heights it would have taken days to climb, even if routes of ascent could be found. This place where he leaned with his boots planted in a layer of sand had never harbored another human before him. It was as though he had been forced to experience in actuality what he had only pretended to feel that dawning with Miranda.

When Tiny had finished with his views, he packed camera and tripod back in his rucksack, plucked the yardstick from the heap of stones that held it upright, and they retreated along the narrow shelf, crept around the obstruction, and clambered through another slot onto a platform that was protected from the wind. There a desiccated juniper furnished material for a fire. Again Tiny tended to his camera while Asa and Jefford collected a pile of broken branches.

Tiny joined them at the fire, opening a rubber sack containing a rubber envelope, from which he extracted a number of developed photographs. He handed these to Asa. There were views of Vasey's Paradise, Redwall Cavern, several of Nancoweap and the Little Colorado, and many other Canyon views. One showed the crowd of Hoya, with old Hyrum Logan in the forefront, and the tragic figures that were Esther Bingham aboard a mule, and Poche beside her.

The landscapes were luminous, as though Tiny had been able to capture the Canyon light. Often the yardstick had been strategically placed in the foreground, to show the scale.

"These are very fine!" Asa said.

Jefford examined the views also, passing them back to Tiny. "Ah, this is marvelous!" he said of the group of Hoya.

"It is the purpose of photography to enchant the eye," Tiny said.

"These are not the views essential to the survey," Jefford told Asa. "Those are noted and keyed in the surveyor's log and will not be developed until Tiny has returned to his studio."

"Photography is also a method of recording topography," Tiny said, shuffling the photographs back into their envelope. "If they tried to run a continuous transit line with levels and contours, we'd be in the Canyon a year. Photographs are the next best thing to being here."

"Clarence King found that photographs were useful for other purposes as well," Jefford said.

Jefford had accompanied King on the 40th Parallel Survey years ago. Asa was irritated by the geologist's harping on his notable friends, as though everyone else was diminished by his connections.

"Scenic views were made into books to be shown to members of the government in the hopes that funds would be provided to continue the survey. The photographs were a more compelling argument than any facts or figures."

Tiny tucked the rubber envelope back into the larger bag. "I am recording topography for the survey," he said. "But I am making scenic views for another purpose."

Asa understood that he was to inquire of that purpose. His hands were sweating. "What purpose is that?"

"We hope to be able to persuade the Congress to establish the Grand Canyon of the Colorado as a national park," Jefford said.

"As was done with the Yellowstone." Tiny waved a hand to indicate the gulfs of space below them. "Thus it would become the property of the nation instead of a gang of Denver magnates."

Asa rubbed the palms of his hands on the knees of his trousers. "But what about the railroad?"

"Do you think a railroad should be run through *this?*" Jefford asked, color in his cheeks, a sheen of sweat on his bald head.

"We are here to survey for Charley Daggett's railroad," Tiny said. "But Will and I have a higher purpose."

"And a good conscience," Jefford said.

Asa stared out at vast spaces, profound depths. It seemed that with

Daggett dead his loyalty was owed to Jake Buchanan. But Daggett had deluded them as to the purpose of the expedition.

"Clare King often said that he exposed himself to nature as one uncovered a sensitized photographic plate," Jefford went on. "He said he would withdraw from scientific observation and let nature impress him with her mystery and glory. With those emotions that tremble between wonder and sympathy."

Asa took a deep breath.

"We are the Brotherhood of the Cut Stump, Tiny and I," Jefford said. "We are inviting you to join us."

He went on: "The stump is the American symbol of progress and destruction. The virgin wilderness of this continent is the creation of the Master Architect. It has been claimed that the nation's riches are His gift to His chosen people. From the beginning, settlers have sought to transform that wilderness into a garden, but their success is destroying the natural paradise that was the gift. We think that the cutting must cease before the Almighty ceases to bless us."

Jefford had spoken solemnly, but there was that patronizing edge to his words.

Asa remembered the mines in the Rockies above Denver, some of them Daggett's, with their tailings destroying mountainsides and creeks. Maybe he had felt these considerations then and thought of it only as envy of rich men. And yet America *was* the mines and railroads, the tailings and the cut stumps, as well as the virgin wilderness!

"Longinus said that what exceeds the common size is always great and amazing. The Canyon exceeds the common size, does it not?"

"Of course," Asa said, irritated again.

"I am trying to discover what you feel about all this," Jefford said, waving a hand as Tiny had done. "Do you feel it is grand and lofty?"

Asa nodded.

"Has it a force you cannot withstand? Does it make such impressions on your mind as cannot easily be forgotten?"

"Well, certainly!"

"Is there a sense of danger here? Does it make you *tremble?*"

"I don't understand—"

"It is sublime, is it not?" Jefford said, and leaned back with his arms folded and an expression of having won the game.

"I suppose it is."

"The sublime is different from the merely magnificent. It affects the heart as well as the eye. It concerns one's relationship to his Maker."

Asa found himself trembling, but not in the way that Jefford meant. He asked what they wanted of him.

"It is difficult for a photographer to catch the sublime on glass," Tiny said, grinning at him. "I've done my best." He indicated the rubber sack in which was stored the envelope of his selected Canyon views. "Just so you'll know what's in this, so it don't get lost if there's a smash."

If he accepted the fact that the scenic views were more important than those dedicated to the survey itself, then he had been seduced. "They are beautiful photographs," he said.

"You are a student of Major Powell's *Canyons,*" Jefford said. "As you no doubt know, the Major is presently director of the Geological Survey. He is also a member of the Public Lands Commission. He is an honorary member of the Brotherhood of the Cut Stump!"

"Mr. Daggett considered Major Powell his enemy," Asa said. He was pleased to see Jefford's startled expression. He felt suddenly swollen with anger that these two would think they could trap him by invoking the sublime. The fact that they were *right* only infuriated him the more.

"I cannot accept membership in your Brotherhood," he said. "Mr. Daggett's son is my best friend, and I am proud that Jake Buchanan trusts me."

They glanced at one another. Tiny shrugged.

"I believe you will come around to our way of thinking," Jefford said.

Asa shifted to face away from them, gazing out at the sublimities of the Canyon. His face was burning as though Jefford's prediction had already come true. He did not trust the geologist, even though he was in the right, and he did trust Buchanan, who was in the wrong.

"It is a matter of loyalty," he said.

"It is a matter of where loyalty is justly due," Jefford said.

Asa slept badly, shivering even wrapped in his blanket, and gazed into the red embers of the fire. He wakened from a dream of Miranda

Straw. She was dressed in white buckskin, her hair in braids, her papoose on her hip. She was pointing insistently, like the guide Sacajawea pointing the way west to Lewis and Clark, pointing as though he should understand the significance of her gesture. His groin was painfully inflamed, and he hunched himself fetally in his blanket, gazing up at the inconceivable vast of darkness. The silence was absolute until there was a sigh from one of the other sleepers.

How had he known to waken at this moment? Was it this moment that Miranda's shade had been pointing toward so insistently? Far to the east, outlining buttes and caprock, was the first pale green illumination. Slowly, slowly, the sky came alight. *Let there be light!* The wonder of that decree from Genesis seized his mind. The pale green merged with pale blue, which faded as the first arm of the sun was raised above the horizon. Rays flashed through the crenellations.

If only Miranda were here to share this dawn, how much more capable and genuine he would be in expressing his poetical thoughts!

The vertical earth began to glow. Scarlet sandstone and sulky red marble became incandescent with the light, as though with inner fires, which merged with the blue cast of the air. The fantastic wrinkling of canyons and ravines, of ridges and buttresses, was struck by living fire, turning shadows blacker than black, the whole in movement, in constant change, as the light advanced and shadow retreated, changing form, shrinking and enlarging, the whole diurnal phenomenon a moving panorama.

Down the great central abyss the sun poured like glory onto galleries and amphitheaters that took fire in turn like flowers opening for the day. He glanced aside to see Jefford and Tiny sitting up similarly, similarly watching in silence. The grand ensemble struck him as the visual equivalent of a heavenly choir sounding its first, sonorous harmonics, bold and wild, and yet with some measurable symmetry the human eye could record but never grasp, even while the heart understood.

He closed his eyes to shut it out.

They boiled a pan of coffee and consumed the remainder of their biscuits and bacon, watching the risen sun continue to compress the shadows further down into the gorge. They returned to the descending cleft on the ledge and made their way down brushy slopes back to the groves of dwarf trees, where he halted to scrape resin into the pail. Then downward again, almost trotting where the way was gradual and, when it steepened, clambering down as down a ladder, eyes frequently turning from the depths below to the heights above.

When they returned to camp, Morphy and Hyrum were still at work on the prow of the *Lass,* shirts off in the noon sun. When Buchanan raised his pipe to greet the three returning from the heights, Asa felt a flush burning his cheeks, as though the Deerslayer must discern that he had been tempted by the Brotherhood of the Cut Stump.

In the Gorge 6

ASA HADEN

Asa was fearful that they were running rapids they should be lining, but he was less able to resist Buchanan's impatience than he had been Daggett's. He knew there would be an upset. He did not see Tiny knocked out of *Miss Saucy* by a side wave, but he saw the two heads in the white water. Morphy pulled the photographer in his soaked overall sprawling up onto a low ledge, then half dragged, half carried him to a higher one.

Asa steered for a stretch of beach. He ran back up the ledges, Hyrum hobbling arthritically behind him. Buchanan and Morphy had Tiny slung over a rock, arms, head, and legs hanging, rocking him trying to squeeze the water out of him.

Fists clenched, Asa prayed that this ill-begotten survey to which he had pretended loyalty would be finished before anyone else was drowned.

Hyrum knelt beside Tiny's hanging head. "Lord!" he called hoarsely. "Hear thy servant, Lord! Save this man!"

Tiny spouted muddy water. He convulsed, his head jerked up. Morphy helped him turn and sit upright. The photographer cursed, spewed more water, and scrubbed his arm over his mouth. He gazed blearily around him.

Buchanan's astonished eyes met Asa's.

"Thank thee, Lord," Hyrum said.

That afternoon, Buchanan shot a bighorn sheep, and the crew of the survey feasted on mutton and drank a cup of whiskey to Tiny's survival. They camped on a broad bank a day's run from Kanab Canyon by Morphy's reckoning.

"Ain't much of a rapid," Morphy said. "Unless there's some more rocks fell off the cliff there."

"We'll run *Miss Saucy* in at last light and leave the *Lass* upriver a way. I'll get up on the cliffs early and take a look-see."

"You can't think Esther's husband is still after us," Will Jefford said.

"Fact is, something happened at Shinumo," Buchanan said, squinting at the geologist.

"I'm the one to go, Jake," the old man said. "It is maybe me he is after."

"Think that's who it is, do you?" Buchanan said.

Hyrum looked from Asa to Buchanan. His big hands kneaded at each other.

Buchanan beckoned to Asa, and the two of them walked along the water's edge, away from the others.

"Had some parley with Pat Morphy," Buchanan said in a flat voice. "Told him I was sick of worrying about him every time my back was turned. Told him I'd be doing the survey a sorry turn if I had to kill him before Callville, but I would do it if I had to.

"I have got pretty good in my life at nothing happening to me," he went on. "But we have lost four so far coming halfway. Maybe we'll lose somebody else. This crazy duck. Or the River. If something happens to Will, I can take over the transit. If it is Tiny the girl can work the camera. If it is Hyrum somebody else will have to cook. If it is Pat we are short a strong back. If it is you we are short more than that. But the *Lass* and her load have to get to Callville. Hook or crook."

After a moment he added, "If it is me, I have left a note in the log that Will is to take over the alignment, you are to super."

"I'm sure that will not be necessary," Asa murmured. He could feel the sweat on his forehead cooling in the dry air.

"You know what we are here for. You will have to write a report of the survey with the photographs and the alignment all laid out to show the thing is *feasible.* Just get it to Denver." It was the opposite side of the Cut Stump.

Buchanan wiped the back of his hand over his mouth. "The survey sprung a bad leak when Esther drowned."

"Yes."

"We hope it will all hold together to Callville, don't we?" Buchanan said, and laughed, maybe at the expression Asa found on his face. It was as though the Rock of Gibraltar was confessing the inability to control its own seismic weakness.

"I am fed up with Tiny and Will whispering secrets to each other," Buchanan went on. "Will just naturally thinks he is about fifty percent smarter than anybody else."

Asa felt his face burn painfully.

"I'm going to build this road," Buchanan said. "Will you throw in with me?"

Asa halted. It was as though he could not keep pace with Buchanan and sort out his thoughts as well.

"I am proud that you would ask me," he said.

Buchanan swung around to face him, something vulnerable in his eyes.

"I don't believe I can do that," Asa said. He was shocked that he had said it.

Instantly Buchanan's face was shuttered again.

He knew that the Deerslayer would not inquire his reasons.

While Asa waited with the others on the east bank for a signal from Buchanan, who had crossed to the mouth of Kanab Creek to scout the cliff there, he hiked upriver a way. Strata of shale and sandstone were bent into folds, which were torn by faults and striped in shades of red, brown, and gray. Higher up, the cliffs were ragged with gulches.

He turned up a narrow canyon that wound back from the River. The walls were as smooth as though they had been turned on a lathe. Ferns sprang from the crevices, and splashes of purple flowers stained the rock. Further up, the creek purled through a narrow meadow, and sand glowed golden beneath the water where the sunlight filtered through.

Miranda was seated in the shade of a cottonwood. Her cap was off, freeing her hair. When she saw him she struggled back into the top of her overall. The infant lay beside her, little fists making knitting motions.

Asa stammered that he hadn't known she was here.

"We should have brought a picnic," Miranda said, which he took as an invitation to join her. He seated himself beneath a tree twenty feet away.

"Some sandwiches and iced tea, and a tablecloth and napkins, all in a proper basket," she added.

Memories of the sweet normality of picnics swarmed through him. He said, "My family has not had a proper picnic since my father became ill."

"What is his illness?" Miranda asked.

"He died in February. He was troubled by his circulation. He was also troubled by the state of everything around him. It seems that as one grows older the world becomes a more disturbing place than when one is young."

He winced to think of the disturbing world Miranda knew.

"My father was troubled in that way also," she said.

"He died suddenly?"

"He had an attack while reading his Shakespeare. It was a fitting end." She inclined her face to gaze down at Esther Bingham's child.

Because of her father's death she had been stranded in that mining camp among brutish men.

She asked about his writing. Was it to be a career?

"I am employed to write a history of this expedition for a magazine called *California Monthly,* in San Francisco."

"And will you put me in your history?"

"I will write of meeting you by surprise in beautiful places!"

She laughed her rather coarse laugh. "How pleasant it must be at a college, with the dignified professors and all the young men with fine manners. Were there young women students also? One in particular in whom you were interested?"

"Not at the university, but in Newfield—my home. It was not a happy attachment."

He avoided her gaze by dipping his head and pulling up grasses with his thumb and forefinger.

"I have been reflecting on Esther's life," Miranda said.

"It seems it would have been better if she had been left among the Hoya."

"She was befriended by the wife of the chief," Miranda said. "This squaw allowed her to make a little garden for herself. She spoke often of that garden. She grew beans and vegetables. Some of the others would steal from it, but when she had married her husband they did not do it anymore."

It was from her garden that Esther had been kidnapped. She must not have known to ask for more than a garden in her life. The lives of women were so much more complicated than those of men, which would account for their more complicated personalities. How complicated and how simple had been Esther's life. How complicated had been, was, and would be, Miranda's life!

"You and your father must have traveled widely," he said.

"We traveled in England when I was a child. We lived in Washington City and in San Francisco. In the last years we traveled much in the West."

He found himself confiding in her: "It is my duty to pursue the history of the three men who left Major Powell's exploration at Separation Canyon and were murdered. They were killed by Indians. Paiutes like the Hoya."

She stared at him from the shade of her cottonwood.

"It is believed that these men left the boats because of contention with Major Powell and his brother."

"I know nothing of this," Miranda said.

"Separation Rapids was the worst they had encountered," he went on. "There was no possibility of portaging or lining. They would have to run it. Their rations were exhausted, and they could not know that they were not many days from their journey's end. They were so weakened by hunger they feared that if they did not leave the river by Separation Canyon there might not be another chance."

"And they encountered hostiles!"

"It was claimed that they molested a squaw."

He should not have mentioned molestation!

"I will leave the survey at Separation Canyon," he went on quickly. "Hyrum and I are to parley with the Shivwits there."

Her mouth rounded as though with a gasp. "Does Jake Buchanan *know?*"

"He was told." It seemed important that he seem a dedicated man to her. "It is what I must do."

He was startled by a gunshot.

It proved to be Buchanan, waving his hat from a terrace on the opposite cliff, beckoning to the *Lass* to cross over to Kanab.

With Buchanan scouting up Kanab Creek, Asa found making camp irritatingly lax. The boats were not unloaded with the usual efficiency. Tiny did not head for a photographic site with his camera, and Jefford sat writing in his black notebook instead of setting up the transit. Morphy helped Hyrum assemble driftwood for the fire.

Miranda sat on a log nursing the child. Hyrum brought the coffee to a boil and passed out the hot tin cups.

Later Asa thought it would not have happened had Buchanan been present.

Morphy squatted before Miranda and held up his cup like a beggar.

"How about a little cream in my coffee?"

Miranda ignored him. Morphy smirked around to make sure he was being appreciated. He pushed the cup at her. "Don't give it all to the pickaninny!"

Miranda reached for the cup and dashed the contents into Morphy's face.

He lurched to his feet swiping at his cheeks. "Fucken whore!"

It seemed to Asa that time slowed. He had a glimpse of Tiny's furious face, of Hyrum rising grasping the frying pan, of Will Jefford stepping back away from the fire.

He took one long stride to confront Morphy. "You will control your foul mouth!"

Glaring into Morphy's coffee-stained face that glared back at him, he felt more astonishment than anger.

Morphy pushed him away.

He flung himself at the big man. Morphy sprawled on the ground on his hands and heels.

When Morphy swarmed back to his feet Asa knocked him down once more. He felt the pure astonishment again. He saw Morphy's hand scraping up a handful of sand.

White-hot grit slashed across his eyes. He gasped, hands clutching his face. Dimly he heard shouting. His eyes seemed to be bleeding scalding grit. *He was blinded!*

Then there was an arm around his shoulders, urging him along.

"Shit, I didn't go to do *that!*" he heard Morphy say.

It was Hyrum pushing him toward the creek. "Get down," Hyrum said. He dropped to his hands and knees and Hyrum gently pried his hands loose from his face and splashed cold water onto his seared eyeballs. He realized the gasping sound was coming from his own throat. Somehow he knew that Miranda was close by. He heard voices raised, then Buchanan's cool voice beside him: "Just hold him right there till I get the medicine kit."

He could trust Buchanan to bring his sight back!

His eyes seemed glued with pain when he tried to open them. He pushed a finger at the right one, that did not burn so terribly. He could see a little, blurrily: Hyrum's boot, pant leg, crystal water flowing, Miranda's child's boot and the leg of her overall, which was threadbare at the knee. He knelt there gasping.

Buchanan returned, to bind some buttery ointment over his eyes. Buchanan said in a low voice, "That is one sorry mick boatman."

Some response seemed called for, but he could not summon himself out of a cocoon of fear and pain.

"Don't expect you need to do anything about it," Buchanan said. In Buchanan's world, an eye would call for an eye. Buchanan was asking him not to carry on a feud. For the sake of the survey.

"Thought Tiny was going to shoot him with that toy pistol. Had to take it away from him for good."

He sensed that Miranda was no longer present.

"If you'd been here it wouldn't've happened," he said.

"Keerect," Buchanan said.

❖ ❖ ❖

In the morning, after a night of fear, Asa discovered that he could see out of his right eye. He rerigged the bandage to cover only his left. He heard the clink of the bottles of Miranda's life preserver jacket.

"Hyrum says you will be all right," she said.

"I can already see a little." He indicated his unbandaged eye.

"I am sorry," Miranda said.

"There is no need to be sorry," he said and felt the fleeting touch of her fingers on his arm. "For my part I am sorry that I did not interfere before."

He was a passenger in the bow of the *Lass,* Jefford and Tiny on the oars, Hyrum with the sweep. He could make out that Buchanan and Morphy manned *Miss Saucy,* with Miranda and the child in the stern.

His right eye was sensitive to the sun, so he dozed as they drifted down the placid River. He wakened to Jefford and Tiny arguing.

"I would've shot the big ape!" Tiny said hotly. "But Jake showed up just then. If I'd killed him we'd all've had to walk out Kanab Creek and be done with this damned land grab!"

"I don't believe that popper of yours would kill a squirrel, much less a twelve-stone boatman," Jefford said. "I'm just as glad Jake's impounded it, however."

They headed into a chute, Miranda with the child buttoned inside her life preserver jacket. Hyrum guided the *Lass* to follow in line. They put in for photographs and angles. Asa found a pond to drink from and winced at his reflection. That night Hyrum brewed another decoction of herbs to pack onto his left eye beneath the bandage. Morphy made himself scarce.

The next day Asa had more use of his right eye, so he steered the *Lass,* wearing the cap lent by Miranda to keep the sun out of his face. There were many rapids today, always one more raising its roar around the next bend. The Canyon would narrow, the current pick up speed, white water slash, whirlpool eddies, back-rushing waves, swift plunges, and sudden fountain waves of the kind that had snatched Esther Bingham from the *Letty Daggett* and almost drowned Tiny.

The boat would accelerate down the tongue of smooth water that led into the cabbage patch of whitecaps, rushing barely under control to bounce off the standing waves and spin in the eddies, while Hyrum and Will Jefford bailed furiously. Above, the sublime cliffs soared to their heights.

At night Asa dreamed of leaving the Canyon and climbing out of Separation to the plateau above with the old jack Mormon, out of mile-high walls, out of white water and lining and portages, to gracious meetings with Indians in buckskin and feathers. They smoked a pipe of peace together, and there was no difficulty of communication. Once he dreamed that Miranda was his companion, but the friendly Shivwits turned unfriendly, communication became strained, they drew away from him and gazed stonily on her, as if they knew she was a murderess.

These days she stayed away from him. He thought it was because she did not wish to incite Morphy to jealousy. Maybe Buchanan had warned her. Nights her bedroll was once again laid out close by the Deerslayer's.

They continued down the River day after interchangeable day, halting for the camera to record views and the transit angles. Buchanan and Jefford discussed alignments, Asa and Buchanan consulted on the rapids.

They were running rapids they would have lined earlier. More and more Buchanan leaned against Asa's caution in his impatience to get down the River before strength and resolve crumbled, before there were any more accidents. Asa had found reading in *Canyons* difficult since the fight, and he had to ask Jefford to read to him so that day by day he would know what to expect.

He did not see Miranda pitched out of the stern of *Miss Saucy.* He was securing the *Lass* to a drift log in a rocky cove when he heard the shout. His heart swelled to bursting at the sound, and he straightened to see her head with its slicked down curls bobbing among the whitecaps of the rapid above the cove. She was wearing the life preserver jacket. *Where was Joseph?* Buchanan leaped in beside her with a splash of white water that seemed to hang in the air. Hands beneath her armpits, he boosted her half out of the water. Morphy flung a rope. Then they were sprawled on a sunny ledge. Asa sprinted toward them.

Miranda held Joseph, the water-darkened life preserver jacket collapsed around her overall-clad legs. Joseph's dark little face dripped water. His mouth was compressed into a quarter-inch line, his eyes were open wide. His lips made a blowing motion. Miranda clutched him to her.

"Oh, little Joe, you are so brave!" she whispered.

When he looked into the faces of the others gathered around them, Asa saw that each of them looked as frightened as he felt.

Clouds chased each other over the Canyon. They thickened, lowered, and showed dark bellies. A cool wind whipped up the River. The smooth brown water dimpled with raindrops. Squinting his good eye, Asa was pleased to see Buchanan waving them to the left bank. They put in and made what shelter they could.

It rained all night. He could hear rocks rolling on the slopes above the camp. In the morning he crawled out from under his tarpaulin and walked in the rain out to the edge of the swollen River. It seemed that the whole incline of the gorge was in action. Streams of clear water burst from the higher cliffs and turned into rivulets of mud, which gathered strength as they raced downward. These streams undermined the larger rocks, which slipped from their seats and plunged down. The Canyon sides seemed to be moving like the descent of a vast theater curtain. The larger rocks crashed into smaller ones, which sprang out like billiard balls. The mud, water, and rocks descended the slopes so that it seemed the camp must be buried in a landslide.

But the rain ceased, the motion slowed and ceased as well, and the Canyon fell into a silence broken only by the great hushed rush of the River. And all at once sunlight poured in.

He snatched off his bandage and flung it from him. The clarity was stunning. Everywhere details sprang out at him. The walls were etched with delicate traceries and banded with vivid color. Architectural and sculptural forms stood out in power and dimension. The blaze of sunlight pouring over the fantastic surfaces mingled with the blue haze to turn the air a purple so rich that it made his throat ache, and all the color and form combined to seize and hold him riveted there.

What he had once thought merely formidable had become truly grand, prodigious, majestic, exalted, *sublime!*

CHAPTER 19

In the Gorge 7

ASA HADEN

The cliffs had changed again. The Canyon walls were now much broken and collapsed, pinnacles and spires tumbled down as though they had been demolished by earthquakes. Dull black lava lay everywhere, monuments of it standing in the River, the banks choked with it, and cinder cones standing further back. Asa knew that they were nearing Lava Falls, which Major Powell had called the most severe rapid before Separation.

> "*We make 12 miles this morning,*" Major Powell had written, "*when we come to monuments of lava standing in the river,—low rocks mostly, but some of them shafts more than a hundred feet high. Going on down three or four miles, we find them increasing in number. Great quantities of cooled lava and many cinder cones are seen on either side . . .*
>
> "*What a conflict of water and fire there must have been here! Just imagine a river of molten rock running down into a river of melted snow. What a seething and boiling of the waters; what clouds of steam rolled into the heavens!*"

Buchanan was stolidly chewing on the bit of his unlit pipe as he and Asa gazed down on the chaos of the Lava Falls Rapids. The drop was eighteen or twenty feet here, Asa estimated—the worst they'd seen so far.

This side of the River was a mess of tumbled basalt, and lava in the channel had made an especially vicious snarl of white water. The only clear lane was along the west bank, where a great fold of brown water was thrown back from a collision with the rock wall. In between, the familiar fountains churned up, with a suck of whirlpools in the midst of them. The watery racket was a weight jammed down on his shoulders as he stood on a high ledge gazing over that concentrated fury. At least Miranda could carry Joseph around this particular hell, but the prospect of manhandling *Miss Saucy* and the *Lass* up the shale ridge and down the other side was discouraging.

"Maybe we can skid them over the first rocks, then line them down the far side there."

"Let's do that," Buchanan said. "I don't have to tell you I am damned sick of hoisting boat."

The *Lass,* lined down with Asa aboard fending with an oar, sped down the channel along the far bank without incident, but past it, the oar was trapped under a rock. The handle jammed into his belly so that he was catapulted out of the boat. He was borne downriver at speed, thrashing his arms and legs to try to get his head out of the water.

A body crashed into him. He was caught, his head borne free of the water, he sucked in the sudden blessed air. His savior was Morphy on a rope end, streaming face close to his. Morphy grinned like a gargoyle at him.

Others on the bank pulled them ashore, Miranda watching from a higher outcrop. The *Lass* placidly nudged the bank a hundred feet downstream, with Buchanan aboard.

Asa lay on his back on the sandy ledge, panting and gazing up at the steeps that filled Will Jefford with awe. Clouds drifted across the slot of sky, and two majestic birds soared against the cliffs. Eagles! He watched in wonder the slow-circling raptors, the soft clouds above them, and the heights that contained it all.

It was suffocatingly hot in the open stretches below Lava Falls. Sometimes they floated past fields of lava like ossified running sores in slanting meadows rich with brown grasses and ocotillo throwing out its long shoots. Far back now were the lower scarps with their tints of rose, pink, and warm tan, and further still the buttress walls of high crags poised against the burning sky.

Always in the foreground were the benches that seemed purposefully laid out for the Colorado, Grand Canyon, and Pacific Railroad.

The provisions were reduced to flour, salt, saleratus, sugar, coffee, and a little moldy bacon. As long as the Deerslayer could keep a fresh supply of meat no one would go hungry, but days passed without Buchanan bringing down any game, and Hyrum's fish line lately had produced only ugly, bony creatures that Pat Morphy likened to a paper of pins soaked in oil.

They came to Parashant Wash, where Jefford computed ninety miles to Callville, fifteen days. Ten to Separation.

That night Hyrum led them singing hymns. Asa remembered standing with his mother and father in the white clapboard church in Newfield, mortified by his mother's clear soprano soaring like some filmy cloth above all the other voices, and his father's reluctant rumble—his father so old, his mother so young. Then came the moment when he stopped being embarrassed by the joyous sounds his mother made in her worship and mouthed the first shy notes out of his own throat.

He leaned back against his boulder gazing at the firelit face of the Iron County murderer, with whom he would leave the River in ten days' time. Hyrum tapped the bottom of a pan with a ladle, leading them in "The Old Rugged Cross," "Onward, Christian Soldiers," "A Mighty Fortress," and the rest, his voice the loudest among the men.

Miranda's clear voice reminded him of his mother's. Even Jake Buchanan was singing, bronze glints from the fire moving on his face.

Asa bent his eyes up to the pale cliffs soaring into darkness, thinking of explosives blowing vast sections into the River, half-tunnels slotted into them, and tunnels dug through them. Against his will he had become a sympathizer of the Brotherhood of the Cut Stump.

There was no longer any reason for him to try to parley with the Shivwits up on the plateau above Separation Canyon, but he was determined not to assist in the successful conclusion of the survey.

Since the scare when Miranda had been pitched into the River, he had begun to realize that he must leave the Canyon and the survey at Separation not with Hyrum but with Miranda Straw. For her and Joseph's safety. He would see her to San Francisco.

Jefford urged Miranda to give them some Shakespeare, and tonight she assented. Seated stiffbacked with the swaddled child in her arms, she spoke so softly and naturally, and so much more sweetly than her usual harsh voice, that it was not as though she declaimed, but only related her sad tale:

There is a willow grows aslant a brook,
That shows his hoar leaves in the glassy stream.
There with fantastic garlands did she come
Of crow-flowers, nettles, daisies and long purples. . . .
There, on the pendent boughs her coronet weeds
Clamb'ring to hang, an envious sliver broke,
When down her weedy trophies and herself
Fell in the weeping brook. Her clothes spread wide,
And mermaid-like a while they bore her up;
Which time she chanted snatches of old tunes,
As one incapable of her own distress,
Or like a creature native and indued
Unto that element. But long it could not be
Till that her garments, heavy with their drink,
Pull'd the poor wretch from her melodious lay
To muddy death.

His eyes filled with stinging tears at the memorial to Esther Bingham, and maybe tears stung in more eyes than his own as Miranda's voice ceased and men began to disappear into their bedrolls.

Miranda laid out her blankets beside Buchanan's again, as she had done ever since the fight with Morphy. Asa lay in his bedroll staring up at the slash of stars across the heavens and tried not to think about her.

He was jerked from sleep by a shot and a shout. A figure was running toward the moored boats. He rose and ran also, his feet bruised by the stones on the beach. He saw the bulky shadow of the *Lass* out in the current, Buchanan standing leaning back against her weight. Asa joined him, grasping the painter, cold water lapping around his thighs. Morphy splashed out to help them, and the three of them slowly pulled the *Lass* back to the beach and secured her beside *Miss Saucy.*

"Was it *him?*" Morphy panted.

"It was surely *some*body," Buchanan said.

"Did you shoot him?" Asa asked.

"Guess I missed."

Everyone milled around the remains of the fire, which leaped up as Hyrum stacked driftwood on it. Shadows moved against the luminous rock wall. Jefford was wrapped in his blanket, Hyrum wore his Mormon garment, Tiny drooping drawers that hung on his skinny body. Morphy was shirtless. Miranda in her overall helped Hyrum with the coffee. In the first paling of the darkness Buchanan disappeared up the wash with his rifle, hunting the enemy who was now trying to destroy the boats instead of shooting at the crew of the survey.

"It's that damned Injun again!" Morphy declared.

Asa seated himself next to Will Jefford, who was shivering with a chill even with his blanket wrapped around him and the fire blazing. There was argument as to whether it was Esther's husband who still pursued them, speculation that he had run out of cartridges or lost his rifle in some fall on the cliffs, or maybe it was a crazed prospector who wanted to see them stranded in the Canyon.

It was as shocking to Asa to think of a malevolent presence prowling through the camp as it was to think of one aiming his rifle from the heights.

Jefford said suddenly: "The Lord is terrible and very great. And marvelous in his power!" He spoke in his familiar, sarcastic tone, extending his neck to thrust his face toward Hyrum Logan. "Do you have that in your Saintly Bible, Hyrum?"

Hyrum nodded, squatting beside Miranda. The big smoke-stained coffeepot sat tilted on the grate. Hyrum placed sticks precisely in the fire, building a structure that burst into flame before it was complete. Tiny lounged on the other side of him, Morphy beyond Jefford.

"When the Master Architect made this Canyon, He made the most magnificent place," Jefford said. "The grandest!" His bald head gleamed in the firelight. He was still shivering. Now he sounded more solemn than scoffing.

"He made the whole earth and the firmament as well!" Hyrum said. No question as to *his* solemnity on the subject.

"Look upon the rainbow and praise the Artist that painted it!" Jefford declaimed. "Look upon the glory around us!"

Asa saw Miranda stir and frown at the queer way Jefford was speaking. He himself had come to agree with Jefford's moral opinions on nature and the Canyon, and the Brotherhood of the Cut Stump, but he did not like Jefford haranguing the crew in Buchanan's absence.

"His hand is always visible!" Hyrum said in his rusty voice.

"I have seen some of these side canyons so beautiful you would think the Architect had made them specially for mortal man to glory in," Jefford said. "Travertine and blue water, cottonwoods and flowers. They will have to dam them and drown them."

"What do you mean, they'll have to dam them?" Morphy growled.

"Dam them for a head of water for hydraulic power. Jake Buchanan is thinking railroad, but you can be sure Daggett's Denver gang knows how to look for more profits. They will dam the side canyons and the River gorges, backing up water for electricity and water power. They will clean out the timber for lumber for trestles and dredging equipment. They will bust the Canyon wide open making galleries for the roadbed, and with monitors to wash the gold out.

"With a powerful head of water they can blast these cliffs to mud," Jefford went on. "When a man sees the mess they have made of the Sacramento River, or the American. In California."

"And the Bay!" Tiny said.

"We have been fortunate to see this glory before it was railroaded and dammed!"

Asa wished Buchanan would return with his cool authority.

Hyrum kept pursing his lips as though he were trying to blow a feather off his nose. Morphy glanced past Jefford at Asa and shook his head once. Since his rescue of Asa, he had become proprietorially friendly.

"I was on the 40th Parallel Survey with Clare King," Jefford rattled on. He sounded as though he had gotten into Buchanan's whiskey jug. "I remember our commission still! 'A geological and topographical survey along the route of the transcontinental railroad, to study rock formations, mountain ranges, and the intervening valleys, to examine mines and mineral deposits.' That was our charge! We were to inform the nation of what it possessed in the way of scenery and minerals. We were opening the West! Well, what has become of the West?" He pointed his chin at Tiny.

"It has gone rich man/poor man like the East," Tiny groused.

"It was like the dawn of the world, opening that box," Jefford said. "Buffalo everywhere. Braves beautiful in their paint. Indian maidens! Mountains full of treasure. Sites for grand cities. Marvelous rivers, creeks like crystal."

As Hyrum's fire leaped up, Asa saw that Jefford's face was cut by lines like the erosion of the walls of the Canyon itself. He seemed to have his arms wrapped around himself awkwardly within the blanket. He was ill!

"The Major saw it from the beginning," Jefford said in an exhausted voice.

Major Powell!

"Saw that if it was not settled in an orderly fashion it would all go to smash. There is not enough rainfall out here. There is land that would take a hundred and sixty acres to feed one cow. The only way to hang on to anything is to get it into the public domain before the Daggetts and the syndicates and the Saints railroad and dam it and chop it into city lots. Chew up the mountains and the intervening valleys looking for minerals. And spread out a passel of squatters who will fail and starve in the drought and move along to the next place leaving their tailings behind."

Asa could hear him panting with his emotion.

"What are you saying, Will?" Hyrum asked.

"This country is the Almighty's bounty! It was put here for all of us! By God, it was put here for its own self! What will the Architect say, do you think, that created this beautiful place, this *sublimity!*—and all we can think to do is drive a railroad through it? What will He think of us, who have served Daggett instead of Him?"

Miranda said, "Will, are you ill?"

Jefford fell silent. He seemed to be sleeping, his head leaned back against the rock behind him.

"*Asa!*" Miranda cried.

He grasped the geologist's arm. In the paling darkness he saw the blood on the blanket. He scrambled to his feet. Jefford looked as though he was snoring, mouth drooped open, eyes closed, but he made no sound. Morphy and Hyrum had risen also.

Buchanan had not missed, he had shot Will Jefford, who had tried to destroy the *Lass* with her load of feasibility.

They dug the grave in sandy soil fifty feet up the wash, Buchanan and Pat Morphy taking turns throwing up shovelfuls of reddish sand. It seemed that Buchanan wanted to do most of the work himself. Miranda stood in a willow shade holding the infant, Tiny squatting beside her. When he was not working, Morphy watched with his arms folded on his chest. Asa remembered the night the big man had wept with lust.

It seemed that he had become more able to accept and forgive.

Will Jefford's body, wrapped in the bloodied blanket, rested in the shade awaiting its final repose.

"Maybe you'd recite something? He liked that," Buchanan said to Miranda when he had scrambled out of the hole. He stood, his shirt dark with sweat, mopping his streaming face with his bandanna.

Miranda shook her head once. Then she nodded. She composed her sun-browned features and spoke in the unfamiliar voice:

Our revels now are ended. These our actors,
As I foretold you, were all spirits, and
Are melted into air, into thin air;
And, like the baseless fabric of this vision,
The cloud-capp'd towers, the gorgeous palaces,
The solemn temples, the great globe itself,
Yea, all which it inherit, shall dissolve
And, like this insubstantial pageant faded,
Leave not a rack behind. We are such stuff
As dreams are made on, and our little life
Is rounded with a sleep.

Asa's eyes felt as though they had been scraped when she had finished, and he had a glimpse of Morphy's tear-gleaming, agitated face.

Buchanan leaned on the shovel for some moments after Miranda's voice had ceased. Hyrum stood with his hat in his hands.

Buchanan called for assistance lowering the body into the grave and shoveled in the first heaps of sand before turning the task over to Pat Morphy.

Buchanan squatted in the sun, watching the big man at work. "It was Will set the *Lass* loose at Kanab," he said in a conversational tone.

No one spoke. Asa moved to stand in the shade beside Miranda. When she changed the position of the infant in her arms, her arm brushed his.

"It was Will that wanted to stop the survey," Buchanan said. "Though it was the medicine man that shot George Ritter. That was his medicine, that little skull he left." He paused briefly.

"With the *Lass* gone, we would've had to quit the survey and walk out, and that was what Will wanted." Buchanan spoke softly, as though he was only sounding his thoughts aloud.

Jefford had thought he was defending the Canyon from desecration. It had always been difficult, with the geologist, to know if he was serious or only derisive. He had been deadly serious! Asa could sympathize with Will's strong feelings, but he could not condone the act of betrayal of the faithful lucky boat they had portaged or lined or run through a hundred rapids by now, and of the crew of the survey, and Buchanan.

Jefford had considered his cause larger than any of that, and he was right.

"He had his reasons for wanting to wreck the survey," Buchanan said. He swung around to face Tiny. "Maybe you do too."

"He and I agreed about the railroad," Tiny said grimly. "I wouldn't've agreed to cutting the boats loose." He gestured toward the *Lass,* where his plates were stored.

"You signed onto this survey to do a job of work. And Will did."

"We didn't sign on to make it one man's Canyon."

"Did you know he meant to wreck the *Lass?*" Buchanan asked in his easy voice.

"Guessed it this morning, when he was talking."

"What about your plates? You didn't plan for the plates to be no good, did you?"

Tiny reddened as though he'd been slapped. "If I'd done that, he wouldn't've needed to cut loose the *Lass,* would he?"

Buchanan thought about that, finally nodding but not as though he was convinced.

"Just how do you stand, Tiny?" Buchanan said, looking down and scuffing a boot in the sand. "What about this job of work you are supposed to be doing?"

"I am getting you your views for the feasibility report," Tiny said. "They will be damn fine, too. Don't ask for more than that."

Buchanan nodded again. Then he stared straight at Asa with hot eyes. Buchanan looked *old.*

"Did you know about any of this?"

"I knew how he felt. I didn't know how strongly he felt it." His face was burning.

"How about you, Pat?"

Morphy shouldered his shovel and shook his head.

Hyrum was twisting his hat between his hands.

"Hyrum?"

"He thought he was doing the Lord's work."

Buchanan strolled a few steps past the grave, then turned and came back. His face had an ugly twist to it.

"I thought I had shot the wrong man," he said. "I did not shoot the wrong man. I will shoot anybody else that tries to run this survey up the spout, and that is the word with the bark on it!"

"I will be leaving at Separation Canyon," Asa said.

Buchanan swung toward him. "*What?*" The word had a flat crack to it, like a board hit against a fence post.

"You know that. Hyrum and I are to go up on the plateau to parley with the Shivwits."

"Circumstances alter cases," Buchanan said, squinting at him in the fierce sunlight. "We are shorthanded as it is."

"It was my agreement with Mr. Daggett."

"You can walk out at Grand Wash when there's no more rapids," Buchanan said. His voice grated.

Asa only shook his head. Hyrum wouldn't look at him.

"The *Lass* has made her last portage anyhow," Tiny said. "We could hardly lift her with Will. And *Miss Saucy* can't carry six of us and the plates."

Asa remained silent, content to let the matter simmer if Buchanan would do so also, while he considered the consequences of obstinacy.

"We will take it as it comes," Buchanan said.

Asa wrote in his journal:

September 24, 1882

I am convinced that Miranda Straw and Esther Bingham's child should not be exposed to what Major Powell called the worst rapids he and his crew had encountered.

I am also convinced that the railroad, and the attendant desecrations Will Jefford numbered in his final words, must not be perpetrated upon this place.

Separation 1

JAKE BUCHANAN

Buchanan sat in cottonwood shade with his back braced against a trunk, legs stretched out before him, pipe in his teeth and eyes closed against the brown glare off the River. He pictured the pilot train chuffing along the tracks on the first terrace above and behind him. There he was, in fine black broadcloth, stogie in his jaw, gazing out the window of his car at the Canyon scenery, a rich man capitalist, a big fellow from Denver. He could look forward to seeing the Canyon from a parlor car, but he was sick to death of seeing it from *Miss Saucy.*

Two more days to Separation Canyon, and maybe most of a week after that to Callville on the Virgen.

He switched the picture in his head to the mules and scrapers brushing out the roadbed, working stiffs with picks and shovels, the water donkey with canteens slung over his back, and the super watching the hard labor. The part he looked forward to most was shooting game for the chow line. He had hoped Asa might be a part of it, starting out timekeeping, he and Asa in the kind of conferences they'd had on lining rapids, Asa listening to him tell how to deal with mules, men, and *things.* The boy had turned him down, and he saw Will Jefford's dead hand in it.

Like *that* these days, his mood would turn black. What lay ahead would go bad on him. He would have to bed Martha Daggett. He hated the jelly of that enormous bosom, and the way she flung her head back in her transports so he could look down the black hole of her throat. No wonder Daggett had taken up with his little copper-haired opera singer.

Ellsworth and the others would have to be convinced, looking at his feasibility report and the photographs as he stood before them with his hat in his hands, and squinting up at him with questions while marking their place with their tended-to fingernails: "Now, see here, Mr. Buchanan—"

It seemed it would have all fit together, key into lock, if he could have brought back the White Captive the way Charley Daggett had planned it. He lounged against the tree, breathing hard.

He was too quick to a rage these days. The time-bear was mauling him, backstabbing sons of bitches chewing on him. What I pay for is loyalty, Daggett had liked to say. He had not thought before of the importance of loyalty! So Asa did not want to come in on Buchanan & Daggett Construction because of Will Jefford ranting against the road scuffing up his precious Canyon. He should've figured to shoot the geologist the first time the *Lass* was cut loose!

And Tiny Truesdale picking at him about private property and public lands and rich man/poor man. That grated on his nerves like a fingernail on slate. Any man with get-up-and-go ought to be able to make himself just as rich as his brains and grit could manage, yes, and bust up, too, when his judgment and luck gave out. So the redbellies and the greasers, and the Saints, if it came to that, plain got washed out of the way of white men with the git.

And Pat Morphy laying for him. That was a scrape he could look forward to! Just about the second minute after they stepped out of the boats at Callville, he would take after the jailbird with all the bile he had soaked up coming down the river of corpses!

Stop it! he cautioned himself.

He had let himself sink into a black sulk when Asa had told him no, and worse than that when the boy had said he'd be leaving the survey at Separation. But he would finish the survey, he would fuck Martha Daggett twice a day if he had to, he would swallow his tongue before the syndicate, and he would build the road. He finished what he started.

He recalled that hell-noisy day at Shiloh, when the Reb sniper had creased him in the thigh. He'd waited through the heat of the day, the guns roaring and roaring off to the east, for the bastard to come down out of the tree where he could get a shot at him; tightening his belt around his thigh to stop the blood. When the sniper did come down, he was in high grass where Buchanan could see only the crown of his gray hat moving away through the grass. He had calculated, and squeezed off his shot, and brought down that fellow squalling like a castrated hog.

Asa and Morphy were on the River in *Miss Saucy.* Asa was working out a new way to run rapids, oarsmen facing forward, not backward, so that the boat went down stern first. What power they lost would be made up by being able to see where they were headed.

They backed water until the scout boat was positioned on the tongue above a strong riffle. They started down stern first, pitching and tossing, but keeping in the chute. In the end waves they bent to the oars and swung around upriver again. He saw that they were laughing. He was not pleased to see the two of them such pals. One of the boy's eyes was still a bloodshot mess from the jailbird slinging a handful of sand at him.

If Asa was trying out this new system, probably he didn't intend to leave the survey at Separation.

He had warned him about that! The bile swarmed up again.

"Stop it!" he whispered to himself.

The Fury came in sight. The papoose on her arm had just about become a part of her. He had another surge of bile that she had moved out on him, coming and going as she saw fit: and, when she did return to his bedroll, about as responsive as a dead mule, lying there spread out for him like the whore she'd been. He beckoned to her.

She approached to halt before him. She held the kit with one brown arm. Her face was blank.

"I've been thinking," he said. "You are a good looker of a young woman, do you know it?"

"Thank you," she said in a low voice.

He sucked on his pipe, which had gone out. Beyond the Fury he could see Hyrum and Tiny at the campsite, Tiny talking and moving an arm up and down like a semaphore. Morphy and Asa were making another backwards run.

"I know a professional lady in Denver," he said to the girl. "She could've married half a dozen of the fanciest gents in Colorado. I mean solid citizens. Men Tiny would disapprove of. She don't want to do that just yet. She will pick her time. You are as good a looker as she is."

"Thank you," the Fury said again.

"I see Asa can't take his eye off you. Like Pat."

She said nothing to that, shifting the papoose to her other arm. One small fist showed out of the blanket.

He'd noticed that the Fury had an eye for Asa, too, which didn't please him any more than anything else. No doubt about it, the boy was a fine-looking young fellow, even with his red eye and the fair sprigs of beard that made his face fuzzy-edged.

"If you will come to Denver, I will see you meet this lady. She can do you some help. You would like her."

"Be like her," Miranda said, in that grating voice she had sometimes. It didn't seem to be a question.

The papoose made his fussy cry, and she busied herself rearranging and whispering to him, standing there before him where he had summoned her.

He had a sense of Asa watching from the River.

"You wouldn't want to have the kit with you, though."

Her black eyes flashed up at him.

"If you made money enough you could hire a nursemaid to keep him."

"Yes, I could do that!" Miranda said, a little fiery.

He waved a hand to calm her down. "I mean, if you was going to lead that kind of high life you wouldn't want a redbelly papoose around you, fussing." He was aggravated that she should take his meaning so out of joint, when he was trying to help her in her fix.

"I am grateful for your concern," she said.

"Bring your blankets over by mine tonight."

She raised her face to the sky, where clouds were coasting over. She shook her head, glancing out at the two pushing *Miss Saucy* up onto the beach.

He gritted his teeth on the bit of his pipe, tired of people he was trying to do favors for snooting him. He supposed that after Callville the girl would head for San Francisco with Tiny, Asa would take the cars back east, and everyone else go his own way; slam, bam, thank you, ma'am.

"Him and me is going to have trouble if he thinks he is leaving the survey," he said. "Walking out at Separation."

She appeared to be frozen where she stood.

"You had better talk some sense into him," he said and got up to stamp on down to the boats to have some confab with Hyrum Logan.

That evening Buchanan laid out the map on a flat rock and called Asa over to look at it, to show there was also access to the plateau from the side canyons below Separation Rapids, and Lava Cliffs, the last bad rapid before Callville. He was wound up so tight he was on a plateau of mad, where it was like he was watching himself from the other side of the street.

Asa peered at the map, and scratched at the tendrils of beard on his cheek, and shook his head. "It was my arrangement with Mr. Daggett that I leave at Separation Canyon. Hyrum is to go with me as interpreter. I'm to parley with the chief of the Shivwits about why they killed the three from Major Powell's crew."

"That was when Charley was bluffing about the expedition not being a railroad survey."

"It was what I was employed for."

"You are not employed for that anymore."

The boy just shook his head.

Buchanan closed his eyes for a moment to keep control of himself. He beckoned Hyrum over. "Tell him what you told me."

Hyrum wore his old gray hat. He looked up at Asa from under the brim, standing spread-legged with his white-haired meathooks dangling at his sides.

"Jacob Hamblin is a friend of mine," he said. "When Major Powell come through the second time, he took Jacob with him to parley with Pokray."

Asa took a step back from the map, folding his arms. Watching him, Buchanan could feel his lips stretch till they hurt.

"Jacob said Major Powell wanted to find out about them three that was killed. He said Pokray was wearing a kind of neckpiece of greenbacks, and there was other sign they was the bunch that had killed them. Jacob was always friendly with the Paiutes," Hyrum added.

"The Major asked him what happened," the old man went on. "It'd been said those boys raped a squaw, but the Major wouldn't believe it. He said those was good boys. The Shivwits owned up to killing them, Jacob told me."

Buchanan watched Asa's face, which told him nothing. Asa cleared his throat. "Why did they?"

"The old chief told Jacob it wasn't a Shivwits woman that was raped, it was a Hualapai from across the River. A Hualapai told them three Mericats had raped a Hualapai woman, so they went on a tear looking for white men. And found those three fellows and killed them when they was asleep."

Asa massaged his neck with his hand, staring into Hyrum's face, which was stubbled with white beard that gave it a kind of pale glow. Buchanan set his willpower like a big wrench on a stubborn nut.

"Jacob thought there was something wasn't right about what Pokray was saying, so he kept after him. It seemed the Hualapai squaw was raped two years before. Jacob swore no harm would come if Pokray told the truth, and finally it come out that his band thought those three was prospectors.

"What prospectors means is first some stakes drove in the ground, and then white man all over the district digging holes and tearing up the land. Running off game and poisoning the water holes. And pretty soon the cavalry comes and moves the Paiute along to some new place where there is less game and bad water, and everything either scratches or bites. That is what happens when prospectors come into the country. So they killed them."

The college boy said slowly, "It was Shivwits and Mormons that murdered those wagon train people in Iron County."

Buchanan watched the old murderer move his shoulders like he was shaking something off. He gazed straight back at Asa. "It was Pokray's band that killed those three of the Major's."

He could hear the rasp of the boy's breathing. "And Major Powell forgave them for it," he said.

"If he was going down the river a second time he surely didn't want that bunch hostile."

It was time to stick an oar in. "What he is telling you is that it is useless to go up there how many years later trying to sniff out cold trails. When you don't know two Paiute words and the old chief is dead anyhow, like as not. And you surely ain't going to have an interpreter."

"My understanding with Mr. Daggett was that I leave the survey at Separation Canyon." Asa was looking straight at him, and he *meant* it.

Buchanan felt the bile surge up to almost choke him. "I believe your understanding was with Will Jefford," he said.

Hyrum stepped back with a hand held up as though to stop trouble. Asa folded his arms on his chest.

"I don't believe there is a court that would fuss me for shooting Will Jefford," Buchanan said. He wiped the back of his hand over his lips. "I'm talking about people trying to sink the survey."

"I don't believe you will shoot me," Asa said. He gave Buchanan the full bore of his blue eyes and turned aside. Buchanan felt his fingernails digging into the palms of his hands as he watched the boy move square-shouldered away.

"You will not do that," Hyrum said.

"I will do what I have to," he said.

In Lower Granite Gorge at first the schist and granite walls were low. The talus slopes above them were studded with barrel cactus and prickly pear, and ocotillo in such regular rows that they seemed to have been planted by a gardener. The dark walls were decorated with delicate flutings. The boulders in the River were so polished they resembled sleek water animals grazing.

They were back in the granite again, with very rough water, but still the tops of the cliffs, and the terraces, seemed to have been designed for the roadbed of a railroad.

And so they came to Separation Canyon, and its rapids.

❖ ❖ ❖

Buchanan went up on the granite with Asa, Tiny, Morphy, and Hyrum, to look down on the rapids. He could feel the power of them through the soles of his boots. It was as though his anger at Asa Haden and this one more pure hell of a trial to face mingled with the trembling of the rocks.

The rapids were formed by the sluff from two large canyons that met at the River exactly opposite each other, like the transept of a church. The River boiled through a slot between cliffs that were a hundred feet high on this side, four hundred on the other. A portage was impossible, even if they still possessed the manpower. Letting the boats down on lines was also impossible, as Asa had read in his waterlogged book. The current drew in at the head of the rapids, where there were huge boulders on both sides, and flung itself over the first fall. Then it drove against the higher cliff and down a second step. The rush of the current around from the right, and the fall, created such a welter of spouting, bucking, thrashing waves in a mass of yellow foam as they had never seen before on this mad river. From that point on, the current battered against the lower cliff in one long, furious boil over a slant of rock bottom, to disappear, still raging, around a point.

It made his teeth ache to look down on it.

"*Jaysus,*" Morphy said, peering down with his hands braced on his knees.

"It is a Holy Terror," Asa said.

Tiny retreated as though it was dangerous even to look down upon the fury beneath them. His face gleamed in the sun.

"I am not going to die in that!" the little man said. "I am not such a fool!"

He scowled at Tiny in disgust. The photographer had lost his grit, like the three from the exploration.

"I am not a damned fool!" Tiny said. He had jammed his hands into the pockets of his overall, where his fists bulged.

"What'll you do, stay here and rot?"

"I'm not going down there," Tiny said in a calmer voice. Hyrum's face was gray with apprehension. Asa looked grim.

"We'll run it in the morning," Buchanan said.

CHAPTER 21

Separation 2

ASA HADEN

About eleven we come to a place in the river that seems much worse than any we have met in all its course. A little creek comes down from the left. We land at first on the right and clamber up over the granite pinnacles, for a mile or two, but can see no way by which to let down, and to run it would be pure destruction. . . .

We find that lateral streams have washed boulders into the river, so as to form a dam, over which the water makes a broken fall of 18 or 20 feet; then there is a rapid, beset with rocks, for 200 or 300 yards, while on the other side, points of the wall extend into the river. Below, there is a second fall; how great, we cannot tell. Then there is a rapid, filled with huge rocks, for 100 or 200 yards. At the bottom of it, from the right wall, a great rock projects quite halfway across the river. It has a sloping surface extending up stream, and the water, coming down with all the momentum gained in the falls and rapids above, rolls up this inclined plane many feet, and tumbles over to the left. I decide that it is possible to let down over the first fall, then run near the right cliff to a point just above the second, where we can pull out into a little chute, and, having run over this to safety, if we pull with all our power across the stream, we may avoid the great rock below. On my return I announce to the men that we are to run it in the morning.

Asa was the last to leave the crag from which they had looked down on Separation Rapids. Hyrum halted him with a hand clamped to his arm as Buchanan, Tiny, and Morphy clambered down over the rocks toward where the boats were pulled up on the beach this side of a tangle of willows.

"I cannot leave with you," Hyrum said.

Asa already knew that. He was still shaken from looking down on that yellow violence of crashing waves, where there was no alternative to running the maelstrom. It would be thought that he was leaving because, like Tiny, he had run out of grit.

"You must take her with you," Hyrum said. The pale, blank eyes stared into his. "She must not go into that rapid. With the babe."

Asa nodded.

"She has taken the orphan babe for her own," the old man continued. "Fed it from her breast, tended to its needs. She has done more than that!"

He blew out his breath and said, "What do you mean?"

Hyrum shook his head once. "She is redeemed!" he said, in that demanding voice with which he had prayed over Tiny's drowned body. His eyes glistened.

"How are her boots?" Asa asked. How many days of walking out of Separation Canyon, then north across the plateau to the Mormon settlements? At least he did not have to try to find the Shivwits band, for questions that no longer needed to be answered and a missing journal he must have always known was a delusion.

"They will have to serve," Hyrum said.

He knew that if he and Miranda were to walk out, Tiny would come also, who had announced that he would not go down Separation Rapids. Morphy would join them out of hatred of Buchanan. And Buchanan had announced his intentions.

He could feel the sweat drying on his face like spider fingers. He thought of Oramel and Seneca Howland and William Dunn at this same juncture. Hyrum stepped back away from him, his eyes still fastened on his.

"She must go with you."

"I know that," he said, nodding.

He found Miranda in the grove of willows on the right bank of the creek. She was seated leaning against one of the trunks, her cap off. The bundle of the infant lay beside her.

She rose as he approached, brushing twigs from the seat of her overall.

"You must come with me!" he said.

In the silence he could hear the roar of the rapids. Miranda touched her fingers to her chin in a gesture that reminded him of Esther Bingham. He saw the blanket shift with Joseph's movement.

"You have not seen the rapid we must face," he went on. "You and Joseph cannot risk it. I almost drowned the other day, when Pat saved my life. In a rapid that was nothing to this one. You might have drowned when Buchanan went in after you. I have determined that I will not run any more rapids than I contracted for, and you must not submit yourself to this. Or the child!"

He paused to listen to the voice of the River. Miranda was staring at him as though he owed her more of an explanation.

"My sentiments are the same as Will's!" he said firmly.

"I don't know what you mean!"

"I will stop the railroad if I can!"

"Because you do not wish the Canyon despoiled."

"You said to me once that one must accept the blessings the Almighty has sent," he said, nodding his head toward the swaddled child.

When he had looked down from the granite upon Separation Rapids, he had understood why the Howlands and William Dunn had left the exploration. They had come down the River from Green River Junction, more than three times as far as the Daggett survey, with three times as many rapids. They were half starved. They must have been as at odds as was the crew of the survey. And they were half mad also from their deprivations and hardships. And perhaps their courage was failing.

"I cannot let you and the child go down those rapids," he said again, gazing into her face.

"Of course we will come with you," she whispered. He saw that her eyes were blank with fear.

"I promise to bring you safely to San Francisco," he said.

She shook her head almost imperceptibly, and he realized that the fear was for him.

After supper Captain Howland asks to have a talk with me. We walk up the little creek a short distance, and I soon find that his object is to remonstrate against my determination to proceed. He thinks we had better abandon the river here. Talking with him, I learn that he, his brother, and William Dunn have determined to go no further in the boats.

. . . All night long I pace up and down a little path, on a few yards of sand beach, along by the river. Is it wise to go on? I go to the boats again to look at our rations. I feel satisfied that we can get over the danger immediately before us; what there may be below I know not. From our outlook yesterday on the cliffs, the canyon seemed to make another great bend to the south, and this, from our experience heretofore, means more and higher granite walls. . . .

I wake my brother to tell him of Howland's determination, and he promises to stay with me; then I call up Hawkins, the cook, and he makes a like promise; then Sumner and Bradley and Hall, and they agree to go on.

Buchanan leaned against the prow of *Miss Saucy,* chewing on the bit of his pipe, watching him approach. Asa could feel his cheeks burning in the powerful sun.

"I will be going," he said. He had spoken so softly he thought Buchanan might not have heard him, so he repeated it. He started to speak again of his contract with Daggett, when Buchanan interrupted:

"It is a contract with Will Jefford!"

He shrugged. He said, "If we learned anything from Esther Bingham, it was to *let things be!*" If he had learned anything from Will Jefford, it was that the men who had made the nation great must be prevented from ruining the country.

"Miranda and the child will come with me," he added.

Buchanan's lips tightened into a scar. "It is only four, five days to Callville," he said calmly. "Take you more than that to get out to the settlements."

"I will not let Miranda go down that maelstrom."

"*Maelstrom,*" Buchanan mimicked. He turned toward the campsite, where Asa could see Tiny and Pat Morphy setting up the dark tent. When Buchanan turned back, his eyes were pits of madness, as Will Jefford had been mad in his way; as the three who had left the exploration must have been mad, and Major Powell as well.

"Tell me," Buchanan said, leaning against the bow of *Miss Saucy.* "What do you think you are going to do with her and the papoose? Take her home and marry her?"

Asa did not reply.

Buchanan scrubbed the back of his hand across his mouth. "She had the chore of whoring for her father's liquor in Eureka. Did you know that? Then after he died she had to fuck muckers for the cash to get her out of Eureka. Her pimp stole all her money, so she shot him."

"That is not the issue," he said.

Miranda had come out of the willows, carrying the child. Buchanan shouted her name.

She approached them warily. Her knees showed through the worn fabric of her overall. She halted, looking from one to the other, the blanketed child held to her chest.

Buchanan said in a flat voice, "Tell him who you've been spreading your legs for these nights."

Her face was a small contemptuous knot beneath the cap. Her eyes looked straight into Asa's, as though to insist that he understand what *men* were like.

She is redeemed, Hyrum had said. "It doesn't matter," he said.

"Tell this fool boy what is going to happen to him if he tries to wreck the survey here!" Buchanan said, his voice rising.

She shook her head again.

"Tell him I will kill him!"

"Tell him yourself," Miranda said in her harsh voice. She swung away, heading for the camp. Once she broke into a trot, her small, burdened figure diminishing.

"You did not use to be a man who would say such things," Asa said.

Buchanan glanced down at the pipe in his hand. The bit had snapped from the bowl. He flung the pieces toward the river.

"You did not use to be a damned Judas like Will Jefford! The survey is going through! The railroad is going through! Cars will run down the Canyon bringing coal to Los Angeles and passengers to admire the views you think are so fine. Everyone will be better for it. Something will be built that *wasn't,* before. I have heard you say so yourself!"

"Mr. Daggett wanted me to write about this journey," Asa said. "I will write why this Canyon must not be destroyed. I will tell the nation what a treasure it possesses here. For the people must know!"

"You are the loony college boy I thought you were when I first saw you," Buchanan said. He held his right fist in his left hand, cracking the knuckles.

Asa had been watching that fist, and when Buchanan detached it from his other hand, he swung his own a moment ahead of it.

The blow caught Buchanan high on the shoulder. He stumbled away but swiftly crowded back. Asa hit him again, full in the face, but Buchanan jammed so close to him that he could hardly swing his arms, and he had to keep ducking and backing. Buchanan swung a leg to trip him. He shouted as he fell. Pain shot like a red-hot bar up his leg. Buchanan stood over him, enormously tall, his boot swinging back again. Trying to lame him!

He flung himself on that leg, clutching it with both arms, grabbing Buchanan's belt. Suddenly Buchanan was down. Asa staggered to his feet, an instant ahead of Buchanan. He swung his right arm as though it was an iron bar with an iron ball at the end. When his fist struck flesh and bone he could feel the jar all the way to his shoulder.

Buchanan fell sprawling on the slant of beach at the river's edge.

Asa managed to stand erect. His face ached, and his ribs, and his leg. He was gasping for breath.

When Buchanan raised his head his face was bloody. Slowly he rose to his knees and started laboriously to his feet. He stood erect, swaying. When he started toward Asa the slant of the beach carried him backward instead. He tottered, flailed his arms, and flopped on his back into the River.

Asa lurched down the slope and into the water after him. He snatched at Buchanan's foot as Buchanan was swept into the current. The boot slipped through his hands, and he stumbled out into brown water. The current thrust against him. He could hear the roar of the rapids. This time he caught Buchanan's ankle. The two of them were carried along the bank toward the promontory that stood at the entrance to Separation Rapids.

Holding Buchanan by the belt he thrashed wildly to propel them closer to the bank.

He felt rock beneath his feet. He teetered there a moment, his strength against the strength of the current, until with a groan of effort he forced their way into shallower water. He dragged Buchanan ashore and collapsed on the sand.

Buchanan's face streamed bloody water. He pulled himself into a sitting position, coughing and spitting. Leaving Buchanan seated there with his head in his hands, his shoulders heaving, Asa limped on up the Canyon toward the campsite in the Canyon heat. The sun glinted off rock faces like mirrors signaling.

The four others watched him as he came over the rise. Hyrum squatted behind his fire, which sent up its first wisps of smoke. Tiny and Pat Morphy, seated on their bedrolls, gazed at him as though they knew something he did not. Miranda stood behind them. He halted before them, dripping water.

"I hear we are going out," Morphy said.

"I'm going!" Tiny said, with his triangle of beard thrust out.

Hyrum was constructing his structure of artfully placed sticks so that the flames leaped up among them. Asa realized that the others looked at him as their leader.

"I don't know how long it will take," he said, squatting also. "We will have to bring water for four or five days."

"There must be maps," Tiny said.

"What's the pigfucker say?" Morphy wanted to know.

"I expect he will go on to Callville."

"I will go with him," Hyrum said in his rusty voice. He didn't look up from his firemaking.

"That is one grizzly bear of a rapid," Morphy said. "That is the worst buster we have come on yet. He can't run that in the *Lass* without a sweep oar." He grinned, showing teeth and gums.

"We could do it in *Miss Saucy,*" Hyrum said.

"He can't take all Tiny's plates in the scout boat."

"He could come back for them overland."

"Tell you what," Morphy said, grinning. "If he leaves those bales of Tiny's plates here, that medicine man of Esther's will sneak down and just naturally smash them to smithers."

Asa could feel his shirt drying on his back in the intense sun. Miranda's eyes never left him. She held one of her palms flattened over the child, to quiet him if he cried.

"We will leave in the morning," he said. "We'll take every water container we have." Tiny would bring his packet of special photographs. They would have to take turns carrying Joseph. They should take along one of the rifles, in case they encountered hostile Shivwits.

Buchanan appeared over the rise. All eyes turned to him. Moving slowly, he went to kneel beside his bag of personal effects, regaining his feet with difficulty.

"We are going out with Asa!" Morphy called to him.

Buchanan turned with Tiny's little derringer in his hand. The side of his face was swollen, and he daubed his bandanna at the corner of his mouth. He never glanced toward Asa.

"*You*'re not," Buchanan said.

"Fuck I'm not!"

"You and me and Hyrum's taking the *Lass* on down."

"Fuck that!"

"It's come on down the River with Hyrum and me or stay here and rot. You are not walking out."

"What the fuck do you mean?" Morphy said through his teeth.

Buchanan pointed the barrel of the derringer like pointing a finger at Morphy's knee. "I can blow your knee off, or you can give me one of your boots. Your pick."

"Pigfucker!" Morphy said.

Asa felt defeat like a dead weight on his shoulders. Buchanan had won, and all he could salvage was that he himself would not finish the survey, and Tiny and Miranda with him.

"Take it off," Buchanan said.

Cursing, Morphy unlaced his left boot and removed it. Keeping the derringer aimed, Buchanan took it from him.

"*Pigfucker!*" Morphy said again.

"We'll run it in the morning," Buchanan said again. He pocketed the little revolver and tucked Morphy's boot under his arm. "We've got some repacking to do, Hyrum. We'll pull *Miss Saucy* as far up the creek as we can and leave her."

Morphy sat gazing down at his filthy stocking foot and single boot. Buchanan's eyes brushed past Asa. He was a man who finished what he started.

When Hyrum and Buchanan had headed back down toward the boats, Buchanan carrying the boot, Morphy scrambled to his feet. He snatched up a stone and flung it after them.

"*I'll kill you!*" he shouted.

August 28. . . . At last daylight comes and we have breakfast without a word being said about the future. The meal is as solemn as a funeral. After breakfast I ask the three men if they still think it best to leave us. The elder Howland thinks it is, and Dunn agrees with him. The younger Howland tries to persuade them to go on with the party; failing in which, he decides to go with his brother.

. . . Two rifles and a shotgun are given to the men who are going out. I ask them to help themselves to the rations and take what they think to be a fair share. This they refuse to do, saying they have no fear but that they can get something to eat; but Billy, the cook, has a pan of biscuits prepared for dinner, and these he leaves on a rock.

. . .The three men climb a crag that overhangs the river to watch us off. The 'Maid of the Canyon' pushes out. We glide rapidly along the foot of the wall, just grazing one great rock, then pull out a little into the chute of the second fall and plunge over it. The open compartment is filled when we strike the first wave below, but we cut through it, and then the men pull with all their power toward the left wall and swing clear of the dangerous rock below all right. We are scarcely a minute in running it. . . .

We land at the first practicable point below, and fire our guns, as a signal to the men above that we have come over in safety. Here we remain a couple of hours, hoping that they will take the smaller boat and follow us. We are behind a curve in the canyon and cannot see up to where we left them, and so we wait until their coming seems hopeless, and then push on.

They separated into two camps. In the upper one were Asa, Miranda Straw, Tiny, and a silent, white-faced, single-booted Pat Morphy; in the lower, Buchanan and Hyrum Logan, who were transferring cargo to the *Lass* and lightening the scout boat so that it could be taken up Separation Creek to be abandoned there. Asa trudged down the slope to help them slide *Miss Saucy* up the bank and to ask Buchanan for a rifle and some cartridges in case they encountered hostiles.

Buchanan wouldn't look at him. His cheek was swollen and darkened, and his face glistened with sweat. "I'll leave it on the rock over there in the morning," he said.

Hyrum cooked biscuits during the afternoon, and he and Miranda divided these among the two parties, as Major Powell's crew had divided their more meager store. Tiny filled water bottles and canteens at the creek that murmured down through the rocks to the River. He mourned his camera that must be left behind like *Miss Saucy.*

Hyrum brought a map to the upper campsite, and he and Asa pored over it. The nearest settlement appeared to be about sixty straight-line miles to the north. There were mountains intervening, but Hyrum thought they were not a range.

"There will be farms and ranches nearer," Hyrum said. "It is the Mormon way to live in town but farm outside."

"We are depending on you," Tiny said and laid a hand on Asa's shoulder.

"Hyrum must go with him," Asa said.

"It is owed," Hyrum said.

Morphy sat on his bedroll with his stocking foot extended out before him. "We'll see what is owed," he said.

At first light Morphy, wearing his single boot, picked his way down the slope to the *Lass.* Asa followed him to collect the rifle and packet of cartridges Buchanan had left on a flat rock near the willow thicket.

Back at the campsite, Tiny and Miranda had prepared for the walk out. Joseph was swaddled in a kind of pack sack that Hyrum had fashioned. Tiny carried his small case of special views slung from a belt over his shoulder, and three canteens. Asa had filled all the empty bottles of Miranda's life preserver with creek water and hung it from a juniper snag along with a light pack, rolled blanket, and the rifle.

While Tiny and Miranda, with the child in the back sling, started slowly up the Canyon, Asa climbed to the crag that overlooked the first drop of the rapids. In the *Lass* Morphy sat at the port oar and Hyrum stood with the sweep while Buchanan pushed off. Buchanan seated himself beside Morphy with a swift, practiced motion, and the lucky boat accelerated as the current caught her. Buchanan and Morphy dug in with their oars as though to speed her more swiftly into the dangers ahead.

An early mist lay in the chasm between the rock walls as the *Lass* slipped down the tongue of smooth water. Ahead of them scarves of phosphorescence were flung up, and white water scoured in great sweeps over the slanting rock further along. From where he stood Asa could see the start of the second drop, beyond the slant rock, but nothing beyond that. The whooping of the water was deafening.

Morphy and Buchanan rowed strongly, and Hyrum leaned on the long oar. They came onto the slanting rock high up and, drifting sideways now, rebounded with the rebound of the water, starting down into the second drop pitching wildly.

Asa raised an arm in a salute just as they passed from view. There was no hand free to respond.

How could he set his will on their survival, the old murderer, the jailbird, and the Deerslayer, but against the survival of the lucky boat and its cargo? The three should wash up in Callville aboard a raft made of the battered planks of the *Lass,* like the horse thief White, the first man to descend the River through the Grand Canyon.

He limped on up the Canyon among the sun-gleaming rocks, to join Tiny and Miranda for the long walk out.

CHAPTER 22

San Francisco 7

MARY TEMPLE

"I believe it was a better poem as I wrote it," Octavius Coogan said, sitting opposite her in the afternoon sun that streamed across the table. He wore a red flannel shirt, with his tall sombrero in his lap.

She looked down at the sun on her pale-skinned hand. "You seemed to respond to my suggestions," she said.

Octavius frowned at the September *Monthly* on the table. On the cover were the eye on California and the table of contents, which included his long poem *Theseus* as well as articles by Bowman Rowlands and James McMurdo.

"Now that I see my poem in print, I wish I had stood by my convictions. You are very persuasive, Mary."

It seemed more complaint than compliment. "Mr. Daggett was interested in your work," she said.

"Such a tragedy!" he said, clucking. "What is to become of the *Monthly?*"

"Beau is temporary publisher."

Octavius clucked again. "Was not Jamey unnecessarily severe in his rebuttal?"

"Perhaps."

"Is Beau in the City?"

"He is in Denver seeing Mr. Daggett's widow."

Octavius leaned to expectorate into the spittoon. "And how is the Byron Fund?"

"I have collected three thousand dollars. I am in correspondence with Mr. Derwent."

She was proud of her efforts, and of the response. The fund seemed the only uncomplicated good in her present life.

Octavius steepled his long fingers together. "And will you soon be taking it to England?"

"I cannot. My sister and her infant are arriving here soon."

"I believe you will always find reasons why you cannot."

She cautioned herself not to show her emotions to an irritating, pretentious poet. She would not even remind him that his promised contribution had never been sent.

"Perhaps you will permit me to take the American Fund to Patrick Derwent then. I long to return there, Mary. My wits have been quite barren in Auburn. Nevvie is so eager to come and stay with you again," he added.

She shook her head firmly. "This little house will have all the occupants it can contain when my sister arrives. And I would have no time for Nevvie, much as I love her."

Octavius looked shattered. "You would not do that for me, Mary?"

"I have just explained that I *can*not."

"If you will not yourself carry the American Fund to Hucknall Torkard, let me carry it across the Atlantic, as I carried the laurel wreath you and I wove in Sausalito."

She felt fussy and quibbling, and aggrieved at the treatment of women by men. She was aware that feminine hysteria was close to the surface. How could Esther's arrival occur just at the time when the fund was almost complete and her position at the *Monthly* very likely to be lost because of Mr. Daggett's death and Beau's enmity? The stars had conjoined to allow her to visit England with real purpose—and at the same time to prohibit that visit. She had been close to losing control of herself in the days since Beau had departed, as though those last terrible scenes must play themselves over and over in her mind's eye, each time with a revision of the words she had spoken.

She said, "Octy, I have done the work, and I believe I deserve what credit is to be had. I do intend to visit England—as we have discussed endlessly—but I simply cannot leave until I discover my sister's state and situation, and see how much of my care she will require."

He scowled at her as though her sister's state and situation were an irrelevancy. "It was my arrangement that you be appointed the American secretary-treasurer," he said. "Surely you remember that."

"I intend to deliver the fund to Mr. Derwent myself! I have still five letters out and am awaiting responses."

"I suppose one is mine," he said, pouting. "It's simply that I must preserve every penny toward my voyage of rejuvenation." He sighed and said, "I don't know what I can do with Nevvie. I was counting on you, Mary."

"Take her with you. Maybe she will be courted by a belted earl."

He glared. He bent to ring the spittoon again. "I have heard a rumor that you and Beau Rowlands have embarked upon an intimacy. Is that perhaps the reason—"

"Beau Rowlands does not care for fair-skinned women. You must not listen to Waldo's rumoring!"

When Octavius Coogan finally departed with his copy of the *Monthly,* crossing the offices in his stately gait, a refuge in England's green and pleasant land seemed to Mary indistinct and improbable.

She was sitting at her desk, pen in hand, when she heard someone come in the door. She thought instantly that it was Ramón, and she rose to lean on the back of her chair, breathing hard as she faced the entry. Beau Rowlands swaggered into the room. He wore a black greatcoat and a black slouch hat. His face was pale within the dark U of his beard. His lips slanted into a grin of greeting, and the relief was so great and so complex that her knees almost crumpled beneath her.

He strode forward to fling an arm around her and kiss her on the mouth. His breath was rank with whiskey and cigars.

"You are back from Denver!" she said weakly when he released her.

"Yes, back!" He brought a bottle of wine out of the pocket of his coat, held it up for her approval, and retreated into the kitchen to draw the cork and bring glasses. They sat opposite each other at the little table that looked out on the traffic of scows on the Bay.

She asked if he had seen Mrs. Daggett.

"Saw Martha, saw Ira Ellsworth," he said, nodding. "There is a problem. Isn't there always a problem?" He laughed too long and wiped the back of his hand over his lips.

She sipped her wine.

"The problem," he said, "is a coalfield near Grand Junction that is worth millions if the coal can be brought to the consumer, but worthless if it cannot."

"Will they proceed with the railroad?"

"Not at this time, probably." He mimicked a deep, pompous voice. "'If the feasibility report is absolutely nonpareil, it will be considered, of course!' So the coal, at this time, remains worthless."

He gazed at her bright-eyed. He looked feverish. Maybe it was the whiskey.

"The expedition should arrive at Callville within days," he said. "With the nonpareil feasibility—and your sister, of course. Jake Buchanan is a man to be reckoned with in Denver circles. Will Jefford's opinions will be listened to weightily, for he is a weighty geologist. The photographic reconnaissance will be of the greatest value. Your sister's assessments will be sought."

"You are derisive," she said.

"I deride the vanity of human wishes!" He almost shouted it and banged his fist on the table so that the bottle and the glasses jumped.

"The railroad will *not* be built, then."

"Alas, Martha Daggett does not feel the need to increase her considerable fortune. She does not think of herself as one of the master builders of the nation. She sees no need to assist a young partner of her husband's or to honor unwritten contracts. The fact is, she heartily disliked her husband and all his works, and I can't blame her for it! She speaks of endowing a chair of moral philosophy at Cornell in her son's name," he added.

He raised his hands, palms up. "Nor does she feel the necessity of maintaining a monthly magazine in California."

So casually, the news of the death of the *California Monthly,* when she most needed an editor's income to support her sister and her sister's child. There were many magazines and newspapers published in San Francisco, but she was not sanguine about a woman's employment in the editorial field. Perhaps she could find employment as a typesetter, or she would have to seek her old position at the Mercantile Library, at half her present salary.

She could feel a weight of sorrow for Beau that his great purpose had failed. But he had risen from adversity before! She asked about the Encino Mine.

"I am bound to go there," Beau said. "It is a very rigorous journey. By steamer to Guaymas, thence overland. Mules! How I dread that journey!" He laughed again. "Do you know, Mary, I feel as though I never want to make that journey again."

She felt a chill she didn't understand.

She could not ask about his old-gold, archaic mistress who awaited him there. Nor could she reproach him for their last terrible encounter, for her thin lips with the sensation of her teeth behind them—like a skull!

"Surely you don't have to depart immediately. You are so tired, and thin."

"After one night with my modern American girl!" he said, laughing, showing his good teeth.

She managed to return his smile.

"I must borrow some money," he said.

"I have a hundred dollars in the bank. Maybe a hundred and fifty."

"What about the Byron Fund?" he said, still smiling.

"Oh, no."

"I will repay it, of course."

"Oh, no, Beau. It is a trust."

"You do not believe I will repay it?"

"I believe you would if you could."

"You are convinced of my failure, then."

Tears heated her eyes. She prayed that he was merely teasing her. But his eyes were steely.

"You are going to rebuild some falling-down old church in England? *England!*"

"Beau, the money has been collected from twenty-eight poets in this country, on the earnest of my good name. I cannot do anything with the money but turn it over to Patrick Derwent of the English committee for the reconstruction of the church at Hucknall Torkard."

When he poured more wine his hand shook, and drops spilled on the tabletop. He licked his wrist. "*Why?*" he said.

"Because it is the resting place of a great poet! Because the church is ruled by a crazed rector whose purpose it is to see Byron's grave dishonored rather than honored!"

"I suppose Yosemite should then be kept holy in honor of the Caledonian water ouzel when he has stopped kicking other people's buckets and kicked his own."

When she tried to interrupt, he raised his voice over hers: "As I suppose the Grand Canyon should be preserved in memory of Charley Daggett!"

She tightened her lips against her teeth. "They should be preserved because they are beautiful places that must not fall prey to careless destruction! And Hucknall Torkard should be preserved because it is the tomb of a great poet!"

Beau waved a hand as though dispelling a fog between them. There were reddish glints in his eyes. "Mary, I am drowning in debts. I have debts in San Francisco that must be paid before I dare depart for Sonora. I have terrible debts! I am in irons! You must trust me with the fund!"

She shook her head, sick to the bottom of her hopes.

"'Loved I not honor more!'" he sneered.

She nodded miserably.

Beau raised his hands, palms up, again smiling in a way that made her want to close her eyes. "Well, my dear, let us not let my ruination interfere with our evening together! More wine?"

She held out her glass. He poured, spilled, and apologized.

He seemed almost himself when they went out to a little Bohemian restaurant on Kearny Street, and at home afterwards, he made love to her as though there had never been any contention between them. But something in her held back this time, and there was a brusqueness and impatience on his part. She almost wept because the joy had gone out of the pleasure.

When she woke in the night, his place beside her was empty.

She rose, calling to him. There was no light anywhere in the house.

She threw on her clothes in the darkness and rushed outside into the Russian Hill night, crying his name. When Mr. Lau appeared out of his basement rooms, she gasped that Mr. Rowlands must have gone to an opium den again.

"I go!" Mr. Lau said and disappeared down the hill, hurrying. Past the black bulk of Goat Island she could see the pale string of lights that was Oakland.

She waited in her parlor for Mr. Lau to return, savaged by terrible premonitions. Beau's greatcoat still hung on the coatrack, and she lifted it down and folded it and held it against her breasts.

Mr. Lau returned hours later to report that Mr. Rowlan' was nowhere to be found.

In the morning Beau's clothes were discovered on the cliff above the little beach at the foot of Larkin Street. They were neatly folded. Later in the day his body was brought ashore at the Embarcadero by the schooner *Emma Ransome.*

Waldo Carrington took care of the notification of Bowman Rowlands's relatives in New Jersey, of the funeral, and the interment.

Mary wrote to Octavius Coogan advising him that she would be grateful if he would carry the Byron Fund to England for her, but that she could not offer to care for Nevvie because of her sister's imminent arrival.

Shivwits Plateau

ASA HADEN

The way led northward toward a mist of low mountains that glowed purple in the sun and never seemed any nearer.

They had been walking for two days over long swales of smooth rock where clumps of brush clung to patches of soil. Water lay in pockets in the rock, congealed into a transparent jelly that could be licked and chewed after the insect carcasses had been picked out. They were almost out of biscuits.

Asa plodded over the rock with Miranda suspended from his shoulders by two loops of belts that must bite into her thighs as they bit into his shoulders. He could feel her breath on his neck, and they were glued together back to breast by their mingled sweat. Tiny trailed them, carrying Joseph in his blanket cocoon on his back, and the rifle suspended from his shoulder on its strap. They had argued about discarding the rifle, for no hostiles, nor anyone else, had been sighted in this huge bleak place.

Neither Asa nor Tiny was a good enough shot to bring down any game, but they had decided to keep the rifle in order to celebrate their ultimate rescue with a salute.

Miranda's feet, wrapped in filthy cloths, stuck out ahead of him. Her boots had disintegrated the second day. She had tried to walk with her feet stockinged and bound, but the binding had quickly worn away so that her feet bled, and there were no more shirttails to cut into stockings. So he had rigged his and Tiny's belts into a harness. Twice he had fallen. She had not complained. They rarely spoke, bludgeoned into half-consciousness by the terrible sun.

From time to time Joseph cried. Miranda's milk was running low. The child's hunger seemed more terribly pressing than their own. They nooned out of the sun, under a crag of pink rock thrust out of a canyonside like the prow of a ship. At the foot of the crag Asa scraped with a stick until he uncovered damp and then continued to scratch until he had a minuscule flow of water puddling.

"How do you know to do that?" Miranda asked.

He supposed he had read it somewhere. He scraped a depression in the sand to contain the water, and presently there was sufficient to spoon into an empty canteen. Tiny sat nearby with his boots planted in the sand and his head in his hands.

It was difficult to wait out the hours of the sun in its zenith, for there was an urgency to keep moving before hunger weakened them further.

Miranda held Joseph to her pale breast, neatening his hair while he sucked, fussed, and jerked his head from side to side. "There, there, Little Joe," she whispered. Presently he slept.

"Leave us here," she said to Asa. "We can't go on like this. Go for help. It can't be far. You said so yourself."

He shook his head and grinned at her. "Your packhorse is raring still."

"Don't leave us," Tiny said. "We would not know how to get water out of the rock without you."

Miranda looked comically disapproving. Some of the stains on her foot bandages were dried blood. She settled the sleeping child on the sand beside her. "I just want to be sensible," she said.

"Allow me the responsibility for sensibility," Asa said.

She smiled at him.

Tiny brought a stack of photographs out of his waterproof packet. He passed them one by one to Miranda, who handed them on to Asa. There were silvery views of cliffs, stylites rock, fantastic formations, rapids, leaps of water. There were other views as well, which he had not been aware that Tiny was recording. There was Miranda standing on an outcrop over space in her overall. Her hair was shaken loose like a tumbleweed of curls, her face unsmiling but very pretty. There was Mr. Daggett in his admiral's uniform, with a hand slipped between the buttons of his tunic and a solemn expression between his sideburns, which flew out like pale flags. There was the crowd of Hoya at the Little Colorado, looking like creatures patted together out of mud. A close view of Esther Bingham's head displayed the tattooed traceries on her chin. Another revealed her as hugely pregnant. Poche was holding her arm, his face shadowed by the stiff brim of his hat. There was Will Jefford with his bandanna knotted on his head, grinning as he brandished his pick at a flower in a rock wall. George Ritter frowned severely beside his transit. There was Pat Morphy aboard *Miss Saucy,* caught squinting over his shoulder from his oarsman's seat. Hyrum Logan squatted behind his cookfire. There was himself leaning against a rock, absorbed in Major Powell's book, which he had left behind at Separation Canyon. There was Jake Buchanan posed against the prow of *Miss Saucy,* pipe in mouth, gazing out at the River.

Tiny replaced them in his packet. They had discussed making a book of his photographs and Asa's journals that would impress the Congress with the beauties of the Grand Canyon of the Colorado and the necessity of preserving it in its natural state.

But he had lost the game to Buchanan, and the *Lass* carried the alignment notes, survey figures, and Tiny's photographic plates down the River to Callville, and ultimately to Denver. Unless they had perished on the way.

"We'll get somewhere tomorrow," he said bravely.

"Where's somewhere?" Tiny wanted to know.

In the late afternoon, they started on. Asa helped Tiny with Joseph's backpack and assisted him with the rifle and a canteen, like a general correcting the dress of a subaltern. Tiny's face was slick with sweat and stubbled with whiskers.

"You'll get us out of this, won't you?" he said, half joking.

"Tomorrow," Asa replied. Tiny helped Miranda into her saddle, legs through the belts that had chafed Asa's shoulders raw, her body pressed to his, her feet in their filthy bandages thrust out like twin bowsprits.

"Hayfoot, strawfoot," he said, and started on, counting steps. In this raddled country of gleaming rock and eroded draws there was often a ledge, like a gift from heaven, where he could rest Miranda's weight for a few minutes of relief. She was braced on one of these when the child began to cry steadily, and Miranda was able to nurse him without the exhausting procedure of releasing her from the belts. There was only so much strength left, and it must be expended as efficiently as possible.

"We'll be there tomorrow, Little Joe," Miranda whispered. "The captain promises!"

The purple mountains lay across the horizon like smoke as the sun crept down the burning sky. In the cool of dusk he could take more steps without resting. There were no more ledges here, and he rested bent over with Miranda sprawled on his back and Tiny squatting beside them looking up into his face with his sun-blistered mouth framed in his tricorn of beard and moustache. He was not sure Tiny believed that he could bring them to safety.

"Just one foot in front of the other till we get there," he panted.

"We don't even know where there is," Tiny said.

He managed to grin at the little man, with Miranda's weight pressing upon him. "There is where, when you get there, you don't have to carry freight anymore."

"I'm sorry I'm so heavy," Miranda said.

"You're not a bit heavy."

"The others are probably in Callville already," Tiny said. "Drinking whiskey and talking about us."

"If they got there," Miranda said in a muffled voice.

That night they slept on a sandy patch in the miles of scattered rock and thornbush, huddled together. The blanket had been discarded soon after Miranda's boots and the water-bottle jacket. They shared the last two biscuits, breaking them carefully into three parts. They had seen one dwarf deer profiled on a ridge. It had waited patiently while Asa untangled the rifle sling from Joseph's pack straps but had leaped pole-legged away before he could take aim.

In the night he became aware that Miranda was sobbing, lying between him and Tiny, with Joseph in the crook of her arm. He didn't know how to reassure her other than to pat her leg. "We will get there today," he whispered. "Don't despair."

"It's not that," she whispered back. "It's that I never had friends before."

She turned slightly toward him so that he could feel her breath on his cheek. He could tell when she slept by the rhythm of her breathing.

In the morning light, the purple mountains were no closer, but the terrain had changed. They were out of the red rock onto sandy soil spotted with saltbrush. Asa congratulated his luck again, for he was unable to walk a straight line anymore, and his staggers would seem to be directed to threading his way through the brush. He could feel the tendons in his knees catch, hesitate as though this time they would fail and pitch him and Miranda forward. But they did not fail, and he placed one foot before the other, hayfoot, strawfoot, fifty paces and rest. He could feel Miranda's breath on his neck.

"There was something wrong with her," she whispered. "She couldn't lift her head. She was too small and her head was too *big.*"

"You don't have to tell me this," he panted.

"I must tell someone! There was something terribly wrong with her. I'd done everything I knew to get rid of her. I'd damaged her terribly, I'd *destroyed* her. I have to tell you—"

She was thinking that she might die! Quickly he said, "We will get out of this. Please don't despair!" He staggered on. He could feel her head pressed to his back, her breath on the nape of his neck.

"*Look!*" Tiny called out, as he lurched through the clear spaces between the bushes. Asa had already seen the feather of dust rising between them and the mountains. He had thought it something manifested out of pure *wish.*

He swiped his tongue across his cracked lips. He felt the shift of Miranda's weight as she straightened and the sudden cool between their separated bodies. Joseph's thin, hungry crying began.

"We're there, Little Joe!" Miranda said.

Now Asa could make out a team and wagon, a horseman moving to join it. He gave thanks.

Still he was startled when Tiny discharged the rifle. Instantly team and wagon and horseman ceased their motion.

He shouted and waved an arm, and staggered on.

"Don't forget," Tiny said behind them. "It was a *man* that carried you fifty miles on his back."

CHAPTER

24

Callville

JAKE BUCHANAN

The *Lass* drifted down the broad River between cliffs that moved further and further apart, past the Grand Wash Cliffs, the last of the cliffs, out of the Canyon and into open country, carrying the three of them who had finished the survey: Jake Buchanan, Pat Morphy, and old Hyrum Logan.

Buchanan knew he should break out the whiskey to celebrate, but Hyrum wouldn't touch the stuff, and Morphy was in such a temper he would probably gnaw the neck off the jug.

He and Morphy sometimes rowed a few strokes and then halted for some more admiration of *flat* scenery. It was like the doors opening to let them out of the penitentiary. Morphy kept silent, stewing on pure meanness and payback, not even bothering to give him the ugly looks he had been screwing his face into since Separation. No doubt he was thinking of devilments that would salve his grievances. Hyrum seemed depressed and slow, here at the end of their journey, as though his damnable guilt that had been put out to pasture for the few weeks of the voyage had now leeched onto him again.

He reflected that there was nothing so insubstantial as dangers past. A whole furious moment of life had been caught up in that sideways slide down the slant rock at Separation, and whether they could get the bow pointed downstream before the fall at the bottom of it; no way of knowing what was past the fall. What was past it was a welter of white water flung up like fireworks, but the *Lass* plowed on through somehow, and the whole of Separation Rapids was done with in about two minutes' time. There was one more rapids after it, which Major Powell had warned of: Lava Walls. It was a rapids that back in the Marble Canyon days would've had them conferring ashore and tossing out bits of driftwood to show the currents, confabbing about a portage while Charley Daggett stamped up and down in his impatience. But here it was only *the last one.* He and Morphy pulled on the oars like killing snakes, and with Hyrum's gray head bent in strain over the steering oar, they were through. Even Morphy joined in the yell of triumph.

Buchanan's shooting luck and eye had come back too, and that night they had feasted on broiled mutton.

But now, out in open country, there was the queer feeling that he should sit himself down to figure out what he was going to do with the rest of his life, when he *knew* what. He was going to build a railroad. He was heading for Denver with the survey documents and Tiny's photographic plates to present to Ira Ellsworth and the syndicators. And to present to Martha Daggett whatever he had to. It made him deep tired even to think of those parts of it, which had to happen before the road building began. But even the roadbed had become as insubstantial as dangers passed, as though Will Jefford's poison had infected that also.

There would be no one in Callville with a payroll. He had about two hundred dollars left from his expenses in Grand Junction and Eureka, which they would split three ways as they had split the biscuits with the college boy Judas and his crew.

Asa had tried to wreck the survey at Separation, but he, Jake Buchanan, had finished it. Now he was floating down a river safe as a lake with Tiny's plates and all the survey and alignment documents, and the description of the mineral claims they had made before they'd quit doing that. The feasibility materials were all present and accounted for, and *good.*

A speck showed up ahead of them on the broad River, which enlarged to two straw-hatted men in a rowboat.

Two half-grown boys, they turned out to be. They held up fishing poles with lines trailing in the water, gawking at the *Lass* bearing down on them. Buchanan yelled across the water: "Callville down this way?"

The older boy waved an arm downriver. "Is you them Daggett boats?" he called back.

"Keerect!"

"Thought you was all drownded!"

Morphy spoke up in a gravel voice: "Not all!"

They drifted on past. The sun glinted like brass on the muddy River. Off to the northwest was a range of mountains as insubstantial as the past and the future. At Callville the Virgen River fed in from the north, and there was a steamer that came upriver from Fort Yuma.

Presently Buchanan could make out a spidery reach of pier and a cluster of buildings at the north end of it.

They closed slowly on the pier, not rowing, Hyrum steering. It was as though now their arrival must be held off, for it opened a whole box of problems and mess.

Four people had collected on the pier, two others hurrying out to join them, men in broad-brimmed sombreros and two women in bonnets, one with a parasol against the sun. It looked like a reception committee, and he saw Morphy's nutcracker jaw relent a bit, though Hyrum looked as down in the mouth as ever, leaning on the sweep to bring the *Lass* in to the pier and casting glances at the people waiting there.

The span of muddy water between the *Lass* and the pier narrowed to nothing. Three sunburnt rowboats were moored further in, pitching in the gentle chop of the River. A fat man with a full beard appeared to be in charge of the reception, grinning down at them and making motions like pulling on a rope.

The shot set everyone on the pier ducking and dodging. At first Buchanan thought it was a part of the festivities, but there were shouts and a scream. Hyrum keeled forward over his oar. Blood spouted from his neck. The old man sprawled half off the *Lass,* with an arm and his head over the side. He slid on into the River.

Buchanan snatched the rifle out of its boot at his feet. The son of a bitch had waited them out and killed Hyrum! With the rifle in hand he leaped onto the pier.

A big woman with a dark moustache shrank away from him, staring down at the water where Hyrum had gone in. The bearded man was opening and closing his mouth like a beached fish.

"Who the hell was that?"

"Been here two weeks, just sitting waiting," the bearded man stuttered. "Thought he was some relative of yourn!"

A fellow in a big hat was running in the street beyond the pier, and Buchanan took out after him. His heels pounded on the splintery wood like mauls. He came into a Mormon-broad street with weathered wood buildings on either side. Big-hat had disappeared up a block. He sprinted up the street, breathing hard. Two men had come out on the boardwalk before the general store.

A black horse swung out of an alley, Big-hat aboard, leaning forward over the horse's neck and swinging a whip like a jockey. It was about a hundred yards. Buchanan raised his rifle, tracked the horse a second, and shot him through the head. Man and horse sprawled in the street in a fountain of dust, the big hat rolling away. Buchanan trotted on. The sniper had one leg pinned under his horse's carcass, his rifle raised.

"Drop that!" Buchanan said.

The rifle dropped. The sniper was a long-haired, towhead boy of about eighteen, with a smear of moustache and beard that made his face look dirty. He struggled to free his leg as Buchanan came up, finally sliding his foot out of his boot. He stood hunched before Buchanan with one boot on and one off. He was about five feet tall, a bowlegged kid with a fraud of a snarl on his face and his mouth trembling. He raised his hands shoulder high.

"Don't shoot, Mister!"

"It was you shooting at us from the cliffs!"

The boy's mouth worked in the beached fish way. "I never!" he protested. "I just come on down here when I heard he was on the River!"

So it had been Esther's husband after all.

"Who's he?"

"Hyrum Longwell!"

"What'd you want to shoot him for?" But he knew.

The boy wiped the back of his hand over his mouth. "I saw Matt Hite shoot my momma. Hyrum Longwell was there killen too!"

"Iron County."

"Yes, sir," the boy said. He pushed a cowlick back from his forehead. "They killed my momma and daddy," he said. He reassembled his snarl. "Gimme to some fucken farmer that treated me like shit! I swore I would get Matt Hite and him when I got my growth. And I done it!"

Hyrum had known this was awaiting him at Callville, but he had chosen to come on down the River rather than walk out with Asa Haden. There seemed reason enough to ventilate this boy, who didn't seem to have got his growth even yet, but when he thought about Shivwits braves and painted-face Mormon militia killing Missouri folk in Iron County, he thought he might have swore about the same thing.

"You got feathers to stick in his hair?" he asked.

The boy dropped a hand to his vest pocket, but quickly raised it when the rifle muzzle jerked at him.

Buchanan called up to the men on the boardwalk, "Any law in town here?"

A deputy produced himself, walking with that slow deputy pace as though they'd relieve him of his star if he hurried. There was some conversation about stringing the boy up to save the trouble of transporting him to St. George.

When he thought of Pat Morphy alone on the *Lass,* Buchanan set out back along Main Street in a hurry. The sun burned like shellac on his face. Past the buildings, he could see the broad sweep of River beyond the end of the pier. The *Lass* was out there with a single figure aboard.

Buchanan slowed to a walk when he saw he was beat. Morphy waved an arm at him from the *Lass.* It was a long shot from the end of the pier, but possible. He raised the rifle, but let it drop, then leaned on it like a cane. The barrel was still hot.

They had brought Hyrum's body up on the planks and covered him with a tarpaulin. The shape of the body beneath the stained canvas didn't look much bigger than the boy avenger's.

Morphy wrestled one of the black waterproofed bales of Tiny's plates up on the rail of the *Lass,* and tipped it into the water. It went in without a splash. Morphy raised both his arms. Then he began scattering papers over the water. He sailed notebooks clipping out over the ripples until they dived in. Then he brought up another bale and balanced it on the rail. He pushed it in and flung his arms up again, all the while diminishing in size as the *Lass* drifted with the current. Now he was out of range.

Jake Buchanan leaned on his rifle and watched the big boatman tip another bale of photographic plates over the side. The boat was riding considerably higher now, Morphy and the *Lass* growing smaller and smaller, floating away down the broad Colorado River toward tidewater.

CHAPTER 25

San Francisco

EPILOGUE

Mary Temple sat with Waldo Carrington at the oak table in the *California Monthly* offices to look over the material that would be included in the final issue of the magazine. The widow of Charles P. Daggett had decreed the suspension of publication after the October issue.

Before them on the table were stacks of manuscript pages. The thickest was Asa Haden's journal of the Daggett Colorado River expedition, which had been scheduled to spread over three issues. Now it would have to be compressed into one.

She herself had produced only one poem since her affair with Beau Rowlands had begun, and she was dissatisfied with "Cupid Touched Me."

There was a Hawaiian pastiche by Waldo, and Jamey McMurdo's water ouzel piece. She had written Mark Twain, Bret Harte, and Henry Park to ask for fiction to publish in the last issue of the *Monthly* but had no responses as yet. There was a story of the old rancho days by a woman from Santa Barbara that was fine but overlong.

Asa's River journal would take up almost half the issue. The writing was effective, and the theme important. Beau Rowlands, as acting publisher, would surely have rejected it.

An obituary of Charles P. Daggett would be included.

"I will obtain the obituary from the *Alta California* and embroider upon it," Waldo said. "'This great mover and shaker' and etcetera!"

"Beau was to have written it," she said.

Waldo tented his fingers together, closed one eye, and gazed down his nose at her with the other. "Have you considered writing an obituary for Beau?"

"I have tried to write a poem," she said. "The promise of the West. The promise of a bonanza. The promise of tomorrow. The devastations of humanity and of nature that accompany the bonanzas. It became hopelessly didactic."

"Suicide implies a terrible despair," Waldo said, who had never liked Beau. "Were we not a part of that despair? Jamey's attack *was* vicious."

How could she discuss this so calmly? She held her chin up. "Beau's piece was shameless propaganda. What would he have done if we had refused to publish it?"

"You knew him better than I, my dear," Waldo said, and would not meet her eye.

"He would have insisted," she said. "And what would we have done if he insisted?"

"Resigned with a great deal of commotion."

"He would never have allowed Asa's journal to be published."

Waldo nodded, frowning.

"He thought that we had betrayed him," she went on. "That *I* had. But the West had betrayed him. He said that in the West great wealth could come only to those with sufficient capitalization, and I think he had despaired of great wealth. And the *Hutchinson* decision was a blow to his authority as a mining engineer.

"I loved him," she added.

"And I know your love is not lightly given," Waldo said. His manicured hand patted hers, his scent of cologne brushed her nostrils. "My dear!" he said.

She went to stand at the window looking down on the busy scene of Montgomery Street. Gazing back at her from the far sidewalk was a tall man in a black frock coat and a plug hat. He had a little goatee beard, and he stood with one hand behind his back and one slipped between the buttons of his jacket as though he were posing for a photograph. His gaze was so intense that she retreated from the window as though her privacy had been invaded.

"We will have a final issue celebrating Nature over Man," Waldo said behind her.

Nature over Woman, in her own case. It was as though the watcher's intent stare had penetrated to her secret. It would require steel nerves for her to grow obviously pregnant in San Francisco. Certainly Waldo, at least, would know who the father was, and Octavius, and Jamey. Moreover, pregnancy would negate any chance of employment as a librarian, and she must find a way to earn a living for herself, for Esther's child, and for her own.

When Waldo had inquired how she was enjoying motherhood, meaning her acquisition of Joseph Bingham, she had laughed and said, "Oh, aunthood merely, surely!" But motherhood was coming as certainly as spring followed winter.

"So romance has blossomed between young Haden and the young woman he rescued," Waldo said.

In his journals, Asa had said of Miss Straw only that she was harassed by violent men in a mining camp and had to be rescued.

"She was carried many miles upon his back. Thus, Miss Straw says, she knows his every vertebrae very well and has found them good. She has located her aunt, who runs a boardinghouse—somewhat disreputable, I gather—south of Market."

"And you will assist the boy with the book he and Al Truesdale are planning?"

"I will certainly caution him to find his own style and not play the sedulous ape to Major John Wesley Powell's. Al Truesdale's photographs will prove a great boon. The purpose of the book, you understand, is not disguised as Mr. Daggett disguised *his* purposes. It is to persuade the Congress to make the Grand Canyon of the Colorado into a national park along the lines of the Yellowstone."

"Thus the Phoenix spreads her wings before she is consumed," Waldo said.

The three companions of the long walk out of the Grand Canyon called upon her that evening, with the purpose of seeing little Joseph Bingham. She supposed that they could be called the Grand Canyon Trio, as once she, Waldo, and Henry Park were known as the California Triad. The slim young woman moved gingerly on feet still healing from her trials. Her black curls were confined by a silk headband in the newest style, and she wore a gray dress with a rather dowdy short jacket with a fur collar. Her closed, small face was a little sullen, a little antagonistic, and her careful steps contrasted with her nervous movements, as though she was always thinking of getting on to the next thing in her vitality. But it seemed that many moments could not pass without the flash of a swift, sweet smile at Asa Haden.

Miss Straw had visited Esther's child daily for the first week, so fiercely possessive that Mary had feared a conflict with her, discovering maternal instincts in herself that had surprised her. But it seemed that Miranda had come to accept the aunt as proper parent, no doubt with Asa Haden's counsel.

That young man had grown a fair moustache that made him look older and steadier than the youth who had appeared at the *Monthly* offices three months ago. His tan suit appeared too small for him, as though his shoulders had grown inches in breadth in his term on the River. Nor could he pass many moments without holding out a hand to help Miss Straw to a seat, or to her feet, or to guide her into a room or out of it, as though with her lamed feet she could not manage alone. Mary remembered all too well that need of touching in that brief stanza of her life when her own vitality could be released only by the feel of Beau. She chided herself for her jealousy of young love.

Al Truesdale wore a proper dark San Francisco suit, a dark cravat with the red wink of a stone in the pin. He looked very Frenchified with his neat moustache and beardlet, and she saw that he too warmed his hands at the warmth the young couple generated.

Mr. Lau's relation, whose name was something like Li-lee, brought Joseph upstairs. The child was dressed Chinese style, in a gray felt suit that looked stiff as armor and red shoes with golden inserts. His eyes were set in his head in an oriental way, and with his black hair, coloration, and dress, he might have been a Grant Street infant. Baby Joseph had a way of looking at her with an absolutely steady gaze that made her feel transparent.

Li-lee stood in her blue Chinese shift with her hands clasped before her bosom, watching Miss Straw holding the baby. Miss Straw's small, hard face had melted utterly.

"Will you forget me, Little Joe?" she whispered. "Please do not forget me, Little Joe!"

The timbre of Miss Straw's voice, when it deepened from her habitual sharp tone, brought tears to Mary's eyes.

"You will always be welcome here, Miss Straw."

"I know, and thank you, Miss Temple," the girl said. She was not much older than Nevada Coogan, but such a different female being.

Asa Haden's hand, which always hovered close, pressed her shoulder.

"What about me?" Al Truesdale complained. "Asa may have carried you a hundred miles, but it was me carried the young mister, don't forget."

"You must never forget Tiny either, Little Joe," Miss Straw whispered.

Asa announced that they were bound for the Adelphi Theatre to see the famous Catherine Clare play Imogen in *Cymbeline.*

Miss Straw, still holding the child to her breast, managed to strike a pose with only the slightest gesture of her free hand:

For your protection I commend me, gods.
From fairies and the tempters of the night,
Guard me, beseech thee.

Li-lee looked relieved when Joseph was surrendered to her, and whispered to him in Cantonese. Miss Straw gave her a chilly look but smiled brilliantly at Mary.

"Guard him, beseech thee," she said.

"Yes, my dear," she said. She understood what was meant when Asa had written that Miss Straw had been harassed by violent men in a mining camp. So young!

Asa announced that it was time for them to depart for the theater, giving Mary one powerful blue glance. Al Truesdale preceded the young lovers, Asa following with an arm surrounding Miss Straw's narrow back. The hand-me-down jacket was gallantly worn. Their voices were still audible when they had passed out of the house. She exchanged smiles of relief with Li-lee.

"Joseph," she said, pointing.

Li-lee's attempt at the name produced a sound like "Hossess." The child fussed and pushed his face at her silk bosom, and Mary indicated that she was to seat herself. Li-lee perched on the settee and unbuttoned the frogs of her bodice while Joseph, immobilized in his stiff suit, rooted for her breast. Li-lee beamed down at him. One of her front teeth was missing, which gave her grin a raffish charm.

Inexpensive as were Li-lee's services, Mary was going to be hard put to afford them.

There was a knock, and she went to answer the door. A tall man stood before her, doffing his hat. He had graying sideburns down to his billy goat beard, and a pale, shaven upper lip. He was the man who had stared at her so intently from across Montgomery Street.

"Mrs. Jiménez, I presume?"

She hesitated, before she said, "I am Miss Temple. I was Mrs. Jiménez."

"My name is Harrison Scott, of Scott and Brown, attorneys-at-law. I am your husband's attorney, Mrs. Jiménez. May I come in? I have important business with you."

She stood aside for him to enter and followed him into the parlor. She felt a peculiar helplessness, as though moved by forces not of her own will. Mr. Scott hesitated in the parlor, looking down at Li-lee and Joseph.

Mary directed him to the table at the window, which showed the black pool of the Bay. He seated himself with a sweep of coattails.

"You have chosen not to respond to my communications, Mrs. Jiménez."

She seated herself opposite him.

"Did you even read my letters?"

"I thought they were from my husband. He has sent me letters I did not wish to read."

"Mrs. Jiménez, I have represented your husband for fifteen years in his struggle with the Land Commission and the courts, and I hope eventually to receive recompense for my services."

She wondered if he had come to her for money.

"Title now lies at the discretion of the Supreme Court," Mr. Scott continued. "And I am fully aware that I will not be paid if the decision goes against Mr. Jiménez's interests.

"Mrs. Jiménez, the home rancho is all but lost already. He has borrowed heavily against it, at ten percent compound interest. The other two grants are not so encumbered, but like many of the land grants in the vicinity they were made to friends of Pío Pico—the last Mexican governor."

Mary said that she had once met Governor Pío Pico. Li-lee watched her worriedly from the settee, Joseph cradled to her breast.

"The governor was in the habit of antedating the land grants he issued. This makes them very vulnerable. The titles to Santa Margarita and San Ildefonso are not specifically clouded, but in fact there is a general cloud over all the Pío Pico grants. The Land Commission awarded title to your husband, but the federal attorney routinely appeals the awards to claimants. And continues to do so throughout the court system."

"What has this to do with me, Mr. Scott? My husband and I are permanently separated."

"Your husband is in failing health, Madam."

She murmured something.

"The decision on the title to Santa Margarita and San Idefonso will be forthcoming at the next court session. Madam, Santa Margarita in particular will command enormous value one day because of its proximity to Los Angeles. To the Jiménez heirs. To you and yours." He gestured with a large hand toward the settee.

"If the justices were to see that these ranchos were to become the property of a living, breathing *American,* with a generation to follow, it would be enormously effective for our cause. May I ask if that is Mr Jiménez's child?"

"He is my sister's child."

Mr Scott blew out his lips in a sigh. "And is your sister resident with you, Madam?"

"She is dead. The child is resident with me." She felt her spread fingers touch her stomach.

"I must reiterate that the successful conclusion of title to the ranchos will be of the utmost importance to your heirs. The child's name, Madam?"

"Joseph."

The lawyer's teeth showed in a stiff smile. "He will be the little Don José. He will ride his pony in his ranchero suit at the head of parades.

He will lead a very fortunate life, Mrs. Jiménez."

"Mr. Scott, I must tell you that my husband has physically abused me. I will not be so abused again!"

"I believe I can guarantee that you will suffer no abuse."

"I must also tell you that I have no money," she said weakly.

"That will be taken care of."

The ranch house at Las Golindrinas came to her clearly, like a stereoptic view. No doubt it was more run-down that when she had known it. She remembered the crumbling adobe, the smell of honeysuckle in the arbor, and the drowsy sound of the bees, the swoop and dart of the swallows along the rock wall, the warm, pleasing stench of the stables, and the beautiful horses stamping and feeding there—though of course they must be gone by now. But the fume of smoke from Ramón's cigar drifted to her also, and the stink of his whiskey breath combined with that of rotting tissues. In failing health!

Her lips tightened painfully as she envisioned Joseph in his fiesta suit and sombrero heavy with metallic embroidery on his pony. And Beau's child!

And Mr. Scott said, "Madam, it is our duty to help to preserve old California as we have known it." He leaned back comfortably in his chair with his teeth showing in his beard like bird eggs in a nest, to accept her capitulation.

Waldo Carrington regarded her over his tented fingers, as she told him what she would do.

He looked appalled. "You will return to Los Angeles to care for a husband you detest!"

She said, "I am no longer a young woman, dear Waldo. I cannot hope for *the* solution, only *a* solution. Besides, *my* attorney thinks Santa Margarita will be very valuable one day. *My* children will be wealthy rancheros!" She almost laughed out loud to think of Beau's child growing up on a hacienda, remembering how he had pled with her to join him on a hacienda in Sonora.

"It is a life Beau would have admired!"

"I suppose it is fitting that your little half-breed nephew will inherit these ranchos."

"There will be another heir," she said and folded her arms over her bosom.

His eyes bugged at her.

She said, "It would be humiliating for the Poetess of Russian Hill to suffer the very obvious physical changes that precede motherhood in San Francisco. In April," she added.

"So!" Waldo said.

"So!" she said. He looked so comically embarrassed that she began to laugh.

"You have mail, Mary." He passed her a letter that had come from Henry Park, a request for one of her Tamalpais poems for *Atlantic Monthly.* It would be the most illustrious magazine in which her work had appeared.

She breathed the warm air of appreciation, even though she knew she was in good part appreciated for her female self as much as for the quality of her verse. The ambiguities of the future were buoyed up by the consciousness of the life within her.

In the horsecar on her way home she wept for her lost love. The verses that had come to her in his memory were dry and inadequate, pathetic merely—Cupid and his longing nymph, the bower they had gladdened—poetry itself in this instance a kind of queer, temporizing bridge between a tattered past and a future that mocked her with its crystalline gleams.

She would memorialize her love not in verse but in prose, a novel! *The Californio* by title, Don Fernando a flawed good man, noble despite his embitterments, scarred by old tragedies of family, nationality, and conquest, and the young American schoolteacher, daughter of emigrants by the southern crossing, whose love would redeem his true nobility. Beau! It came to her intact—plot, character, and setting, the hacienda Las Golindrinas, the sparrows scouring along the ancient walls, the hum of bees, the beautiful equine flesh, the peons tugging their forelocks and crossing themselves as Don Fernando passed by them, even the old-gold mistress! All of it for Beau, for her children, for herself.

❖ **THE END** ❖

NINETEENTH-CENTURY EXPLORATIONS OF THE GRAND CANYON OF THE COLORADO RIVER

1858 Lieutenant Joseph Christmas Ives, with a military party, explores upriver from Callville, a steamboat station at the juncture of the Virgen River, as far as Havasu Canyon.

1867 James White arrives at Callville on a raft, claiming to have floated through the Canyon from the San Juan River in fourteen days, after an encounter with hostile Indians.

1869 Major John Wesley Powell explores the Colorado River, from Green River, Wyoming, to Callville. Three of his men, Oramel and Seneca Howland and William Dunn, leave the exploration at Separation Canyon and are murdered by Indians.

1871–1872 Powell's second expedition, under the command of Almon H. Thompson, proceeds from Green River as far as Kanab Canyon.

1889 The Denver, Colorado Canyon, and Pacific Railroad Survey proceeds from Green River, Utah, to South Canyon, where the expedition is aborted after the deaths by drowning of the president of the proposed line, Frank M. Brown, and the boatmen Peter Hansbrough and Henry Richards.

1889–1890 The Stanton Expedition of the Railroad Survey continues in new boats from Crescent Wash (now North Canyon) to Yuma, Arizona Territory. This was the first expedition to be equipped with life jackets.

1896 The *Panthon,* with George Flavell and Ramón Montéz aboard, voyages from Green River to Yuma, Arizona Territory. This was the first expedition for no practical or exploitative purpose.